# The Variety Girls

Betty Firth grew up in rural West Yorkshire in the UK, right in the heart of Brontë country... and she's still there. After graduating from Durham University with a degree in English Literature, she dallied with living in cities including London, Nottingham and Cambridge, but eventually came back with her own romantic hero in tow to her beloved Dales.

**Also by Betty Firth**


**Made in Yorkshire**

*A New Home in the Dales*
*War Comes to the Dales*
*A Wartime Christmas in the Dales*
*A Wartime Wedding in the Dales*
*A Little Miracle in the Dales*
*Brighter Skies in the Dales*

**Sweethearts of the Forces**

*The Variety Girls*

# The VARIETY GIRLS

## Betty Firth

First published in the United Kingdom in 2026 by

Hera Books, an imprint of
Canelo Digital Publishing Limited,
20 Vauxhall Bridge Road,
London SW1V 2SA
United Kingdom

A Penguin Random House Company
The authorised representative in the EEA is Dorling Kindersley Verlag GmbH. Arnulfstr. 124,
80636 Munich, Germany



A CIP catalogue record for this book is available from the British Library.

ISBN 978 1 83598 476 5



Cover design by Diane Meacham

Printed and bound in Great Britain by Clays Ltd, Elcograf S.p.A.

Look for more great books at
www.herabooks.com | www.dk.com

*To all my friends in Harden Players, for happy times spent both on stage and off.*

# Chapter 1



*29th March 1940. Bradford, West Yorkshire*

Molly Clough felt a painful tug at her scalp, and bit her lip as she attempted to disentangle her straw-coloured hair from the automatic loom she was bending over. Somehow, a lock had managed to escape the rag curlers she wore under her headscarf to wind itself around a spinning bobbin.

She muttered curses at the loom while she tried to free herself. Why did this always seem to happen, no matter how tightly she pinned her curls in place? It was a wonder she had any hair left on her head, she had lost so many to these infernal machines in the seven years she'd been working as a weaver at Taylor's Mill. The ruddy things could scalp you if you weren't careful – or worse.

There were four looms under Molly's care, among the many that stretched in rows across the flagged floor. The thunder of these black, oily monsters reverberated against the thick stone walls. Mill girls quickly grew accustomed to the clatter, however, even becoming glad of it. It meant they could chat to their friends without drawing the attention of Mr Shackleton, their overlooker. You learned a particular way of gossiping when you worked in a mill: as much lip-reading as speech, letting instinct guide busy hands while you hopped from loom to loom.

Molly was glad the overlooker wasn't around to see her fumbling with her hair. He'd dock her sixpence if she was forced to stop the machine, and that was a tanner she could ill afford to spare. It was needed for the trip to the pictures she'd promised her little sister Daphne tomorrow, so the bairn could enjoy her regular weekend swoon over Errol Flynn. No matter how many times Daph saw *The Adventures of Robin Hood*, apparently it still wasn't enough.

Of course, there was always one way to get yourself out of trouble with old Shack, as the millworkers called him – but it'd be a cold day in hell before Molly would consider *that*.

'Do you ever wonder how much of our hair ends up in the cloth?' she asked her best friend Rita, at work on the set of looms beside Molly's.

'I reckon they could get a double-breasted suit and matching waistcoat out of the amount I've lost since we started here,' Rita mouthed back. She nodded to a portly, blue-overalled figure swaggering down their alley, thumbs in its pockets and chest puffed like the master of all it surveyed. 'Heyup. Shack on the prowl.'

'Oh heck.' Molly couldn't free her hair in time to avoid the overlooker's critical eye, but she'd be damned if she was going to pay sixpence for it. She grimaced as she yanked the stray lock from her scalp and let it join the weft feeding the machine.

Having freed herself, Molly took a second to mop her sweat-slicked brow with her hanky before resuming work. The mill was as hot as Hades once the machines had been running for a while.

'You know, Reet, I reckon Luddites had it right,' Molly observed. 'Bloody evil things, these are.'

'Lord who?'

'*Ludd*ites. That's what they called these millworkers who broke up the machinery because they were going to lose their jobs to it.'

'What, here?' Rita asked, with a surprised look at some of the other weavers.

Molly laughed. 'Not our workers, daft lass. This was in the olden days, when George III was king.'

Rita gave her an awed look. 'Ee, you know some posh words, you do. I hardly understand you half the time. Where do you learn all this stuff, Moll?'

'I don't know. Books and things,' Molly said with a shrug. 'They're not really posh. You just haven't heard them before.'

'You should've tried for a place at the grammar when we were bairns. I bet you could've been in the Houses of Parliament or summat by now.'

Molly smiled. 'And who would've paid for that? Santa Claus?'

They stopped speaking and focused diligently on their work as Shack approached.

'Miss Clough. Miss Duffy,' he greeted them. 'Let's see how we're getting along this morning.'

He peered over Molly's shoulder, getting rather closer than he needed to as he examined her work, then cast a cursory glance at what Rita was doing.

'All right, ladies, good job,' he said heartily, although Molly suspected he was secretly disappointed there was nothing that might give him an excuse to dock them a few pennies – or worse, summon one of them to his private room for a 'talk'.

She expected Shack to move on, but still he lingered, beaming affably.

'Well, what are we up to tonight?' he asked, lifting his voice over the sound of the machines. 'Jigging until dawn, no doubt. It's the Majestic you girls usually go to after work, isn't it?'

'Sometimes,' Molly said cautiously.

'Don't blame you. Only young once, eh? You might not think it to look at me, but I enjoy a visit to the dance halls myself on occasion.'

As if to prove it, he danced a few steps with an imaginary partner in his arms. Rita stifled a giggle, but Molly didn't feel much like laughing.

Did the man ever take his wife with him when he went out? Molly doubted the long-suffering Mrs Shackleton was her husband's first choice of partner, for dancing or anything else.

'Actually, sir, Molly and me were planning to have early nights,' Rita said sweetly. 'Friday's still a work night, even if tomorrow's a half-day. We don't want to be tired on the job, do we?'

Molly nodded. 'I'd as soon curl up with a book as go dancing.'

'What?' the overlooker said in amiable disbelief. 'Why, you're like a pair of old maids! When I was your age, I'd be kicking up the dust into the early hours. You ought to come out with me sometime, ladies, and let me show you how it's done.'

To Molly's great relief, the millowner, Mr Taylor, appeared at the door of his second-floor office and looked over the balcony to beckon his overlooker upstairs. Shack looked irritated at having his conversation interrupted, but he quickly smoothed his expression into a simper.

'It seems I must take my leave, Miss Clough,' he said to Molly. 'Perhaps I'll see you at the Majestic one of these days, eh? Don't forget to keep a spot free on your dance card for me.'

'Yes, sir,' Molly said flatly.

The overlooker patted her bottom before going to join Mr Taylor. Molly ignored this, focusing on what she was doing. She'd found this was the best way to deal with these unwanted touches. Even a flinch could be seen as encouragement.

'How does he know we go to the Majestic?' Rita asked as soon as the man had gone, lowering her voice to speak once more in the way the mill girls had developed to gossip privately while they went about their work: a sort of carefully enunciated murmur, with lip shape as important as sound in understanding one another.

'He's been eavesdropping on us in the canteen, I suppose,' Molly mouthed back. She shivered, reliving the horrible feeling of Shack's hand on her bottom. 'We'll have to find somewhere else to go out if he's going to start following us there. What are you really doing tonight?'

'There's a new musical comedy on at the Royal, *Road to Singapore* – Bob Hope and Bing Crosby. Do you fancy it? Some of the other girls are going so we can tag along with them.'

'Nay, I'm at our pub,' Molly said absently as she changed a spent pirn on the loom beside her. 'My grandad wants me to do a few merry numbers for the boys, get them in the mood for opening their wallets. Payday today.'

'At the pub again?' Rita examined her friend's tired looks with concern in her pretty green eyes. 'That's three nights this week. I know it's family, but it's a lot for your grandad to ask when you're on your feet all day. It's not like you're getting paid for it.'

Molly shrugged. 'It's practice, isn't it? And Grandad usually slips us a few bob if he has a good night.'

'I could understand if you enjoyed it. I mean, I aren't saying you've not got a good voice because you have – better than Gracie, even.'

'No one's better than Gracie, bless her sainted name,' Molly said reverently. She turned from the machine to give her friend a squeeze. 'But ta, love.'

'You don't enjoy it though, do you?' Rita persisted. 'Don't seem like it's worth making yourself ill for, working nine-hour days then singing your lungs off at the Boot and Slipper all night with those old devils fondling your backside whenever your grandad's got his back turned.'

'My backside's dealt with worse,' Molly said, with a significant jerk of her eyes towards Shack, who was back on patrol. 'Don't worry about me, all right? Stage fright's just… part of earning my stripes as a performer. I won't always be that way.'

'I've seen what you're like before you sing. If you're shaking like that just for your grandad's old boozer, how do you think you'll cope at the Albert Hall?'

Molly laughed. 'I wouldn't book the place just yet. I'm not fool enough to set my sights much higher than the better class of working men's club. You know, the sort where they hardly ever throw broken bottles if they don't fancy you.'

'Why do you want to be a singer if it gets you so flayed?'

Molly paused to consider this.

'Because… because there has to be *more*, you know?' she said. 'More than Taylor's and Bradford and…' She gestured vaguely through air rendered thick by the lint that made them cough. 'Well, all this. Nowt to life but weft and shuttles and fighting off randy overlookers for a pathetic few bob a day.'

'Oh. I see.'

Rita fell silent, focusing on her work.

'I didn't mean that the way it probably sounded,' Molly said in a softer voice. 'I don't mean I think I'm too good for it or owt. It's just… well, you know what I mean.'

'Do I?'

'You must do. The mills sapped the life out of my dad and I'll be blowed if they do the same to me. If there were summat else you could do to keep food on the table, summat that could take you to exciting places and introduce you to interesting people, wouldn't you?'

'Aye, happen so,' Rita admitted. 'Must be nice to have a talent you can use to make your way. Wish I weren't such a dunce.'

Molly shook her head. 'Why do you always do that?'

'What?'

'Do yourself down. That's your dad talking, that is. Don't forget all them class prizes you won for handwriting when we were at school. All my handwriting ever got me was the slipper from Miss Lawrence for turning in unreadable work.'

Rita scoffed. 'Oh, *handwriting*. Where's nice handwriting going to get me when I've noan got the spelling to go with it?'

'And you're bonny as a film star to boot,' Molly said, choosing to ignore this. 'Ida Lupino's got nowt on Rita Duffy. I'd swap with you any time, Reet.'

'Give over.'

'I would, honest to God.' Molly smiled archly, nodding to a lad who was watching them as he fixed a 'smash' – a warp breakage – on a stopped loom. 'Harry Castle thinks so too, see? Look at his little pink cheeks while he's gazing dreamily at you, bless the boy.'

Rita shook her head. 'Oh, hold your whisht. He never is.' But she was smiling.

Shack was almost within earshot again. Molly tried to look as though she was focusing intently on her weaving.

'We'd both better hold our whisht before he finds an excuse to get us in his room,' she murmured. 'Listen, how do you fancy calling in at the pub after you've been to the pictures? I'll make sure you get a drink on the house.'

'What, on us own?' Rita said, sounding worried. 'It's a bit rough, that place – no offence or owt.'

'You've been before.'

'Not without a lad to look after me. My dad'd play pop if he heard I'd been in the Boot and Slipper by missen.'

'Well, don't tell him then,' Molly said with a shrug. 'Grandad'll make sure you aren't bothered. We can hide in the saloon and you can tell me about the film. That way I'm not missing all the fun.'

'Aye, all right.'

Rita fell silent as the overlooker once again ambled in their direction. Molly was sure he came down their alley five times more often than any of the others.

She tried not to catch the man's eye, although she could see well enough he was trying to catch hers. It unsettled her, the way he came over so often. The way he looked at her. He didn't always stop to make conversation, but always she could see him looking.

Mr Shackleton had a reputation among the men who worked at Taylor's. Strict but fair is old Shack, they would say with an approving nod. A hearty, affable sort, who'd do right by you if you did right by him. The sort of bloke you wouldn't mind going for a pint with. An eye for the ladies, but that's all in fun.

Among the women workers, however, the man had a different reputation, although fear for their jobs kept it confined to whispers. All Taylor's girls knew that Shack was a man you ought never to allow yourself to be caught alone with. His wandering eye and roving hands had been notorious ever since Molly had started work at the mill: just fourteen years old and fresh out of school.

Shack had always been liberal with his attentions, doling out unwanted touches and oily compliments to any young woman he encountered. Yet lately, it seemed that he had been singling Molly out from among the other girls. Too often she caught the mingled scent of stale tobacco and last night's beer on his breath, and felt his horrible little toothbrush moustache tickle her cheek as he leaned over her.

She didn't know why he should pick her out. There were far prettier girls working at Taylor's – Rita, for example, with her glass-green eyes, film star curves and flaming hair. And yet it was Molly his gaze was drawn to. Her he watched constantly, smiling an unpleasant little smile.

It wasn't the lecherousness in his gaze that worried her. That was present whichever girl his eye happened to fix upon. It was a sort of earnest, proprietorial expression he reserved only for her that really made Molly's flesh creep – as if he didn't just want her. As if he *owned* her.

It only made her more determined to be free of this life. Free of Taylor's, free of this dirty old town, ready to spread her wings out in the world.

Molly Clough had plans. She had talent, she knew it. Perhaps she couldn't be a star, because that kind of thing didn't happen to girls like her, but she could be *something*. And she would be something. Yes she would, if it killed her trying.

*Chapter 2*

It was dusk by the time Molly began making her way home. The silence outside felt eerie, as it always did when the sound of the machinery that was such a big part of her life suddenly ceased.

Everything seemed so dark nowadays. Molly felt like she had never known true darkness until the blackout. There were no welcoming lights shining from the windows of pubs and hotels as there would have been this time last year. Life would be going on as usual behind the blackout shades, but from the outside, the city looked... well, dead.

It seemed so pointless, when there was nothing happening. Why should people have to break bones tripping over sandbags and risk getting run over by trams, all for nothing? In case the Germans worked out where they were and dropped another batch of propaganda leaflets on them? Let Jerry drop his paper bombs, and help grateful housewives to light their fires. It wasn't like this was a real war – not like the last war, when men had been dying in their hundreds every day.

Molly's father had been one of the men who had come home from that war. It felt so laughably absurd – that he should survive the horror of the trenches only for the mill to finish him off. Except that it wasn't laughable at all. It made her want to cry.

The doctors had told them it was his lungs. Whether it had been the gas of Ypres that was more to blame or the wool dust in the poorly ventilated rooms of the mill, they hadn't deigned to say. To Molly, her father had just seemed to fade away after he had become too ill to work.

She had sat with him a lot towards the end – it had seemed to comfort him to have his children nearby – and tried to smile

9

while she listened to the wheezing whistle of his once strong tenor voice. He had talked of his childhood, of a little brother he had lost, and his lifelong love of music. But she had never heard him say a word about the war.

Anyhow, that war hadn't been like this one. Some people had been calling this new war the Phoney War, but Molly preferred the name coined by some wag in the press – the Bore War. That was exactly what it felt like: just dull, dull, dull. As dark and dull as the streets of her home town had become.

Everyone had been terrified back in September when the prime minister had announced that for the second time this half-century, Britain was at war with Germany. They had turned horror-stricken eyes to the skies, imagining the hell that might rain down at any moment as the fury of the Luftwaffe was unleashed. Would it be firebombs? Would it be gas? Was this the end of the world as they knew it? The theatres had been closed, the cinemas shut down, the football grounds emptied – every place where people might congregate and make themselves easy prey for German bombers had been given the order to close their doors.

Every place, that is, except the churches. Oh yes, people had needed the churches. Folk who had never whispered a prayer in their lives had been on their knees the Sunday after war came. Molly knew this because she had been on her knees right beside them, pleading that they might all be spared.

And then… nothing had happened. No war had materialised, no fighting: just paper raids, and a lot of headaches and shortages. World leaders exchanged insults with Hitler over the airwaves while their weapons gathered dust. Gradually the places of entertainment had reopened, blacking out their windows and carrying on as before. Boys in khaki who called themselves soldiers but had never been proven in battle twiddled their thumbs across the Channel, with nothing to do but smoke cigarettes and try to learn enough French to persuade the local girls to give them a tumble.

Molly's nineteen-year-old brother Ted was among them. He made her laugh with letters about the scrapes the lads got into, but they'd barely had a sniff of a fight. It all felt like such an anticlimax.

Molly felt guilty that she almost wanted the war to begin in earnest. This limbo state just made her perpetually anxious – as if she was forever waiting for carnage to be unleashed. There needed to be a war so there could be an end to the war, didn't there? They couldn't carry on like this forever.

She glanced up at the drone of a plane overhead.

One of ours or one of theirs? Daphne would know. She was a whizz on planes, that lass – could tell you the make, model and engine capacity just from its silhouette or the sound it made. She had a scrapbook into which she was painstakingly gluing cigarette cards and newspaper cuttings showing each type of plane, both Allied and Axis.

That's what this Phoney War had done to them. Made it all a game. Daph collected fighters and bombers the way that, before the war, she'd collected stamps. But it wouldn't be a game if Goering decided to swap his bundles of propaganda leaflets for raining fire and poison gas.

Molly quickened her steps, suddenly anxious to be at home.

–

Mam was by the living room fire when Molly arrived at their little terrace. It was a cosy scene: Mam in her chair, Geoffrey the cat lying across her shoulders like a tatty fur stole, with Daphne sitting on the rug between her mother's knees while Mam brushed her long hair. The wireless trilled out soft chamber music that Mam hummed unconsciously along to, and an appetising smell of pan haggerty floated through from the kitchen: mingled scents of toasted cheese, crispy bacon and succulent fried onion that made Molly's mouth water.

Daphne's hair was fairer than either Molly's or Ted's, who both bore their late father's straw-like shade of light brown. Unlike her older siblings, the baby of the Clough family was a true blonde

– storybook princess hair, their dad had called it. At fifteen, Daphne was inordinately proud of her thick, glossy locks and wore them as long as her mother would let her get away with.

'Now then, love, will you not let me take just a few inches off?' Mam was pleading when Molly came in, struggling to pull her brush through a knot.

'Oh, Mam, give over,' Daphne said. 'You say that every day.'

'I spend more time unknotting thy hair than I do keeping house, our Daph. We'll be living in squalor soon, and me sitting amongst the filth and rats with no time for owt but playing lady's maid to Madam Rapunzel.' She pressed a kiss to the girl's crown.

Daphne giggled. 'You won't really make me cut it though, will you?'

Mam sighed. 'Nay, child.'

'How many brushes is that?'

'I've lost count with your mithering of me. Eighty, I think.'

'You have to do a hundred. It says in my girls' beauty book that for truly beautiful hair, it must be brushed a hundred times each night.'

Molly smiled as she put her handbag down on the dining table. She knocked over a heavy steel caliper belonging to her sister that had been propped against the table and bent to set it right again.

'You spoil her, Mam,' she said to their mother, making a conscious effort to soften her voice. Days among the clattering looms left her prone to speaking rather too loudly after clocking out – always the sign of a weaver, folk would say. 'Tell her to stop being such a vain little miss and get a job.'

'Oh, let her be,' their mam said. 'There'll be time enough for jobs when she's done with her schooling. She's a bairn yet.'

'I'd been working a year at her age.'

Mam sighed, her eyes drifting to Daphne's calipers against the table. 'Aye, well, I'd a sick child to nurse, and your dad too ill by then to work. I'm sorry, love. You know we'd have loved to send you to the grammar school if we could've afforded it.'

'Now, you know I didn't mean it that way.' Molly came over to give her mother a kiss. Sarah Clough was young yet, barely forty, but her still-handsome features were careworn and pinched after years of worry and hard work. 'I was after teasing Daph, that's all. You've nowt to feel guilty about.'

'I don't feel bad on our Ted's account. He couldn't be done with school fast enough, that lad. It's you girls who got the brains for the family.'

'Don't worry about me. I'll make my way one way or another. And if not, Daph will just have to support us with her giant brain and good looks.'

'I will,' Daphne announced importantly. 'You won't catch me working in a stupid old mill. I'm going to get a proper posh job.'

'As what?' Molly asked, smiling. 'A hairdresser's mannequin?'

'No. I'll be a…' Daphne paused. 'A courtesan.'

Their mam spluttered. 'You'll be a *what*?'

'A courtesan. You know, ladies of the court, like the ones who attend on the queen and princesses. I'll wear a pointy hat and a wimple, and Moll and Ted will have to bow to me and call me m'lady.'

Molly laughed. 'That's a lady-in-waiting, you daft apeth.'

'Oh.' Daphne looked puzzled. 'What does a courtesan do then?'

'I'll tell you when you're twenty-one,' Mam said firmly, drawing the brush through her shining hair. 'Ninety-eight, ninety-nine, a hundred. There. Finished.'

Daphne looked dubious. 'Are you *sure* you did a hundred?'

'I probably did twice that many, the number of times your blethering made me lose count and start again.'

'I brought you this, Daph,' Molly said, producing a card from her coat pocket. 'Rita saved it for you from her Player's.'

Daphne took the cigarette card eagerly. 'Is it the Dornier Do 17?'

'No, the Junkers Ju 88.'

'Ooh, ta! I've been after that one for ages.'

Mam stood up, dislodging Geoffrey, who gave her a dirty look before stalking off to the kitchen with as much dignity as a glorified scarf could muster. She went to examine her eldest daughter, taking Molly's face in both hands.

'You look tired, our Molly,' she said in a low voice.

Molly patted the leathery yet tender hand against her cheek. 'I'm all right. A few late nights singing for Grandad.'

'Hmm. Has that old goat at work been bothering thee again?'

'He came over a few times, trying to find out where we go dancing, but he didn't try owt. I've asked Reet not to leave me by myself with him if she can help it.'

'That's right, you girls look after each other, and don't be afraid to take it to Mr Taylor if it happens again. He's a good man.'

Molly recognised the truth of this. It was only thanks to Mr Taylor that the family had been able to send Daphne to the local grammar school – the first of the family to take her School Certificate. The millowner had offered to pay them a small monthly allowance when Molly's father became too ill to work, and continued to support them financially until Daphne's schooling was done. It was guilt as much as kindness that had spurred this act of generosity, the cynical voice in Molly's head whispered – not that Taylor had ever admitted the mill was responsible for the lung affliction that killed her father, but he knew it well enough. Still, it was more than many employers would have done.

'Taylor's got a real blind spot when it comes to Shack though,' Molly told her mother. 'All the men at work have. They reckon it's just horseplay, the way he is with us girls.'

Mam shook her head darkly. 'Men. They're all in it together. I wish there were summat else for you, love. I hate to think of you at the mercy of someone like that.'

'Perhaps there will be, one day.' Molly smiled. 'A well-paid job somewhere exotic, so I can get a suntan while I'm keeping you and Daph in the lap of luxury.'

'We can but dream.' Mam pinched Molly's cheek. 'My clever lass. There's nowt in this mucky old town half good enough for thee, that's certain.'

'I'm glad someone thinks so.' Molly kissed her mother on the forehead. 'Just keep saying your prayers for me.'

'It's not right, the way men have things all their own way. Shame we have to wait for the next life to see these… these beggars get their comeuppance,' Mam said, with a glance towards her youngest daughter as she hastily adjusted her language. 'That Shackleton would never dare try owt if your dad were still with us, or if we had your brother at home. His sort think it's a licence to take advantage when they know there's no man of the house.'

'We don't need a man of the house,' Daphne said fiercely. 'If this Mr Shack tries to take advantage of Moll, we can fight him ourselves.'

Molly narrowed one eye. 'And what do you know about it, babby?'

'Can you stop calling me that? I'm fifteen, for goodness' sake.' Daphne tossed her glossy hair. 'I'm a woman.'

Molly snorted. 'You're a fathead.'

'You're the fathead, fathead. Anyhow, I know what that means all right, "take advantage".' She gave a knowing nod.

'How do you know what it means?' Mam demanded.

'Well, Tilly Woolf next door had a cousin try to take advantage of her, she told me – only when I asked her what that meant, she turned red and said her mam told her she wasn't to tell. So I knew it meant kissing or she'd never go that colour. Anyhow, she said if they ever do it, you're to kick them in the whatsits and run off. I could kick the Shack man in the whatsits easy, and with my calipers on it'd really hurt.' She frowned. 'Where are his whatsits anyway?'

Molly raised an eyebrow at her mother, who suppressed a smile.

'You're getting too grown-up for your own good, young miss,' Mam told Daphne.

'She ought to know though, Mam,' Molly said. 'It could keep her safe.'

'Aye, happen so,' Mam said with a sigh. 'Better to lose a little of her innocence than not know how to defend herself if the time has to come.'

'What ought I to know?' Daphne demanded. 'Stop talking about me like I'm not here, it's annoying.'

'I'll have a talk with you in bed tonight,' Molly said. 'But not now. It might put you off your tea.'

'We ought to be sitting down to eat,' Mam said. 'Come to the table, girls, and I'll serve up.'

She left them and went into the kitchen.

'Oughtn't you to be wearing these, Daph?' Molly asked, nodding to the calipers against the dining table.

Her sister groaned. 'I don't have to wear them *all* the time, do I?'

'If you want your legs to get straight and strong you do, like the doctor told you. You'll need good legs when you're a lady-in-waiting at Buckingham Palace, won't you?'

'They weigh a million tons though, and they make me itch worse than wool stockings. Folk'll say I've got leg nits.'

Molly shook her head, smiling. 'Leg nits. Only you, Daphne Clough.'

'Anyhow, Mam said I could take them off while I was having my hair brushed.'

'You ought to put them back on before you put weight on your legs though. Here, I'll help you.'

Daphne didn't object as her sister knelt by her and buckled her into the hated braces. She looked wistfully at the bent, spindly legs poking out from under her school skirt.

'Do they still let you be a lady-in-waiting if you've had polio?' she asked Molly.

'Of course. As long as you haven't got anything infectious you might give the princesses.'

'Stop teasing. I bet they don't.'

Molly frowned as she looked up from the buckles to meet her sister's eye. 'Now why would you think that?'

'I don't know. I just bet they don't, that's all, like when I wasn't allowed to be a Girl Guide patrol leader even though I was the oldest. I bet they don't let you be one of them lady ferry pilots either, like what Pauline Gower is.' A faraway look appeared in the girl's eyes. 'I'd love to do that.'

Molly smiled. 'I see. So you're going to be up flying Spitfires and Hurricanes after a hard day serving caviar at the palace, are you?'

'No. Because they won't let me, because my legs don't work properly.' Daphne rubbed her eye aggressively. 'They won't let me do owt good when I finish school, even if I've got my certificate. I'll be a charity case and have to live in a dustbin.'

'No wonder Mam and Dad called you Daph. Short for daft-as-a-brush, I reckon,' Molly said. 'You're a grammar school girl. That means summat. You'll be able to do owt you want.'

'It won't matter what school I went to if I can't walk properly.'

'What about Mr Roosevelt? His legs don't work but that didn't stop him becoming the president, did it?'

'Yes, but that was in *America*.'

Molly had been ten when the talkies arrived in Britain to change entertainment forever, but her little sister, six years younger, couldn't remember a time when her world hadn't revolved around the magic of Hollywood. She murmured the name 'America' in the same hushed and hallowed tone as someone else might speak of Shangri-La.

'It isn't the same for you anyway, because your legs are going to get better,' Molly said firmly, fastening the final buckle. She gave her sister a stern look. '*If* you stop being an ass and keep wearing your calipers like Dr Anderson told you, your legs'll be as strong as mine in no time.'

'When will they be as strong as yours?'

'I don't know, do I? Just soon, that's all.'

'You promise?'

Molly leaned forward to kiss her sister's forehead. 'I promise.'

# Chapter 3

Two hours later, Molly was sitting on a stool in her dressing room, her hands pressed flat on her knees as she tried to control their shaking.

She made herself call it a dressing room. It was foolish, she knew, but she thought that if she could train herself to use the proper words, she would be less likely to embarrass herself if she ever did get a professional engagement. In actual fact, her 'dressing room' was the broom cupboard at the Boot and Slipper pub, where her grandad Sid – her late father's father – was the landlord.

Still, there was a mirror in it. And she did get dressed there, so it was technically the truth even if she did have to share it with spiders and bottles of Vim.

Molly wondered whether she would ever feel ready for a professional engagement. Sometimes, if she had a spare copper, she bought a copy of *The Stage* and gazed longingly at the advertisements for variety acts. She might even go as far as circling one. But she had never mustered the courage to request an audition.

How could she, when her only experience was in her grandad's pub, and even there she couldn't face the familiar regulars without shaking? She usually managed to get through her act without drying up, but an audition was something else. A panel of strangers, judging her… she shuddered to think of it.

Even if she made it that far, it seemed like such an impossible dream. Molly knew she had some talent, but always a voice whispered that something like that could never happen to someone like her. All there was in her world, all there had ever been, was the mills. Generations of her family had worked in them. It felt as though Molly's brain went on strike whenever she tried to picture herself in another situation, as if it was just too huge to comprehend.

But Gracie had been like her once, hadn't she? Just a working-class northern girl, possessed of a lucky combination of guts, talent and a determination to make it into the spotlight. And if Gracie Fields could do it, why not Molly Clough?

Molly took a few deep breaths as she tried to calm her panic. It was nearly time to go out there.

There was nothing to do but keep practising, she supposed. Try to build her confidence, and hope that one day she would feel ready.

A knock sounded at the door.

'You coming, lass?' a gruff voice demanded. 'Filling up fast.'

'Aye, I'll be right there, Grandad,' Molly called back.

She lifted one hand and watched it shake. Her heart thumped against her chest, sending ripples right up to her throat, and her stomach churned with dread. You'd have thought she was going to war, the way her brain reacted to the prospect of singing for a handful of half-cut men who barely registered her presence while they amused themselves with darts and dominoes. Everything in her body screamed *run, run, run*, and it was all she could do to overrule it.

Molly couldn't help asking herself at times like this if Rita wasn't right – if it was all worth it. She usually felt more settled after the third or fourth song, the music seeming to quell the terror in her heart, but the stage fright beforehand was such a horrible sensation. It almost felt like having the flu: her cheeks hot, her body trembling. But experience would bring a cure, surely. She couldn't imagine Gracie getting herself into such a state.

Molly took another deep breath and exhaled slowly through pursed lips, then smoothed her curls and went to take a seat at the piano in the public bar.

The pub was busy that night. It was Friday: payday for the mill-workers.

Molly recognised the usual crowd. Bill, Terry and Keith, old friends of her father's, propping up the bar and almost fall-down drunk already. There was a gang of smartly dressed men who worked at the department store across the road, a handful of boys she recognised from Taylor's and a few soldiers. It was rare these days that you ventured into a public space without encountering a scattering of khaki. One of them, a lone soldier nursing a pint at a table near the piano, smiled vaguely as she took a seat at the instrument.

Of course there were no ladies in, other than Molly. The pub did have a saloon bar, screened from view by panels of oak and thick stained glass, where women and other folk with pretensions to respectability could go for a drink without exposing themselves to the wild excesses of the public bar. But women rarely visited the Boot in spite of that, and certainly not without a man to accompany them. The place had a reputation for being 'rough' – somewhere women didn't go.

That was why her grandfather was so keen to have Molly tickling the ivories whenever she had a free evening. Sid was desperate to add a veneer of respectability to the place, and he felt that replacing punch-ups with sing-songs would be a good start.

Molly hoped Rita wouldn't forget her promise to come in after her film. She felt braver with her friend nearby.

'All right, you lot, shut thy gobs,' her grandad called from behind the bar. 'Here's our Moll to entertain you again, not that you reprobates deserve it, so make sure you show your appreciation with a big hand.'

'And after that you can keep your big hands to yoursen, unless you want a thump,' Molly said with an arch grin, fighting her panic as she attempted to summon a bit of personality. That was what they wanted, wasn't it? Not just a good voice or a pretty face. Someone they felt was like a pal, or a sweetheart. Someone who could make them laugh.

Sure enough, there was a satisfying gale of drunken laughter in response to her joke. It was accompanied by a smattering of applause, which was heartening even if it was somewhat thinly spread.

Molly again noticed the young soldier sitting near her. He was good-looking in a boyish sort of way, with rather untidy dark brown hair – somehow he had evaded the customary short back and sides – and a warm, inviting smile. If he had looked vague when he caught her eye before, he seemed alert now. All his attention was fixed on Molly as he waited for her to start singing.

That was a rarity for a start. She was background music really: a sort of human wireless. Most of the men continued to talk amongst themselves as she sang and played. Molly wasn't used to being the main event, but this lonely soldier seemed to have nothing better to do tonight than let her entertain him.

Well, so be it. It would be an experience to have an engaged audience, even if it was only one person.

'Here's one for all the soldier boys who're missing their sergeant majors tonight,' Molly said, hoping to impress her uniformed admirer with a military theme, then launched into 'Kiss Me Goodnight, Sergeant Major'.

She could hear her voice quavering, and tried not to think about the room full of men. Instead she focused on the boy watching her from his table, making him her whole audience. It felt easier that way, kidding herself she was performing for just one man.

By the third song, Molly had started to feel more relaxed. She gave them 'Sally, Pride of Our Alley', 'The Biggest Aspidistra in the World', 'Wish Me Luck as You Wave Me Goodbye', then 'Boiled Beef and Carrots' and a few other music-hall tunes for the old gents. She ended with a couple of George Formbys and 'Beer Barrel Polka' as a finale – a favourite with soldiers and civilians alike, with quite a few men joining in.

There was a sufficiently hearty round of applause when she finished, but to Molly it sounded more polite than appreciative. Or was she letting her lack of confidence whisper in her ear? Plenty of them had been singing along, after all, although how much of that was down to the quality of her performance and how much to the beer, she couldn't say. It was hard to gauge how popular she really was among the Boot's patrons, who knew full well that it wasn't a good idea to upset the landlord by booing his granddaughter off stage.

The boy who'd been watching her didn't applaud, Molly noticed. He had kept his eyes fixed on her all through her performance, smiling when a song merited it, humming along with the catchier numbers and generally responding exactly as she would wish. But now she was finished, he didn't join in the clapping. He just watched her curiously, an unreadable expression on his face.

Molly beamed when she saw that Rita had come in, accompanied by young Harry Castle from the mill – her long-time admirer. They were watching from the back, applauding enthusiastically, and Molly waved before indicating that they should go into the saloon to wait for her. She didn't leave the piano stool, however. She always waited for her grandad to tell her whether he wanted her to do a couple more numbers before she disappeared.

Sid was busy behind the bar, but the young soldier got up and approached her. Although actually he wasn't that young, Molly noticed as he drew close. The way he smiled gave him an air of youth, but she supposed he must be about twenty-five.

It was an odd uniform he had on. There was no insignia to show what regiment he belonged to. Molly recognised the material as good-quality officer serge – you tended to notice these things when you worked in textiles – but he had no shoulder pips or collar badges to indicate his rank. It was strange for his uniform to have nothing on it at all. Was he employed as a tailor's mannequin at the department store over the road?

'Um, hello,' he said when he reached her, looking a little bashful. 'I wanted to tell you how much I enjoyed your music.'

He didn't have the local accent, Molly noticed, or any accent that she might have expected to encounter in the Boot and Slipper. To her inexperienced ear he sounded like he could be a lord or something, with his rounded vowels and sounded aitches.

It was lucky he had a uniform on. An accent like that could get you into trouble in a place like this, if you were a civvy. Even with things as they stood, Molly could see a few of the mill lads casting dirty looks in their direction. Clearly they thought this young soldier was getting above himself by talking lah-di-dah to the only girl in the public bar, who they naturally considered theirs by right. Still, the man's uniform and Molly's relationship to the landlord ought to keep the pair of them safe. None of the regulars were drunk enough to risk the consequences of starting a fight with a soldier, and they would be even less keen to do anything that might get them barred.

Molly was anxious not to get drawn into conversation with a stranger when she had friends waiting, but she found herself intrigued by this young man with the fancy accent and unidentifiable uniform. There was a mystery about him, and she would very much like to know what it was.

'Ta, love,' she said with a smile. 'It was nice to sing for someone who seemed to appreciate it. That's a bit of a novelty in this place.'

'You sell yourself short. I wasn't the only one who appreciated it – not by any means.'

'Oh, they're just humouring me because it's my grandad's pub. Still, I managed not to shatter any glasses so I hope it wasn't too terrible.'

'Gracie Fields fan, are you?' the lad said with a smile.

'You might say so.'

Molly paused. Her grandad had caught her eye and given her a nod, which meant she was free to join her friends. The last thing she wanted was to give the young soldier any encouragement if he had amorous intentions. When posh boys like him showed an interest in lasses like her, it was rarely with anything honourable in mind. But she would like to satisfy her curiosity about where he came from, and how he had ended up drinking alone in her grandad's pub.

'I've not seen you in here before,' she said. 'You don't sound like you're a Bradford lad either. On leave?'

'Not exactly.'

She scanned the bare uniform. 'You're not a deserter, are you?'

He smiled. 'No, not that either. Go on, you can have one more guess. If you don't get it the next time, the penalty is you have to let me buy you a drink.'

Molly couldn't help smiling. 'In that case, it's better if I don't guess. I've got friends waiting for me. Are you going to tell me who you are before I go, or are you enjoying playing the part of "mysterious stranger in the pub" too much to let it drop?'

'I've got no objection to telling you who I am, if you'll extend me the same courtesy.' He held out his hand to her. 'Jack Forrester. I'm a Londoner by birth, although I don't have what you might call roots these days.'

'Margaret Clough,' Molly said, standing up to lightly shake the hand he offered. 'That's Molly to my friends. Bradford born, Bradford bred and been bugger all anywhere else unless you count Blackpool.'

'Don't mince your words, do you?'

She shrugged. 'You don't get far putting on airs round here, lad. I talk as it comes to me. Sorry if my vocabulary's not as ladylike as what you're used to down in London.'

'Really?' he said with a smile. 'You're sure you're not trying to shock the poor southerner on purpose, just to laugh in your sleeve about his blushes?'

'Perhaps I am. Is it working?'

Jack pressed a hand to his forehead in a comically affected gesture. 'I'm practically swooning into my smelling salts.'

Molly grinned. It had been a while since anyone had flirted with her – properly flirted, as opposed to the greasy attentions of Shack at work or the bottom pinches she got from the men in the pub. Cautious though she had vowed to be with this new acquaintance, she was forced to confess she was rather enjoying it.

She took out a cigarette and fumbled for a match, her hands still shaking with residual nerves. Molly was only an occasional smoker, but she always felt in need of one to calm her down after performing. She flushed when she noticed Jack Forrester watching her tremble, but he didn't say anything. He merely took out a cigarette lighter and politely lit her smoke.

'So then, Margaret-known-as-Molly Clough,' he said. 'Is it Miss or Mrs?'

'That's rather a personal question.' Molly exhaled a cloud of smoke as she scanned the featureless uniform. 'What about you? I suppose the name goes with a rank, doesn't it?'

'That's rather a personal question.'

She smiled. 'All right, if that's how we're playing this game. It's Miss.'

'And just plain Mr for me. No rank to boast of, although you might say I'm a sort of officer.'

Molly frowned. A *sort* of officer? Surely an officer was something you either were or you weren't. She was feeling more confused by the second. Her new friend, on the other hand, was grinning as if enjoying himself. It was clear he relished keeping her in suspense.

'All right, mysterious Mr Jack Forrester, you've got my attention,' Molly said. 'Are you going to tell me what your big secret is?'

'What, and have you run away as soon as all my glamour and mystery have evaporated? Let me buy you that drink, then I'll think about revealing all.'

'I really can't,' Molly said, realising to her surprise that she did feel some regret about this. 'Like I said, my friends are waiting for me to join them. That wasn't an excuse. Perhaps another night though.'

He shook his head. 'Afraid not. I'm going back to my billet tomorrow.'

'Where are you billeted?'

'London.'

'Oh. Well, it seems it wasn't to be.'

'You might sound a little more cut up about it,' he said with a smile. 'You can wound a chap's feelings, talking that way.'

'I'm sure you'll get over it. I really ought to go.' Molly stubbed her cigarette out in the ashtray on the piano, then hesitated. 'Look... Mr Forrester.'

'Jack, please.'

'Jack then. I have to ask, or it'll haunt me to my grave – what are you doing in here on your own? No offence, but you're not much like our usual patrons.'

He shrugged. 'If you must know, I'm here to hear you.'

Molly frowned. 'Me? What do you mean?'

'I came to town to visit the Alhambra. I was at a loose end tonight and I heard a whisper in my guest house that a half-decent lady singer was performing at a pub nearby, so I thought I might as well stop in.'

'Someone really said that about me?' Molly asked, blinking.

'Yes, there were a couple of old chaps jawing about you in the dining room. It sounded like you were a bit of a draw. I'm very glad my steak was tough or I might have left the table before I'd had a chance to eavesdrop.'

'And you genuinely liked my act?'

'You've got talent, definitely. A little raw and unpolished, and you'd do rather better if you stopped trying to imitate Gracie Fields' personality and showed off more of your own. I'd certainly have liked to see more of it.'

Molly stared at him, puzzled. 'I can't believe you came in tonight just to hear me sing. Why?'

'Because that's my job – at least, it's part of my job.' Jack turned sideways so she could see a black tab on the shoulder of his uniform, embroidered with white letters. 'Here's your final clue. If you don't guess my secret this time, Miss Clough, I'll be sorely disappointed.'

Molly squinted at the tab in the low pub light. *E-N-S-A…*

'ENSA!' she said. 'You're with ENSA? The entertainment organisation?'

'I knew you'd get there in the end.' Jack reached over to his table to pick up his cap and put it on. Molly noticed that this, too, bore a brass badge with E-N-S-A incorporated into it. 'I'm a crooner with a concert party, entertaining the troops, but I do a little talent spotting on behalf of the organisation as well. That's why I'm here. I was sent to adjudicate at an audition call for professionals at the Alhambra. We consider semi-professionals and amateurs too though, and we always need decent singers.'

'You can't mean me?'

'Why not? ENSA's desperate for acts at the moment. There are a lot of bored, homesick men here and abroad in dire need of entertainment while they wait for the balloon to go up. If you've ever dreamed of employing your talents professionally, there's never been a better time to get a foot in the stage door.'

'Yes, but… I've got no experience. I'm not on the variety circuit or owt. In the daytime I'm a weaver in a mill, and at night I sing here. For my grandad,' Molly finished feebly.

'All that matters is that you've got talent,' Jack said. 'Plenty of acts touring with ENSA had done nothing more adventurous than a church hall revue before this war began. Now they're treading the boards over in Europe for hundreds of appreciative soldiers.' He paused. 'Well, some of them are appreciative.'

Molly stood in stunned silence as Jack pressed a card into her hand. He took his greatcoat from the back of his chair and started putting it on.

'I ought to go, before I overstay my welcome,' he said, with a sidelong glance at a group of men flashing him resentful looks. 'Think about it, won't you? It's ten quid a week if you get in.'

'Ten quid!'

'That's right: ten for performers and musicians, four for chorus. There might be overseas work too, if you've ever had a hankering to travel.' He finished buttoning himself up and nodded. 'Well, good luck. I hope our paths will cross again, Miss Clough.'

# Chapter 4

Molly remained where she was for some time after Jack Forrester had left. After a while, she sank down on to her piano stool again. A couple of the men who had been glaring at Jack endeavoured to get her attention, but Molly ignored them. None pressed the point, knowing Sid would sling them out if she complained they had been getting fresh.

She looked at the card in her hand. It bore the NAAFI crest and the same winged ENSA insignia Jack had worn on his cap, as well as a name, address and telephone number. The name was 'Dennis Walmsley, assistant to Mr Dean', and the address was that of the Theatre Royal on Drury Lane, where ENSA had its headquarters. Molly didn't know the name Dennis Walmsley, but she knew who Mr Dean was. Basil Dean was the director and producer who had founded ENSA to provide entertainment for the troops, shortly after war had been declared.

Molly was well aware of ENSA, of course – the Entertainments National Service Association, although the popular joke among servicemen was that the initials really ought to stand for Every Night Something Awful. Her brother Ted had attended several ENSA concerts over in France, which had been made compulsory by his commanding officer. Ted was happy to go though, no matter how bad the show, since there were usually a couple of pretty girls in the concert party to make it worth his while. For the soldiers of the British Expeditionary Force, with nothing much to do but polish their rifles and wait for the war to begin in earnest, any sort of entertainment must be a relief.

Molly turned the card over. There was nothing on the back.

What did this Jack Forrester expect her to do? Did he want her to traipse all the way to London on the off-chance of an audition, bindle stick over her shoulder like Dick Whittington?

She wondered if she ought to be flattered that he had thought her worthy of the organisation. Or should it be the opposite? Ought she to be insulted? ENSA was something of a joke, after all. But all Molly actually felt after the strange encounter was dazed.

Could it have been a pick-up line? The man had certainly seemed keen to buy her a drink, and he'd proved a very competent flirt. As she had reflected when he first approached her, when posh boys paid attention to girls like her, it usually meant they had mischief in mind.

But then he had run away right after pressing the card on her, never to meet her again. While her brain whispered that she ought to be careful, Molly couldn't help feeling disappointed that Jack hadn't arranged to see her on a future occasion. No doubt he flirted with a lot of young women in the course of his work, but he had been rather amusing.

After looking at the card again, weighing up whether it was worthwhile hanging on to the thing or if she should leave it in the ashtray, Molly tucked it into her handbag and went to seek out Rita in the saloon bar.

—

Molly found her best friend at a table in the corner, giggling as Harry whispered something in her ear. From the colour of Rita's cheeks, she suspected it was something naughty.

It made Molly smile, seeing them together. Harry had been making sheep's eyes at Rita for months, but despite Rita giving him as much encouragement as she could, he had never plucked up the courage to make a date with her. He was a confident enough lad normally – both Molly and Rita had known him since schooldays – but Rita's good looks tended to make even the cockiest young man shy around her, as if doubting he could ever be worthy of such a beauty.

If it hadn't been for that odd encounter with Jack Forrester, Molly would probably have slipped away and left Rita and Harry to enjoy their evening. She had to tell someone about it though, or she was sure she might burst with the strangeness of it. Besides, Rita had seen her now, and Molly knew her friend wouldn't let her sneak off.

'Evening,' she said, taking a seat. 'Did you not go to the flicks with the girls then, Reet?'

'Oh no, I did.' Rita nudged Harry, who was busy nuzzling her ear. 'This one was in the ticket queue with a couple of lads from work, so we thought it made sense to go as one big group. Didn't we, Harry?'

'We did, aye.' Harry left Rita's ear alone and nodded to Molly. 'Heyup, Moll. Cracking show, that. Tell you what, you've got some lungs on you.'

'Ta,' Molly said, smiling at him. 'What made you come along?'

'Couldn't let Rita come in here on her own, could I?' He smiled sheepishly when Rita nudged him. 'And, er, she said what a treat it'd be for me to hear you sing. So naturally I couldn't say no.'

Molly laughed. 'All right, I'll believe you. How was the film?'

Harry grinned. 'Didn't see much of it.'

'Ah. Like that, was it?'

'Oh, get away with you, embarrassing me,' Rita said, nudging him, although she was smirking just as much as Harry. 'If you want to make yoursen useful, lad, fetch Molly a drink. She must be parched after all that singing. I wouldn't mind another either.'

'I won't say no to a half of milk stout,' Molly said. 'Tell my grandad you're with me and he won't charge you, Harry.'

'Really? In that case, I'll come again.' Harry stood up. 'Back in a minute, ladies.'

'Did you see who were here before?' Rita asked in a low voice as soon as her beau had left them alone.

'Who?'

'Shack. I spotted him when we came in, standing around on his own.'

Molly grimaced. 'Really, Shack was here? I didn't see him.'

'He kept his hat on but it was definitely him. I think he left before you finished though. Has he never been in before?'

'Not when I've been here.'

'He came in for you. I'm sure he did,' Rita murmured. 'He seemed determined to find out where you go of an evening earlier.'

'Perhaps,' Molly said uncertainly. 'It could be coincidence though. How would he know I play here?'

'He knew where we went dancing, didn't he? And there's plenty of lads from the mill who are regulars.'

'I suppose so.'

Rita rested a hand on Molly's. 'You ought to watch yoursen,' she whispered. 'Stay with me and Harry tonight. Don't walk home alone, all right?'

'I'll be OK. It's only quarter of a mile.'

'Humour me, please. It's not only him. You never know who's lurking in the blackout.'

Molly squeezed her friend's hand. 'All right, for you then.'

It was a question Molly had often pondered – just how dangerous was their overlooker? He was lecherous, yes, but how far would he push his luck with the women who worked under him? Certainly there was worse to fear from him than a pinched bottom. Molly well remembered an occasion when she was just fifteen, still naive in the ways of men, and had found herself alone in Shack's office. When he had attempted to press a kiss on her then, she had escaped back into the mill. What might have happened if she hadn't managed to evade him? Would it have stopped at a kiss?

That was the problem: all the girls at Taylor's whispered that you should never be alone with the overlooker, but few dared speak openly about why. He had the power to hire and fire at will, so it was rare anyone made a complaint against him – it wasn't worth the risk. The few women who had complained to Mr Taylor about Shack's behaviour had found themselves quickly jobless. You just had to stick close to your friends and hope for safety in numbers. But if he had come to the pub especially to find Molly, where else might he follow her to?

It might be coincidence, of course. He hadn't necessarily come here tonight to seek her out. But... what if it wasn't?

Molly looked thoughtfully at the distorted shapes of the men in the public bar through one of the saloon's thick stained-glass panels.

'You know, it isn't so much for my own sake that I worry about men and what they can do,' she murmured to Rita. 'It's our Daph I can't help thinking about. She's starting to look ever so grown-up, Reet.'

Rita frowned. 'She can't be courting already? I thought she wasn't sixteen yet.'

'She's not, and naive for her age at that. I suppose that's natural, when she's been kept at home so much. But she looks like a young woman, and that worries me. I tease her about getting a job, but honestly, it scares me to death that she'd ever be in the hands of someone like Shack.'

'She is a bonny little thing,' Rita said quietly.

'Aye, and don't she know it?' Molly said with a half-smile. 'That's what I mean: it's the worst combination. Bonny, innocent, and her legs too weak to run away if someone like him ever did try to... you know, take advantage.'

'Will she be able to get a job with her bad legs?'

'She'll have to work doing summat, unless I can somehow earn enough to support her. The bit of money Mr Taylor gives us to keep her at school will stop once she turns sixteen. I don't think Daph realises how hard it is to manage on my wages and what our mam can bring in from charring.'

'She'll get her certificate all right, won't she?' Rita asked.

'Aye, she'll have no trouble there. She's got plenty of brains. Still, even with a grammar school education, she might struggle to find a good job unless her legs get stronger. She can only walk a short way without crutches. It's a big improvement on where she was five year ago, when she couldn't walk by herself at all, but…' Molly pressed her eyes closed. 'She still seems so helpless,' she whispered. 'Such a child.'

'Poor bairn,' Rita said feelingly. 'It don't seem fair. Daph getting ill, and then your dad not long after.'

'She doesn't realise how helpless she is, that's the worst thing.' Molly smiled as she thought about her sister. 'Honestly, Reet, the kid's fierce enough for owt. You should've heard her threatening to fight Shack when our mam was worried he'd been trying it on with me. I'd hate for her to ever have to change. I hate the idea she has to learn how unfair the world is, and how much exists that can hurt her. But Daphne's nearly a woman, and I know me and Mam won't be able to protect her from everything.'

'At least a decent education ought to keep her out of the mills,' Rita observed.

'That's exactly what worries me,' Molly said in a low voice. 'He knows about her. Shack. Told me he could put a word in with old Taylor about finding a place for her at the mill, all jolly and pompous as if he were doing me a huge favour – summat where she'd not be on her feet too much, he said. I told him she was staying at school and we were set on her being a secretary. But if she finds it hard to get owt and me and Mam are struggling, she might feel obliged to take whatever's on offer, you know? Especially after Mr Taylor's been good to us and paid towards her schooling.' Molly shivered. 'I'd walk the streets before I'd let my sister work for Shack.'

Rita shook her head. 'You don't mean that.'

'Don't I though? I bloody do. I'd do anything to keep our Daph out of his hands. Anything.'

Harry returned with two halves for the women and a pint of bitter for himself, halting their conversation.

'What're you two lasses looking so serious about?' he asked. 'Not been talking about me, I hope.'

Rita smiled. 'There are other topics of conversation, Harry Castle.'

'Well, what is it?'

'I was going to talk about this,' Molly said, taking the ENSA card from her handbag and putting it on the table.

Harry picked it up. 'E–N–S–A,' he read. 'What's that stand for?'

Rita shook her head. 'Don't you ever read the papers?'

'Not if I can help it. I'm sick to death of hearing about the ruddy war. I'll have to hear enough about it after I get my call-up.'

'Oh, don't,' Rita said, shuddering. 'I can't bear to think of you marching off to war, Harry. Let's hope it's all over before they need you.'

He gave her a kiss. 'I never knew you cared, Reet,' he said softly. She flushed a little as she returned the kiss.

Molly smiled. 'Do you two want to give me ninepence and send me to the pictures? That's what my mam and dad used to do when we were kids and they wanted time alone.'

'Sorry,' Rita said with a smile. 'Go on, tell us about your card. I'm sure Harry can keep his lips to hissen for five minutes.'

'I had a horrible feeling you were going to say that,' Harry muttered.

'Honestly, it's all right if you want to be by yourselves,' Molly said. 'I'll go home and tell you about it at work tomorrow instead.'

'You will not,' Rita said firmly. 'I told you, I'm not having you walking home on your own.' She turned to her boyfriend. 'Harry, sit on your hands and move over. Then if you behave tonight, I'll let you take me to the pictures on Saturday just us two.'

'Will you sit on the back row with me and not complain if I slip the usherette a few bob to point her torch the other way?'

'Love, I'll even chip in sixpence.'

Harry smiled, and sat on his hands as instructed. 'All right, I'll behave. But you promised, mind.' He turned to Molly. 'What's the card for then, Moll? Is this Dennis Walmsley bloke the soldier we saw talking to you?'

'No,' Molly said. 'But that was who gave me the card. Jack Forrester.' She took a sip of milk stout. 'And don't let the khaki deceive you. He isn't a soldier.'

'He was quite good-looking, wasn't he?' Rita observed. 'Was he after you?'

'I'm… not sure. He did offer to buy me a drink, but he ran off pretty quickly when I said no. He's billeted in London so I doubt we'll bump into each other again. Anyhow, he was too posh for the likes of me.' Molly gazed at the card. 'Shame, really. He was a bit of a laugh.'

Rita picked up the card. 'There's an address on here. Maybe he wants you to write to him.'

Molly shook her head. 'That's ENSA's address, not his.'

'What is this ENSA?' Harry asked. 'Aren't they them shows on the wireless?'

'I swear the boy lives under a rock,' Rita said, rolling her eyes. 'They put on concerts for the troops, don't they, you barmpot? It stands for… well, I can't remember what it stands for, but that's what they do.'

Molly nodded. 'Our Ted's been to a few. He says they're all right, but he's easily pleased. If there are girls showing their legs, he's happy.'

'What's that got to do with this boyfriend of yours, Moll?' Harry asked, removing one of the hands he'd clamped under his thigh so he could sip his pint.

'That's who he is. He's a civvy, not a soldier – that was an ENSA uniform. He told me he was a crooner with a concert party. He scouts for new acts too. That's why he was in town: to oversee some auditions at the Alhambra.'

Rita frowned. 'You're not saying he was after recruiting you for ENSA?'

'I don't think you need to sound quite so surprised,' Molly said. 'I'm not that dreadful, am I?'

'You're not dreadful at all. But ENSA – aren't they supposed to be… well, you know, a bit third-rate?'

'The shows on the wireless are all right, if you like that type of thing,' Harry said. 'Gracie Fields, George Formby and that.'

'Aye, they put the ones with the big stars on the wireless,' Rita said scornfully. 'My cousin Debbie's in the ATS and she says the ones they get are nowt but blokes trying to whistle like bluetits and ventriloquists with their lips moving.' Rita paused to extract a cigarette from her pack of Player's and light it. 'Every dismal end-of-pier act who was chucked out of work when they closed the seasides is in ENSA now, Deb reckons. And the lads and lasses in their squadron *have* to go. Their commanding officer made it a rule that concerts are treated the same as a parade – except Deb says she'd rather square-bash for four hours in the rain than have to sit through some of them.'

'Our Ted's CO made them compulsory too,' Molly said. 'They can't all be rubbish though. The good acts were put out of work along with the bad when they shut down the holiday resorts. Some of them must be putting on decent shows.'

'They probably save those for the officers' mess and inflict the rest on the poor sods in the NAAFI canteen,' Rita said. 'You're too good for them, Moll.'

Despite her friend's confidence in her, Molly couldn't allow herself to believe this. ENSA might be a joke to a lot of people, but they had talent in their ranks despite their reputation, and some big stars too. Gracie was in ENSA, for a start. Jack Forrester had said Molly had talent, yes, but he'd also said it was raw and unpolished. ENSA's standards may be low, but she couldn't believe they were low enough to consider an untrained pub singer with no professional experience and almost debilitating stage fright.

'What's it pay, this ENSA thing?' Harry asked.

'Hmm?' Molly roused herself. 'Oh. Ten pound a week.'

Harry spluttered on his beer. 'How much?'

'That's what that bloke Jack told me. Ten for performers, four for chorus.'

Rita stared at her. 'Bloody hell!' She flashed an embarrassed glance at Harry. 'I mean, um, blumming heck.'

Harry grinned. 'Don't worry, love. I had no illusions you were a blushing flower.' He shook his head. 'Ten quid just for belting out a few tunes. Tell you what, wish I'd kept up the chapel choir when I were a bairn.'

That was another thing that triggered Molly's ever-active self-doubt. Ten pounds seemed like so much money. Maybe not to someone as plummy as Jack Forrester, who she wouldn't be surprised to learn had a country estate filled with butlers, but to the likes of Molly Clough it sounded like a small fortune. She earned less than two pounds at the mill, all of which she handed over to her mother, plus an extra six or seven bob on piecework that she was allowed to keep for her pocket money. It wasn't much for a forty-eight-hour week amidst the heat, dust and noise of the weaving shed. What a thing it would be to earn five times that amount! It felt impossible that anything she was capable of could be deserving of such riches.

What couldn't she do with ten pounds a week though? She could take care of her sister, pay for a specialist doctor, their mam could give up the hateful charring that gave her so much pain in her back...

'It does sound a lot of money, doesn't it?' Molly said dreamily.

'I had no idea ENSA performers were paid so well,' Rita said. 'And he's invited you to go to an audition, has he, this admirer of yours?'

Molly hesitated, thinking back over her conversation with Jack Forrester. Now she reflected on it, she wasn't sure the word 'audition' had ever been mentioned. Jack had said she had talent, had told her ENSA needed singers, had given her the card. But he hadn't said in so many words what he wanted her to do. Surely if he really thought she had a chance, he'd have been more specific about her next steps?

'Not exactly,' Molly said. 'He just said he liked my singing and gave me this card. I've got no idea if I'm supposed to ring them up or write or what.'

'For ten pound a week? I'd run out and find a phone box now, love,' Harry said. 'Warble "Biggest Aspidistra" down the line until they give you an audition just to get rid of you.'

'It'll be at least half a dollar for a trunk call to London. I'm not made of money, Harry.'

'I'll lend you the half-crown. Just as long as you promise to remember me when you're famous.'

'I'm worried I've got the wrong end of the stick, that's all,' Molly said. 'Jack told me he liked my voice but it was raw, whatever that means. Happen he was trying to tell me I ought to get more practice. Maybe have some proper voice training, as if I could afford owt like that.'

'Or maybe it was all a line,' Rita said, pursing her lips. 'He is a man, at the end of the day.'

Harry nudged her. 'Oi.'

'Yes, I thought about that,' Molly admitted. 'Still, ENSA is something to consider. If I did decide to go for it though, I'd probably only get one chance. I don't want to waste it by rushing into anything.'

'You've said that about every chance you've had so far,' Rita pointed out. 'You've come into work raving to me about any number of singing jobs you've read about, you get as far as writing down the address, then you lose your bottle.'

'One-night stands, that's all. Not regular jobs, with proper pay and a future.'

'It's all experience, isn't it? And money, which is more than you get playing here. I reckon that's just an excuse.'

'It's not an excuse. I want to be sure I'm ready when I do it.' Molly shivered. 'I have these horrible visions.'

'Of what?' Harry asked.

'Mostly of audition panels giving me the raspberry. Sometimes there's one of those giant shepherd's crooks yanking me off stage while dogs howl at the stage door.'

Harry laughed. 'You're daft, you are. How can you sit there singing and not know you're good at it?'

Rita gave him an approving smile for these words of encouragement, and consented to close the gap she had imposed between them. Harry stretched an arm around her shoulders.

'There's good enough for the Boot and there's good enough for garrison theatres in front of hundreds of men,' Molly said. 'And then there's my nerves. What if I faint or throw up, or my knickers fall down, or they pelt me with soggy tomatoes?'

Harry shook his head. 'You've put far too much thought into this, lass.'

'They wouldn't do that,' Rita said. 'Not now tomatoes have gone up to a shilling a pound.'

'Really, you think that's all that'll stop them? I'd be just as upset if it were turnips.' Molly sighed. 'Oh, but ten quid a week though. My mam and sister could live like queens if I were on ten quid a week.'

Harry finished off his drink. 'Better to take a chance than spend your life wondering what might've been, if you ask me.'

'He's right,' Rita said. 'Since we were all at school, you've been talking about getting out of Bradford and seeing the world. Well, this could be your chance. The war won't last forever. It might not even last while next month. Grab the opportunity while the going's good, love.'

Molly raised an eyebrow. 'What happened to "you're too good for them, Moll"?'

'Not at ten quid a week you're not.' Rita stubbed out her cigarette. 'Look at it this way. If you try for ENSA and it don't work out, you'll be no worse off than you were before. But if it does, it could be everything you've ever wanted. Travel. A good wage. All the things you've always talked about.'

'Well, yes, but… it just feels so unlikely. That it could happen to me, I mean.'

'There you go again, talking yourself out of it.' Rita leaned over the table to seize her friend's hands. 'There aren't many ways out for lasses like us, Moll. You're lucky – you've got a talent. For God's sake, use it.'

'Hear, hear,' Harry said, toasting the sentiment with his beer. 'You'd be a prize twit if you let a chance like this get away.'

Molly couldn't help thinking she would be a prize twit too. But still there was that image of the audition panel, sitting there, judging her. Of hundreds of truculent men forced to attend a concert they didn't want to be at, their resentful eyes fixed on Molly… she could feel herself trembling just thinking about it.

'I'll give it some thought,' was all she felt able to say as she tucked Jack's card into her handbag.

## Chapter 6

Molly did give it some thought. She thought about it all the next morning at work, and that afternoon when she took her sister to the New Victoria Picture House. She was so deep in thought that she didn't even notice when the finale music for *Robin Hood* started to play. She roused herself when Daphne nudged her in the ribs.

'What's up with you?' Daphne demanded as the house lights came up. 'You've hardly said a word all afternoon. You didn't even make that sighing moany noise you usually do when Will Scarlet comes on.'

'I do no such thing.'

'You do. Like this.' Daphne rolled her eyes as she did an impression of a pathetic juddering sigh, a noise Molly was sure she had never made in her life. She couldn't help laughing.

'Well, Patric Knowles is a very handsome man,' she said. 'Not quite as handsome as Clark Gable, but if you will make me come and see this picture every Saturday then I ought to have someone nice to look at. And he's a West Riding lad.'

'I don't know how you can look at him when Errol's on. He's much better than Will Scarlet, and old big-ears Gable.'

'Come on.' Molly helped her sister to her feet, glancing at the cinema-goers filing out around them. 'You're going to fetch the pair of us a clout, talking about Clark like that around all these lasses. I'll buy you a cup of tea at the cafe.'

'And a bun?'

Molly smiled. 'We'll see.'

'Have you got any spice left?' Daphne asked hopefully. 'I finished mine.'

'Go on then.' Molly handed over a paper bag, which her sister seized on gleefully. On cinema days, their mother always made up a bag each of what Daphne called Coconut Dip: a mix of sugar, desiccated coconut and cocoa powder, into which a wet finger could be dipped and sucked. Portions were smaller now than before the sugar ration, but Mam still managed to keep a bit out of their twelve ounces for the weekly treat. Molly, knowing her sister's weakness for sweet things, generally left hers untouched so Daphne could have a second helping.

Daphne's crutches were under the seat, and Molly handed them up to her. When the cinema had cleared, Daphne swung herself down the aisle with a deftness born of much practice.

'Don't lean too heavily on your sticks,' Molly warned as they waited for the foyer to empty so they could exit. 'You ought to put as much weight on your legs as you can bear to, Daph. It helps build the muscles, the doctor says.'

'Oh, stop nagging. It hurts, all right?'

'I know it does, but you want them to get strong, don't you?'

'Suppose,' Daphne muttered. 'OK, I'll try.'

She shifted her weight, grimacing. Molly knew Daphne hated to put weight on her legs when they were out in public, not only because of the pain but also the self-consciousness the child felt about the way it caused her legs to bend. But the doctor said she had to build up her muscles if she was ever to be free of crutches and calipers for good.

They exited the cinema into the dull, grimy streets of Bradford. To Molly, her home city always felt like a sort of industrial forest, with soot-black chimneys in place of trees, cobblestones instead of grass and whey-faced, underfed people huddled in overcoats instead of wildlife. Outside of the annual Bowling Tide festivities in August, the place could feel so bleak and colourless, especially since war had arrived to switch off the lights. It made her long all the more to see new places, new faces – for a life beyond the one she had always known.

Molly's eyes narrowed when she spotted a gang of lads in their shirtsleeves loafing outside the Alhambra theatre, hassling the girls who went by.

Actually, perhaps a jungle was a more appropriate comparison than a forest. The city certainly had its share of predators.

She took her sister's arm to guide her out of sight of the gang, but it was too late. One of the boys had spotted them and gave a scoffing laugh.

'All right, bowlegs?' he called to Daphne. His jeer transformed into a wolf whistle when Daphne turned to glare at him, however. 'Here, you're not bad for a cripple, are you, blondie?' He winked. 'Tell you what, love, I've got summat over here you can hold on to for support.' The rest guffawed appreciatively at this specimen of their mate's sophisticated wit.

Molly gave the boy a look that could have withered a bunch of daisies. She took Daphne's arm and hurried her away.

'Just ignore them next time,' she said. 'That's what they want: attention. Ignoring them hurts them more than rising to the bait, even if it's just with a mucky look.'

Daphne shrugged. 'I don't care. Sally Crowther at my school says that when boys tease you like that, it's because they like you.'

'You what?'

'That's what Sally says. She's got three boyfriends already, even though she's only my age. She says it's a compliment when men pay attention to us and we ought to be flattered if they whistle and shout, or if boys pull your hair to make you cry and daft stuff like that. It's a sort of flirting, she says.'

Molly stopped walking and took hold of her sister's shoulders. 'Don't you *ever* listen to anyone who tells you rubbish like that, d'you hear? Ever.'

Daphne blinked at her sister's earnest tone. 'Lots of girls at school say stuff like that though.'

'Then lots of girls are talking through their hats.'

'Why are you so cross about it, Moll?'

'Because… because it gives lads free rein to treat you like muck, that's why. If someone loves you, or even just likes you, they don't treat you like that. They don't insult you or pick on you or try to hurt you. They sure as heck don't make you cry. They show you respect. When you start walking out with boyfriends, our Daph, I want you to remember that. Will you?'

'All right. If you're going to get all upset about it.'

Daphne looked puzzled by her sister's sudden outburst. She couldn't see what was in Molly's mind: her worries that her bonny little sister – fearless, confident but oh so much more vulnerable and sheltered than her peers – would be easy prey for any man who wanted to abuse her.

'Sorry.' Gently, Molly brushed an escaped hair from her sister's face. 'I hate it when girls your age are told lies like that, that's all. Once you start believing them, boys think they can treat you however they like. It's only because I love you that I get protective, you know, babby.'

Daphne smiled. 'What're you talking soft for?'

'Oh, I don't know.' Molly held on to her sister's elbow as a tram trundled by, then guided her across the tracks. 'Thinking about the future, I suppose. You and Mam. Me.'

'That's why you've been quiet all afternoon?'

'Aye, suppose it is.' Molly paused, remembering what she had copied down from the noticeboard at work that morning. 'I've been thinking about the mill.'

'Are you going to leave?' Daphne said, her expression turning black. 'You should. I hate that old place. It killed Dad and now it makes you miserable all the time.'

'It don't always make me miserable. Rita's there, and my other friends.'

'Huh. They should leave too. Everyone should who works in a mill, then we can close the ugly, evil things down. Making everything smoky and dark and smelly.' Daphne glared at a chimney pumping out black smoke in the distance, as if she could demolish the thing through sheer strength of will.

'And what will people do then, sing for their suppers?' Molly asked. 'There's not much work for folk like us apart from the mills, Daph. There never has been. You'll find a better future now you've had a decent education, but it's too late for me.'

'No it isn't. Because you *can* sing for your supper, can't you?' Daphne said. 'You could make money singing if you wanted. You're as good as anyone off the wireless.'

Molly smiled. 'That's not what you normally say.'

'That's just teasing,' Daphne said dismissively. 'You could, you know. I don't understand why you don't.'

'Let's not talk about it in the street,' Molly said, putting an arm around her sister's shoulders. 'I don't want every Tom, Dick and Freddie knowing my business.'

They had reached the cafe where they usually stopped after a trip to the pictures. Molly did like to make a day out of it for Daphne when she could afford to, and her grandad had done well enough the night before to slip her five bob from the till with strict instructions to spend it on herself and her sister. Daph had precious few treats in life, and while they might tease each other to pieces like any siblings, Molly knew her little sister looked forward to their special time together on Saturday afternoons.

Inside the cafe, Molly helped her sister into a seat and claimed the one opposite. The waitress who approached them was new, Molly noticed. Her face crinkled with pity when she saw Daphne's crutches propped against the window and the heavy metal calipers clamped to her legs.

'Aww, bless the lamb,' she said in a hushed voice to Molly. 'Lame, is she, the little girl?'

'She is,' Daphne said brightly. 'Her ears still work as well as ever though. And she isn't a little girl.'

Molly couldn't help smiling, although she had some pity for the waitress's flushed cheeks. The woman meant well, she supposed. People often meant well. It's a shame that meaning well seemed so rarely to translate into doing well.

'That was naughty, wasn't it?' Daphne said in an undertone after they'd ordered and the waitress had gone to fetch a couple of fruit scones and a pot of tea.

'Well, maybe a little,' Molly said. 'She wasn't trying to be unkind. Still, you were entitled to be cross. Happen she'll know better for next time.'

'Why do people think my legs not working properly means I must be deaf as well? They talk about me to you and Mam as if I'm not there.'

'Honestly, Daph, I wish I knew. It's just one of the strange things about people. They don't mean to be rude.'

'Don't they? Then they should jolly well try harder not to be.'

'I wonder what the scones will be like today,' Molly said, attempting to move the conversation on to happier subjects.

'I only had about two currants in mine last time,' Daphne observed glumly. 'I don't mind that, but I miss how sweet and crumbly they used to be.'

'It's difficult now sugar and butter are rationed. We should count ourselves lucky things aren't any worse.'

'I can't wait till the war stops and we can have proper sweet things again.' Daphne fixed her sister in a stern gaze. 'Anyhow, don't think I'm going to let you off telling me what you've been quiet all day for. You promised, Moll.'

'All right. But you mustn't say owt to Mam yet, OK?'

Daphne swelled, proud to be sharing a confidence.

'Cross my heart,' she said, doing so. 'Is it that Shack man?'

'No. Well, it concerns him a little.'

The waitress came back with their tea. While she was pouring, Molly reached into her handbag. She took out the note she had scribbled that morning and the ENSA card Jack had given her and laid them side by side.

'What are they?' Daphne asked, trying and failing to read her sister's handwriting upside down over the teapot.

'My future. I'm hoping one of them will be, at least. I'm just not sure which.'

Molly was silent as she looked from one to the other.

'Tell me what they mean then,' Daphne demanded impatiently. 'I hate mysteries. That's why I always read the last page of an Agatha Christie first.'

Molly looked up at her sister in shock. 'You don't really, do you?'

'Course. I'd go mad if I didn't know who'd done it right away.' She shook her head. 'You're a monster.'

'Are they about singing for money like I said? If they are, you should definitely do it. I would.'

'Go ahead,' Molly said with a laugh. 'You could make your fortune out of people paying you to shut up.'

'They wouldn't, they'd beg for more. I've been practising. Here, listen.'

Daphne cleared her throat and burst into a rousing chorus of 'There'll Always Be an England', singing at the top of her voice. The other customers turned to look, some with amusement, others with irritation, but most quickly looked away when they saw Daphne's condition. A few continued to watch, however, grinning – the sort of people you found everywhere, who never said no to free entertainment regardless of quality. If only Molly could be sure it was that sort who would make up the lion's share of any ENSA audience, she would apply in a heartbeat.

Daphne had a soaring voice, strong and clear like her sister's, but she had a habit of drifting seriously off-key. Molly put her hands over her ears as Daphne warbled through the song, hitting the occasional right note more by chance than intention.

'All right, all right, stop before you get us thrown out,' she said, laughing.

Daphne stopped, grinning. 'You did tell me to go ahead.'

'I didn't think you actually would! You're mad, you are.'

Daphne smirked at the staring customers. She bobbed her head in a bow and there was some scattered applause: more for her nerve than her singing, Molly suspected.

'I'm much better than I used to be though, aren't I?' Daphne asked. 'They clapped. You heard them.'

'Aye, they clapped when you stopped. You might learn a lesson from that.' Molly shook her head. 'Does nowt embarrass you?'

Daphne shrugged. 'People look at me anyway. I'd rather feel like they're looking at me because I'm being interesting than because my legs don't work.'

'You're an odd little thing,' Molly said with a smile. 'Not that I'd have you any other way. I'm not sure how you can possibly be my sister though.'

Daphne sipped her tea. 'Me neither. I reckon Mam and Dad actually stole you from the monkey house at Blackpool Tower.'

'Ha ruddy ha. Seriously, how do you do that? Sing with everyone looking at you, bold as brass? I can't sing a note in front of people without shaking. If there's a trick to it, I'd love to know what it is.'

Daphne pondered this.

'I think the trick is in being different already,' she said. 'I've been different most of my life. If I'd been upset every time people paid attention to me, I'd have been miserable all the time. So I just decided not to be upset about it, that's all. If they want to look at me, let them, and I'll make sure I give them summat worth looking at.'

'I wish I could do that,' Molly said wistfully.

'It's easy. You just have to stop caring what people think of you. Then you can do owt you want.'

'Easy for you. Not for me. I'm not that sort of person.'

'I bet you haven't even tried properly.' Daphne picked up the scribbled note. 'What does this say then? I can't read your rubbishy writing.'

'It's an advertisement that was on the noticeboard at the mill. I copied it down.' Molly took the note and read it out. '"Bright, tidy girl with a head for figures needed as wages clerk. Apply direct to Mr Taylor. £140–£150 per annum, according to ability. Training provided.'"

'What's that got to do with you?' Daphne asked.

'I was thinking of applying, wasn't I? My arithmetic's pretty good, and Taylor knows I'm reliable after seven year with the company. There's nowt to lose by putting myself forward. It'll mean ten bob a week extra for us, and it gets me out of the weaving shed.' Molly's brow lowered. 'Away from Shack.'

'It's not what you want to do with your life though, is it?' Daphne asked. 'You always said you wanted to see the world.'

'There'll be a time for that, I hope. I'm only twenty-one, and not courting yet. Nor will I be either, while there are things I want to get done.'

'Not even if Clark Gable asks?'

Molly smiled. 'Well, maybe for Clark. But I'm not expecting him to sweep me off my feet just yet.'

'Hmm.' Daphne pursed her lips as if sceptical about this. 'What's the little card for? Is that a job too? You said one of them was going to be your future.'

Molly looked at the ENSA card, tracing the letters in the organisation's insignia with her fingertip.

ENSA could mean travel, just like she'd always dreamed of. And money, real money – the sort of wage that meant her sister could get the high-quality medical care that might make all the difference to her adult life. New people; new places; a life away from Bradford and the mills. But at the same time, a career based on her talent as a singer seemed so impossible – so distant and unreal. It couldn't be part of ordinary, unexceptional Molly Clough's future, she was sure.

Even if by some miracle she applied and was successful, wartime entertainment felt highly insecure as a career. As Rita had said in the pub, the war might end any day. Taylor's may not be perfect but Molly at least knew she had a job there for life, with a small but reliable salary. While part of her felt she would be mad to throw away her one opportunity to make it as an entertainer, a louder, more sensible part of herself told her she would be a fool to give up a steady job for the chance of a career in show business that might last a matter of months.

The wages clerk job, on the other hand, was something real – something better than what she had at the moment, and something she actually had a chance of achieving. Yes, Molly could believe in the wages clerk job. It would mean more money to support her family, even if it wasn't the ten pounds a week Jack Forrester had dangled like a golden carrot in the pub, and it would allow her to escape Shack's clutches. The fact her overlooker had been lurking in the Boot and Slipper worried Molly more than she was willing to let on.

'It… nothing,' she said, in answer to Daphne's question. 'Just a dream, that's all. Just a daft dream.'

Molly tore up the card and left the pieces in the ashtray for the waitress to dispose of.

# Chapter 7

'This is an April Fool, isn't it?' Rita said to Molly the following Monday at the mill.

'Course it isn't.'

'Then you must be off your chump, love.'

'I beg your pardon?'

'Ten quid a week, Moll. Ten quid a week!' Rita shook her head. 'You ought to be put away, you ought. I've a mind to ring up the funny farm right now and ask them to send the men in white coats for you.'

'You're talking like the ENSA thing was a guaranteed job offer,' Molly said. 'It wasn't, Reet – far from it. Am I really going to bet my future on the words of some bloke in the pub who was probably only trying to get a look at my knickers?'

'Why not at least try? This could be your big chance to make summat of your life. Seriously, what have you got to lose?'

'The cost of an expensive trip to London? My job, if Shack gets to hear of me looking for summat else behind his back? My dignity?'

'Oh, *dignity*,' Rita said with a snort. 'What's dignity worth? I'd sell mine for ten bobs' worth of stockings and a packet of cork-tipped fags.'

'I like to think mine's worth a bit more than that,' Molly said. 'Anyhow, maybe you can't put a price on dignity, but you can on a third-class ticket to London and it's thirty-five bob. Thirty-five bob that I haven't got. Then there's the cost of a boarding house when I get there, since I'd have to stay the night. I'm not parting with more than a week's wages for the privilege of having a bunch of strangers laugh in my face.' Molly glanced up to the balcony where the offices were. 'There's Taylor going into his room. Mind my looms for a minute while I give him my application, would you? I ought to do it while Shack's taking his break.'

'Aye, all right,' Rita said glumly. 'I still reckon you're making a mistake though.'

Molly hurried up the stairs and knocked on the door of Mr Taylor's office.

'Come in,' came the soft-spoken instruction. Molly patted the pocket of her overall to make sure the envelope she had stashed there hadn't gone astray, then went in.

Mr Taylor was at his desk, squinting through his round spectacles as he wrote something down. He looked up at her with a vague smile.

Molly rather liked the kindly old gentleman who owned the mill. He expected his people to work hard, but he also regarded them with an almost fatherly affection that left them in no doubt they could go to him if they were ever in need. He had been good to her family over the years, and she would always be grateful to him for enabling her sister to get an education.

Mr Taylor had one major fault, however, which was that he would insist on seeing the best in people. This might not be considered a character flaw in most folk, but when the people Taylor was determined to see the best in included his lecherous overlooker, it was a definite black mark. He had a blind spot when it came to Shack that – benevolent old gent that he was – Molly couldn't help holding against him. There had been at least two girls in her time at Taylor's who'd had to leave their positions after making a complaint about Shack's behaviour, because Mr Taylor couldn't or wouldn't believe his seemingly affable overlooker was at fault.

'Now then, it's young Molly Clough, isn't it?' the millowner said, smiling warmly. Mr Taylor prided himself on knowing the name of every worker in his mill.

'Yes, sir.'

'And how's that sweet little sister of yours? Daphne, wasn't it? Getting on well at school, I hope?'

'She is,' Molly said with a smile. 'Top of the class for everything, cribbing like mad for the summer exams. And she's not so little any more. She'll be sixteen this August.'

'Sixteen already! Time is running on.' He gestured to a chair. 'Well, is there something I can do for you, my dear? Your family isn't in any trouble, I hope?'

'No, but it's kind of you to ask.' Molly took the seat he had offered. 'I mustn't linger. I left another girl minding my looms. I just came to bring you this. Um, the advertisement said to apply directly to you.'

She handed over the envelope, which contained her letter of application for the wages clerk job. Molly hadn't known quite what to include in this but she had given it her best guess, presenting details of her school marks in arithmetic and some extracts from her reports, pointing to her reputation at Taylor's as a fastidious and reliable worker. She had been careful all the while to show off her best handwriting – such as it was – and get her spelling right. She had also taken special care with her appearance, to show how neat she could be.

'Oh,' Mr Taylor said, blinking as he read the letter. 'Why, Miss Clough! I had no idea you were ambitious.'

'Is it all right, sir?' she asked anxiously. 'I mean, of course I understand if I'm not what you're looking for. If you want someone a bit... well, a bit posher. But I have worked here for seven years, and my family have worked for your family for three generations. I'm always on time, always neat and careful, and you can see from my school marks that I do have some brains for all that I'm not—'

The millowner held up a hand, smiling. 'Now, now, don't get yourself into a lather. You have every right to apply. Of course, I must wait until I have all the applications before giving the matter my careful consideration.' He lowered his voice. 'But between the two of us, I should say you stand a very good chance.'

'Really?'

'Oh yes. Don't think I haven't watched you. A little too fond of chatter, perhaps, as you young girls tend to be, but I don't like to be strict with you as long as it doesn't affect your work. I know you're often first at your station in the morning, and never in a hurry to clock off. I know you've hardly taken a sick day in the seven years since you came to us. I've noted that you never neglect to close your shafts when you leave your looms. Yes, Miss Clough, I have observed you. A conscientious girl, and a bright one too, I believe.'

Molly beamed. 'Oh, thank you! If I can only be considered…'

'And your overlooker speaks very highly of you,' Mr Taylor went on, sliding her application letter into a card file.

Molly frowned. 'Shack— Mr Shackleton does?'

'Indeed, quite glowing reports. I'm sure he will be happy to provide you with a written reference. Should this prove satisfactory, which I have no doubt it will, then… but we must do things properly.' He winked at her over his spectacles. 'Let us just say you have no cause to lose any sleep over it. You may return to your work now, Miss Clough.'

Molly stayed seated. 'So… whether I'm considered for the job will depend on what Mr Shackleton says?'

'It is the usual procedure to ask for a reference from the overlooker, yes. But as I said, I doubt this will be a problem. I get the impression you're something of a favourite with him.'

'Yes.' Molly got to her feet. 'Yes. Thank you.'

—

'Well? What did he say?' Rita mouthed when Molly returned to her looms.

'Hmm?' Molly roused herself. 'He said I had a good chance. In fact, he almost seemed to be suggesting the job was as good as mine, although he didn't say it in so many words.'

'Oh.' Rita sounded disappointed. Molly had no doubt her friend had hoped for a different outcome, since Mr Taylor's refusal to consider her for the pay clerk job might mean a change of heart about ENSA. 'Well, that's hardly a surprise. He must know you're too clever to waste down here. What happens now?'

'Nowt for a bit, until the deadline's passed. Only...' Molly's gaze had fixed on Shack, who was doing his rounds. 'Only Taylor has to get a reference for me. That's all.'

Whenever Molly's eyes weren't on her work, she followed Shack with them, waiting to see if he would be called into Mr Taylor's office to discuss her reference.

Lunchtime came and went, however, and although Shack had been up and down to his own office a few times, she hadn't seen him speak with his boss.

Perhaps it would be OK, but the idea of needing Shack to speak in her favour unsettled Molly. She would be answerable to someone else if she got this job, in another part of the mill. She would no longer have anything to do with her old overlooker, which, even more than the increase in pay, was what had drawn her to the job in the first place.

But Shack wouldn't like that, would he? Molly grimaced as she thought of that strange, proprietorial, almost proud look he sometimes fixed on her, as if she belonged to him. As if she were his mistress, almost. That felt so much more frightening than the purely animal looks of desire she had sometimes been subjected to from men.

Would the man try to sabotage her attempt to better herself by giving her a bad reference – try to keep her in the weaving shed where she was under his control? She wouldn't put it past him.

Molly's stomach lurched as, close to the end of the working day, she saw Mr Taylor emerge from his office and beckon Shack to him. The overlooker scurried upstairs obediently.

It felt like an age before Shack emerged from the boss's office, with the big clock above them ticking closer to six. What had they been saying in there, Molly wondered? Taylor had said he needed a written report. Perhaps he was making Shack write it there and then.

When the overlooker finally came out, Molly scrutinised his face from under lowered lids. She had no wish for him to see her looking at him, but she was dying to know how the conversation had gone. It was hard to make out his expression, but he didn't look angry. If anything, he looked rather bucked up.

Shack glanced down at her, and Molly quickly averted her gaze.

'Nearly time to punch the clock, thank heavens,' Rita said. 'Here, what do you say to a quick drink with me and Harry in the Bell next door? Might as well enjoy it while you can, before you get too nobby to mix with the likes of us.'

Molly smiled. 'I don't think I could be that nobby if I tried. I'd love to, if I wouldn't be intruding on you lovebirds.'

'Don't be daft.'

Molly jumped as she registered footsteps nearby. She hadn't noticed Shack come downstairs. He was approaching her with an expression of beaming, slightly smug benevolence on his round, red face.

'Oh Lord,' she mouthed to Rita. 'The buzzer's about to go as well. Don't leave me alone with him if everyone disappears, all right?'

'I won't if I can help it,' Rita mouthed back, with a worried glance at the overlooker.

'Well, Miss Clough, I'm told you've been stricken by a violent case of ambition,' Shack said when he reached her. He didn't sound any different to how he usually did. If he was angry about her going for another position behind his back, he was hiding it well.

'I applied for an office job, yes,' Molly said uncertainly. 'Did Mr Taylor—'

'He spoke to me about it. I'm to write you a reference, it seems. I told him I'd have it on his desk first thing tomorrow.'

The buzzer sounded to signal the end of the day, and the other workers made a beeline for the time clock to punch their cards.

'And… will that be all right?' Molly asked Shack hesitantly.

'Of course.' The overlooker's face wore an expression of studied nonchalance. 'But I wonder if you wouldn't mind stepping up to my room for a moment before you go home? There are a few matters I'd like to discuss.'

Molly looked at Rita in panic.

'I ought to come up with her, sir,' Rita said. 'Me and Molly always walk home with Harry Castle, one of the smash hands. It isn't safe for girls like us to be out alone in the blackout.' Her tone became slightly pointed. 'After all, you never know what sort of men might be around.'

'Nonsense,' Shack said heartily. 'I'll ensure your friend makes it safely to her tram stop, don't you worry. Now run along and clock out, there's a good girl. You can take Miss Clough's card too.'

Rita gave Molly a helpless look. She couldn't defy the overlooker outright.

'I'll wait for you at the pub, all right?' she murmured as Molly reluctantly handed over her punch card. 'Don't walk home by yourself.'

Rita went to join Harry, who was waiting for her.

'I oughtn't to stop long,' Molly said to Shack. 'My mam and sister are expecting me at home.'

'I'll be as brief as I can. Please, follow me.'

Not being able to see any way out of the situation, Molly did so.

# Chapter 8

She didn't like it though. The last time Molly had been caught alone in Shack's office, she had been able to get away when he had attempted to kiss her. But that had been in a mill full of people, when he wouldn't dare push his luck too far.

Not so now. Now the looms were silent, the workers gone, the building dark and empty. Molly supposed Mr Taylor was still in his office – at least, she hadn't seen him leave – but there wasn't a single other employee in the place. And Taylor's office was on the other side of the building…

'Please, have a seat,' Shack said when they reached his room. He closed the door behind him and, more significantly, drew the bolt.

The fact that he even had a bolt on his office door was enough to make Molly shiver. It hadn't been there the last time she had been alone with him. He must have fitted the thing himself…

'I'd rather stand,' Molly said, lurking as close to the door as she could without looking shifty. 'As I said, I can't stay long. My mam and sister will worry if I'm not home at the usual time.'

Shack shrugged. 'Have it your way. How is that little sister of yours? Still doing well in her schooling?'

'She is,' Molly said, struggling to keep the chill from her voice. Funny how the question sounded so much more unsettling coming from Shack than it had when Mr Taylor had asked. 'We're expecting great things from her.'

'Well, as I told you before, we'd always have a place for her at Taylor's. Something worthy of her talents.'

Molly felt her skin twitch. She hadn't been lying when she'd told Rita she would make a living walking the streets before she'd let her sister fall into the clutches of a man like Shack. When he had pressed his attentions on Molly once before in this room, when she was just fifteen, she had run away from him. Daphne couldn't run.

Shack sat at his desk, shuffling through some papers. For the first time in a long while, Molly regarded the man closely.

Her overlooker always reminded her of a character from Dickens: an avuncular Mr Pickwick, round, red-cheeked and jolly, with an impression of having overindulged in the finer things during his forty or so years on the planet. The men at work liked him for his seeming good nature, his raucous jokes and his willingness to stand them a pint if he bumped into them in the pub. They often ragged him about his notorious eye for the ladies. Shack laughed as heartily as anyone, as if it was all good clean fun despite the wife and children he had at home.

But it hadn't taken Molly long to realise that the man's amiability was merely a mask to hide the brutal desires he pressed on any girl unlucky enough to fall into his hands. It was all there in his eyes. Shack might have the manner of a kindly uncle, but his eyes showed the monster inside.

'Thank you, but my sister has other plans,' she said coolly. 'What was it you wanted to speak to me about, sir?'

'Merely to assure you that the reference you need won't pose any difficulties,' he said, without looking up. 'I felt you would sleep easier knowing I intended to give you a good report.'

Molly blinked. 'Oh. Really?'

'Of course. You've been a good worker for me, and you're a neat, clean little girl. I'll be sure to mention that when I write your reference.'

Molly felt rather bewildered. She hadn't expected him to be as cooperative as this. She was sure he'd be angry at her attempts to escape him, but he seemed quite content with the situation, sitting at his desk not even looking at her. Why did he need to summon her to his office just to tell her that though? He could have said as much on the shed floor, and left her to go home with Rita.

'Well, thank you,' she said. 'Am I free to go, sir?'

'Yes, in a moment.' Finally he looked up, his expression grave. 'Of course, while I'll be sure to give credit where credit is due, I'm afraid I will have to present your record in full. I hope you won't take it personally, Molly. I owe it to Mr Taylor to be entirely honest about your conduct.'

Molly, he had called her. On the floor, it was always Miss Clough. Not even her Sunday name of Margaret, but Molly, the name her friends and family used. Alarm bells rang in the back of Molly's mind.

'What record?' she asked, edging a little closer to the door.

She had seen him bolt it, but it wasn't locked with a key. If he tried something, could she get out in time? Good God, but if he were to attempt to force himself on her, here in this empty mill with no one to hear her screams…

Shack slid a piece of paper from a pile and stood up.

'You've been a good girl for the most part, but there are a few exceptions,' he said. 'Sixpence docked pay for not returning from your break in a timely fashion, 4th July 1933.'

July 1933? That was the month she had started work here. Had he really kept records of any little breach of the rules for as long as that?

'Twenty minutes late to work, 11th January 1935,' he continued, skimming his list.

'What?' Molly stared at him. 'That was the middle of winter! I trekked through three feet of snow to get to work that day, and made the time up.'

'Nevertheless, I'm obliged to report it. There are half a dozen similar incidents. And then there was the time you failed to clock in at all, with the loss of a day's wages: 10th February 1937.'

Molly shook her head in disbelief. 'Are you joking? That was the day my father died!'

'I know. And I do understand,' Shack said in a conciliatory tone, stepping closer to rest a hand on her arm. 'I don't want to have to report these things, believe me. But a man must do his duty, my dear, no matter how unpleasant.'

Molly looked at the fleshy red fingers on her arm.

'Oh,' she said tonelessly. 'It's this game, is it? This was why you looked so smug when you asked me to come up. Of course you did.'

'I beg your pardon?'

'You're going to say you'll leave those things out if I… if I'm nice to you. That's what you're going to say. Straightforward blackmail. I ought to have guessed.'

He took hold of her arm, holding it in a firm grip. His face was close to hers.

'It isn't like that,' he said, in a voice suddenly breathy and hoarse. 'It's simply that I have to do something. Don't you see that, Molly?'

Molly winced at the fingers digging into her flesh. 'I'd be grateful if you'd let go of my arm please, sir,' she said in a low, even tone.

'Do you know what it does to me, seeing you every day? Do you know how hard it is? Of course you do. You must do.' His rancid breath was hot on her cheek.

'I never meant to make you feel like that,' was all she could think of to say.

'The hell you didn't. I saw you that night in the pub. All those men watching you – wanting you. You were lapping it up. I swear it was all I could do to control myself.' His eyes had fixed on hers, on fire with lust and narrow with resentment. 'You're all the same, you girls. Act the whore, torture a man till you drive him half mad, then cry victim when he can't help himself any longer – as if that wasn't what you wanted all along.' The grip on her arm tightened, bruising the flesh. 'Well I won't have it, d'you hear me, young lady? I won't have it.'

'Please,' she whispered, her eyes stinging with tears of pain and fear. 'Let me leave. Let me go home. I won't apply for the clerk's job. I'll stay here, if that's what you want, and tell Mr Taylor I changed my mind.'

'What I want is to get you out of my head. I don't know why I can't stop thinking about you, why you're different from the rest of them, but if I don't have you just once, I feel like I'll never be free of you.' His voice had become almost a growl. 'Do you hear me, Molly? Just… once.'

'I'll scream,' she murmured. 'I'll scream and I won't stop screaming until someone comes.'

He grinned unpleasantly. 'No one will hear you. Old Taylor's as deaf as a post, and there's a lot of mill between him and us. These walls are solid stone.'

'Don't think I won't tell him. I'll tell everyone.'

'No one will believe you. You can be sure of that.'

He pulled her to him roughly and pressed a hard kiss to her lips. Molly struggled against him, but he was a large man, and powerful. She couldn't get free of his grip, no matter how hard she tried to wrench herself away.

Her brain was screaming. He was wrestling with her while he kissed her, trying to drag her to the floor, and Molly could tell that this was something he'd done before – perhaps many times before. With one hand he pushed up her skirt and wrenched at her stockings, tearing one with his fingernails and snapping her suspender. A sob bubbled in her throat, prevented from escaping by the hard lips on hers.

Oh God. This was it. He was stronger than she was. She couldn't fight him off. He was going to take her, right here on the floor, and no screams would bring her help. The door was bolted and she couldn't get away…

Would it hurt? People said it could hurt. People said it could break you, if the man didn't care what he did to you. Molly experienced a swell of nausea, and gagged in her throat.

He was still wrestling with her, trying to pull her down. Molly resisted with a strength born of pure terror. Once he had her prone, he could easily overpower her – pin her with his bulk. But as long as she remained upright, there was a chance.

Daphne's words from a few days ago sprang into her head. *If they ever do it, you're to kick them in the whatsits and run off…*

Molly did the only thing she could think to do, with the one part of her body that still had free movement. She brought her knee up as hard as she could to connect with the front of the overlooker's trousers.

The effect was instantaneous, and very satisfying. Shack let out a sharp groan and clutched at his tender area, bent double with tears streaming down his face. Molly grinned with relief at finding herself free, but she didn't have time to dally. She unbolted the door and ran out, straight to the nearest accessible place of safety – Mr Taylor's office. Shack would soon recover and pursue her, but while he might be stronger, she was faster. She needed to get to where there were people, as soon as she could.

# Chapter 9

Mr Taylor was working at his desk when Molly burst in. She slammed the door behind her and leaned back against it, panting hard.

'Miss Clough!' the millowner said, staring at her. 'My goodness, what on earth is the matter?'

Molly couldn't answer for a moment.

'Please,' she gasped, clutching her stomach. 'He's... coming. You have to... help me.'

'Whatever can be wrong?' Mr Taylor took in her torn stocking, which had rolled down below the hem of her skirt, her dishevelled hair and smudged lipstick. 'You look a state, my dear. Did you injure yourself?'

'It's... Shack.' Molly took a moment to catch her breath, gulping in the air.

'Shack? What is a shack?'

'Mr Shackleton, I mean.'

'He's long since gone home, I should imagine. Did you need to speak to him?'

'I already spoke to him.' She hesitated, looking at Mr Taylor. Molly knew he hated to hear a bad word against his overlooker, but he was a kind man. Surely he would believe her. After all, the evidence was right before his eyes. 'He did this. He attacked me.'

Mr Taylor frowned. 'Young lady, if this is a joke then I must say I find it in rather poor taste.'

'I swear to you on the Bible, sir, he did this. He... if I hadn't managed to fight him off, he'd have... hurt me. You must understand what I mean.' She looked at him with pleading eyes. 'You have to believe me. He said... he said no one would. But you have to, this time.'

'Miss Clough, this is a serious accusation.' He stood up. 'But perhaps it's a misunderstanding. Yes, I'm sure it must be that.'

Molly laughed in disbelief. 'A *misunderstanding*? The man tried to rape me!'

Taylor fixed her with a stern look. 'I see no reason for coarse language, young miss.'

'Coarse... I don't believe this!' Molly forced herself to be calm. 'Right. Ask him yourself. He's still in his office, I suppose, clutching his unmentionables. I'd like to hear him lie about it to my face.'

'I shall. It's only right he be allowed to tell his side of the story. Come along and we'll have this out.'

Molly walked behind Mr Taylor to Shack's room, her head whirling. It felt so unreal. How could she appear in the man's office, dishevelled, half undressed and clearly scared out of her wits, and *still* be told it was all her imagination? What world was this she lived in?

Molly expected to find Shack still recovering from the blow she had given him. However, when they entered his office, he was buttoning his mackintosh – a little red in the face, but otherwise back to normal. She ought to have kneed him harder.

'Oh. Good evening, sir,' he said to Mr Taylor, with a convincing expression of surprise. 'Did you want me for something? I was about to head home to the missus.' He chuckled. 'No doubt I'll be in for an earful if I let the tea go cold.'

Mr Taylor glanced at Molly, who was shaking her head at the brazenness of the man. 'Ah, Mr Shackleton, I'm glad I caught you. Now then, I'm afraid there's some little... unpleasantness we must deal with. Is it correct to say that you spoke with Miss Clough here a short time ago?'

'That's right, sir,' Shack said, radiating innocence. 'Is anything wrong?'

'Do you mind telling me what your conversation was about?'

'Well, I knew that Miss Clough would be worrying about the reference she needed from me. I wanted to reassure her that I intended to write her a glowing report, so that she could take the happy news to her family.' His face assumed an expression of deep sympathy. 'I know things are difficult at home, with her father passed and her little sister crippled. I didn't want to add to the child's worries.'

'Did you… touch her at all? Anything that might have been misconstrued as… well, as something other than it was?'

'I don't think I… oh yes, I did put my hand on her arm,' Shack said vaguely, as if the memory was just coming back to him. 'The girl was upset — that was my fault. Thoughtlessly I made a reference to her father's death, which of course brought back bad memories. I put a hand on her arm to console her.'

'So it was a misunderstanding,' Taylor said, with palpable relief. 'I was sure it must be.' He looked at Molly hopefully, almost pleadingly, as if desperate for her to confirm this so the whole unpleasant business could be swept under the carpet.

'It certainly was not a misunderstanding,' Molly snapped. 'I know exactly what happened.'

'You dispute this version of events, Miss Clough?'

'Well… no, not entirely,' Molly admitted. 'That is to say, he did summon me here to say he was going to write me a good reference, and he did mention my dad dying and put his hand on my arm. Then he tried to blackmail me for my favours, and when that didn't work, he attacked me.'

Shack blinked at her. 'Attacked you! My dear, are you feeling quite well?'

A look of indulgent impatience passed between the two men: an expression of masculine solidarity at the nonsense of women. This more than anything made Molly wish she had a few more knees with which to dish out whatsit-related justice to the whole pack of them.

'Don't you bloody dare stand there lying to my face about it, you bastard,' she said through gritted teeth. 'You know what you did. And you know that you've done it before, to other poor girls.'

'Miss Clough! I must protest,' Mr Taylor said, staring at her in shock. 'Is there any need for this sort of language? I mean, really!'

Molly laughed. 'I can't believe I'm hearing this! The man tries to rape me and you're swooning over naughty words? What is *wrong* with you?'

Taylor's expression turned cold. 'I think you've said quite enough, young lady.'

Molly tried to force herself to calm down.

'Look, sir, you've been kind to my family,' she said in a quieter voice. 'I think you're a good man – or part of you is. But you just won't see what's under your nose, Mr Taylor. The girls who work here live in fear. Every one of us is afraid to be alone with the overlooker, because we know what happens if he gets you by yourself. And you, who've been told over and over what his true nature is, just put your hands over your ears and turn the other way because you can't bear to confront anything sordid or seedy.'

'I said that's—'

But Molly wasn't done. 'Why do you hide from this?' she demanded. 'Because the man cracks a few jokes, pats his belly and chuckles like bloody Santa Claus? Believe me, he's far from harmless. Ask May Chiltern – except you can't, because she resigned when you wouldn't listen to her complaint about him. Ask Barbara Slaithwaite – except, oh no, she was pushed out for blowing the whistle too, wasn't she? They can tell you who Shack is. He's a monster, Mr Taylor. If you ever emerged from your ivory tower and actually listened to the girls who work for you, you'd know that.' She narrowed one eye. 'Except you do know that, don't you, sir? Deep down, you must know you're lying to yourself.'

Taylor looked uncertain. He turned to his overlooker with a pleading look. Shack flashed the millowner an ingratiating smile.

'You know how these girls are, boss,' he said. 'You brush their arm in passing, and the next minute they're screaming blue murder. They take everything the wrong way.'

'Yes,' Mr Taylor said hesitantly. 'Yes, I suppose they… might. That does sound likely, doesn't it?'

'Are you really so weak as to give in to him?' Molly demanded. 'Can you not see when you're being manipulated, damn it?'

'Do calm down, my dear, and try to restrain your language,' Shack said, but Molly ignored him.

'I know you want to hide from this, Mr Taylor, but you can't,' she said. 'Don't you see? You can't, or it'll happen again – and again and again. It'll keep happening for as long as you let this man be in a position where he can make it happen. You're a father of daughters. Think about how you'd feel if it happened to one of your girls, and the men responsible for her safety turned a blind eye as you're doing now.'

Shack shook his head sadly. 'Don't be too hard on the girl over this, sir. It seems to be some sort of mental breakdown. I suppose pressure at home, the lame sister—'

'Is this part of my mental breakdown?' Molly demanded, gesturing to her torn stocking. 'Or this?' She rolled up her sleeve and thrust out her arm so they could see the bruises made by Shack's fingers.

Shack raised an eyebrow. 'You aren't claiming I'm responsible for all these? How long would you like to suggest I've been beating you, Miss Clough?'

Molly looked at her arm and flushed. It was true there were a number of other bruises there. It was easy to get a bang working with the looms, and she often had small bruises on her arms and legs. But only the five indentations on her forearm were fresh.

'Don't listen to him,' she said to Mr Taylor. 'I didn't get these from the machines. They're finger marks – you can tell by looking at them.'

Taylor blinked. 'Finger marks?'

'That's right. He held me so hard he bruised the skin, and it was sheer luck that I was able to get away before he went any further – that and a well-aimed knee. You *have* to sack him. He's dangerous.'

Mr Taylor looked undecided for a moment. Suddenly he seemed helpless, like a little boy whose world was collapsing. It was clear that nothing in his life had prepared him to deal with something like this.

'Try to be kind, sir,' Shack said, with an affected sympathy that made Molly wish she'd kneed him a second time for good measure. 'She's under a lot of strain.'

'Yes. Yes, we must always be kind to those beneath us.' Taylor clung to the suggestion as to a lifeline, and the helpless look on his face turned into one of indulgent pity. Molly knew, when she saw that expression, that it had been no good. He would never listen, to her or anyone else. Mr Taylor had a mind that would see only the good in things. Anything dark or painful was essentially invisible to him.

'Miss Clough, I think you had better take a day's holiday tomorrow,' he said. 'Mr Shackleton is right: you've clearly been overworking. Rest assured you won't lose any pay. I can't have my staff making themselves ill.'

'I don't want pay!' Molly's voice was choked with hurt and frustration. 'Haven't you been listening? I want you to sack this bugger!'

He looked stern. 'I do wish you would refrain from using these vulgar expressions. It's hardly becoming of a young lady, especially a Taylor's girl. Don't forget, you carry the reputation of the business with you wherever you go. I feel I've been very fair, given your unseemly behaviour.'

'You're really not going to do anything, are you?' she whispered. 'You're just going to let him keep doing this, to other poor girls. Young girls who can't defend themselves, like my sister. My mam was right; you bastards are all in it together.'

'Miss Clough—'

'Don't give me *Miss Clough*. I've had enough of your damn lectures. If words are more upsetting to you than what your friend Mr Shackleton tried to do to me tonight, then you need to take a long, hard look at yourself.' She drew herself up. 'In fact, here's a bit more vulgar language for you. You can stick your bloody job, Mr Taylor. You can shove all your jobs up your overfed arses, the pair of you. Please consider this my notice.'

With that, she turned on her heel and swept out.

# Chapter 10

Molly managed to maintain her air of dignity until she was outside. Once she was sure no one could see her, she burst into tears.

What had happened in there? What had she said? She could barely remember. It was like a dream – a nightmare.

But she remembered what she had felt. His hand on her arm, gripping so tight she couldn't get away. His hot breath on her cheek. His hard, brutish lips forcing a kiss on her as he wrestled her to the floor…

Suddenly, she felt sick. A hard cramp surged in her abdomen, similar to the ones that came with her monthlies. She darted down the snicket between the mill and the pub next door, clutching her stomach as she retched, but nothing came up.

The darkness felt so much more frightening than it had before. Molly had been proud to feel she could take care of herself, even in the blackout. But after what had nearly happened to her tonight, she was imagining cruel, eager male eyes watching her from every shadow.

She longed to be where there were people, and warmth and light and safety. After mopping her eyes and mouth with her handkerchief, Molly hurried into the Bell pub.

She wondered if Rita had already gone home. Molly didn't know if the scenes in the mill had lasted minutes or hours, but it felt like an eternity since her friend had left her. She found Rita still waiting, however, sitting at a table with Harry.

Molly joined them and sank exhausted into a seat.

'I was just going to come and look for you,' Rita said. 'I thought you must've walked home alone, you were gone so long.' She frowned. 'Where's your coat, Moll?'

'Left it at work.'

'Are you all right? You look dreadful.'

'Been better,' Molly muttered.

A black look settled on Rita's face. 'It was him, wasn't it? Shack. What did he do to you?'

'This.' Molly stuck out her leg to show them her torn stocking. 'And this.' She displayed the bruises on her arm. 'And worse, if I hadn't managed to get away. He'd have… gone all the way, Reet. He tried to.'

'Oh my God!'

'Shack?' Harry shook his head. 'Nay, he's harmless. I know he's got an eye for the girls but it's just a cheeky pinch on the bum here and there, that's all.'

Molly glared at him. 'Do not test me tonight, Harry Castle. I've had just about enough of men telling me I'm a silly little goose who can't possibly know what it feels like when someone tries to force himself on her. I know what happened, OK? I was there.'

'All right,' Harry said, blinking. 'Sorry, Moll. I didn't mean owt by it. Did he really try to… you know?'

'He did.'

'I never should have left you alone with him,' Rita whispered. 'Moll, I'm so sorry.'

'Let me get you a drink, eh?' Harry said. 'You look all in.'

Molly closed her eyes. 'Yes. Ta.'

He went to the bar. Rita moved her chair closer to Molly's so she could wrap an arm around her.

'What happened, love?' she asked in a hushed tone.

'He tried to… to drag me down. He was strong, Reet. He'd have hurt me if he'd done it, I know he would.'

'That bastard,' Rita muttered. 'I knew he was a dirty old goat but I never thought he'd take it that far.'

'Oh God. If my first time with a man had been like that, with him… If a baby had come of it…' Molly felt again the swell of nausea, and swallowed hard to push it down.

Rita gave her a reassuring squeeze. 'Don't think of it, Moll. You're safe now. How did you get away?'

'I kicked him somewhere painful and ran off to tell Taylor,' Molly said wearily. 'But it didn't matter. He just lectured me about swearing and told me I must be overtired.'

'He's really not going to sack him, even after that?'

'Of course he isn't. He's too weak. He'd rather let the bastard keep getting away with it than face up to what's been happening right under his nose.' Molly's eyes widened as the other events of the night broke through her daze. 'Oh hell. I'm unemployed.'

'You what?'

'I…' Molly looked at her friend with a frantic expression. 'Reet, I think… I think I told Taylor to shove his job up his fat arse.'

'You never did!'

'I did. I know I did.'

Rita regarded her with admiration. 'By, that were brave. Daft, but brave. Proud of you, Moll.'

'Never mind that. I've got no job, Rita! Mam and Daph are relying on me. No other mill is likely to take me on now either – not once they hear how I left Taylor's.' Molly rubbed her face. 'Oh my word, what was I *thinking*? Why did I have to let my temper run off with me like that?'

'After what Shack tried to do? You were right to.'

'Whatever will I do? I might never get another job. Not after this.'

'Happen Taylor'll change his mind, after he's calmed down.'

'He won't. He's determined to believe I'm a liar, and I insulted him.' Molly swallowed a sob. 'I've made a mess of everything, Reet,' she whispered. 'He'll stop the money he gives us for Daph now too, after what I said to him. I don't know how I dare tell my mam.'

'Well, if you need summat fast then it don't have to be the mills, does it?' Rita said evenly. 'There was the ENSA thing.'

'Don't talk daft.'

Rita handed Molly a handkerchief so she could clean up her face. 'Why not? You need a job, and it were good money.'

Molly mopped her eyes. 'I'd never get in.'

'You've got nowt to lose by trying, have you? Ten quid a week, Moll.'

Molly considered this. It was true that she had little left to lose, now. Was it at least worth making a telephone call? Even the few bob it would cost to place a trunk call to London felt precious now she was out of work, but if she was offered an audition… Her family needed money, and ten pounds a week could prove a lifeline even if the war only lasted a few more months.

'I threw away the card,' she mumbled.

'That don't matter. You remember the name of the theatre they use as headquarters, don't you? Just ask the operator to put you through.'

'I'll… I'll think about it.'

—

Molly asked Rita to come home with her, and be there while she told her mother what had happened. She was dreading telling Mam that she had no job to go to the next day. Not that Mam would blame her, but Molly knew her mother wouldn't be able to hide her fears for the future.

She couldn't help feeling responsible – not for what Shack had done, but for the way she had behaved afterwards. She hadn't needed to insult Mr Taylor, and it had been beyond foolish to impetuously quit her job like that. In doing so, she hadn't only thrown away her position at Taylor's; she had seriously jeopardised her chances of finding another job anywhere else.

The family lived on Molly's wage, along with the extra they got from Mr Taylor for Daphne's schooling and medical care. Without that, all they had coming in was a few bob from

Mam's charring job. If Molly couldn't find something quickly, it wouldn't be long before they were destitute. Daphne would be forced to give up school and take whatever job her disability would allow her to get, just to keep the family afloat.

Molly didn't doubt her sister would be able to find some work, despite her lameness. The child was pretty enough for the pictures. But the sort of man who would employ a young girl for that reason alone – especially a girl who could hardly walk unaided – was exactly the sort Molly wanted to protect Daphne from.

Molly scowled, her guilt turning to anger when she thought of what her little sister's future might now hold. How absurd it was that *she* should feel guilty, that *she* should be punished – she, who tonight had nearly suffered the worst fate it was possible for a woman to suffer. Shack was at home, she supposed: content at his hearth in a pair of warmed slippers, and his wife on hand to bring him any little thing he wanted. Molly doubted he would lose a moment's sleep over what he had tried to do to her.

'Are you sure you want me to come in?' Rita asked when she, Molly and Harry reached the Cloughs' terraced house.

'I'll feel better for having you there.' Molly sighed. 'She'll cry, I suppose. She'll hug me and tell me everything's going to be all right, then she'll cry on her own in the kitchen when she thinks I can't hear. Poor Mam. I must give her so much worry.'

'Want me to wait for you, Reet?' Harry asked.

'Nay, I don't know how long I'll be,' Rita told him. 'You get on home.'

'Sure? Don't like you walking home by yourself.'

'Give over, it's only the end of the street. Even I can't get into trouble over that distance.' She gave him a kiss. 'I'll see you tomorrow.'

There was no sign of Mam or Daphne when the two women entered the house.

'Mam?' Molly called. 'Are you in? I brought Reet back with me.'

'Aye, in your bedroom with Daph and the doctor,' her mam's voice called from upstairs. 'Come up, girls.'

They climbed the stairs and squeezed into the small bedroom that Molly shared with her sister. Daphne was sitting on their bed, looking a little frightened while Dr Anderson felt her calf muscles. Their mother sat by her, watching with ill-concealed anxiety.

'Heyup, Rita, love,' Mam said, standing up to give her daughter's friend a hug. 'You'll stay for your tea, I hope. It's chops and mash.'

'Nay, Sarah, I wouldn't take your precious meat ration. I won't say no to a cuppa though, when the doctor's finished,' Rita replied.

'Our Molly tells me you're courting.'

'I wouldn't quite call it courting yet,' Rita said with a smile. 'But I have been walking out with a young man I'm starting to think well of.'

'I hope he's good enough for you, that's all.'

'That's what I'm trying to find out.'

Mam turned to Molly and frowned.

'Summat's wrong,' she said at once. Molly had fixed her hair and lipstick and reattached her snapped suspender with a safety pin, but her mam could always tell when something wasn't right with her children. 'What is it? Where's your coat?'

'It's nowt,' Molly said. 'Well, it's summat, but I'm all right. Left my coat at work, that's all. I'll tell you about it when Dr Anderson's gone.'

The doctor had taken out a hammer to test Daphne's reflexes. When he was done, he put it away in his black bag, frowning.

'Well, Doctor, what's the report?' Molly asked, trying to keep her voice light for Daphne's sake. 'Will she be running a marathon this summer, or will it have to wait until after Christmas?'

Dr Anderson continued to look serious. 'May I speak with you and your mother in private, Miss Clough?'

'Why do you need to do that?' Daphne demanded. 'Summat's wrong, isn't it? I'm getting worse, aren't I, Doctor?'

The doctor summoned a smile. 'Nothing of that nature. Actually, I'm very pleased with your progress. Just a business matter, that's all.'

Daphne still looked suspicious, however.

'Don't worry about Daph,' Rita said to Molly and her mother. 'I'll look after her until you're done.'

She sat by the bed and took a piece of tied string from her coat pocket. 'Our Jemima taught me a new way to do Cat's Cradle the other day,' she said to Daphne. 'Want to see?'

Daphne shrugged, as if she were far too grown-up to care about such childish things, but she was still little girl enough for her eyes to kindle at the prospect of what was secretly her favourite game. 'You can show me if you want.'

Molly and her mother followed the doctor out on to the landing.

'Is that true, what you told Daph?' Molly asked in a low voice. 'Are her legs getting better?'

'Certainly her muscle strength is improving month on month,' the doctor said. 'I'd have liked to see a little more development, but she's definitely headed in the right direction. Has she been keeping up with her exercises?'

Mam nodded. 'Molly and I make sure she does them every day.'

'It hurts her though, poor bairn,' Molly said with a sigh.

'It's the only way, I'm afraid,' Dr Anderson replied.

'You said there was a business matter,' Molly said, casting a worried look at her mother. 'Your fees… they're not going up again?'

'Not this time, but I can't guarantee it won't be necessary in the near future.' The doctor took off his glasses and pinched the bridge of his nose. 'Even professionals are being affected by this wartime cost of living. But that wasn't what I wanted to talk to you about.'

'Well, what is it?' Mam asked.

'I know your family has little in the way of spare funds, Mrs Clough, but Daphne's iron calipers are very old now. The modern aluminium type would provide her with much better support, and be lighter and more comfortable too. My worry is that if she continues to build muscle without adequate support to keep her legs straight, she may regain the use of them but remain forever bow-legged. If there was any way you could raise the money…'

'How much are these new calipers?' Molly asked.

'Not cheap, I'm afraid. New ones would cost at least forty pounds, but I may be able to find a used pair for you in the twenty to thirty range.'

'Thirty pounds!'

'Doctor, it would take us years to save that kind of money,' Mam said. 'Our Molly only brings in thirty-five shillings a week from the mill.'

'I know. I'm sorry. The best I can offer is to help you find a pair as cheaply as possible, but it would be highly unlikely they'll be any less than twenty pounds. It could make all the difference to Daphne though, both in terms of her comfort and her future prognosis.'

Mam rubbed her head. 'Well if our Daph needs it then we'll have to find it, that's all. Thank you, Doctor.'

When the doctor had left, Molly turned to her mother.

'Where on earth will we find twenty pound, Mam? No one in the family has got that sort of money to lend us.'

'I know, but if Daph needs new calipers…' She paused. 'Mr Taylor's always been good to us, hasn't he? Happen if you speak to him tomorrow, he'll be willing to help.'

Molly frowned. 'Ask him for a loan, you mean?'

'Aye. I feel sure he'd advance the money on your wages if he knew we were in trouble, and we can pay him back at five bob a week. Things'll be tight for a while, Lord knows, but if it gets Daph better then it's just what we'll have to do.'

Molly hesitated. 'I… I'm not sure how I feel about asking him, Mam.'

Mam put a hand on her arm. 'I know it's humbling, love, but what choice have we got? This is for your sister.'

'I know.' Molly sighed. 'Aye, I know.'

Mam looked into Molly's face. 'Summat is wrong, I can tell. What's up, our Molly? Has that Shackleton been bothering thee?'

'He has, but it's all right. He didn't do owt to me. I'm a bit shaken, that's all.'

'You ought to tell Mr Taylor about that old devil,' Mam muttered darkly. 'I can't believe you'd get into trouble for it. Have a word when you ask him about the money tomorrow, eh?'

'I'll… think about it.'

Mam cocked her head, one eye narrowed. 'There's summat else. What is it, love? You know you can always tell your mam.'

Molly hesitated. Her mother looked pale and drawn. What with Daphne's legs, Ted on active service overseas and Molly's attempts to fend off Shack's unwanted attentions, Sarah Clough must lose a lot of sleep for worrying about her children.

'No, there's nothing else,' Molly said at last. 'I'm tired, that's all.' She kissed her mother's forehead. 'And don't worry about the money for Daph's calipers, Mam. I'll get it for us, one way or another.'

'Well, are you ready?' Rita asked the following day, squashed next to Molly in the telephone box across the road from Taylor's Mill. Molly had arranged to meet Rita during her dinner break, so she didn't have to endure the nerve-wracking experience of making a call to ENSA alone.

She hadn't been able to bring herself to tell Mam or Daphne that she had now entered the ranks of the jobless. Mam had so much on her plate that Molly couldn't bear to add to her worries. That morning, she had got up, dressed for work as usual and left the house, but she hadn't gone to Taylor's. Instead she had spent the hours in Bradford Central Library, trying to find solace in books.

If this phone call led to an audition, then she would come clean about everything. And if it didn't... God only knew what she would do if it didn't.

'I feel like I do before I sing,' Molly said, holding up a trembling hand. 'What if I make a mess of it, Reet?'

'You won't. Just give them your name, tell them what you can do and ask if they'd be interested in seeing you. And don't forget to mention your mate — what's his name?'

'Jack Forrester,' Molly murmured.

'Right.' Rita squeezed her arm. 'You can do this, Moll.'

'Maybe I should just go to Taylor and apologise. He might give me my job back, if I admit I was in the wrong. He might even feel guilty enough about turning a blind eye to what Shack gets up to to agree to the loan for our Daph's calipers.'

'And what then? Shack won't leave you alone, now you've humiliated him. Anyhow, why should you admit you were wrong when you weren't?'

'Because it's a man's world, and that's how we survive in it.'

Rita smiled grimly. 'Say that again, and pretend it's your sister you're talking to.'

Molly sighed. 'I can't, can I?'

'Then toughen up and make the call. It is just a call, remember. It's not an audition.' Rita pressed the receiver into her friend's hand. 'Do you remember the theatre to ask for?'

'Theatre Royal, Drury Lane,' Molly said automatically.

'And I've got five bob in small change here,' Rita said, shaking her purse. 'I raided our Jemima's bottle money. Mam lets her keep half what she gets when she takes Dad's empties back. It'll only be enough for six minutes though, so don't ramble too much.'

'Thanks, Reet. I will pay you back.'

'Never mind that. Get yoursen some work first.' Rita slid five sixpenny bits into the slot. 'Here we go.'

Molly dialled zero and asked the operator to put her through to ENSA at the Theatre Royal. Her stomach started doing somersaults as she heard the phone ringing. Finally, a young woman answered with a bored-sounding, 'Good afternoon.' Molly pressed Button A to speak.

'Um, hello. I mean, good afternoon,' Molly said, flashing a panicked glance at Rita, who nodded encouragingly. 'I wanted to... that is, can I speak to Mr Dean's assistant?' She hesitated, flustered, as she tried to remember the name on the card. 'David... no, Dennis. Dennis Walmsley.'

'Who wants him?' the girl asked suspiciously.

'I, er... Jack Forrester told me to call. He gave me Mr Walmsley's card and said I was to arrange an audition.'

'Mr Forrester? In that case, I'll put you through.'

Except Jack hadn't actually said that, had he? All he'd done was drop puzzling hints. Already Molly was beginning her ENSA career – if she was to have such a thing – with a lie.

A male voice came on the other end of the line. 'Yes?'

'Are you Mr Walmsley?' Molly asked.

'I am. How may I help?'

'I, er, I've got your card. That is, I used to have it, but then I… lost it. But I really did have it. Jack Forrester gave it me.'

Rita mouthed the word 'rambling'.

'Sorry,' Molly said to Dennis Walmsley. 'Sorry, I'm nervous. I mean, not that I get nervous a lot. I don't get nervous on stage.' *Lie number two…* 'I just… I'd really like an audition for ENSA, if you and Mr Dean thought I was worth one. Um, please.'

'Well, that was rather a lot to take in,' Mr Walmsley said, sounding amused. 'Did I hear you mention Jack Forrester?'

'Yes.' Molly seized on the name gratefully. 'He came to hear me sing, in my gran— in a club in Bradford. He said ENSA was desperate for singers of my calibre and gave me your card.'

'And your name is?'

'Dorothy.'

Rita stared at her. Molly shrugged in bewilderment. She had no idea where that name had come from either. Suddenly it had occurred to her panicked brain that you probably didn't get very far in show business with a name like Molly Clough.

'Dorothy what?' Mr Walmsley asked.

'Dorothy, er…' Molly looked around wildly, until her gaze fell on a billboard showing a butler holding a silver tray of cigarettes. 'Dorothy… Kensitas. Miss Dorothy Kensitas.'

'Kensitas?' the man on the phone said in surprise. 'Like the cigarette brand?'

'Yes. Just like that.'

'That's unusual.'

'Well, it's common in my family.' Dorothy Kensitas, formerly Molly Clough, let out a nervous laugh that quickly faded.

'And what is it that you do, Miss Kensitas?'

'I sing and accompany myself on the piano. Mostly I sing Gracie Fields numbers, plus a few George Formby and Arthur Askey.'

'All right.' Molly could hear the scratch of his pen as he wrote this down. 'And you entertain professionally, you say? You have experience on the variety circuits?'

'That's right.' The weight of her falsehoods beginning to crush her, Molly felt compelled to add, 'I don't have bags of professional experience, but I've been performing for a few year now in the pubs and clubs round our way.'

The pips sounded to let her know her three minutes were nearly up, and Molly waggled her eyebrows at Rita. She put a handful more sixpences into the slot.

'You, er, don't want me to sing now, do you?' Molly asked Mr Walmsley.

'The performance side of things isn't my area. Your best option, Miss Kensitas, would be to apply in writing to your local ENSA organiser. He'll be able to tell you if there are any auditions for semi-professionals coming up near you. If you give me a moment, I'll find his address.'

'If there's any chance of an audition sooner, I'd be very grateful. I'll travel if I need to. I'm, um, keen to get started.'

'Well, keenness is always appreciated.' Dennis Walmsley paused. 'You say it was Mr Forrester who recommended you contact us?'

Molly grimaced. Whatever had possessed her to give a fake name? If this man or his famous boss were to ask Jack whether he thought she was any good, he'd never have heard of Dorothy Kensitas.

'That's right,' she said. 'He might not remember me now. I was using a… a stage name the night we met. But if you could let me talk to him—'

'I'm afraid his company is on tour.' There was a pause while Mr Walmsley leafed through some pages. 'Well, Miss Kensitas, I believe we can fit you in this week. How does Thursday at two o'clock sound?'

Molly blinked. 'Thursday? What for?'

'For your audition, of course. You did say you wanted to be seen as soon as possible?'

'Well, yes, but I thought…' Molly took a deep breath. 'Never mind.'

'All right, Thursday at two, here at the Theatre Royal. It will be a four-person panel taken from one of our concert parties with a suitable vacancy, and there'll be a piano provided. The very best of luck.'

The phone clicked off as he hung up.

Molly turned a panicked look on Rita, still gripping the receiver in white knuckles.

'Well?' Rita said.

'They… they want me to go down,' Molly whispered. 'Down to London. For an audition.'

'Arghh!' Rita gave her a hug. 'I told you, didn't I? I knew they'd want to see you.'

But Molly was too dazed to rejoice. 'I was so sure they'd say no.'

'When will you go?'

'The audition's Thursday at two, they said. I'd have to travel down tomorrow and stay overnight.'

'Tomorrow! That isn't much time to get ready.'

Molly rubbed her brow. 'Oh my word. I told them I had years of professional experience, Reet. I said Jack had invited me to arrange an audition. I gave a fake name…'

'I heard, and a ruddy daft one at that. What on earth for?'

'It just occurred to me I ought to have a name that sounded a bit more glamorous, like you get in the films.' Molly groaned. 'They're bound to find out I fibbed if they talk to Jack. What will I do?'

'Jack won't land you in trouble, I'm sure,' Rita said. 'I think the bigger question is: how are we going to raise the money for your trip by tomorrow?'

—

Somehow, the money for the journey to London was cobbled together. Molly raided her meagre pot of rainy-day savings:

about ten bob in an assortment of shillings, sixpences and thrup-penny bits. Rita did the same, contributing eight-and-six. Harry, floating on the fluffy pink clouds of requited love, chipped in a whole pound. Other friends were touched for a small loan, until a sum of fifty-five shillings was stashed in Molly's purse. She hoped it would be enough to cover a third-class train ticket, meals and some cheap accommodation.

It felt like so much money though. Molly glanced furtively around her as she queued for the ticket office at Bradford Forster Square station late on Wednesday afternoon, feeling as if her heavily laden purse was burning a hole in her handbag. She had never had fifty-five shillings in one go before.

There was one pound note that she felt particularly guilty about: a gift from her mother. Mam had taken it from the money she was saving for Christmas and told Molly to put it towards the material for a new coat, which she could purchase on her way to York. That was where Molly's family believed she was going: to visit a newly married schoolfriend, Susan, during a holiday from work. Molly just couldn't bring herself to admit that she had lost her job at the mill, plunging them all into potential poverty, so she had told her mother that the coat she'd left at Taylor's had been lost – which it as good as had been. Rita said it hadn't been in the cloakroom where Molly left it, which meant it must have been put with the lost property in Shack's office. All too aware of what could happen to the women who entered that room, Molly refused to ask her friend to reclaim it.

If the ENSA thing came off, perhaps Molly could pull herself out of this mess and find a way to provide for her family again. If she couldn't… well, it was payday on Friday. When she came home from another day sitting in the library with no pay packet to hand over, she would be forced to confess to her mother what she'd done. And then there was the coalman due his money on the Saturday, and always another bill on the horizon. There were only so many times they could hide behind the settee and wait for the knocking to stop…

It was a gamble, she knew it. Fifty-five shillings against the prospect of a ten-pound-a-week salary. Ten pounds would quickly provide enough for Daphne's new calipers, and Molly would have the opportunity of a lifetime – to make her living in the world of entertainment. But if the ENSA thing didn't come off… nearly all the money in Molly's handbag would need to be paid back. It was a lot of money to bet on what might end up being nothing more than a foolish dream.

Molly didn't know how she would explain to her mother if she came home without a job. She would have to reveal that she had taken money under false pretences, had lied about where she had been, and that she had been concealing the truth about her work situation for days. Her mam would be worried to death if she knew her twenty-one-year-old daughter was travelling alone to the capital, to be put up in some seedy boarding house.

Molly was sure she had never told a lie to her mother in her life before. She had always felt she could tell Mam anything – until now, when she was oppressed by the horrible feeling she had let her family down. She had told a packet of lies to Mr Walmsley at ENSA as well. What was happening to her? She had always prided herself on being an honest, truthful person. Apparently all it took to corrupt her was desperation.

Oh, but wasn't it absurd? Suddenly the utter ridiculousness of where she was and what she was doing hit Molly like a slap round the face. Her, in ENSA! Her, in France entertaining the troops! Her, taking centre stage in a garrison theatre like Gracie or some proper singer. And she had the audacity to be here in the ticket queue, waiting to go to London as if this was a thing that could conceivably happen. What had she been thinking? Had she convinced herself she was in fact Dorothy Kensitas, whoever that glamorous stranger might be, and forgotten she was just plain Molly Clough from the mill?

'Where we off today then, pet?' the man in the ticket office asked cheerily when it was her turn to be served.

It wasn't too late to walk away. She could still abandon this madness, go home to her mam and sob the whole story out on her shoulder.

But then what would happen? Could she bear to go cap in hand to Mr Taylor, apologise for doing absolutely nothing wrong and beg him for her job back? Could she stand having to humiliate herself to Shack, and accept his repulsive advances just to keep earning thirty-five bob a week doing a job she hated in a city she had been longing to escape all her life? To have her little sister fall into the man's hands one day, perhaps?

No. Never that. Never as long as she lived.

'London,' she said firmly to the man in the ticket office. 'A third-class ticket to London, please.'

# Chapter 12

Molly arrived in London in the depths of the blackout, and was forced to invest some of her remaining funds in a cab to get her safely to her lodgings. She didn't have the confidence to wander the streets of a strange city in the dark, hunting for the right bus or tram.

The boarding house wasn't too disreputable, but Molly quickly discovered that there was a reason it was cheap. In fact there were four reasons: the perpetual smell of boiled cabbage, the layer of greasy dust on every surface, and the two women she had to share a room with – one of whom snored loudly and the other of whom had a very relaxed attitude towards personal hygiene. Still, it was a bed for the night.

Molly left the place at ten the next morning, although her audition wasn't until two, leaving her case behind to collect later. Since she had borrowed heavily to come on a trip that might amount to nothing, and since she had no money to waste on getting around, she decided she would walk to Drury Lane and take in a few of the sights. This was her first trip to London, and if she failed to get into ENSA, it would very likely be her last.

The Theatre Royal was some three miles from where she had stayed the night, but Molly let her feet wander rather than going there directly. She followed signposts to famous landmarks or, where there were no signs, she attached herself to gaggles of sightseers in the hope they would lead her to something worth seeing.

It all felt so… big. Bradford had always felt big in a cramped sort of way, but it was nothing like this. Apartment buildings and department stores several storeys high rose up seemingly to the clouds. The streets were thronged with people of all classes – even during the working day, when at home the majority of the population would be locked inside the mills. Pubs, restaurants and cafes came to life once Big Ben chimed midday, thrumming with merriment despite the early hour, while the broad ribbon of the Thames sliced the city in two.

London wasn't what you'd call clean – of course not, it was a city – but it felt light and airy compared to home. In Bradford you could look in any direction and see half a dozen huge, black chimneys against the horizon, hemming you in like the bars of a cell. Nearly every building was covered with the soot of more than a century past, and the dreary terraced houses huddled together as if for warmth. Here there was a sense of... expansiveness, Molly supposed. It was crowded and built up just like any city, but it felt like there was room to breathe in a way there wasn't at home.

There were still those faces, so tragically familiar to her – tired, broken, bitter working men and women, and the dead-eyed, dead-end kids whose only future was to end up just like them. Molly had seen hundreds of faces like that, her own father among them, and had only prayed she and her siblings wouldn't become just three more. But here there was something else. It was in the music that spilled from the cafes and pubs, the cheery calls of the market traders and the bawdy singing of street-corner loiterers still drunk from the excesses of the night before. Here there was life, and joy in life – the kind that didn't go to sleep when the lights went out.

True, Bradford had pubs and working men's clubs enough, and cinemas and dance halls and a couple of theatres, but it always felt like a place built for work. Life had to be squeezed into the small slivers of time between earning enough to keep yourself and your family fed. London felt different. It felt like somewhere life came first. Molly longed to explore it further; to be absorbed into the city's mass and become a part of it.

It wasn't long before Molly had wandered to the area that had the most charm for her personally: the West End. She took in the sights around Charing Cross, Covent Garden and Leicester Square, then shivered deliciously when she realised she was in Soho. The place was heavy with the mingled scent of fresh fruit and vegetables, food from a dozen different countries, the ink and paper of the print shops and the sweet, exotic perfume of the women of the night – and day, as it seemed here – who frequented the streets. Mam would play merry hell if she knew her eldest daughter was exploring those disreputable streets alone, but Molly's curiosity drove her on.

For so long she had been fascinated by the bright lights of the capital and now here she was, right where it all happened. Who knew what stars had walked where she was now walking? She passed theatres whose names sounded vaguely familiar – the Windmill, the Palace, the Prince Edward – and wondered which of her idols had played there, and if she would ever be able to emulate them.

In one street, however, Molly found not a building but a pile of rubble, lying between an Italian restaurant – Cortesi's – and the George and Dragon pub. She looked at this for some time, pondering what building had once been there and what had happened to it.

Eventually, a young man in a white apron came out from the restaurant next door, possibly hoping she might be hungry enough for him to lure her inside.

'Everything all right, Miss?' he asked cheerfully, with the hint of a foreign accent mixed in with the cockney she had got used to hearing during her walk around the capital.

Molly tore her gaze from the rubble to look at him. He was Italian, she realised with another shiver of excitement. Around her brother's age, perhaps eighteen or nineteen, and rather good-looking – tall and dark with nut-brown skin.

She tried not to stare too obviously. Molly had met very few Italians, other than the men who travelled with the fairs. There seemed to be a lot more foreigners in London than at home, which made the capital seem all the more exotic and exciting. She couldn't wait to tell Daph about it all.

'I only wondered what had happened to this place,' she said, nodding to the rubble. 'It looks like it blew up or summat.' She flushed when she noticed the lad grinning. 'Some*thing*, I mean. Sorry.'

'You talk however it comes natural, Miss, same as we all should,' the boy said. 'What do they call you? Sounds like you're a long way from home.'

'M— um, Dorothy.'

'Ah. No wonder you're a long way from home. Blew in on the wind with your little dog too, eh?'

Molly smiled. 'Sorry to disappoint you but it's Kensitas, not Gale.' She cleared her throat self-consciously. 'Like the fags.'

'Angelo Cortesi. Pleasure to meet you, Dorothy.' Molly noticed how Angelo had moved instantly to first names. She was sure nothing so formal as a 'Miss Kensitas' could ever sound right in the mouth of this warm and cheerful young man.

'Oh,' she said as he shook her hand, glancing at the sign over the restaurant he had emerged from. 'Cortesi's... this is your place?'

'It's the family's. My grandparents opened it after we came over from Italy in twenty-four, when I was just a tot. Now my grandad's gone, my grandmother and my dad run it together. She cooks, he manages things.' He smiled. 'And I'm just the errand boy who waits on tables and dreams of better things.'

'The food certainly smells good.'

'Best in London, girl. Tell your friends, eh?' Angelo nodded to the rubble she had been looking at. 'Respectable young lady like you wouldn't have wanted to go in there though.'

'Wouldn't I? Why?'

He lowered his voice and leaned closer. 'Dirty bookshop.'

'Blimey! Really?' Molly felt again that thrilling shiver of something new and forbidden. She had no idea such places existed.

'That's right, seriously blue stuff – I mean, so the boys tell me,' Angelo said, in a tone of not very convincing innocence. 'My nonna would've said I'm not too big to thrash if she'd ever caught me in there. We've been overrun round here for weeks now: young lads searching the rubble for "salvage".'

As if on cue, a boy of about thirteen appeared from amongst the debris. He turned red to the roots of his dusty ginger hair when he saw the pair of them watching him, hastily shoved a very singed paperback book into his pocket and scurried away.

Molly laughed. 'So I see. What happened to this place?'

'Jerry plane dropping leaflets come down with engine failure. Dornier Do 17. Dad said we were lucky to get away with only half our roof being knocked off. Could easily have been Cortesi's that got flattened that night.'

'Oh Lord!' Molly stared at the pile of dust and stone with new eyes. 'You mean it… was anyone inside?'

'Not in the shop. Closed up for the day.' Angelo looked sober. 'There was an old couple asleep in the flat above though, and the German pilot bought it too, although don't suppose we're allowed to feel too bad on his account. Three other Jerries baled out and were taken prisoner. Makes you think, don't it?'

'Those poor people,' Molly said softly.

'Gawd knows what it'll be like if the Luftwaffe really decide they've got it in for us.' He shivered. 'Bombs on London, can you imagine? It don't bear thinking about.'

'No,' Molly said vaguely, still staring at the rubble. 'No, it doesn't.'

After a moment of solemn silence, Angelo returned to his former cheeriness. It never seemed to desert him for long.

'Well, where are you off to this fine spring day?' he asked. 'Don't do for a young lady like yourself to be hanging round these streets. There's rough sorts about.'

Molly smiled awkwardly. 'I'm trying to find the Theatre Royal on Drury Lane, only I've got a little lost seeing the sights. It's all right though, I've still got an hour and a half. My appointment isn't while two.'

'Ah, you're with the ENSA lot, are you?'

'Not yet, but I'm hoping to be. That's why I'm here. For an audition.' Molly found that confidences somehow came naturally

with Angelo. She lowered her voice so she could get at least one
fib off her conscience. 'And I'm really Molly Clough. Dorothy
Kensitas is a stage name. Don't tell anyone, will you?'

Angelo grinned. 'Suits you a lot better. Well then, Molly, if
you're going to be with ENSA, you'd better come in for some
lunch. Official ENSA dining establishment, is Cortesi's.'

Molly blinked. 'Is it?'

'Well, maybe not what you'd call official, but it's where all the
Drury Lane gang come when they're peckish. Dad gives them a
special rate. Reckons it lends us a bit of glamour, being patronised
by entertainers.'

Molly hesitated. 'I'd like to, but I do have to make sure I'm at
my audition on time. I don't know which way to go from here.'

'Don't worry about that, it's only a couple of streets away. You
can walk it in ten minutes. I'll point you in the right direction
when you've had something to eat.'

Molly couldn't deny that the smells drifting from Cortesi's
were very enticing.

'Um, I haven't got all that much money either,' she told
Angelo, flushing slightly. After paying for her accommodation,
breakfast, the cab last night and a return train ticket, only six
shillings of her original fifty-five now remained to keep her fed
and watered until she made it home again.

'This once, it's on the house,' Angelo said. 'Bring you luck,
eh, darling? Ever eaten Italian food before? Course you haven't.
In you come and have some of my nonna's pollo alla cacciatora.
That's chicken stew to you.'

Refusing to listen to further protestations, Angelo half guided
and half dragged Molly into Cortesi's.

## Chapter 13

Molly couldn't deny she felt better after having eaten. She'd only had a slice of toast at the boarding house, nerves over her audition suppressing her appetite, and it hadn't been until she had caught the delicious scent of the Italian food that she'd realised how hungry she had become.

She had wondered how her tastebuds, reared on a diet of plain, stodgy English fare, would cope with the flavours of Italian cuisine, but the chicken and tomato stew Angelo's father served to her had been delicious. The British were wont to regard garlic with suspicion as something foul-smelling and foreign, but Molly had enjoyed the subtle tang it added to her meal. She had even gone so far as to beg Angelo to share the recipe so she could make it for her mother and sister, but he had only winked and said it was a family secret.

It wasn't only the meal that had improved her mood. Angelo's company had been very welcome too. It was hard to feel nervous about her audition in the glare of his infectious grin. Molly had been introduced to his father, who beamed on her with a smile much like his son's and begged in halting English that she would come again after she joined ENSA. The Cortesi family seemed to take it for granted that this was definitely something that would happen.

Molly had been made to feel so welcome at Cortesi's that it felt like she had friends here already. ENSA didn't seem like such a distant dream now she had eaten where the ENSA people ate, and made friends with some of their friends. While she could feel the familiar stirrings of stage fright as the time for her audition drew nearer, she no longer felt like she had placed herself somewhere she couldn't possibly belong.

After her meal, Angelo gave her directions to Drury Lane. Finally, at a quarter to two, Molly found herself outside the Theatre Royal. She gazed up at the imposing classical facade and sucked in a breath.

Lord, it was so big! She felt quite dwarfed by it. The warmth and companionship Molly had experienced in the Cortesi family's cosy little eatery started to dissipate as she thought of the ordeal ahead. She could feel herself beginning to tremble.

She had to be strong though. She mustn't let herself forget that she needed this job. But oh goodness, why had she let Angelo persuade her to eat? It only meant she was more likely to throw up.

Molly tried to calm herself with a few stern words.

She could do this. She had sung and played in front of people dozens of times, and although she'd always been nervous, she'd managed to avoid either vomiting or getting jeered off stage. This time wouldn't be any different. She wouldn't let it.

What was it Daphne had said, the day she had sparked that mixture of embarrassment and admiration in her sister by bursting into song in the cafe? *You just have to stop caring what people think of you…* Which might be a lot easier if the opinion of the people in question didn't have the power to shape your entire future.

Molly thought of all the times she had sung in her grandad's pub, and when she'd felt the least nervous. After pondering, she decided it was probably that night Jack Forrester had come in. She had been anxious, but the stage fright had seemed to quieten more quickly than usual.

Why? What had been special about that night? Was it because Jack had been actively listening to her, in a way the pub's patrons rarely did?

Eventually, Molly concluded that it wasn't just because Jack had been an engaged audience. It had been because she had singled him out, and sung as if for him alone. For the first time, she had been able to shut out the room full of people and make her performance all for this one man who seemed to be on her side.

There was no guarantee any of the audition panel would be on her side, of course. But if she picked out whichever one seemed friendliest and tried to sing only for them, perhaps that would help her get through it.

Molly thrust her hands into the pockets of her borrowed coat to conceal their shaking, squared her shoulders and marched inside.

There was a middle-aged woman seated in the repurposed ticket office, in a khaki uniform like that of the ATS. It was distinguished by the same black ENSA tabs as Jack Forrester had worn, and the brass cap badge of the organisation. She gave Molly a warm smile, which instantly made her feel a little better.

'Afternoon, my love,' the woman said. 'Now then, is it Miss Kensitas? I've got a young lady of that name pencilled in for two o'clock.'

Molly started. She had all but forgotten the stage name over her meal at Cortesi's. If the woman hadn't pre-empted her, she'd have blundered in and given her real one.

'Er, yes,' she said.

'Well, go on up.' The woman nodded towards an impressive staircase between two marble pillars that branched off into two at the top. 'Best of luck.'

Her attitude was very relaxed. She seemed to take it as read that Molly knew exactly how things worked at ENSA, and the layout of the theatre. Perhaps this was what things were like in the world of entertainment.

'I haven't been here before,' Molly said. 'Which room do I need?'

'Up the right-hand stairs and second on the left, sweetheart. There's a sign on the door. They'll call you in when they're ready for you.'

'Thank you.'

Cautiously Molly crept up the huge, opulent staircase, grimacing with each footstep. The carpet was beautiful red plush with gold trim, so soft that her sturdy shoes left footprints on it. She felt as if she ought to have removed them and gone up barefoot.

Molly soon located the right room. The plaque on the door read 'Stage Manager's Office', but there was a piece of paper hanging down that must have come unstuck. She held it up. Written on it were the words 'Forces Follies Audition Room'.

She sat on a chair outside, feeling suddenly shabby in her best Sunday dress and the borrowed coat that hung loose on her conspicuously uncurvy frame. In the midst of white marble friezes, velvet furnishings and crystal chandeliers, Molly couldn't help feeling like exactly what she was: a mill girl playing at being a singer. The confidence she had felt when she had been with Angelo was long gone, and she felt once more that she was somewhere she could never hope to belong.

Someone was in with the audition panel already; Molly could hear their act through the door, which was slightly ajar. Another lady singer, it sounded like. She certainly had a strong and distinctive voice, if rather husky. She was singing a comic song, 'Nobody Loves a Fairy When She's Forty', in a manner full of humour and character.

Molly wondered if she and the woman were in competition. Perhaps there was only one opening for a female comic singer in the Forces Follies, which she assumed was the name of the concert party they were auditioning for. Did ENSA have such a thing as a reserve? Might she be asked to audition for a different company if this one didn't want her, or would it be an outright rejection? She had no idea how it worked.

Eventually the woman finished, amidst applause from the audition panel.

'OK, gorgeous, you're in,' a male voice said. 'We'll write to you with details of where you're to report, all right? Give us a bell if the letter doesn't turn up by next week.'

Molly blinked. Was that all there was to it? Sing a song, some applause, then you were accepted for a ten-pound-a-week job just like that? She hoped it would be as easy for her – assuming there was still a job going.

A heavy dread settled on her. Would they send her home without auditioning, if the position had been filled? Would it all have been for nothing? It had cost her so much to come here, in cash and in courage…

A moment later, the woman who had just auditioned emerged. Molly couldn't help staring. Partly this was because of the singer's pink-sequinned, feather-trimmed dress, which was guaranteed to draw the eye, and partly it was because of her unusual breadth and height – she must be well over six foot. But it wasn't only those things.

She had been able to belt out a tune, certainly, but… well, unkind though she felt to think it, Molly couldn't help but notice that the woman was no looker. Far from it, in fact. Not that that should matter if someone had the pipes, but it usually did – or it did when men were making the decisions. ENSA really must be desperate for acts.

'All right?' the singer said in a deep, gruff Lancashire accent.

'Um, hello.'

With no sign of embarrassment, the woman began rummaging in her sizeable cleavage. After exploring her brassiere for some considerable time, she produced a packet of gaspers and shook one out. Molly stared.

'Oh, sorry,' the singer said, holding out the packet. 'Not very gentlemanly of me. You want one?'

'No, thank you.' Molly's puzzlement lifted as the penny finally dropped, and she laughed. 'You're a female impersonator.'

'Female impressionist, love. Female impersonator's summat else.'

'Is it? What's the difference?'

'No one's going to mistake me for the real thing is the differ-ence. Female impersonators are all about creating an illusion.' He produced a book of matches and lit his foul-smelling cigarette. 'Whereas I'm a bloke in a dress and everyone knows it. That's the gag, see?'

Molly felt slightly embarrassed at how long it had taken her to cotton on to this, but then she supposed she'd lived a pretty sheltered life.

The female impressionist came forward to shake her hand, cigarette clamped between his teeth. As an afterthought, he reached into his padded cleavage for a long holder encrusted with paste jewels and shoved his fag in the end. 'Nobby Peters, or Dolores de Diamond when I'm on stage. What do you do then?'

'Um, I'm a singer. I play the piano too. Not very well, but enough to accompany myself.'

'Well, break a leg, lass. Hope you make it.' Nobby nodded goodbye then stomped heavily down the corridor in his feathers and sequins like a cowboy disguised as Ginger Rogers, smoke billowing from his cigarette.

# Chapter 14

It seemed an age before Molly was called in to her own audition. She had no wristwatch, but she guessed it must be well past two o'clock.

Why the wait? Did the panel just enjoy making her sweat? Because if so, they'd be thrilled to see how well it was working. Her hands were shaking so badly that she had to sit on them.

Eventually, however, the door opened and a woman's head appeared. The face under the ENSA cap was young, framed by dark curls, and not unfriendly. However, it had a look that reminded Molly of her mam's old moggy Geoffrey. When Geoffrey decided to bestow his approval on someone new, he would rub against them and purr like they were his best friend. But there would be a period of wary standoffishness first while Geoffrey sized them up, and that was how the ENSA woman seemed to be regarding Molly.

'Miss Kensitas, I presume,' she said in a businesslike tone. 'Tabitha Daley. We're ready for you.'

Tabitha had a clear, forthright voice, naturally resonant, as if she were used to giving commands. She sounded like the captain of a girls' hockey team, or someone who rode to hounds. A 'yoiks' or 'tally-ho' seemed like it would come naturally to Tabitha Daley.

Molly grasped her handbag in both hands, hoping this would keep them steady, and followed Tabitha into the audition room.

Inside were three other people seated behind desks. A chair had been placed on the other side, facing the panel. Behind it was a small piano.

Tabitha slipped into a seat next to her fellow judges. Molly, not having been given any instruction, continued to hover. Self-conscious about the way she was gripping her handbag, she slipped one hand into her coat pocket instead, then instantly withdrew it when she realised how inappropriately casual this must look. Tabitha Daley noticed her fumbling, Molly was sure. She looked like a woman who noticed things.

There were four judges: two male, two female. The younger of the men flashed her a small smile.

'Sit, please, Miss Kensitas,' he said, nodding to the chair in front of the desks. Molly did so.

None of the others looked up. The older man seemed to be making notes. Could they be about her? She hadn't said a word yet, let alone sung one.

Molly took in the appearance of the judges while she waited for them to pay attention to her. Tabitha was the only one wearing an ENSA uniform. The others were in civilian clothing, although of a Bohemian sort. The man who had spoken wore a black woollen jumper, half-moon glasses that were far too old for him and side-combed hair. He had a pale, studious air that didn't seem to belong to the world of entertainment.

The second woman was dripping silk scarves and expensive-looking jewellery. She was excessively pretty, Molly noticed, with luxurious jet-black hair. She reminded Molly of the silent film actress Clara Bow, who in her childhood she had thought the most beautiful person she had ever seen. The woman had a somewhat snooty expression, however, looking down the length of her nose at Molly as if unimpressed by what she saw.

The other man was middle-aged, diminutive but stocky, wearing a loud checked suit and spotted bow tie that would suit a comedian – except that he looked far too stern to possess such a thing as a sense of humour. All but this man were quite young, with the oldest perhaps twenty-seven or twenty-eight.

Only the studious young man smiled at her. Molly flashed a tremulous smile back. If she was going to choose someone to be the person she played to today, then this seemed to be the one closest to being on her side.

'Would you like anything before we begin, Miss Kensitas?' Tabitha asked. 'A glass of water? A cigarette?'

Cigarette. Why hadn't Molly accepted Dolores de Diamond's offer of a gasper outside? It might have calmed her nerves, and stopped her worrying about the smell of garlic on her breath. It might also have made her feel sicker than she already did though, and she hadn't wanted to tempt fate. Anyhow, it was too late now – for water, cigarettes or anything else. The way her hands were trembling, anything she tried to drink would go all over her. She'd be liable to set fire to herself if she attempted to smoke.

'No, thank you,' she said.

'Now there's no need to be nervous,' the studious young man told her, glancing at the hands gripping her bag. 'We're all friends here.'

'I'm not nervous.' Molly realised she had said that rather too abruptly. She cleared her throat. 'I mean, um… shall we begin?'

'Well, let me introduce everyone to start us off,' said Tabitha, who seemed to naturally take charge of any situation. 'We're all with the Forces Follies ENSA party: one of the first parties formed under the organisation. As I said, my name's Tabitha Daley. I play the accompaniment for our artistes. This lady is Madame Chastain, a dancer, formerly of Sadler's Wells. She's top of the bill so do excuse her swollen head.' The Clara Bow lookalike gave Molly a chilly nod. 'Philip Brooks, our manager' – she gestured to the studious young man – 'and finally David Harper, our compère and resident comic.' Here she indicated the grumpy man in the loud suit, who didn't bother to nod.

So the young man in the spectacles, Philip, was the troupe manager and not a performer. Molly wondered that the man called David wasn't the one to manage them. He looked like a manager sort.

'Like most ENSA units, we're a seven-hander – or we aim to be,' Tabitha went on. 'It can vary as we lose people to the call-up.

There's myself and Philip in addition to the performers, of course. You'll meet the rest if you make it.'

'Nice to meet you all,' Molly said. 'Dorothy Kensitas.' She forced herself not to wince as she spoke the unfamiliar name.

'We're aware of that,' Madame Chastain said coolly. Molly looked at her with surprise. Madame Chastain spoke in cut-glass English that wouldn't sound out of place on a member of the royal family. From the woman's name, Molly had been expecting a French accent.

'Yes, I know.' Molly gave a nervous laugh. 'I, um, just felt I ought to join in rather than sitting here with nowt to say for myself.'

She bit her tongue as soon as the dialect word slipped out, but it was too late. Madame Chastain immediately began scribbling in her notebook, her smirk barely concealed.

'Well, I don't think we need to ask where you come from,' Philip said with another friendly smile. 'I'm a Leeds lad myself. Makes me feel homesick to hear a local accent.'

Molly could have hugged him for wanting to put her at her ease, but his words only made her more self-conscious. She had been trying so hard to show good elocution. Clearly she had been failing miserably, even before the unfortunate 'nowt' escaped.

'Jack Forrester sent you then?' David demanded gruffly.

'Yes,' Molly said. 'I mean to say, he was the one who encouraged me to apply for an audition.'

'Said he'd never heard of you when I asked him.'

Molly flushed. 'He… he might've forgotten. I was singing under a stage name the night we met.'

'What was it?'

'Um, Molly Clough.'

'Huh. Damn funny stage name.'

'They like it in the clubs back in Yorkshire. It sounds… homely.'

'I'll say it does. So you're a professional entertainer, are you?'

'Semi-professional,' Molly said, trying not to flinch. It wasn't a complete lie, was it? She got the occasional few bob from her grandad when he'd had a good night, which she could call a fee of sorts.

'Where have you performed?' Philip asked, pushing his spectacles up his nose.

Molly hesitated. If she told the whole truth – that her entire show business experience was in a single pub owned by a close relative – she'd be out on her ear before they'd even heard her sing. But the more fibs she told, the more she was setting herself up for trouble if she got caught out. Could she get away with being vague and hope they moved on?

'Oh, here and there,' she said in what she hoped was a breezy tone. 'Pubs and working men's clubs, mostly.'

'Any theatre work?'

'Um…' Molly hesitated, then decided if she was in for a penny, she was in for a pound. 'Well, I was a Sunbeam. At the Alhambra.'

Madame Chastain raised an eyebrow. 'You were a child performer?'

'Yes. Briefly.'

'You must be able to dance as well then.'

'Yes, a little – I used to – but I don't dance now. It's my singing people seem to like.'

'Any more recent experience?'

'Well…' Molly tried to conjure up the name of some small local theatre she could claim to have performed at. There was the City Varieties in Leeds, but it was too well-known. Philip would certainly know it, if that was his home town. What other names did she have stored in her brain? 'Do you know, um… Shipley Playhouse?'

Philip raised an eyebrow. 'You've played there?'

Bugger. She hadn't thought they'd have heard of the place. She'd never even been – she only knew the name because she remembered Rita being taken there by a boyfriend once. She had assumed from Rita's description that it was relatively humble, but clearly it was more impressive than she'd thought.

'Yes. Just once. Very, very low down the bill.' Molly gave a nervous laugh. 'Practically off the bottom of it, in fact.'

'Wines and spirits,' Philip said with an understanding nod. 'We've all been there.'

Molly assumed this must be some variety term rather than an offer of a drink. She smiled vaguely.

She was trembling all over now: not only her hands but her whole body. The short interview had set her so on edge that she didn't know how she was going to fumble her way through the songs in her repertoire. Nevertheless, she stood and went to the piano.

'Do you have your music?' Tabitha said, in a kinder voice than before, which told Molly she must have noticed the state she was in. 'I can turn the pages for you.'

'No,' Molly said absently as she took a seat at the instrument. 'My dad taught me to play, but he never learned to read music and nor did I. I do it from memory, sort of.'

Philip raised his eyebrows. 'You mean you can play by ear?'

'I'm… not sure. I just know the music for the songs I sing. I listened to it over and over on my friend Rita's gramophone until I could do it.'

There was a short muttered conversation among the panel, then Philip nodded to her.

'What're you going to give us then, kitten?' he asked. 'Just a couple will do.'

'I thought "Greatest Aspidistra" and "Beer Barrel Polka". People seem to like those best.'

'All right, whenever you're ready.'

Molly took a deep, shuddering breath. All she wanted now was to run away. No amount of focusing her attention on the friendlier members of the panel would be enough to conquer her overwhelming panic. But she couldn't run away, could she? She closed her eyes and let her fingers move instinctively over the keys as she started to sing.

Molly had no idea how she got through that performance. Her brain seemed to take itself off for a little holiday, as if it had had about as much as it could bear. She could hear her trembling voice like it belonged to someone singing far away. She could hear the tinny plonking of the unfamiliar piano as she fumbled for the right keys. It all seemed to be happening independently of her, as though her body was being piloted by someone else. When she had finished her second song, she just sat there, numb, trying to remember how her arms and legs worked.

There was no applause, as there had been for Dolores de Diamond. No chummy chat, and the immediate offer of a job. The panel just looked at her.

'Well, thanks for that,' Philip said after what felt like an eternity. 'If you'd like to wait outside, Miss Kensitas, we'll call you back when we've reached a decision.'

—

Molly felt like an automaton as she got to her feet and left the room. She pulled the door closed but it stuck in the same place as before, remaining slightly ajar. She didn't bother trying to pull it to, but went to sit on the chair she had occupied previously.

It was going to be a no, she supposed. She knew she had performed badly. Funny how she couldn't seem to feel anything.

The interview part of it had been excruciating, and she had seemed to get drawn into one falsehood after another without having any intention of telling further fibs. As for the singing… well, she had been able to hear herself: her usual strong, clear tone becoming a pathetic, frightened warble under the influence of nerves. They had been humorous songs, but her performance had been neither fun nor funny. And if she couldn't cope with an audience of four, how on earth had she thought she could entertain whole theatres full of weary, jaded troops?

The daze started to lift, and she swallowed a sob as she faced up to the fact that it had all been for nothing. She had been right when she had told herself she would get nowt for her trouble but jeers and pain if she made this trip to London. She had never wanted her mam so badly.

There was a hum of voices from behind the door. Molly wasn't usually one to eavesdrop, but some bloody-minded impulse to really put the seal on her humiliation seemed to egg her on. She shifted her chair forward, leaning towards the crack where the door stood ajar, and tried to make out what was being said.

'Well, my loves, if that's the best we can do, we might as well give up now,' a polished, girlish voice that Molly recognised as belonging to Madame Chastain was saying.

'The kid was nervous,' Tabitha said. 'Don't be too hard on her, Di. She had a good voice underneath it, I thought.'

'I thought so too,' Philip said. 'My worry is whether she's got anything original to offer. Every company in the organisation seems to have someone taking off Gracie Fields. I would like the Follies to be a little more original. Still, we might make something out of her.'

'She looked frightened to death, didn't she?' Tabitha observed. 'Voice quavering like an opera singer. Poor thing.'

'You know, chaps, we ought to let them perform before we start grilling them,' Philip observed. 'It isn't fair to get them quaking in their boots and then expect them to do their best work.'

'It's the only way to test them under performance conditions,' Madame Chastain said primly. 'If they can't manage the four of us, how will they cope when they're being heckled by a NAAFI full of raucous soldiers? It takes nerves of steel to handle a service audience. You know that, Phil.'

'She can play by ear though, and she's taught herself her accompaniment.' Tabitha was speaking again now. 'That's impressive with no formal training. What did you think, Little Davy?'

'Flat,' the second male member of the panel said, somewhat brutally.

'Now that's not fair. She was in tune, whatever else you might think of her.'

'Not that sort of flat. I mean flat chest, flat personality, flat everything. Don't matter how well she can sing if she ain't got nothing else going for her. The troops'll tear us to shreds if we put out playbills promising them birds and turn up with a shrinking waif like that. They'd get a bigger thrill out of Dolores.'

Molly could feel her face burning. She wanted to run, to get away from this place and these awful, humiliating words, but it felt as though she was rooted to the spot.

It was Philip's turn to speak next. 'I thought she was a pretty little thing.'

Davy snorted. 'Really? Would you take her to bed?'

'Rather a moot point, luvvie,' Philip said.

'Well I wouldn't,' Madame Chastain announced. 'Little Davy's right. The Follies need sex appeal, not some skinny kid. The face is quite pretty in a pale, underfed sort of way, I suppose, but she hasn't got a curve on her.'

'She must've impressed Jack,' Philip pointed out. 'And he's not easily impressed.'

'Not enough to stick, it seems. He'd never heard of her when Davy asked him.'

'The girl said she was using a stage name.'

'Yes, how very convenient. She probably picked Jack's name up in some club and used it to wangle herself an audition.'

'The kid looked half-starved,' Davy observed. 'What do they feed them up in whatever northern hellhole she comes from?'

'Gruel for every meal, I imagine,' Madame Chastain said with a tinkling laugh. 'Tabby, did you see her hands?'

'I know, she couldn't stop shaking,' Tabitha said. 'I remember being the same way before my first big audish.'

'That wasn't what I meant. I was talking about the calluses, and the dirt under her fingernails, and the bruises on her wrist. No doubt she does some horrendous working-class job during the day then goes home to get a beating from the boyfriend at night.'

Molly tugged self-consciously on her coat cuff, cursing herself for not wearing gloves. She did usually, but there was a stain on the pair she had brought so she'd left them in her case.

'That ghastly northern accent as well!' Madame Chastain went on, sounding gleeful as she enumerated Molly's many failings. 'I could barely understand her.'

'Nothing wrong with a northern accent,' Philip said stoutly, although there was little of Leeds in his own polished speech. 'Official accent of music hall, practically.'

'Those days are gone. Move with the times, cherie.'

'Accent aside, I thought she spoke very clearly,' Tabitha observed. 'Enunciated well, I mean. Good, resonant tone that ought to carry.'

Molly sat up a little straighter. Yes, at least that was one thing she didn't have a problem with. Years of speaking in such a way that Rita could tell what she was saying just from the shape of her mouth meant she rarely mumbled, and talking over the clatter of the looms had given her volume.

Madame Chastain wasn't impressed, of course.

'Oh yes, you could hear every dropped H as clear as a bell,' she said. 'They must be starved for glamour in the clubs up there if she's their answer to Garbo.'

'Decent legs though,' Little Davy said. 'We do need another girl. Maybe if we fattened her up a bit—'

But Molly didn't stay to find out what the panel thought she might be good for if they fattened her up: whether it was the stage, a brothel or a batch of suspicious meat pies. Her cheeks on fire with shame, she grabbed her bag and gas mask and hurried away.

# Chapter 15

The woman in the ticket office said something as Molly rushed from the building, but Molly sped past without answering. The opulent interior of the Drury Lane theatre was a blur of red and gold through eyes filled with tears. She had to get away from this awful place, and those people who'd made her feel as if she was a slab of meat to be appraised. She needed to be by herself, and sob until the crushing despair lifted enough for her to function again.

The street outside was busy, and several passers-by stared at the young woman who ran from the theatre. Molly supposed she must look rather like an escaped wild animal. She felt like one.

Through tear-filled eyes, Molly noticed a narrow passage to one side of the building where she could hide until she had recovered. She nipped down it and slumped against the theatre wall, next to several overflowing dustbins.

Her surroundings were still blurred by tears, but now she was alone, she found they wouldn't fall freely. Her throat felt tight, the sobs she badly needed to let out trapped inside her. She couldn't breathe properly, and gasped as she tried to swallow mouthfuls of the foul-smelling air.

She should never have come. She had told herself she shouldn't, and she had been right. Why on earth had she let Rita persuade her? Of course ENSA wasn't for people like her. The panel had made that abundantly, painfully clear.

Molly let out a strangulated sob as she thought about the words she had heard: so casually cruel, talking about her as if she was a thing rather than a human being. Sneering at her hands, her figure, her accent – her actual performance had hardly seemed to matter.

And this was the world of entertainment she had so idolised. Behind the glitter and applause, it seemed a hard, callous, ruthless place. Molly had never believed herself to be naive, but in this worldly environment, she felt little better than a baby. She was sure she could never be like those people, and talk the way they talked.

She sank on to the hard cobbles, not caring about the state her clothes would be in if she lingered here. An ENSA recruitment poster was on the wall opposite, bearing an illustration of numerous beaming performers.

> Professional and semi-professional artistes wanted for troop entertainments. Join ENSA, the greatest show on earth!

Molly swore at the thing.

Well, it was over. The dream had ended, and in the most brutal way. She wasn't going to be a part of ENSA. She was never going to perform again, after what she had heard the panel say – not at the Boot and Slipper or anywhere else.

ENSA. 'Every Night Something Awful.' 'Abandon hope all ye who ENSA hear.' There must be a hundred and one cracks like that, to be heard wherever servicemen gathered. And Molly had been deemed unworthy of even this much-mocked organisation. It was clear now that she had been kidding herself in choosing to believe she possessed anything like professional-level talent.

What would she do though? She grimaced as she thought of Mr Taylor, and the words she had spoken that day at the mill. But she would have to go to him – to apologise, and beg on her knees for her job back if necessary. What choice did she have? It was the only way she could hope to provide for her family.

Molly pulled out her handkerchief and hastily wiped her eyes when she heard footsteps. She looked up to see someone in uniform approaching. As the figure grew closer, she realised it was Tabitha from the audition panel.

'There you are,' Tabitha said. 'I came out to give you our decision and you'd scarpered. Nora on the door said she'd seen you bolt down here. What on earth is the matter, Miss Kensitas?'

Molly struggled to her feet. Now she had had time to think, her grief had been at least partly replaced by anger.

Who did these people think they were, anyhow? What gave them the right to sneer at her? Yes, her fingernails often had loom grease staining them despite vigorous scrubbing. Yes, her hands were callused, and yes, she had bruises from the machine she operated. That was the consequence of a hard day's work – a thing she would bet Madame Chastain had never experienced in her life. Perhaps she was skinny, because with Daph's medical bills to pay and a salary of only thirty-five shillings a week, she couldn't always afford the privilege of three square meals a day. And yes, she had a Yorkshire accent, because she came from bloody York-shire. According to them, her major crime wasn't being a bad singer, or even being unattractive. It was being working class.

Well, Molly had endured a lifetime of people trying to make her feel like nothing because of that. But her dad had drummed into his children that they were as good as anyone else, and she wasn't going to stand being spoken to that way by this bunch of elitist prigs who thought they were better than her.

'What do you think is the ruddy matter?' she demanded of Tabitha.

Tabitha blinked. 'I'm sorry?'

'I heard what your delightful panel said about me. That door don't close all the way. Well I recently left a job where I was made to feel like a tart just for existing in the gaze of a man, and that was nowhere near as humiliating as the way you lot were talking about me. I told them to shove their job up their arse, and now I'm saying the same to you. Sod your ENSA, Miss Daley, and sod you as well.'

Molly made to push past her so she could storm off, taking what little was left of her self-respect with her, but Tabitha put a hand on her shoulder.

'You heard all that?' she said in a low voice.

'Course I heard. I might be poor but I aren't deaf, love.'

'I'm sorry. We didn't know you could hear us.'

Tabitha at least had the decency to look ashamed. Well, good. So she should.

'I heard it all,' Molly said. 'I'm ugly, I'm skinny, I'm common… what else was it your Madame Thingummy said? No, never mind. I can remember.'

Tabitha flushed. 'Diana shouldn't have said those things. We had no idea you were listening.'

'Do you think that makes it better? That's worse!'

'Look, you mustn't take it personally. Di's like that about everyone.'

'And the man you called Little Davy?'

'Oh, pay no attention to him. He lost what charm he had at the Somme.'

'He made it sound like I was auditioning to be a pick-up girl, not a singer. Do you know how that felt?'

'He's hard-headed, that's all,' Tabitha said. 'I know it must sound cynical, but it does matter – whether the boys fancy you. Service audiences don't care if you're there to juggle, tap dance or do impressions of Hermann Goering while swinging upside-down from a trapeze. All they care about is that they hardly see a woman all day and they want something pretty to look at. It gives them something to talk about in the NAAFI afterwards and it gives them something to dream about when they go to bed – something besides the war. It's the concert parties with good-looking girls that fill the most seats, no matter how abysmal they might be in other respects.'

Molly thought of the letters she'd had from her brother about ENSA concerts, and was forced to admit this was probably true.

'Why do you think Diana's top of the bill?' Tabitha went on. 'She's no great shakes as a dancer, for all her claims she was with Sadler's Wells.'

'It was humiliating,' Molly muttered.

'I know, and I'm sorry. I promise you, Little Davy's really not as bad as that conversation made him sound.' Tabitha nodded to the ENSA poster on the wall. 'The thing is, he believes it: all that stuff about doing our duty and boosting morale. I mean, we all believe it to an extent – at least, it's nice to think we're doing our bit – but the truth is, most of us are here because we were thrown out of work when the venues on our old circuits were closed or requisitioned. Not Little Davy. For him, it's all about giving the troops something to buck them up.' She shrugged. 'And he happens to think the best thing for bucking up a young soldier is a pretty girl. I doubt he's wrong at that. He's the only one of us who's ever actually fought in a war so I suppose if he cares a bit too much, that's his prerogative.'

'And the posh girl, Diana – what's her excuse?'

'Being too beautiful for this world,' Tabitha said with a wry smile. 'But she's not so bad when you get to know her – neither of them are. Di's OK when she doesn't let her ego get the better of her, and Davy only talks tough in auditions because he's obsessed with making the Follies the best they can be.'

'Well it's clear what they thought of me anyway. Now if you don't mind, Miss Tabitha Daley, I need to go home and prepare myself to beg my old boss for my job back in the hope he'll loan me enough to pay for my little sister's new calipers.'

Tabitha frowned. 'This would be the boss who made you feel like a tart?'

'No, that was the overlooker who tried to force himself on me.' Molly wasn't quite sure why she was saying all this, except that now her hopes had been dashed, she had no reason to bite her tongue. 'The boss is the millowner who turns a blind eye to it.'

'My word!' Tabitha said, staring at her. 'Oh, you poor little chick.'

'Spare me your pity, love. And you can take this back to your friends when you tell them you've delivered their rejection.' Molly flicked two fingers up and again made to leave, but again

Tabitha stopped her. She didn't look offended. In fact, she was smiling.

'You know, if you'd shown pluck like this in your audition, it would've been an easy yes,' she said. 'Do you really know Jack Forrester? Di thought you might have made it up.'

'I know him. We met while I was playing at my grandad's pub. I wish to goodness now that I'd never set eyes on the man,' Molly added bitterly.

'He didn't remember you.'

'He'll remember me as Molly Clough. That's my real name. Dorothy Kensitas was a stage name I made up when I telephoned for an audition.' Molly leaned back against the wall with a weary sigh, her anger disappearing as quickly as it had arisen. 'I thought it might make me sound glamorous.'

'It doesn't suit you.'

'No. I suppose I'm not the glamorous type.'

'And have you really performed at Shipley Playhouse?'

'No. And I was never a Sunbeam, and I've never played the variety circuits or any professional job. My career peak is the time I came second in a local talent show to a man who did farmyard impressions. I'm an amateur — less than an amateur. I play in my grandad's pub after work, that's all.' Molly gazed blankly at the smiling concert party on the ENSA poster. 'At least, I used to.'

Tabitha leaned against the wall beside her. 'You didn't need to lie to impress us, you know. You're not at all bad.'

Molly gave a grim laugh. 'Now who's lying?'

'Honestly. Phil thought you had talent and so did I. Even Di and Little Davy admitted you had a decent voice, and everyone was impressed that you'd taught yourself to play your accompaniment.' Tabitha turned to look at her. 'I doubt we got the best of you today either, did we? You looked frightened to death.'

'I do get nervous,' Molly admitted, wiping her brow with her handkerchief. 'Today was a thousand times worse than usual though. I was already shaking, and then that interview... well, I'm sorry for wasting your time.' She paused. 'At least, I'm sorry for you and Philip. The other two can go jump off a bridge.'

Tabitha laughed.

'Did you say you had a sister who needed new calipers?' she asked.

'You're not going to pity me again, are you?'

'I promise I won't. I'm just interested.'

'Yes,' Molly whispered. 'I wasn't going to get in touch after Jack gave me an ENSA card. I was sure I had no chance of getting in, and it felt so foolish to imagine someone like me doing summat like that. Then I left my job at the mill after what happened with the overlooker, and when the doctor said our Daph needed these new leg braces, I thought…'

'What have you got to lose?' Tabitha said softly.

'That's it.'

'And then we made you feel like this.' Tabitha laid a hand on her arm. 'I'm so sorry. It was unforgivably rude, and very unkind. We didn't know you could hear us, but that's no excuse.'

'I just want to go home,' Molly said with a small sob. She felt as helpless as a child, alone in this strange place. 'I want to go home to my mam.'

'Of course you do, sweetheart.'

'She don't know I'm here. She don't even know I lost my job. And she deserves better than having me lie to her, after everything she's sacrificed for the sake of us bairns.'

'How much are the calipers?'

'At least twenty pound for a used pair,' Molly said in a toneless voice. 'I don't know how we're going to find money like that.'

Tabitha paused. 'Well… it's irregular, but it might be possible for Phil to arrange an advance on your wages. If that's going to help.'

Molly blinked. 'On my what?'

'Your wages. That's if you still want to work with us.' Tabitha smiled. 'I didn't actually come out to give you a no. I came to tell you that the panel had voted in your favour. Three to one – Phil and I talked Davy round in the end. We're taking a risk, but at least two of us could see that you had better in you than we saw today.'

'Are you joking?'

'Certainly not. And you know, Miss Kensitas – sorry, Miss Clough – I'm almost glad in the end that we upset you. At least now I've had a glimpse of the real you. If Davy had seen you telling me off, he'd know there's nothing flat about you. Once you've got those nerves under control, I have a feeling the boys are going to love you.'

Molly stared at her. 'You can't mean it.'

'Why can't I?'

'But… I performed badly. I lied about being semi-professional.' Molly grimaced. 'And, um, I just used a very rude gesture to you when I was cross. Sorry about that.'

'I've spent the last six months touring army barracks. Believe me, I've experienced worse,' Tabitha said with a smile. 'Like I said, you had no reason to lie. The only thing we ever cared about was that you had talent, and I'm persuaded you do. Will you take the job?'

'I mean, if you honestly…' Molly took a deep breath. 'Yes. Yes, I… I'll take it.'

'I hoped you'd say that. Now if you'll come back inside, Phil will go through some paperwork with you. Then all you need to do is go home and wait for the official letter.'

## Chapter 16

Molly travelled home in a daze. It wasn't until she changed trains at Leeds that the day's events started to sink in, and even then it felt like half dream. She had to keep peeping into her handbag at the banker's draft Philip had arranged for her – a whole thirty pounds, her first three weeks' wages as a professional entertainer. She had felt herself rich on the journey down with a mere fifty-five shillings. Now she felt like a bootlegger in some American gangster film.

And even more important was the other document she had stashed in her bag – her contract with ENSA, signed over a sixpenny stamp to make it all legal, bearing her signature and that of Basil Dean. Just seeing his signature above her own, testifying to the fact that she had finally realised her dream of becoming a professional entertainer, sent shivers down her spine.

Molly expected to find her family in bed when she arrived home at nearly midnight. When she entered the living room, however, she discovered her mother still awake: knitting in the fireside gloaming, with Geoffrey around her shoulders as usual. Daphne was sleeping with her head in her mother's lap. Mam looked up to smile softly at Molly.

'Welcome home, love,' she said quietly. 'Glad to have you safe again.'

Molly couldn't help feeling a pang at the comfortable domestic scene, and her mother's soft and loving words of welcome. She had been so focused on her ambition of getting into ENSA that she hadn't stopped to dwell on what would follow. She had dreamed of escape for so long, but now it hit her just how hard it was going to be to separate herself from her loved ones.

Still, at least she would have the comfort of knowing she was providing for them. A small smile illuminated her face when she thought of the banker's draft, and how Mam would rejoice when she saw it.

'You'd no need to wait up,' Molly said softly, so as not to wake Daphne. 'I've got my key.'

'Our Daph insisted,' Mam said with a smile, resting a hand on the sleeping girl. 'And I must admit, I wanted to make sure you came back safe to us before I turned in. How was York, love? Did you get the material for your coat?'

Molly grimaced. She'd forgotten about that.

'Well, no,' she said. 'But there's a good reason.'

Daphne awoke at that moment, the sound of their voices breaking through her dreams. She beamed when she saw her sister, and immediately snatched up one of the crutches so she could push herself to her feet. She limped over to Molly for a hug.

Molly smiled as she bent to kiss the golden hair. 'I'd almost think you'd missed me, babby.'

'Maybe a little,' Daphne said. 'But don't be smug about it, or I swear I won't miss you a bit next time you go away.'

Again, Molly felt that pang of impending separation. She would have to break the news now. The official ENSA letter might arrive any day, notifying her that she was to join her unit. But for a moment she just held her sister tight, blinking back a tear.

'You should be in bed,' she said quietly. 'It's school in the morning.'

'I can't sleep if you're not next to me. It feels funny. Anyhow, I was worried you might have been murdered on the way home.'

Mam laughed. 'She's been to York, love, not Chicago. We need to stop you spending so much time at the pictures.'

'Actually…' Molly began, then stopped. She didn't want to disturb her sister's sleep with news that might upset her. 'Daph, why don't you visit the outhouse first, then you can go get your nightie on? I want a word with Mam before we all go to bed.'

Daphne looked at her suspiciously. 'What for? It's not about me, is it?'

'No it's not about you. Not everything's about you, incredibly. It's about me, and not for little girls' ears.'

Daphne drew herself up. 'I'm not—'

'Yes, I know, you're exceptionally grown-up,' Molly said with a smile. 'I promise it's nowt exciting, all right? Just boring stuff about the material for my new coat. Go get ready for bed and I'll be there in half a minute to help you unbuckle your calipers.'

'Hmm. Well, all right. But it's no use trying to keep secrets from me. I always find them out in the end.' With a last suspicious glance, Daphne swung herself out of the room.

'Well, love, what is it?' Mam said to Molly when they were alone, putting her knitting to one side and dislodging Geoffrey, who stalked off. 'Nowt happened untoward on your trip, did it? I thought I could trust your friend to look after you, and it didn't seem so far to travel by yoursen.'

'Nothing like that.' Molly smiled at her. 'I brought summat back for us, that's all.'

Mam shook her head. 'Now you didn't ought to be spending your little bit of money on presents.'

'I didn't. Not exactly.' Molly reached into her handbag and took out the banker's draft, which she presented to her mother. 'Here.'

Mam almost dropped it when she saw the amount written there. 'Thirty pound!'

'That's right, for Daph's new calipers. Didn't I tell you I'd get it for us?'

Mam stared at the piece of paper in her hand, as if she couldn't believe she was holding it. 'But where on earth… thirty pound, mercy me! Is this all from Mr Taylor?'

'Mr Taylor had nowt to do with it. It's not a loan, Mam, it's mine. I earned it – that is to say, I will earn it. It's an advance on my wages.'

'I don't understand, love.'

Molly took a deep breath. 'This might come as a shock, but I've summat to tell you. About the mill and me and… and where I've been the last two days.'

—

Mam looked rather dazed when Molly had finished her tale. Her brow soon clouded as the facts sank in, however.

'That Shackleton,' she muttered darkly. 'That old… that old devil! He ought to be locked up. He ought to be hanged, preying on young girls. I've a good mind to… to… I don't know what I've a good mind to do, but I'll think of summat. If your dad were here, he'd haul him out into the street.'

'I know,' Molly said. 'I can't believe Mr Taylor's going to let him off scot-free.'

'I don't suppose the police would do owt if you reported it. Not when it's his word against yours.'

Molly sighed. 'No.'

Mam's gaze drifted back to the banker's draft. 'But… did you really go all the way to London on your own?'

'Aye.'

'Oh, that gives me the shivers, that does,' Mam said, hunching. 'Here, come sit by your mother where I can feel you safe and sound.'

Molly sat on the rug and rested her head on her mother's knee, just as Daphne had been doing. She sighed while Mam stroked her hair, feeling as if the dirt and stress of her long journey were being brushed away by that familiar, comforting touch.

'I'm sorry,' Molly whispered. 'I know it was wrong to lie. I just felt I couldn't come clean until I'd fixed the mess I'd landed us in. I knew how worried you'd be, especially after what the doctor said.'

'You didn't land us in owt. It was him. Shackleton.' Mam scowled at the thought of him. 'I wish you'd told me where you were going though, love. You're young to go all that way on your own, and to stay in a boarding house too! I'd have come with you if I'd known, and asked Peggy Woolf to put Daphne up with her Tilly.'

'I'm not that young, Mam. At least, I don't feel young.'

'Young folk never do.' Mam looked at the banker's draft again. 'I'm not sure I like this, our Molly. Not that I aren't grateful for the money, but to have you go so far away, and live among theatre folk. People say all sorts goes on in the theatre. Don't sound like a life for a lass what's been brought up proper.'

'What else can I do? Go back to the mill and wait for the next time Shack finds a reason to get me alone?'

'Mmm. "Out of the frying pan and into the fire" is a phrase that springs to mind.'

'I'll be all right. I doubt the theatre world can be more dangerous than Taylor's.'

'Perhaps.' But Mam sounded doubtful still.

'It's ten pound a week,' Molly said, a note of pleading in her voice. She felt like she needed her mother to be pleased for her, even if Mam couldn't be happy about losing her. 'You can give up charring, and Daph don't need to worry about finding work the minute she finishes school. She can do some secretarial training and wait for her legs to get stronger. And you know singing for my living is what I always dreamed of.'

Mam sighed. 'I'd hoped you might find summat closer to home, that's all. London's a long way off.'

'I won't always be in London. We'll be touring a lot of the time, and I'm sure I'll be able to come home regular. Then once the war's over, I'll have enough experience to get work locally. I know I can earn enough to keep us all, once I've got a foot in the door.'

Mam smiled a little wistfully. 'Happen your future might not look quite the way you think. There'll be a lad come for you before too long, young Molly. Make sure you pick one who's worth tying a future to.'

'I'm in no hurry to pick any of them.' Molly looked up, and felt a jolt of guilt when she noticed her mother's eyes had filled with tears. 'I'm sorry, Mam,' she said softly. 'I'll miss you and Daph to pieces, honestly, and Rita too. It's just... I have to do more with my life than stay in Bradford, or I'll spend whatever years I've got left wondering what might have been.'

'You're right. It's what I always wanted for thee – a life out of the mills.' Mam sighed again. 'But I wish you bairns didn't have to fly the nest quite so close together. First Teddy, now you. Even my baby's a young lady now, as she's anxious to keep reminding the pair of us.' She took Molly's hand to give it a press. 'I'll never hold you back, pet, you know that. But just remember that whatever happens, you'll always have a home with your mam.'

—

Molly was rather emotional after the scene with her mother. She took her time visiting the privy in the yard, feeling the need for a little cry. When she eventually went into the bedroom she shared with her sister, she found that Daphne had unbuckled herself from her calipers and put herself to bed, where she was reading a mystery story.

'Ugh, sorry,' Molly said. 'I hadn't meant to be such a long time. I ought to have been here to help you with your calipers.'

'That's all right,' Daphne said. 'I need to get used to doing it myself for when you're gone.'

Molly looked up from rummaging in her suitcase for her crumpled nightdress. 'Where am I going then?'

Daphne put down her book. 'When you go off to live in London, I mean.'

'Have you been eavesdropping?'

'Not on purpose. I was in the kitchen giving Geoffrey his milk. You're quite loud, you know.'

Molly sighed and went to sit on the bed by her sister. She put an arm around her and Daphne snuggled into it.

'I'm sorry,' she said quietly. 'I was going to tell you tomorrow. I just didn't want to upset you before bed. Are you cross?'

'A bit.' Daphne looked up at her. 'But you should do it. You should go off and sing for all the soldiers, and be on the wireless and get famous and marry a film star. I would.'

Molly smiled as she thought of Daphne's singing. 'You would, would you?'

'I'll miss you a bit though. When you're gone.'

Molly looked down at her sister. She was smiling in her usual careless fashion, but her eyes looked damp.

'Talking soft, babby?' she said quietly. 'I thought you didn't approve of it.'

Daphne shrugged. 'It's allowed for tonight.'

'I'll miss you too,' Molly said, kissing the top of her hair. 'I wish I didn't have to go. I mean I want to, but... I don't at the same time. Everything I've ever known is here. All the people I care about.'

'You shouldn't feel guilty about it.'

'How did you know I felt guilty?'

'You always do about summat.'

Molly whispered a sigh as she looked around the familiar little room: the threadbare brown carpet, the faded wallpaper almost every inch of which Daphne had covered with pictures of aeroplanes and movie stars. On the chest of drawers sat Molly's old doll Jessie, as she had for years past.

Where would she be sleeping this time next month, Molly wondered? The thought of her shadowy new billet and the strangers she would be sharing it with produced a feeling not unlike the familiar stage fright.

'Anyhow, you're daft to feel guilty,' Daphne said with a yawn. 'If I could sing like you, I'd run away and make my fortune so I could live somewhere good.'

Molly smiled. 'Like where?'

'Blackpool,' came the prompt answer, as Molly had known it would. Apart from Hollywood, Daphne felt there was no more wondrous place in the world than Blackpool. 'And once you're rich, me, Mam and Ted will come to live with you in your big house and we can eat candy floss and go to the pictures all day.'

'All right, we'll do that. Sleep now, Daph. It won't be many hours until it's time to get up for school.'

Daphne burrowed under the covers. 'I hope I can still sleep when you're gone.'

'I hope so too. I'll leave Jessie for you to cuddle, OK?'

Daphne pulled a face. 'I can't sleep with a *doll*. Tilly Woolf will laugh at me summat awful.'

'I'll tell you a secret.' Molly bent closer to whisper as she tucked the covers around her sister. 'Tilly Woolf never needs to know.'

'What did you see in London?' Daphne asked sleepily. 'Did you see where the princesses live?'

'I did, and Nelson's Column and Big Ben. And I saw the theatres where the stars play, and a shop that had been destroyed when a Dornier Do 17 crashed into it. The plane had been taken away but I saw some pieces of the fuselage.'

'Crikey!' Daphne's eyes sparkled. 'Wish I'd seen it. Did you see any Jerries?'

'No. They'd all been taken prisoner except the pilot, who was killed.'

'What else did you see?'

'Well, I made friends with a nice Italian boy,' Molly told her with a smile.

'Ooh!' Daphne shuffled up, even more interested in the Italian boy than she had been in the air crash. 'Is he handsome? Did he make love to you in Italian? Can he play the violin?'

Molly laughed. 'He is handsome, but I don't think he plays the violin and the only Italian he spoke to me was about food. His family run a restaurant. When I'm settled, you and Mam can visit and I'll take you to try their delicious meals.'

'Tell me more about the Italian boy. What's his name? How old is he?'

'His name's Angelo and he must be about our Ted's age, I suppose.'

'Angelo,' Daphne said slowly, trying the name out. 'I'm glad he's called Angelo. That sounds like a handsome name.'

'I promise I'll tell you all about him tomorrow after school, but you need to rest now, Daph. It's very late.'

'All right.' Daphne gave another yawn. 'I'm proud of you though, for getting into ENSA. I'm proud of Ted too, for going to fight in the war. Only don't tell him I said so.'

'Well, we're proud of you. Our clever little sister.'

'Will you sing me to sleep?'

Molly smiled. 'You've not asked me that in a long while. I thought you'd got too big for it.'

'Aye, I have, but you'll be gone soon so I want you to do all the things you always did. Sing the one you said was Dad's favourite.'

Molly stroked her sister's hair as she sang the lullaby her father had sung to her when she was a tiny bairn: 'Sleep, Baby, Sleep'. Daphne was fast off in moments but Molly kept on singing long after her sister was in the land of dreams, stroking the silky golden hair that soon became damp. Yet despite the tears that fell, Molly felt her voice had never sounded so soft and sweet.

# Chapter 17

Molly's official letter from ENSA arrived just five days later. She had felt like she was on the edge of her nerves waiting for it to arrive – as if, even with her contract and the banker's draft, it couldn't really be real until she was summoned to her unit.

She had no idea what to expect. The troupe manager, Philip Brooks, had said a lot about how things worked while she was signing bits of paper, but Molly had been so dazed to be offered a job that it hadn't really sunk in. She vaguely remembered there had been something about a house in London where the other girls were billeted, and something else about arrangements for touring, but it was all a mush in her brain now. Molly wondered if they might be sent on tour right away – perhaps even overseas, to entertain the boys in France.

The prospect of that was doubly terrifying. Not because she would be going near the fighting, since there was precious little of that going on. To be honest, she had barely given a thought to the war. But the idea of being shipped to a foreign country when she had never left these shores in her life, with people she hardly knew and an act she'd barely rehearsed… she would rather face the German guns.

With no job to occupy her and a dozen frightening thoughts buzzing around her brain, Molly attempted to distract herself with housework. She insisted that her mother sit and rest, and let her take care of the chores while she was at home to do so. Which was why she was about as lacking in star quality as she could be, in a pinny and headscarf with dust from the kitchen grate all over her, when the letter that marked the beginning of her professional singing career arrived. Molly bore it to the living room with all the pomp and circumstance it deserved.

'Is that it?' Mam asked, looking up from the socks she was knitting for Ted.

'Must be. It's got the NAAFI crest on it.' The Navy, Army and Air Force Institute, which provided canteens and shops for the armed forces, operated in partnership with ENSA, so Molly knew this must be an official communication.

'Open it then.'

Molly grimaced. 'I… no, not yet. Later on.' She went to put it in her dad's bureau.

'Why, for goodness' sake?'

'Because it'll be real once I open it. It'll mean I'm really going.'

'You want to go, don't you?'

'Yes, but… I don't know. Just let me finish my jobs. When Daph's home from school, we can all read it together.'

Mam shook her head. 'You're daft, you are. You must get it off your dad. Owt else come?'

'Aye, a letter from Ted.' Molly took the envelope bearing her brother's name, rank and service number from the pocket of her dusty pinny. 'It's addressed to us all. Shall I read it out?'

'Do, and save me finding my glasses.'

Molly opened the letter and read it aloud. '"Evening all, or morning all, or whatever time of day it is when you open this. Mam said my last letter took six weeks to get home. Let's see if this one can beat it."' She looked at the envelope for a date. 'Well, it did, but not by much. Looks like he wrote it at the start of March.'

'What's he been up to? Mischief, no doubt.'

'"Nowt much happening still, but we keep ourselves entertained,"' Molly read on. '"Hewitson got himself into a spot the other day when we were marched off to yet another ENSA show. There was a bevy of girl dancers and he made a bet with us that he could click with the best-looking one in the NAAFI afterwards. They usually stop in to say hello, but the ENSA men take good care of their girls and make sure we humble Tommies never get a look-in. Anyhow, Hewitson struck lucky this time. The ENSA blokes were all tiddly so they weren't on guard like usual – I think they must've been passing round a flask to keep out the cold. Well, Hewy seized his chance and was on the bonny girl dancer like a wolf on a sheep. He's a tremendous show-off and piled on the charm for this lass while sending winks behind her back to his pals, but no luck. The girl wasn't interested. Then you'll never guess what – her boyfriend turned up! Turns out she's as good as engaged to our drill corporal. The corporal couldn't exactly put Hewy on a fizzer for chatting up his girl when the man had no idea, but he certainly had the evil eye on him. I reckon he'll find a reason to give Hewy latrines next week. Serve him right for showing off."'

'Isn't it funny how in his letters, our Teddy is always such a good boy while all his pals are getting into trouble?' Mam said with a smile. 'I'm sure there's a lot more goes on at his barracks than he tells us about.'

'Unless the army's reformed him, which seems pretty doubtful,' Molly said, laughing. 'There was barely a week went by at school that he wasn't in some scrape.' She looked at the letter again. 'I wonder if there's a chance I'll be sent to where Ted is. It'd be wonderful to see him.'

Mam shivered. 'Oh, don't talk of it. The thought of you so close to the enemy, and at the mercy of all them soldiers an' all. It makes me feel faint.'

'Ted says the ENSA men look after their girls.'

'Mmm, until they've had one over the eight. Besides, they might be worse than the soldiers for all we know. You be careful, our Molly.'

'I will.'

'Has Ted got owt else to say?'

'"Tell our Daph I got her some real French perfume off one of the local girls,"' Molly read. '"I'd have got you all some but she only had one bottle to sell, and I know Daph's the vainest. Don't worry, I'll make sure I come home with presents for everyone. Love to you all, and hugs and kisses to Mam. I don't suppose Daph and Moll care much for their brother's hugs and kisses, so they can be satisfied with perfume and a clip round the ear. All my best love, Teddy."'

Mam smiled. 'Well, he's a good boy for all his wild ways. Army life seems to suit him.'

'I hope he can come home soon,' Molly said fervently. 'I can't feel at ease with him over there being a soldier, even if this isn't much of a war.'

'Your dad used to talk about France and Belgium sometimes,' Mam said dreamily as she resumed her knitting. 'In the last war, I mean.'

Molly frowned as she put away Ted's letter. 'Did he? I never heard him.' She couldn't recall her father ever discussing the last war in her hearing.

'Before tha were born, lass.' Mam paused mid-row. 'He never did talk of it much though, even to me. None of those boys who came home did. But it haunted them, all the same.'

'I wish to God it were done with and everyone safe back at home.'

'Aye, so do I, love. So do I.'

—

Later on, Mam went out to fetch Daphne from school while Molly blackleaded the living room fireplace. Mam returned not only with Daphne, spry in her new lightweight calipers, but also Rita.

'Look who we ran into,' Mam said. 'I thought you wouldn't object to us asking her back for the grand ceremonial opening of your letter.'

Rita looked her friend up and down. 'Looks like you must've opened it already. They're sending you to a minstrel show, are they, Moll?'

'Very funny.' Molly took out her handkerchief and wiped the smears from her face. 'Do we have to open it now?'

Rita came forward to give her a squeeze. 'You'll have to open it sometime, love. Suppose it says you're to report for duty tomorrow? They might court-martial you if you don't turn up when you're meant to.'

'It's not the army, Reet. I don't think you can be thrown in the nick for desertion from ENSA.' Molly paused, frowning. 'Unless you can. I suppose it is national service, even if it's a civilian organisation.'

'Better not take the risk. Go on, open it.'

'I will.' Molly paused. 'In a minute, when I've put the kettle on.'

'Ugh, you're sooooo slow,' Daphne said, rolling her eyes. 'If you're going to take all this time about it, I'll open it.'

'Er, you will not. I don't see your name on it, Daphne Clough.'

'All right, do it then, before we all die of suspense.' She shook her head. 'See, this is exactly why I read the last page of mysteries first.'

Rita gave her a shocked look. 'You don't, do you?'

Daphne shrugged. 'I don't know why everyone's always so surprised about it.'

'Appalling, isn't it?' Molly said to Rita. 'I'm toying with the idea of disowning her.' She went to fetch her letter from the bureau. 'Right, I'm opening it. Are you all happy?'

'Ecstatic,' Rita said. 'Well, where are you going?'

Molly opened the envelope with her eyes closed, dreading what might be written there.

Supposing it didn't include information about where she was to go? Supposing the panel had been swayed by Madame Chastain after she had left, and were writing to withdraw the job offer and demand repayment of her advance – an advance she had already spent?

'For pity's sake, child, open your eyes and read it,' Mam said impatiently.

'Yes. All right.'

Molly opened her eyes slowly and skimmed the letter, then let out a sigh of relief.

'It's all right,' she said. 'It's not France. It's London.'

'That's not as good as Paris,' Daphne said. 'I thought you'd want to go to France more than anywhere. Wouldn't it be wizard if you got to sing for Ted and all his mates?'

'I would like to go overseas, but not until I've had a chance to rehearse and get to know the others in my unit.' Molly looked again at the letter. 'I'm to be given a room in one of ENSA's grace-and-favour houses with the other Follies girls, and rehearse for a new revue before we go on tour on the 7th of May.' She looked up at the others. 'That's less than a month away. Will it be enough time to work out what I'm doing, do you think?'

Rita put an arm around her. 'You'll be fine, love. Just trust your gut.'

'If I trust my gut, I'll throw up on someone.'

'All right, then don't trust your gut. Trust your friend Rita when she tells you that you're brimming with talent, beauty and charm and you can completely, definitely do this.' Rita nodded to the silent wireless set. 'And one day, when you're on that thing singing for the world, I'll say "I used to know her when she was nobody."'

Daphne, her attention drawn to the wireless, went to turn it on.

'Thanks, Reet,' Molly said with a smile. She looked at the letter again, then drew another piece of paper from the envelope. 'Here's a travel voucher to get me to London. They want me to join them within three days.'

'Mercy, so soon!' Mam said, clutching at her hair. 'That's no time to get you packed and ready.'

'Don't worry. I've not got much to bring.'

'No doubt you've not thought of half what you'll need. Now, let me go see what's in the old trunk.' Mam bustled out in search of linen and towels.

Daphne seemed distracted while this chatter was going on, frowning at the wireless. Someone was talking, but Molly had filtered it out while she focused on her letter.

'You all right, babby?' she asked.

Daphne nodded to the wireless. 'What's that he's saying about an invasion?'

'Invasion!'

Molly darted to the set and turned the volume knob. A BBC announcer was speaking.

> …pledged every possible assistance. To repeat: it is confirmed that German troops have invaded Norway and Denmark. Bergen, Trondheim and Narvik in Norway are occupied, and the whole of Denmark is now in German hands. Oslo is also said to have been captured following heavy aerial bombardment. The Norwegian government have given orders for general mobilisation, and Norway and Germany are confirmed to be at war. Britain and France have pledged every possible assistance.

'The buggers have invaded Norway,' she muttered.

Rita slipped her hand into Molly's. 'Denmark too. And it sounds like they've already surrendered.'

'What does it mean?' Daphne asked, looking worried at the sudden solemnness of the older girls. 'It's not near where Ted is, is it?'

'No.' Molly summoned a smile. 'No, Ted's a long way from there. It's just Hitler flexing his tiny muscles, that's all.'

'Will it be all right?'

'I… don't know. But Ted's safe.'

But the unspoken words *for now* hung heavily in the air.

–

'Now are you sure you've packed everything you need?' Mam asked two days later, as she, Rita and Daphne waited with Molly at Forster Square station.

'I think I've packed enough for two Mollies,' she said with a laugh, gesturing to the two large cases she was taking down south.

Mam had insisted she take her own bedding and towels, despite the ENSA letter saying everything of that nature would be provided, 'in case they weren't clean', plus crockery, cutlery and a selection of improving books. She seemed convinced that 'theatre folk' – pronounced in a tone dripping with suspicion – would immediately try to drag her innocent daughter into their louche, debauched lifestyles and felt that a small Bible and two volumes of *Pamela* might help keep Molly on the straight and narrow.

Seven pounds remained from Molly's advance after paying for Daphne's calipers and settling her debts, five of which Mam had tried to press on her, but Molly had refused to take more than three. She was sure that even in the expensive capital, three pounds ought to be enough to keep herself until she was paid again in three weeks' time. After all, she was used to surviving on little, and Mam and Daphne would need the money more than she did.

Daphne was crying helplessly, her usual careless attitude nowhere to be seen.

'Don't, Daph, please,' Molly whispered. 'You'll only set me off, and before you know it we'll all four of us be wailing our heads off.'

'I… can't… help… it,' Daphne sobbed. 'Everything's going to be… different now.'

Molly stepped forward to hug her.

'I'll visit,' she promised. 'I'll write all the time too. And Rita's promised to take you to the pictures every Saturday on my behalf so you can blow kisses to Errol Flynn.'

Rita, struggling with emotion of her own, summoned a wobbly smile. 'That's right, with tea and scones in the cafe afterwards. I know it won't be the same, Daph, but I promise we'll have fun.'

Daphne didn't seem to hear this as she held on to her sister with an iron grip.

'I wish I could go with you,' she whispered.

'I wish you could too, babby,' Molly said. 'I'll write two letters a week and tell you all the gossip about the people I meet and where we go, so it'll be almost like you're there. And if I do go to France and see our Ted, I can bring back the perfume he bought you.'

Even this couldn't console Daphne, however, who continued to sob pitifully. She was prised gently off Molly by her mother.

'Let others say their goodbyes, love,' she said softly. 'Your sister's train will be here soon.'

Rita stepped forward to hug her friend. She was crying too now, and so was Molly.

'I'll miss you,' she whispered. 'Don't forget your old friends when you start making new ones, eh?'

'Never,' Molly said fervently. 'You were the first friend I ever made. Nobody could take your place.' She managed a smile. 'And don't you forget me when you're so lovey-dovey with Harry that you can't think of owt else. I want a letter a week at least, Reet, so I can admire that beautiful handwriting.'

'And correct the spelling as you did when we were at school,' Rita said with a laugh. 'Good luck, my love. We'll all be here waiting for you when you come home.'

Molly could hear her train in the distance.

Her mother stepped forward last of all. 'Another baby bird flying out into the world,' she whispered as they embraced. 'I don't think I'll ever get used to it.'

'Flying away, but not for good,' Molly said as she squeezed her tight. 'We'll all be together again soon – Ted too. I'm certain of it.'

'I hope you're right, love. I feel like I'm missing a part of myself when you bairns are off somewhere I can't keep you safe.' Mam let her go as the train pulled in. 'But you have to grow up and find lives of your own, just as me and your dad did. It's selfish of me to want to keep you forever. Just remember when you're away how proud we are of you, all right?'

'I will, Mam. I love you.'

'I love you too, sweetheart.' Mam gave her a push towards the train. 'Now go on, off you go to conquer the world.'

Her loved ones swam in a sea of salt tears as Molly waved from the train. She kept her eyes fixed on them until they were mere dots, but soon they, like the chimneys and soot of her home town, had faded far into the distance as Molly sped towards London and a new life.

# Chapter 18

Molly's journey south was dogged by delays. She tried to sleep when they were shunted repeatedly into sidings, but sleep refused to come. The faces of the people she had left behind, wet with tears, preyed on her mind, and the delays worried her too. The guard refused to tell the passengers the reason for them, citing 'careless talk', but Molly wondered if it was due to the movement of troops. Could it be to do with the invasion of Norway and Denmark, which had seemed to mark a turning point in this so-called Phoney War?

Her fellow passengers spoke of the news in hushed whispers right along the carriage. They talked of what it would mean for the war, whether Norway had invited her own fate by remaining too neutral, and whether Mussolini would now join his ally Hitler in the fight. Molly tried to block it out so she could sleep, but she couldn't.

It made her think of Ted, and the enemy creeping closer as it sought to conquer and subdue still more of Europe. One week ago, all Molly had wanted was for the war to carry on long enough to give her a chance as an entertainer. Now, she was wracked with guilt for harbouring such a thought. If Norway had fallen, who might be next? Belgium? France? Even Britain itself? Surely such a thing could never happen.

And yet he wouldn't stop, would he? Hitler. He was so much stronger than Molly could have imagined, before this all started when he had seemed more like the creation of a music-hall comic than a real threat. Not so now. She shuddered to think of German tanks in Bradford, and a swastika flying over their old town hall. It felt impossible, but no doubt the Norwegian and Danish people had felt it to be impossible until the day it became reality.

The worst thing was in being forced to watch these things unfold while powerless to do anything about it. It made one feel so utterly helpless.

-

It was late when Molly arrived at King's Cross. Once again she chose to part with some of her precious funds rather than try to navigate buses, tramways or the underground system in the blackout. Perhaps one day the streets of London would be as familiar to her as those of Bradford, but for now, the idea of traversing them in total darkness filled her with fear.

Molly's billet was in Covent Garden, close to the theatre district: an exciting prospect for a girl who all her life had dreamed of the West End. The Forces Follies manager, Philip, had given her to understand that it was a private home whose occupants had evacuated to the countryside in anticipation of air raids, and had leased their empty house to ENSA for the duration. Perhaps they later regretted this, since no air raids had materialised, but it was too late to back out now. It wasn't long before Molly's cab drew up outside the address: Number 12, The Larches.

She wasn't sure what she had been expecting. Something grander than her own terrace home, certainly, but still comparatively humble. She was surprised, therefore, when the dimmed lights of her cab fell on an impressive Georgian townhouse – surprised and a little intimidated. Molly could imagine Daphne going into raptures about the idea of occupying such a princely abode, but all Molly could think was how nervous she would feel about leaving smudges on the furniture.

The cab sped away into the darkness, leaving her alone. Molly approached the front door and took a deep breath.

Inside this building was the first part of her new life. A new home, albeit only for the four weeks before the Forces Follies were sent on tour, and one that was about as far as she could

139

imagine from her home in Bradford. But even more frightening was the thought of the people she would be sharing her new life with.

Behind this door were strangers – strangers Molly would come to know well in the months to follow, for good or for bad. Would they like her? Would they be friends, rivals – even enemies? Would they look down on her for her class and accent, as Madame Chastain had done, or would they be girls much like her?

She knocked tentatively on the door. A moment later, a woman of about Molly's own age appeared.

The girl's face was more interesting than pretty, Molly thought, with a rather long, freckled nose and a pair of large, twinkling dark eyes set close together. Untidy chestnut hair was piled anyhow on top of her head and she wore an expression of vague good nature. She was dressed in a faded, slightly grubby pink silk camisole that slumped over one shoulder, a pair of French knickers and nothing else. A cigarette in a long holder bobbed lazily in the corner of her wide mouth. In fact, she was the picture of the sort of disreputable theatrical that Mam had dreaded her daughter falling in with, which rendered her instantly fascinating to Molly.

The girl took her cigarette holder out and beamed at her visitor. Molly had barely opened her mouth to introduce herself when the girl grabbed her hand and yanked her inside.

'My darling child, thank Jehovah you've come,' she said heartily in a well-bred accent with a hint of Scottish, throwing her arms around Molly before instantly releasing her. 'And just in the nick of time too. We're having a hell of a to-do in the kitchen. What do you know about cats?'

Molly blinked. 'Cats?'

'Yes, little ones. Well, big ones and little ones. Poor Millicent is yowling her tiny ginger head off, and I must say I feel about ready to join her. She's got one out, but she just stares at the poor thing like she's no idea what to do with it.' She glanced at Molly's suitcases. 'Oh, dump your things any old where and we can arrange rooms when we've seen to Millicent.'

Dazed, Molly left her cases in the hall and followed the woman in the silk camisole. She seemed to have been expecting her, although why she should assume the new member of the Forces Follies was an expert on cats, Molly had no idea.

'Um, I take it you knew I might be arriving today?' she asked.

'No idea, my pet. We get used to people coming and going. What do they call you?'

Molly hesitated, wondering whether to persist with the stage name she had invented that day on the telephone. She still felt her real name was hardly the stuff stars were made of, but she couldn't get used to being Dorothy Kensitas. As several people had now observed, it really didn't suit her.

'Molly Clough,' she said, deciding she was done with fibs. 'I sing and play piano,' she added, her name sounding rather inadequate on its own.

'Fenella Prince, darling.'

'Oh! That's such a good name.'

Molly wasn't sure how that comment had slipped out. It had just struck her how much better Fenella Prince sounded than Dorothy Kensitas, and especially than Molly Clough. She flushed, realising it had been an odd thing to say, but Fenella grinned good-humouredly.

'Kind of you to say so,' she said. 'I've never liked it much myself, but Mother was a Walter Scott fanatic so here we are. Anyhow, we can do introductions and all that rot when we've seen to Millicent. In here, quick.'

She grasped Molly's hand and pulled her to a door. There was a yowling as of an animal in pain coming from behind it, and a hum of excited chatter. Fenella yanked Molly through into a kitchen, where two women were kneeling beside a swollen-bellied and distressed-looking ginger cat who was standing stiffly to attention in a blanket-lined vegetable crate.

'I brought reinforcements, ladies,' Fenella told the other two. Molly recognised Tabitha — now in a dressing gown rather than the ENSA uniform she had been sporting previously — but the diminutive fair-haired woman beside her was a stranger. She had a pretty, mild face, and smiled shyly at Molly.

'Hello,' she said. 'Are you a new girl? I hope you know about cats.'

'Oh Lord, I'd forgotten you were coming this week,' Tabitha said, looking flustered. 'Girls, this is… Dorothy, was it?'

'No, it's Molly Clough again,' Molly said with a smile. 'I thought I'd leave Dorothy behind. She never really felt like me.'

'Well, Molly, you've met me and Fenella, and this adorable little person is Pam.' She indicated the shy girl. 'Di you already know, but she's hiding in our room in case she faints at the sight of blood.' Tabitha nodded to the wailing cat. 'And this is Millicent, the poor love. I'm sorry you had to arrive in the middle of a delivery. We've got a lot of skills between us, but unfortunately they don't include midwifery.'

The cries of the distressed cat broke through Molly's daze at her strange welcome, and she knelt beside the blonde girl with the sweet face, Pam. Fenella knelt beside her, yanking up the strap of her camisole.

'We don't know what to do for her,' Fenella said. 'She belongs to the house owners. They keep her as a mouser. We could see she'd put on weight when we came back from our last tour, but we didn't realise it was kittens until she started making all this noise.'

'She's had one little one already,' Pam said in her soft voice, indicating a black sausage of fur wriggling next to its mother. 'She bit off the bag he was in, but she doesn't seem much interested in him now. No more have come out since then. She just cries, the darling – don't you, my poor pussy willow?' She cooed over the cat, tenderly stroking her silky fur, then turned back to Molly. 'Do you know how it ought to work?'

'Only a very little,' Molly said. 'Our cat Queenie had kittens when I was a girl. But it was a long time ago.'

'Well, that's more experience than any of us have got,' Tabitha said. 'I never owned a pet in my life until we found ourselves joint foster mothers to Millicent. Does she need a vet, do you think?'

Molly rested a hand on the cat's stomach, pressing lightly to see if she could tell how many kittens were inside her. She could feel at least three separate wriggling forms.

She tried to remember the day Queenie, their old cat, had given birth. Molly must have been eleven or twelve the day it happened, during the long school holidays.

That was where Geoffrey had come from: one of five born to Queenie that sunny summer afternoon. If it had been up to their mam, who had always been an animal lover, they'd have had a houseful of cats from that day on, but their dad put his foot down and said they could keep one kitten only. And so it was Geoffrey, the runt of the litter, who stayed with the family while the rest were rehomed with friends and neighbours.

'How long since the first was born?' Molly asked.

'I suppose quarter of an hour,' Pam said.

'I think that's probably a normal gap between births. With Queenie, it was about half an hour between the first and second and even longer between the second and third, then the last two seemed to come out in no time at all. They were all healthy though.'

Fenella whistled. 'Well that's a relief. We had the idea that once one had been born, the rest ought to sort of plop out right after. We were worried they were stuck.'

'What's more worrying is that she's not mothering the first-born,' Molly said, frowning at the neglected kitten. 'Queenie started washing and suckling hers right away.'

The sausage-kitten certainly looked distressed at his neglect, his mouth opened wide in a noiseless wail of complaint. His mother only stared at him curiously, however, as if unsure what he was.

'I know just how you feel, Mill,' Fenella said. 'I'm sure if I had a baby, all I'd be able to do is stare at it helplessly and cry.'

'What can we do to get her to like him?' Pam asked. 'I thought mothers liked their babies automatically.'

'We need to get her instincts going,' Molly said, although she had no idea where this knowledge of cat midwifery was coming from. 'Perhaps… if two of you hold her on her side, gently so as not to hurt her, and I guide the baby to her so he can feed, she might realise what it's all about.'

'It's worth a try,' Tabitha said. 'Ella, help me hold her so Molly can scoop up the little one.'

She and Fenella manoeuvred Millicent on to her side to expose her sagging, milk-heavy stomach and held her there. The cat temporarily forgot her pain in indignation, flashing them resentful looks at this treatment. Gently Molly nudged the tiny kitten to his mother, his mouth gaping, and he fixed on to a teat. Millicent watched him with surprise for a moment, then bent her head to start licking him.

Molly smiled. 'There we go. You can let go of her now, I think.'

Slowly Fenella and Tabitha withdrew their hands, watching to see if Millicent would spring up, but she stayed lying on her side. A fond maternal pride seemed to have appeared on her little feline face as she licked the baby roughly all over, and her wails quieted for a moment in the joy of motherhood.

'Oh!' said Pam, who was at the back end. 'Here's another little one coming. A ginger one this time.'

Millicent, her maternal instincts now awakened, seemed to know what she needed to do. When her second kitten emerged, she immediately released him from his sack of fluid and began washing him as he attached himself to a teat next to his brother – or sister, Molly supposed, although they would have no way of knowing that until later. The cat seemed quite content now, and although she still meowed in a distressed manner when a birthing pain tore through her, she was purring.

It was a strange welcome to her new life, Molly reflected as she watched the mother and babies. She had been so nervous on the train down, thinking about meeting her new billet-mates, living away from home for the first time and what might be waiting for her in London. Delivering kittens as soon as she arrived had been the last thing she expected. And yet she was glad of it, in a way. She would rather tackle something like this alongside these people who were going to be such a big part of her life than sit making awkward, stilted small talk as they attempted to get to know one another the long way round.

She smiled at the two suckling kittens, and their proud mother looking down at them. There was comfort in knowing she wasn't the only new arrival in the house that night. It made her feel less alone.

*Chapter 19*

Everything went smoothly after that. Soon, Millicent had three babies nestled against her flank.

'It's enough to make you broody, isn't it?' Pam said in her soft, mellow voice. Molly wondered what she did with the troupe. She had a voice just made for lullabies.

'Oh Lord, don't say that.' Fenella turned to Molly. 'That's how we lost the girl before you – Maud. She left when she found out she was… expecting a happy event, shall we say. It was quite a scandal when her parents found out. Stuffy church types. Still, Maud seemed pleased about it. Rather her than me, I must say.'

'You mean she wasn't, um…' Molly trailed off, not sure how to phrase the enquiry politely, but Pam nodded.

'The father was some officer she let get her tight after a show,' she told Molly. 'Phil and Little Davy have been extra careful since then, keeping us close whenever we visit a NAAFI or go out to a club. They think it'll give ENSA a bad name if it leaks out that its girls are running wild with amorous soldiers.'

'It's a real pain having a chaperone when there's someone you'd like to get to know better,' Fenella said, pulling a face. 'It's like going out on the town with my dad.'

'Here's another little one coming, I think,' Tabitha said as Millicent gave another yowl. 'Poor thing, it sounds so painful. Definitely a cure for broodiness rather than a cause of it.'

Millicent no longer seemed to need the help of her midwives, and they watched as she dealt with the fourth kitten in her litter: ginger and white like his mother. Soon he was lying with his siblings, being washed by a rough motherly tongue.

146

'I think that's all of them,' Molly said. 'She'll be out of pain now, I hope.'

Pam turned pleading eyes on Tabitha. 'Oh, do let me have them in my room, Tabby. I can keep an eye on them overnight, and make sure they've got everything they need.'

'Are you sure?' Tabitha said. 'They seem noisy little blighters. We've got a full day of rehearsal tomorrow.'

'They won't make me too tired, I promise. Someone ought to watch over them, at least for tonight.'

'Well, all right. I wouldn't take them yet though, Pam. Let Millicent settle into mothering whilst we warm up with a cup of cocoa, then we can see if she'll tolerate us moving them.'

Pam beamed. 'Thank you. I'll put some milk on, shall I?'

'I'll love you forever if you do, darling,' Fenella said with a shiver. 'I'm freezing to death, sitting here delivering kittens in my scanties.'

Tabitha laughed. 'I'm not surprised. Go put a dressing gown on, Ella, for goodness' sake. Poor Molly must feel like running straight back home, being greeted by you with your bosoms half out of your cami and forced to deliver kittens the minute she arrives.'

'It's been memorable, certainly,' Molly said with a smile.

'I'll bank up the fire and we can get cosy while Molly tells us about herself,' Tabitha said in her forthright way. 'We ought to arrange rooms as well.'

'Molly's sharing with me,' Fenella announced. 'If Pam's looking after the kittens and you're managing Di's artistic temperament, I can take care of the new girl.'

Tabitha looked at Molly. 'Is that all right with you?'

'Um, yes,' Molly said. 'Whatever you think is best.'

'That's sorted out then,' Fenella said. 'Molly, you stay here and get warm. I'll put your cases in our room.'

'Thank you.'

'On your way, put your head into mine and Di's bedroom and tell her there's no more blood,' Tabitha called after Fenella as she went to the kitchen door. 'She ought to meet the new additions.'

'If I must.'

It seemed to Molly that Fenella pulled a face before going out.

It was interesting watching the interactions between the women, Molly thought as she observed them going about their tasks: Pam warming milk for their cocoa and Tabitha shovelling nutty slack on the fire. All were relatively young – certainly none looked older than twenty-five, and Pam quite a bit younger – but the other two seemed to look to Tabitha as a sort of house mother, seeking her permission for anything they wished to do. Molly could see why. Tabitha had an air of being able to cope in a crisis that must naturally appeal to someone like Fenella, who seemed to brim with a somewhat scatterbrained energy, and Pam, who had a childlike quality that begged to be mothered.

Molly tried to guess what the women did in the Forces Follies. Tabitha had said she played the accompaniment. But what about Pam, with her soft, soothing voice – was she, like Molly, a singer?

She couldn't begin to imagine what Fenella did. For some reason, Molly found herself picturing the woman on a trapeze.

'Come to the fire, Molly,' Tabitha said, in a firm tone that brooked no opposition. 'You must be half frozen after your journey.'

Molly did feel cold, although the distraction of Millicent and her kittens had given her little time to think about it until now. Gratefully she accepted the invitation, sinking into the chair that Tabitha pushed close to the flames. Pam put a steaming mug of cocoa into her hands, and Molly beamed at her. She was a tiny person: not even five feet in height.

'Thank you,' she said. 'You're all very kind.'

'Have you come a long way?' Pam asked. 'You sound like you're from near me.'

Molly had wondered where Pam might be from. She had a strange accent, seeming to mix bits and pieces of several counties and a small amount of Irish too, but there was definitely something of the north in there.

'I'm from Bradford,' she said. 'Are you Yorkshire as well?'

'Lancashire,' Pam said. 'It's nice to meet a neighbour. I'm sure we won't allow that old war to come between us down here among all these southern heathens, will we?'

Molly smiled. 'Definitely not.'

Fenella came back in, wearing a silk dressing gown that didn't look particularly warm, although it showed off her figure perfectly. She flopped into a chair.

'Diana's not coming,' she said. 'She's got a face full of cold cream and cucumber slices over her eyes. She says she's in no hurry to meet either new girls or kittens and it can wait until she's had her beauty sleep.'

Pam frowned. 'That's not very good manners.'

'Not to mention a waste of our cucumbers,' Tabitha said. 'Those were for sandwiches tomorrow.'

'I don't mind,' Molly said. 'I wasn't expecting any sort of welcome party.'

Actually she was rather grateful to be spared a second meeting with the woman who had sneered at her so harshly. So far she liked all her new acquaintances, and she felt that Diana's presence could only mar the cosy, friendly atmosphere of the kitchen.

Molly sipped her cocoa, feeling it warm her from top to toe. Some of her worry and homesickness started to evaporate as she sat by the crackling fire with these new friends, listening to the purring of Millicent and her babies.

'You've got ever so many questions, I suppose,' Fenella said, lazily lighting a cigarette. 'Ask us whatever you like. If we can answer, we will.'

Molly considered this. She felt like there were a hundred and one things she wanted to know, but now she had been put on the spot, she wasn't sure what to ask. Her eyes were drawn to the cat and kittens, content in their vegetable-crate bed.

'What will happen to them when we go on tour?' she asked.

Pam beamed. Molly didn't think Fenella had been testing her when she had invited her to ask them questions, but Pam was looking at her as if she'd passed all the same. It was clear the girl was an animal lover, and naturally she felt the welfare of these little ones ought to be everyone's top priority.

'The house is always occupied by some troupe or other,' she said. 'The owners ask that they take care of Millicent – feed her and so forth, so she can keep the mice in order – but they don't know about the kittens. I'm not sure we ought to tell them. They might send Millicent and the babies away if they think she can't do her job. She's not really a pet, although she's a sweet, loving little thing.'

'Will whoever moves in be willing to take care of four kittens until they're big enough to leave their mother?'

'They'll make sure Millicent's fed, at any rate. It's a condition of being billeted here. I was planning to ask Angelo to check on them sometimes too – that's a friend of ours.'

Molly sat up straighter. 'Angelo Cortesi?'

Fenella blinked. 'How can you know that? You just got here.'

'I met him when I came for my audition. He found me wandering lost around Soho and gave me a free meal.'

Pam's brow knitted momentarily into a worried frown. Molly wondered why this should be. However, the girl's face quickly smoothed into its customary expression of bashful sweetness.

'You'll fit in just like a jigsaw piece,' she said with a smile. 'We can take you to Cortesi's tomorrow and tell Angelo you're a Follies girl now. We always eat there when we can afford to. His grandmother's a wonderful cook.'

'What do you all do with the Follies?' Molly asked.

However, Tabitha looked at her wristwatch at this moment and her eyes widened.

'Mercy me, will you look at the time!' she yelped. 'It's nearly one, and we've to be at the theatre by nine.' She clapped her hands. 'Come on, ladies, to bed with you. There'll be plenty of time tomorrow to show off your acts to Molly. Breakfast at half past seven sharp.'

Tabitha shooed them to their bedrooms like a mother hen, with strict instructions that they were to go straight to sleep with no chattering so they would be well-rested for rehearsals the next day.

Molly couldn't help smiling. She felt as if she had landed in the middle of a boarding school story for girls. Already she had enough news to fill several pages of the letter she had promised to write to Daphne as soon as she had settled in. Her sister would be fascinated to hear the tale of how Molly had no sooner arrived than she had been called on to help deliver kittens, and the interesting people she had met.

–

Molly slept badly that night. She wished she hadn't started thinking about the letter she was going to write to Daphne. It only made her feel more keenly the absence of her sister at her side, and that she had never felt so far from home. The women she had met had been kind – or in the case of Madame Chastain, at least refreshingly absent – but that didn't stop her missing her mam and sister.

This felt like such a different world to the world of home. The future yawned like a great black emptiness, waiting to be filled with goodness knew what.

Since she was a girl of fourteen, Molly's life had been one of routine: filled with the mill, her family and the little, simple pleasures she had been afforded between long hours of toil. There would be no real routine in her new life. Every day would bring something fresh. A home today wouldn't be a home tomorrow, new people would pass through her life like trains through a station, and tours would take her to places she had only ever seen in pictures. It was exciting, but more than a little terrifying.

And so many men would now be part of her existence! Molly shivered when she thought about the service audiences she would be playing to, nearly all of them male, and all apparently more interested in catching a glimpse of an exposed thigh or daring décolletage than in how well she could sing. She would be expected to chat with these strangers after shows too, and flirt with them probably, which was even more frightening.

It reminded Molly of the girl she was replacing in the troupe, Maud, who had been unlucky enough to find herself in the family way after being charmed by some young officer. Molly liked to think she would never be so foolish, but if her experiences with Shack had taught her anything, it was that some men were adept at hearing a 'yes' when you gave a 'no', no matter how loudly you shouted it. If Mam knew about the fate of poor Maud, she would insist that Molly went home right away and to hell with the ten pound a week.

Molly's room for the next four weeks was a sizeable one: nearly three times as big as her room at home. There were two single beds, one occupied by her and the other by Fenella, who snored softly as she slept. Fenella had dropped off almost as soon as her eyes had closed. She seemed to be someone on whom the worries of the world rested lightly, a quality which couldn't help but make Molly envious.

Molly stretched an arm over the empty space where her sister would normally be, swallowing a sob. She envied Pam her boxful of kittens, even if their presence meant a night of disturbed sleep. It would be a comfort to have a warm, furry presence purring beside her bed.

Funny. Now that she was here, Molly had everything she'd ever aspired to in life. The chance to make it as an entertainer, to provide for her family, to escape the mills and see exciting places, meet interesting people, have adventures. And yet still the homesickness gnawed, the future loomed like some hollow and terrifying thing, and the tears soaked into her pillow.

# Chapter 20

Molly was awoken the next morning by the sound of a shrill whistle, letting out a mix of short and long notes to an unfamiliar rhythm. She sat up with a start.

Could it signal an air raid? Had the Luftwaffe finally started dropping something more lethal than paper?

She glanced around in panic, wondering where she was and why Daphne wasn't by her, before reality broke through the grogginess of sleep.

She was in London, wasn't she? And this... this was the house in Covent Garden where she was to live until the Forces Follies went on tour.

Despite passing an unsettled and tearful night, Molly felt her spirits rise when she remembered where she was. Fenella seemed to have disappeared, but before doing so she had opened the curtains and taken down the blackouts, letting the spring sunshine pour in. Today would show Molly what this new life had in store for her. She felt excitement bubbling, strong enough even to make her forget nerves and homesickness.

Fenella came in, dressed in an expensive-looking – if rather faded – salmon-coloured dress. She looked well-rested, although Molly felt like there were birds nesting inside her own head. Fenella had also found time to apply her make-up and style her hair.

'Rookie mistake, darling,' she said cheerfully. 'Always put an alarm clock under your pillow if you don't want to bathe in cold water. We all have to share the same six inches, so if you're last up, you're left with the soup.'

The whistle sounded again, tooting out its odd little tune.

'What is that?' Molly asked. 'Are we supposed to go to a shelter or something?'

Fenella rolled her eyes. 'Nothing so exciting. It's only Tabby doing "come to the cookhouse door". She's obsessed with making us a tip-top military unit of unparalleled efficiency, just in case ENSA is sent to the front lines to demoralise the enemy with bad jokes and off-key singing.'

'Come to the...'

'"Come to the cookhouse door." It's the bugle call they use on army camps to signal mealtimes.' Fenella shook her fist in the direction of the kitchen as the whistle sound became more urgent. 'I'll have the pea out of that bally thing, so help me God.'

Molly put her fingers in her ears. 'So it means we're to go to breakfast?'

'Yes, and Tabby won't stop blowing it until she's rounded up the lot of us so we'd better get a wiggle on. I swear I feel more like a ruddy sheepdog than a comedienne in this place.' Fenella threw Molly the grubby silk dressing gown she had been wearing the night before. 'You can borrow this, save you hunting through your case, and have your bath after. It'll be cold now anyhow, so you might as well take your time as not.'

Molly donned the dressing gown and allowed herself to be swept along in a tide of Fenella. Her new friend tucked an arm through Molly's as if they'd known one another for years, before leading her to the kitchen. There was certainly an appetising smell in the air, and since Molly had missed tea the night before, she felt ready to do justice to any food that might be offered.

Pam was at the cooker with a towel around her damp hair, frying bacon. Tabitha was standing beside her tooting the whistle, dressed in her ENSA uniform, while Madame Chastain – or Diana, as the other women called her – ate a plate of bacon and eggs in a series of dainty nibbles. Millicent was at her feet, purring hopefully while she watched the progress of the bacon.

'Well, you're here at last.' Tabitha pocketed her whistle and shook her head at Fenella. 'Look at you, Ella, all dressed and curled while poor Molly hasn't had a sniff of the bathwater. I do think you might have woken her and offered her the chance of a hot bath on her first day.'

'The early bird and all that,' Fenella said with a shrug. 'Rookies have to learn the hard way, same as we all did. And must you blow that infernal whistle at us every morning, Tab?'

'If I didn't, I'd never get you out of the house before lunch,' Tabitha said with a motherly smile. 'Now sit down and eat, the pair of you.'

Diana gave a chilly nod to Fenella and Molly as they pulled up chairs. 'Good morning, ladies.'

Molly mumbled a 'good morning' in return. Diana seemed inclined to be polite to her today, but there was a distinct absence of warmth compared to how she had been received by the rest of the women. Molly wondered if it still rankled that Diana had been overruled by the other panel members on the day of her audition.

'Sleep well?' Diana asked, with scrupulous yet icy politeness.

'Yes, thank you,' Molly said, matching her tone. Untrue, of course, but it was the expected response.

'I wish there'd been time for another few hours,' Fenella said with a yawn. 'While you were packing in your beauty sleep, Di, we were up all night with the poor old cat. Didn't turn in until after one.'

'I'm sure the cat could have worked things out for herself.' Diana tutted as Millicent wove around her legs, her milk-filled belly sagging beneath her. 'Shoo now, you greedy creature. You'll do for my last good pair of stockings.'

'Oh, do be kind to her, Di,' Pam said gently, coming over to add more bacon to the plate from which the women were helping themselves. 'She's got her babies to feed now. We ought to give her as much extra as we can while she's nursing.'

'You're too soft-hearted, Pam. All these shortages and we're giving our food away to fill cats' bellies instead of our own.' Nevertheless, Diana took a piece of bacon rind from her plate and held it under the table for Millicent, her expression softening slightly.

'How are the babies?' Molly asked Pam. 'Did they have a settled night?'

'As good as gold, the dears,' Pam said, simpering. 'Hardly a peep out of them. They'll be missing their mother now though. Millicent won't go back to them while there's food so we ought to finish as soon as we can.'

'Yes, eat up,' Tabitha said, taking a seat and helping herself to a fried egg, slice of toast and rasher of bacon. 'We need to leave in an hour, and Molly hasn't bathed yet.'

Fenella didn't need telling twice, immediately diving in to load her plate. Molly regarded the food with awe, however.

She was very hungry, but her mind couldn't encompass the idea of such a big meal first thing in the morning. At home, breakfast usually meant a bowl of watery porridge or a slice of toast. Bacon and eggs, when they could afford them, were the main meal of the day rather than something served at breakfast time. It made Molly feel faintly guilty, thinking of the sparse fare her family would be sitting down to.

It would feel strange for Mam and Daphne with only the pair of them at the table, Molly supposed. No Molly, no Ted, no Dad. She knew it would give her mam more pain than she would ever show, thinking about those empty chairs. The thought of her mother's quiet heartache had Molly blinking back another tear.

Nevertheless, she needed to eat. She took a piece of toast and spread it with a little butter, not quite courageous enough yet to indulge in the luxury of bacon.

'Um, how does it work?' she asked Tabitha. 'I mean with the food. Buying it, cooking it and so on.'

'When we're settled in billets for any length of time, we've got a household pot,' Tabitha told her. 'We each put in six bob out of our wages for the week, and whoever's turn it is on the cooking rota will take our ration books and get the shopping. I'll be touching you up for your contribution later.'

Pam came over with a teapot and poured them each a cup.

'Make sure you savour it, girls,' she said. 'I wouldn't be surprised if they put it on coupons before long. The shortages get worse every time I go to the shops. Honestly, I've started to dread being on cook duty.'

'If Hitler tries for France, Lord knows what might be off the menu,' Fenella said through a mouthful of bacon.

Diana curled her lip. 'Fenella, could you please at least attempt to keep your mouth closed while you eat?'

'We're not at the ruddy Dorchester, Di,' Fenella said, rolling her eyes. 'There's no one here to see us, is there? Let me eat the way that makes me happy.'

'It may make you happy, but I've no wish to watch half-chewed chunks of pig flesh rolling around your mouth while I breakfast.'

'Oh, dry up, darling, do.'

Molly was only half listening to them bicker. She was too busy dwelling on what Fenella had said. A shiver of horror had rippled through her at the idea of the Germans advancing into France. It felt so close, just twenty miles or so across the Channel, and all those poor boys just waiting there – Ted amongst them.

Pam seemed to notice Molly's expression, and came to rest a hand on her shoulder.

'I'm sorry,' she said softly. 'Ella upset you, didn't she? Do you have a sweetheart out there?'

'Not a sweetheart,' Molly said, flushing as all eyes turned to her. 'But, um, our Ted's with them – my younger brother.'

Fenella grimaced. 'Sorry, Molly. I never do think before I open my mouth. I'm sure that won't happen.' She turned to Diana. 'Will it, Di?'

'Of course it won't,' Diana said firmly. 'The Maginot Line's impregnable. Hitler may be half-crazed but from a military point of view, the man's no fool. He'd never throw his forces away on a fruitless invasion attempt.'

'Di's our resident war expert,' Tabitha told Molly. 'I'm ashamed to admit I can't follow half the talk about tactics and politics you get in rooms full of men, but our Diana puts them all to shame. She's wasted as a dancer. She ought to have been a general.'

Diana flashed her friend a smile that by her standards was almost warm. Molly, meantime, felt comforted enough by her confident assurances of no French invasion to help herself to a rasher of bacon.

'Will I have to wear a uniform too?' she asked, glancing at Tabitha's khaki ensemble. It seemed odd that it was worn by some ENSA members and not others. Personally, Molly rather liked the idea of something official to wear.

'If we go overseas, certainly,' Tabitha said. 'That's the main purpose of it: to make us look military, so no over-zealous gendarme mistakes us for spies and hauls us in for interrogation. But in this country, it tends to be worn only when we're on official ENSA business.'

'And Tabby likes to believe she's always on official ENSA business,' Pam said with a smile.

'I think she likes wearing it because it makes her look like she's in charge,' Fenella observed. 'Which she is, of course. I swear she'll have us drilling around Hyde Park one of these days, barking orders like a sergeant major.'

'A bit of military discipline would do you the world of good, young Ella,' Tabitha said sternly, waggling her fork. 'If it weren't for me, I'm sure you'd never get out of bed except to buy cigarettes and go dancing with unsuitable boys.'

'You know me too well, my darling.'

'The worst part is that they make us pay for the uniforms ourselves, unlike the armed forces,' Pam told Molly. 'They're made from officer material too, so they don't come cheap. You don't need to rush to buy one though. It's only vital if they send us abroad.'

Tabitha watched Diana take another slice of toast. 'You're not having more, are you? You'll be too bloated to get into your dress if you stuff yourself with bread.'

'All right, all right.' Diana rolled her eyes as she put the toast back. 'All this deprivation for a measly ten pounds a week. It hardly seems worth it.'

Molly choked on her bacon. 'Are you joking? That's more than I used to earn in a month!'

'Well, yes, I'm sure it seems like a lot to someone like you,' Diana said with a condescending air. 'But it's significantly less than those of us employed by private theatres were earning. I wouldn't expect you to understand' – she gave a little sniff – 'coming from your background.'

'What's that supposed to mean?'

'I meant because you haven't entertained professionally before,' Diana said with a careless shrug. 'No need to be touchy about it, cherie.'

Molly managed to bite back the sarcastic remark that tried to escape, settling for a scowl.

Pam turned off the cooker and came to join them. Millicent the cat, who clearly knew which side her bread was buttered, instantly jumped into Pam's lap to rub her face against her cheek. She was rewarded with another piece of bacon rind.

'She'll be too fat to catch mice if you keep feeding her,' Diana observed. 'You spoil that animal rotten, Pam.'

'She deserves it, the love.' Pam beamed fondly as Millicent thanked her for the bacon with another face-nuzzle.

'Pammy, I swear you'll be packing them into the truck to take on tour with us,' Fenella said. 'Dog acts, yes, but kitten acts? I can't see it taking off.'

'Um, do you mind if I have the last egg?' Molly asked, eyeing it hungrily.

'Help yourself. Everyone else does.' Pam pushed it towards her. 'I wouldn't get too used to bacon and eggs though, Molly. Things tend to be rather different when we're on tour.'

'Oh Lord, yes,' Fenella said, mopping up the last of her egg yolk with the crust from her toast. 'You get real extremes. One moment we're roughing it like soldiers on the march, nibbling dry corned beef sandwiches or cooking kippers over a campfire, then the next we're dining with officers on roast beef and potatoes, sipping fine wines on a chaise longue like the Sheik of Araby.' She glanced at Tabitha. 'Do you remember the young lieutenant who took a shine to you when we were in Béthune, Tab, and sent you that enormous box of chocolate caramels we guzzled between us?'

Tabitha laughed. 'That you guzzled while I watched, you mean. I was lucky to even get one.'

'I can't remember ever feeling so sick during a performance,' Fenella said happily. 'I thought I'd burst on stage and shower everyone with half-digested chocolate.'

Diana pulled a face. 'Must you, cherie? You're putting me off my food again.'

'I don't care,' Fenella announced. 'When my time comes, that's the way I want to go. On stage, making people laugh, full to my back teeth with chocolate caramels.'

Molly was staring at Fenella and Tabitha in awe. 'Were you really in France?'

'That's right,' Tabitha said. 'They sent us over in December to do a Christmas tour. We performed with some big stars too. They tend to slot them into whatever revue happens to be doing the rounds, and our usual routines go out of the window as we work around them. Ella was feed for Tommy Trinder one night.'

'I know, I'll be bragging of it on my deathbed,' Ella said, grinning. 'We had Gracie Fields as guest artiste for one show as well.'

Molly spluttered. 'You've met Gracie?'

Tabitha laughed. 'Sorry, I forgot you were a fan.' She turned to the other women. 'I don't think I told you yesterday but Molly's the most tremendous comic singer, and accompanies herself too. She quite knocked the socks off Phil and me the day she came to audition.'

Diana gave a cough that sounded suspiciously like a snort. Molly chose to ignore it, and quickly diverted the conversation from her supposed musical genius.

'What do you all do in your acts?' she asked.

'You get used to doing a bit of all sorts in an ENSA party,' Fenella said. 'But mostly I'm a comic, which is something of a novelty. Women don't often get to be funny. I do a double act with Little Davy and a solo spot to finish.'

'And Diana dances and I play accompaniment, as I think I told you before,' Tabitha said.

Molly turned to Pam. 'How about you? What do you do?'

Pam blushed slightly, and Fenella laughed.

'With Pam, it's not so much what she does do as what she doesn't,' she said. 'That is to say… but I won't spoil the surprise. I can't wait to see your face, Molly.'

When breakfast was over, Molly went to the bathroom to wash. She couldn't stomach the idea of immersing herself in the tepid water that had been left to her though, dingy with the grime of four bodies before hers. Instead, she managed as best she could with a flannel and the bar of carbolic soap her mother had thoughtfully remembered to pack for her.

Once she was clean and dressed in her best – the same dress she had worn for her audition, which was her only good one – Molly joined the other women in the living room.

'Do we walk to the theatre?' she asked.

'We will today,' Tabitha said. 'It's only quarter of a mile, and our props and things are there already.'

They donned coats and set off. Molly followed as the other women led her through the theatre district, and Fenella fell into step beside her.

'Well, and how do you like us all so far?' she asked, in a low voice so the others couldn't hear.

Molly smiled. 'I feel like there can only be one polite answer to that.'

'We're not a bad bunch. Pam's so sweet that it's impossible to dislike her, and Tabby takes good care of us all despite her bossy ways. I know it's scary living away from home for the first time but you'll grow to love it.'

Molly looked up at her. 'How did you know I was away from home for the first time?'

'I assumed so when I heard you having a little weep last night. Now, don't be embarrassed,' Fenella said, catching sight of Molly's flushed cheeks. 'We've all done it. I'm sure even Di cried her first night with us, despite the fifteen husbands she'd left buried under the flowerbeds back in Lorraine.'

Molly frowned. 'Fifteen husbands?'

'Oh, do ignore me,' Fenella said cheerfully. 'I have the most absurd sense of humour – it's what makes me such a dreadful comic. Lucky it's only ENSA. The men we play to have learned not to expect much.'

Molly watched Diana walking proud and erect alongside Tabitha at the front. 'Your friend Diana doesn't like me much, I think.'

'I sometimes wonder if she likes any of us. Well, no, she loves Pam – everybody loves Pam. She and Tabby row at least once a week, but Di respects her in spite of that. It's obvious she doesn't think much of me though.' Fenella took out a cigarette and fumbled for her matches. 'Then again, I'm not especially fond of her so it all balances out. We mostly manage to keep things civil.'

'Why do you think she doesn't like you?'

Fenella shrugged. 'Suppose I just rub her up the wrong way. Every time I catch her eye she seems to be curling her lip, and I get at least three lectures a day about unladylike behaviour. I don't take it personally and nor should you. Di's one of those women who prefers the company of men, that's all. Hasn't got much time for her own sex. I suppose it comes of the sort of work she used to do.'

'You mean with the ballet?'

Fenella laughed. 'She'd love us to believe it. She insists it's added to all our playbills under her name. But Di's no more a former Sadler's Wells dancer than I am.' Tabitha looked back, frowning at them for dawdling. Fenella glanced sidelong at Molly and pressed a finger to her lips. 'But mum's the word for now. Pam and I will take you to Cortesi's after rehearsal and let you have all the gossip worth having.'

Molly had been expecting Tabitha to lead them to the Theatre Royal, where she had had her audition, so she was surprised when they stopped outside a much smaller, dingier theatre in Soho called The Empress.

'The best we can do, I'm afraid,' Tabitha said, noticing Molly's underwhelmed expression. 'They're holding auditions on the Drury Lane stage so we're in here. The boys will be inside, setting up.'

Molly followed the others in. A passage led to a compact stage with a piano to one side. The troupe manager, Philip, was sitting behind it playing an energetic rendition of 'The Yellow Rose of Texas' while Little Davy and Nobby, the female impressionist – in a staid brown suit today rather than his sequinned Dolores costume – arranged things on the stage.

And there were all sorts of things to be arranged. A half-assembled cabinet painted with moons and stars; juggling clubs; a unicycle; a backcloth of a moonlit garden; a pair of artificial plants, and Lord knew what else. Molly wondered who used what in their act. She could picture Fenella on the unicycle.

Her attention was caught by Philip's playing, which was rather good. At her audition, Molly had assumed from the young man's studious appearance that he was only active backstage, not on stage, but Philip certainly didn't sound like an amateur on the piano. He stopped playing when he noticed the women, and stood up with a welcoming smile.

'Well, that's our two new girls arrived safe and sound,' he said. 'Assuming Nobby doesn't mind being classed as one of the girls.'

'Always happy to be treated like the lady I am when I'm on stage,' Nobby said cheerfully, one of his noxious cigarettes clamped between his teeth as he assembled the cabinet. He nodded to Molly. 'Nice to see you again, love.'

'Bad news on this piano, Tabby,' Philip said, turning to her. 'The low B's off-key and so's the middle C. Keep it soft on them if you can.'

Tabitha shrugged. 'At least it's got a low B and a middle C. I've played on plenty of battered NAAFI instruments with two or three keys missing.'

Little Davy left what he was doing and came over to shake Molly's hand with an almost jovial air, which rather surprised her after what she'd heard him say at her audition.

He was once again in a loud checked suit appropriate to his role as the troupe comic. Molly had never seen him standing before, but now that she did, it was clear how he had come by his name. Little Davy was broad and portly, but in height, he stood only a little taller than tiny Pam. At just five foot four herself, Molly wasn't used to having to look down on people.

'Well, Miss Kensitas—'

'Um, Clough,' Molly said, flushing. 'Sorry. I decided to go back to my— to the name I was using before. But I'd prefer just Molly.'

He blinked. 'All right, Molly it is. We might have to think up something a bit more exciting for the playbills, but you're welcome to any name you like off stage.' He gestured to Nobby building the cabinet. 'As you can see, we all muck in where we're needed. ENSA parties travel light because they have to, and that goes for people as well as props and staging. Any dead weight and it's out, no hesitation.'

'He means it as well,' Fenella said, rolling her eyes. 'I expect he'd abandon me in the middle of the road if I died on my feet one too many times.'

Fenella spoke lightly, but her words worried Molly. Already she could feel the familiar stage fright starting to gnaw at the idea of performing in front of these people. It was almost as nerve-wracking as her audition – more, in some ways. Pam and Fenella had never seen her perform before, and it felt important to impress these new friends. It almost felt like a test – a way of proving her right to call herself one of them.

Just how much truth was there behind Fenella's jokes? If Molly once again struggled in front of Philip, Davy and the rest, would she find herself being told to pack her bags and go home before she had ever played a professional engagement?

Little Davy didn't seem to have noticed her discomfort, however, and carried blithely on.

'We fellers usually tackle the heavy lifting, but it's important never to forget that we're a team,' he said. 'You might be asked to do bits and bobs outside your own turn. The call-up's a bugger for keeping a consistent troupe, excuse my French, and we all sometimes have to fill in for artists who disappear on us halfway through a tour. You might find yourself being sawn in half, or feeding to a comic, or playing accompaniment if Tabby's out of action. That all right by you, missus?'

Molly felt that it certainly wasn't all right by her. She had no idea how to do any of those things. She could probably manage to be sawn in half if they absolutely promised they could put her back together again afterwards, but she didn't know what a feed for a comic did, and as for accompaniment, she could only play her own music. But since the last thing she wanted on her first day was to appear stuck-up, she only smiled and nodded.

'That's why they call it variety, eh?' Little Davy patted her shoulder before going back to help Nobby.

'Speaking of the call-up, have we managed to find a replacement for Carlito yet?' Diana asked Philip.

'Carlito was the crooner we had,' Pam explained to Molly. 'Well, he was Charlie really. He chose an Italian stage name to sound more exotic. Then his call-up papers arrived, he went off to be an airman and we've been without a straight male singer ever since. Honestly, I don't know why we bother to audition men under thirty. We never get to keep them.'

'He'll have defected to some regimental concert party now, I suppose, or been nabbed by the RAF Gang Show lot,' Tabitha said with a disgusted sniff. 'It isn't right the way we keep losing our best men to them, when it's supposed to be our job to provide the troops with entertainment. ENSA really ought to be a reserved occupation.'

'Well, there's not much we can do about that,' Philip said. 'We'll just have to do without until someone suitable turns up. I've asked Jack to keep an eye out.'

'I don't know why you don't do it yourself, Phil,' Diana said. 'You're better than anyone Jack's likely to send us. It's ridiculous to have your skills in the troupe and not use them.'

Philip turned away to call to the men preparing the stage. 'Are we ready to make a start, boys?'

'I think so,' Davy called back. 'Everyone can go on in billing order, and rookies at the end. Nobby last but one, Molly last of all.'

Molly noticed that Tabitha nudged Diana, shaking her head, but Diana just shrugged. She might have spent more time pondering what this signified, and why Philip had turned away when Diana suggested he sing for them, but by now her nerves were making their presence felt. She thrust her hands into her coat pockets to cover their trembles.

'I'm glad you've come, Molly,' Fenella said. 'Saves me being down in the wines and spirits for once.'

'Wines and…'

'Bottom of the bill. That's usually my spot. Come on, let's get ourselves a seat.'

Molly followed Fenella and Pam to seats in the front row where they could watch the rest of the troupe perform. Little Davy got up on stage first, and acted as master of ceremonies to introduce Diana's act. Then Diana herself took to the stage in front of the moonlit garden backcloth, with Tabitha at the piano.

## Chapter 22

'Diana's top of the bill, of course,' Fenella whispered to Molly. 'Oh so much worthier than we humble proles. She told Phil she'd walk if he didn't give her top billing.'

Pam frowned at her. 'Ellie, don't be cruel. I can't believe she said any such thing, or did half the stuff you and Maud were always whispering about her.' She looked at Molly. 'Pay no attention to Fenella, she's a terrific gossip. Diana's really a bit of a sweetheart when you get to know her. And she's terribly fond of Millicent, although out of pride she tries to hide it.'

Fenella snorted. Molly didn't say anything, but she couldn't help but agree with the spirit of that snort. Pam would always be blind to the faults of anyone who was kind to her precious cats. Their chatter drew a censorious look from Philip, and they fell silent.

Molly watched as Diana took off her coat to reveal a clingy, sequinned silver dress. She unfurled a long silk scarf.

'Oh heck,' Molly whispered to the other two. 'Were we supposed to wear costumes? I don't really have one.'

'No, it's not a dress rehearsal,' Pam whispered. 'We can do your kitting out from ENSA stores another time. Some people like to wear what they perform in though, to help them feel more confident.'

'Not to mention that in Diana's case, the costume kind of is the performance,' Fenella said with a grin.

Molly could see what she meant. Diana's costume certainly showed a lot of… well, a lot of Diana.

Diana's dance was in the vein of Isadora Duncan, with Tabitha playing the accompaniment on the tinny theatre piano. The performance did make Molly feel a little better about her own skills. As Tabitha had told her the day of her audition, Diana was really no great shakes as a dancer. Perhaps you could call it a sort of ballet, but there was a lot more running, waving and swaying than what might fairly be labelled dancing, with the long silk scarf doing most of the work. Diana's movements were graceful and fairy-like, but anyone with feet and a scarf could replicate her performance. Molly didn't know much about Sadler's Wells, yet she imagined there was a little more to their style of dancing than that.

Diana was certainly showing off her figure though, including a generous amount of bust, and a shapely leg could be glimpsed through a slit in her dress. She really was incredibly attractive – it galled Molly to admit it, but seeing Diana in her dress and stage make-up, she thought the woman might even be more beautiful than Clara Bow. To boys like Ted, that would be a hundred times more important than skilful dance steps or a poignant, emotional performance.

The men present today certainly seemed to appreciate it. Davy clapped heartily when the performance was over, with Nobby adding a wolf whistle to his applause.

'Thank you, cheries,' Diana said, curtseying prettily.

'Glad to see you've not lost your touch, Di. Still earning your top spot.' Davy grinned at Pam. 'Well, Pammy. Follow that, eh?'

'You bet I will,' Pam murmured, with a strange half-smile.

Philip hadn't applauded Diana's act, Molly noticed. He was sitting a little way from them, making notes.

'So, Phil, what's the verdict?' Tabitha asked.

'Pretty good,' he conceded. 'The boys'll like it, which is the only thing that really matters. Diana, is that the same dress you wore on the last tour?'

'It's the only one I could find in the ENSA boxes to fit,' Diana said, glancing down at it.

Now Molly looked more closely, she could see it was frayed at the hem and missing some sequins, although it certainly did a good job of showing off everything Diana seemed anxious to reveal.

'It's getting rather shabby,' Philip said. 'Nothing in the boxes you could adjust?'

Diana wrinkled her nose. 'Do I look like a seamstress, darling?'

Philip sighed. 'All right, I'll see if the powers that be will consider granting us some funds for new costumes. Otherwise it'll have to do for another tour, so try not to tear it. Pam, your turn.'

'Now you'll see something,' Fenella whispered to Molly as Pam stood up.

'What?'

She smiled. 'Wait and see.'

Again, Tabitha launched into her accompaniment – this time a jaunty festival tune such as one might expect to hear at the circus – while Pam took off her coat.

Tabitha was a perfectly adequate accompanist, but Molly did wonder why Philip didn't perform this function. Little Davy had said there was no room for dead weight in ENSA, and it seemed odd that the troupe would have a manager who couldn't also fulfil a role on stage. She had heard enough of Philip's playing to recognise that he was a cut above not only her but Tabitha too. If what Diana said was true then he was also a talented singer, yet he had seemed anxious to change the subject when she raised it. Molly made a mental note to ask the other women what the story behind this might be when they took her to Cortesi's.

She was glad they had suggested visiting the restaurant. Molly was longing to see Angelo again, as the first friend she had made in the capital. He felt like a bridge between her new life and the old one, somehow.

She quickly forgot about Angelo and everything else, however, as she watched Pam on stage. With little embarrassment, the tiny woman tucked her dress into the long knickers she was wearing and proceeded to perform her act. So entranced was Molly that she even forgot her nerves.

She understood what Fenella had meant now when she had said it wasn't so much what Pam did as what she didn't do. It felt like she could do *everything*. Nearly all the props Molly had noticed on stage were for Pam's act. She turned somersaults, she did conjuring tricks, she tap-danced, she juggled, she played the mouth organ while riding a unicycle, she did stunts with a lasso, and all of it with an ease and poise that suggested she had been performing such feats all her life. For all the woman's shyness off stage, it was clear she was a natural performer.

Pam had an easy, familiar patter too, teasing the audience, joking with them, almost flirting with them. It felt incredible to Molly that the soft-spoken little person she had begun getting to know was one and the same as this daredevil stuntwoman and master conjurer.

'Now for my last trick, I'll need a volunteer from the audience with the daring to enter my disappearing cabinet,' Pam said when she had run through several card tricks that Molly couldn't begin to guess the secret of. 'Oh, no, not you, sir,' she said when Nobby put up his hand. 'I've not got the skill to make the whole of you disappear. I'd hate to be left with a leg on my hands, or a hand on my leg, for that matter. No, thank you, sir, I don't need a practical demonstration. Not without at least being bought a drink first. Yes, you, sir,' she said, nodding to Little Davy. 'I can see from the look in your CO's eye that he's been longing for you to disappear since the day you got here. Do you want to come up?'

Davy, who had obviously done this before, grinned as he allowed Pam to usher him into the cabinet covered in moons and stars. She sealed him inside and ran through more of her teasing patter, before eventually opening the door to reveal he'd gone. There was a gasp from Molly, and a round of applause from everyone else.

'Where is he?' she whispered to Fenella.

'He usually uses it as an excuse to nip to the pub, but his act's up next so I suppose he's in the wings,' Fenella said.

'But… I mean, how did she…'

'I can't tell you that, my pet. Pam'd have my guts for garters. You'll have to ask her yourself.'

Molly shook her head. 'I can't believe what I just saw.'

Fenella smiled. 'All the rookies say that. It's Pam who ought to be top of the bill, not Di and her mad scarves. Her name alone means a lot in this business – at least it used to, and still does to a lot of us.'

'I could have sworn she'd been doing that stuff from the cradle.'

'And so she has, practically.' Fenella put a finger to her lips as Little Davy strolled back on to the stage, hands in his pockets as if he hadn't just been spirited magically away. 'We'd better hush if we don't want a lecture. He gets very sharp-tongued if anyone talks during his bit.'

Molly couldn't help gazing at Pam as with utter unconcern, entirely unaware she had just shaken Molly's world to its foundations, the girl took her seat again. Molly felt quite starstruck to be sitting beside her. She couldn't believe she had delivered kittens with this talented person. She was only barely restraining herself from begging for Pam's autograph.

Little Davy's routine was less impressive. Mostly it was a copy of Max Miller's act, but with anything bordering on blue humour taken out, which made it feel rather bloodless. Basil Dean didn't approve of ENSA members using innuendo to get laughs, Fenella told Molly in a whisper, and insisted all scripts were vetted at headquarters.

At the end of Davy's set, he summoned Fenella to the stage and the pair of them did an old-fashioned cross-talk routine before Fenella moved on to her solo spot.

Molly soon learned that Fenella's particular skill was impressions, and she wasn't half bad at them either. She lampooned all the famous figures of the day, male and female, from Lady Astor to Lord Haw-Haw. When she had run through her repertoire, she invited members of the audience to shout out names for her to mimic. This was where she really had Molly holding her sides, because the impressions Fenella couldn't do were even funnier than those she did well. Her Maurice Chevalier was so hilariously bad that Pam nearly fell off her seat laughing.

Nobby was up next, performing as Dolores with jokes and songs. It felt strange listening to him warble songs like 'Nobody Loves a Fairy When She's Forty' and 'I'll Be Your Sweetheart' when he wasn't in costume.

By that time, however, Molly was in no state to pay attention to Nobby's act. All she could think was that she was on next. In a few minutes, she would have to sing and play in front of all these professionals. The urge to flee was strong, and she fought hard to keep it at bay.

Each of the other Forces Follies members had something. Diana might not be able to dance all that skilfully, but she was beautiful, graceful and glamorous. Pam was a born performer who seemed to be able to do anything. Davy, Fenella and Nobby could each, in their different ways, make people laugh. Tabitha was a better piano player than Molly could ever hope to be, and even Philip, who didn't perform on stage, had significant talents. Molly had never felt more like a mediocre pub singer than she did right then.

She didn't know if she could do it. Not now she had seen what everyone else was capable of. She couldn't bear to think of the pity in her new friends' eyes when they discovered just how talentless she was.

She didn't belong here. They had been kind to her, but she wasn't one of them. They were variety people. Whereas she was just... Molly from the mill.

Pam put a hand on Molly's, clenched tightly over the arm of her chair.

'There's no need to be nervous,' she whispered. 'I know it's not a bit of good saying that because you will be anyway, but we are all on your side, I promise.'

'I want to run away,' Molly murmured. 'I want to go home to my mam. Oh Lord, did I say that out loud?'

'It's just a rehearsal, darling,' Fenella whispered on the other side of her. 'If it goes badly, so what? It's only ENSA, and we've heaps of time to practise together before you have to appear on a real stage.'

'You don't understand. I'm not... I was never meant to be here. It shouldn't have happened.'

'If you're here then it was meant to be,' Pam said firmly. She nodded to Davy beckoning Molly to the stage. 'Just do your best. Once the first one's out of the way, it'll get easier. Won't it, Ellie?'

'That's the way it goes,' Fenella said cheerfully. 'Break a leg, darling. Remember, there's no audience. Only us.'

Molly felt she would prefer a disinterested audience of strangers right at that moment, but she didn't say so. Instead, she took a deep breath and went to Tabitha at the piano. Tabitha didn't relinquish her seat, however.

'Oh yes,' Philip said. 'I forgot to tell you, Molly: we're going to have Tabby play your accompaniment. Not that there was anything wrong with your playing, but it means you can concentrate on singing without distractions. That way, you can work the crowd – give it a bit of oomph, you know? Besides, Tabby's used to managing on the dreadful pianos you tend to find in barracks and aerodromes.'

Molly fought against a sensation of panic. The last thing she wanted was for someone else to accompany her, even if Tabitha was the better player. The piano gave her something to do with her trembling hands, and something to hide behind. Without it, she would feel so incredibly self-conscious and exposed. It would feel almost like being naked.

'I, um, I'd really rather play,' she said. 'It... helps me get the timing right.'

'You won't be playing when we tour,' Philip pointed out. 'You ought to get used to performing as you will then.'

Tabitha looked at Molly's shaking hands, then at Philip.

'I think she ought to play her accompaniment for today,' she said. 'It'll help me to hear her so I can adjust the time and key accordingly.'

'I suppose that is true,' Philip said. 'All right, Molly. Take a seat.'

Tabitha stood up and Molly sank gratefully on to the piano stool. She didn't know what would have happened if she'd had to perform centre stage with no piano to shield her. She'd have fainted, probably. At least now, she could put that ordeal off for another day.

Molly tried to stay focused as she ran through some of her more popular songs: nearly all Gracie Fields numbers. She remembered what Little Davy had said about her being 'flat' and tried to infuse them with a little more personality. It was Gracie's personality rather than her own – hers seemed to have gone off on holiday – but a copycat routine was the best she could do at that moment.

The relief she had experienced on being told she could have the piano went some little way to soothing Molly's nerves, but not enough to stop her voice trembling. Still, she felt she gave a better performance than she had at her audition, and there was loud applause when she finished – suspiciously loud, and nearly all of it coming from where Pam and Fenella were sitting.

It bucked her up nevertheless, even though she knew her friends were only trying to make her feel better. It made her feel there were people here on her side. For a moment, with the sound of her new friends' applause ringing in her ears, Molly could actually feel as though she belonged.

There was little time for conversation after Molly had finished singing. Immediately the performers were split into two groups, one supervised by Tabitha and the other by Philip, as they worked on individual aspects of their acts.

Molly found herself taken to task a comparatively small amount by Tabitha, who was in charge of her group. She was sure the woman was going easy on her for her first day, since Molly was well aware that her act was nowhere near as polished as the others. With the rest of them, though, Tabitha was like a strict schoolmistress, pulling no punches as she outlined everything that ought to be improved.

What most surprised Molly was the way Diana reacted to this treatment. Molly wouldn't have expected her to receive criticism well, but Diana responded with meek obedience to everything Tabitha pointed out. Fenella had said that the two women often argued but there was a mutual respect between them, and it was clear from watching them together that this was true.

'Diana, for pity's sake,' Tabitha said with ill-suppressed frustration as, for a third time, Diana stumbled over the pirouette Tabitha had introduced to her dance – more to show off the low back of her dress than for any performance reason, Molly suspected. 'It can't be making you dizzy. It's only one spin. You look like a drunk elephant trying to dance *Swan Lake*.'

'Sorry, Tabby,' Diana said meekly. 'It's the scarf that puts me off balance. I'll get it right, I promise.'

'See you do. I'll make sure you practise before bed every night until we go on tour.'

'Yes, do remind me. I want to do it as well as I can for the boys.'

Molly wondered if any other member of the group would find Diana so compliant, or if this was something only Tabitha could achieve.

Fenella, who had been in Philip's group, approached them.

'Are you done or what?' she demanded of Tabitha. 'It's gone five, you know. Phil says Pam and I are free to go, but we're not leaving without Molly.'

'Yes, I suppose we ought to get some grub,' Tabitha said. 'Sorry, I got carried away.'

'We are going out, aren't we? It's Friday night.'

Diana shook her head. 'I thought you were exhausted after delivering kittens until the early hours.'

'Never too tired for dancing, darling. Besides, we have to show Molly what a night on the town's like.' Fenella looked at Molly. 'Have you ever been out in London before?'

'Er, no,' Molly said. The idea of it was both intriguing and frightening, and almost certainly not something she would be writing about to her mother. 'I don't have much money though. Just enough for food and essentials, really.'

'Oh, don't you worry about that,' Fenella said blithely. 'You won't be paying for anything. That's what men are for.'

Philip came over with Pam. 'Did you girls say you're going out?'

Fenella rolled her eyes. 'Here we go again. You don't always have to come and keep an eye on us, Phil. I promise I'll keep Molly constantly at my side so no young cad can get her in the family way.'

'And who's going to keep you at their side?' Diana asked, raising an eyebrow.

'I am,' Philip said firmly. 'Sorry, girls, but you know the rules. I won't spoil the fun, I promise. I'll just be around if anyone gets fresh.'

'What if we like them getting fresh?' Fenella muttered.

'Ignore Ella. We'd love to have you along, Phil.' Tabitha turned to Fenella. 'Well, are we going to Cortesi's for dinner before we hit the town?'

'Molly, Pam and I are,' Fenella said. 'You and Di go home to eat. We can go out as we are, but you two need to change. Besides, we want to talk about you to Molly.'

'All lovely things, we promise,' Pam said with a smile. 'We just thought it might be nice to have a little chat with our new girl without Teacher listening in.'

'All right,' Tabitha said. 'Come on then, Di. I'll whip up something from the larder for the two of us.'

Tabitha seemed happy to accept her role as authority figure, and didn't look hurt by her exclusion from the dinner party. Molly thought Diana's face crumpled slightly, however, though she might well be imagining it. Diana seemed to isolate herself from the others routinely, and when she had to be around them, she acted as though she'd rather be somewhere else. She could hardly be upset when they did the same in return.

—

Fenella and Pam each claimed one of Molly's arms as they walked her to Cortesi's. They seemed determined to adopt her, and in this exciting, frightening new world, Molly was quite willing to be adopted.

She felt a wave of relief on entering Cortesi's. She remembered it so well from her previous visit: the delicious scent of the food, the red-checked tablecloths, the flickering candles jammed into wine bottles and the painted frieze of Tuscany that covered one wall. Although Molly had visited only once before, it felt homely and familiar – somewhere she associated with friends.

Angelo was behind the bar with his father, but they didn't immediately notice the new arrivals. They were having a discussion in Italian which, although conducted in an undertone, Molly thought sounded somewhat heated.

'We'll sit down and wait until they notice us,' Pam whispered. 'Best not to interrupt.'

The two women made a beeline for a table in the corner, as if this particular spot belonged to them. It was the same table Angelo had shown her to the last time she had eaten here, Molly noticed. She followed and took a seat between them.

'Are they arguing?' she asked, glancing at Angelo and his dad. She couldn't understand what they were saying, of course, but both men wore grim expressions.

'Yes,' Pam said in a low voice. 'They often do.'

'Really? The last time I was here, I got the impression Mr Cortesi doted on his son.'

'That's the problem. Angelo's determined to go into the army, but his dad doesn't want him to. They're always clashing about it.' Pam's gaze drifted to the father and son. 'You can understand why. No one wants to send their only child off to war, do they? Matteo – that's Angelo's father – lost a brother in the last one. I suppose he's terribly afraid he'll lose his boy the same way.'

'He'll be called up eventually though, won't he?'

'I'm not sure he can be. He's an Italian citizen, although he's been in this country since he was three. People tend to be suspicious of foreigners, especially from countries that are friendly to the enemy.' Pam sighed as she looked at Angelo, his handsome brow knit determinedly while he spoke with his father. 'I can't help taking Matteo's side. I wish Angelo wasn't so determined to go.'

'Pam's desperately in love with him,' Fenella told Molly matter-of-factly as she helped herself to one of the bread rolls in a basket on the table. 'A lot of girls are, but their love isn't pure the way Pammy's is.'

Pam shook her head, smiling. 'Honestly, Ellie, how can you talk such nonsense? I know it's all in fun but do keep your voice down. I'd blush to match the tablecloth if Angelo were to hear you.'

Fenella flashed Molly a conspiratorial look, but as Angelo was approaching the table, she deigned to remain silent.

Angelo was beaming now, as was his father from behind the bar, their quarrel seemingly forgotten.

'Well, if it isn't our star customers.' He nodded to Molly. 'Miss Gale. I'm glad the wind blew you back in our direction.'

Pam frowned. 'Gale? I thought it was Clough.'

'It is,' Molly said with a smile. 'Just a private joke. I'll explain another time.'

Molly noticed again that worried expression she'd spotted on Pam's face when she had first mentioned she knew Angelo. She wondered what it meant. Was Fenella only teasing, or did Pam really have feelings for the young Italian that might make her worry Molly was a contender for his affections? Molly would have liked to reassure her, but it felt rather bold to wade into a conversation about matters of the heart when they were such new friends.

'Dad and I thought you'd abandoned us,' Angelo said cheerily. 'Not seen you for days, girls.'

'We've been busy delivering kittens, among other things,' Fenella told him. 'Nothing personal, Angie.'

He laughed. 'I know you only call me that to make me blush so I'm not going to bother asking you to stop. What do you mean, delivering kittens?'

'I told you our cat Millicent had put on weight,' Pam said. 'Well, it turns out it wasn't from eating too many mice. Now we've got four baby Millicents to take care of.' She beamed at him. 'Oh, you must see them, Angelo. They're the most perfect little things you've ever laid eyes on. I wish I could keep them.'

'And I wish I was a rich man, so I could buy a big house for you to adopt all the strays in London,' Angelo said with a smile. Molly noticed his voice was softer and less teasing with Pam than when he addressed her or Fenella.

'Will you come to see them? The girls and I were hoping you might check on them sometimes after we go away.'

'Any favour I can do you, darling, I'd be happy to oblige. For as long as I'm still here, at least.'

'Your dad hasn't given in, has he?' Fenella asked.

Angelo sighed. 'No. I hate to defy him, but it seems only right I do my bit. I wonder I'm not getting pillowcases stuffed with white feathers delivered every day: a big, strong boy like me hiding at home while others are doing the fighting.'

'I do wish you wouldn't, Angelo,' Pam said, turning her large blue eyes on him. 'Not when you don't have to. What if… well, I wish you wouldn't, that's all.'

'Ah, but it's all part of my plan.' Angelo took her hand and pressed it to his lips. 'How else can I get beautiful girls like you to entertain me for free?'

Pam laughed, blushing slightly. 'Oh, get away with you. I don't know why we let you flirt with us when we know there must be dozens of girls a day who hear your lines before we do.'

'Yes, but they're just for practice so I'll be ready when the real thing comes in.'

Fenella shook her head at Molly, smiling. 'You know, I wonder sometimes why we always come here. The service is terrible. Ten minutes we've been sitting here waiting to be offered some food.'

'All right, I can take a subtle hint as well as the next man,' Angelo said with a grin. 'What do you want then?'

'The usual lasagne for me and Pam,' Fenella said. 'Molly?'

Molly had been looking down the menu, but the names were all in Italian. She wasn't certain yet whether she was ready to take a chance on lasagne or risotto, whatever they might be.

'I'll have the pill… the pole… um, the chicken stew again, please,' she said.

Angelo laughed. 'All right, I'll let you get away with it today. But next time I'm going to insist you tackle something more adventurous.'

'We'll have a bottle of wine too, Angie,' Fenella said. 'We're showing Molly the town tonight.'

'Lucky Molly. I'll give Nonna your order. Dad'll bring your wine over when he's served the other customers.' He left, stopping to give his dad their drinks order on the way to the kitchen.

'Now I'll be in Pam's bad books for scaring him away,' Fenella said to Molly, grinning at Pam, whose cheeks were still flushed. 'I swear I've almost starved to death some evenings, waiting for the pair of them to finish gazing into each other's eyes so I could get some food.'

'Oh, stop your teasing,' Pam said. 'You know he's the same way with everything in a skirt. He flirts with you just as much as me. I bet he'd even flirt with Nobby if he came in here in costume, just through force of habit.'

'Yes, but he means it when he does it with you.'

Pam laughed. 'Molly, if you love me, you'll change the subject before I blush myself to death. What would you like to talk about?'

Molly did have something she wanted to ask. The image of Pam earlier, turning somersaults like some sort of acrobatic machine, was still imprinted on her brain. She couldn't help contrasting it with the girl's shy smiles as Angelo had complimented her.

'I did have a question,' she said. 'I hope you won't think it's bad manners. It's a tiny bit personal.'

'Those sorts of questions are the best way to get to know one another, I always think,' Pam said. 'Not that I'm promising to answer. What is it?'

'It's just… you seem so quiet off stage. But on it you were so… I mean, I've never seen anything like it. I could hardly believe that was you. How do you do that – become a different person?'

Pam shrugged. 'It's an old act and I've been doing it a long time. My mother and father did it before me – except that they sang comic songs too. Unfortunately I didn't inherit the skill. I can't sing a note.'

'We were glad to find there was something she couldn't do,' Fenella said. 'It proves she's human after all.'

'I practically grew up in front of an audience,' Pam went on. 'I was barely six months old when I first appeared on stage. I learned to wear a mask almost before I'd had time to find out what was underneath it.'

'Pam's a Sheridan,' Fenella told Molly, with some pride.

'Oh.' Molly didn't know what a Sheridan was, but evidently it was something rather impressive.

Pam laughed. 'You must stop acting like the name means something, Ella. Why on earth should Molly know the Sheridans?'

'But it does mean something,' Fenella said. 'The Sheridans are a legend in this business.'

'Twenty years ago, perhaps. The world's moved on since then.'

'Um, what is a Sheridan?' Molly asked.

'I am,' Pam told her. 'That's my full name – Pamela Sheridan. We're an old music-hall family. The Sensational Sheridans, we were known as.'

'The Sheridans weren't just a family, they were a dynasty,' Fenella said, her voice reverential. 'Pam's grandfather and great-grandfather worked the halls as well. I was taken to see her parents' act at the Edinburgh Empire when I was a girl. That was what made me decide I wanted to be on stage. I'd never seen anything like it.'

That explained Pam's mixed-up accent, Molly supposed. As part of a family of entertainers, she must have travelled a lot in her childhood.

'And now I'm the last of us left performing,' Pam said with a sigh. 'The one remaining Sensational Sheridan. A relic at nineteen, just like music hall. I suppose the wireless will do for speciality acts like mine in the end, but at least I can have a final fling with ENSA.'

'Relic my foot,' Fenella said stoutly. 'You're the best act on the bill by a mile. Don't tell Tabby, but I'm ten times prouder of sharing a stage with a real Sensational Sheridan than any number of Tommy Trinders.'

Angelo's father Matteo appeared at their table with a bottle of red wine. His English was limited, relying on his son to translate for him, but he beamed affably as he poured them each a glass.

'Chianti,' he said proudly. 'Best of my country. Enjoy, young ladies.'

He disappeared, and Molly regarded her glass warily. She rarely drank wine. It was more potent than the milk stout she favoured, and tended to go to her head. She didn't suppose the Cortesis served milk stout, however, and she would be embarrassed to order such a thing in front of her sophisticated new friends.

The other two were happily sipping their Chianti. Not wanting to be left out, Molly took a sip likewise. The flavour was pleasant, although it burned her throat.

'What about you?' Molly asked Fenella. 'How did you end up on the stage?'

'Oh, my story's not nearly so interesting as Pam's,' Fenella said, lighting a cigarette. 'It's rather a cliché, really. I'm the typical little boy who ran away from home to join the circus — apart from being a girl, of course, and it was the theatre rather than a circus. Still, it's depressingly unoriginal, don't you think?'

'No, it's fascinating. Do you mind telling me why you left home, or is it private?'

Fenella shrugged. 'You're welcome to know if it gives you joy. Mother and Father kept a hat shop in Edinburgh — rather a fine hat shop, which made them aspire to better things for the family. They made enough to send me and my sister to the sort of boarding school that was supposed to make young ladies out of us. Only I couldn't bear being made a young lady of – honestly, the mistresses there were absolute horrors. It was like being surrounded by a dozen Dianas, lecturing me about etiquette and deportment all day.'

'You have to pity them,' Pam said with a laugh. 'I don't envy anyone whose job it is to teach Fenella how to be ladylike.'

'All I ever wanted to do was show off and perform,' Fenella went on. 'I earned good money putting on shows in our dorm at thruppence a ticket, mimicking the mistresses for the other girls. I was mostly miserable though, and Mother would insist on keeping me there despite the fact I was bottom of the class. Eventually, when I was fifteen, I decided I'd had enough of snooty teachers and sore palms from the daily whacks I earned myself. So in the middle of the night I packed a bag, climbed over the school wall, spent my saved-up thruppences on a ticket to London and set out to find myself a job.'

Molly stared at her. 'Blimey!'

'And this is her idea of an uninteresting story,' Pam said with a dry smile.

'Weren't you dreadfully afraid?' Molly asked.

'I imagine I was,' Fenella said rather dreamily. 'It seems a long time ago now. I barely had a shilling left in my pocket after paying for the train ticket. I'd probably have ended up in some dreadful scrape if Little Davy hadn't stumbled over me hanging around his stage door, trying to attract the attention of some bigwig who could give me a job.'

Molly frowned. 'Davy did?'

'Oh yes, he and I are old friends. He felt sorry for me and said he'd try me for a week as a feed – the straight man, you know? Audiences seemed to like the novelty of this naive, gangly kid setting up Davy's saucy punchlines. His act was a lot more risqué back then. That was five years ago, and we've worked together ever since.' She exhaled a stream of smoke and followed it with her eyes. 'We were part of a revue at the Metropolitan on Edgware Road when they closed the theatres, so we toddled along to ENSA to beg for a job along with all the other out-of-work entertainers. A lot of them chose not to renew their ENSA contracts once the private theatres reopened, but I find this life rather suits me.'

'And your parents – do they know where you are?'

'I write them once a year so they know I'm safe, usually when we've stopped for a one-night stand so they can't find me from the postmark,' Fenella said. 'Perhaps they don't care if I'm alive or not after the way I bolted, and they'd certainly be horrified to know I'm on the stage, but they did bring me into the world so it seems only polite. Besides, I want my little sister to know I'm all right.' She smiled slightly as she put her cigarette out in the ashtray. 'She's the only thing about that old life I miss.'

Molly was regarding her new friend with wonder. She couldn't imagine how it must feel to land on the streets of London at just fifteen, alone and penniless. She had been frightened enough to come here even at the ripe old age of twenty-one, with several pounds in her pocket and a home and job all arranged. It seemed nothing could frighten Fenella. And there was little Pam too: so bashful off stage but alight with the fire of generations of Sensational Sheridans as soon as she had an audience. Molly prayed a little of their fearlessness would rub off on her.

'What about you, Molly?' Pam asked. 'What prompted you to make a life in the world of variety?'

'You mean despite my conspicuous absence of talent?' Molly said with a small smile.

'I don't mean any such thing. You're very good for an amateur.'

Molly flushed. 'You could tell that just from hearing me?'

'Oh, not from the way you performed. But nerves like that are usually the sign of someone new to the business.'

Fenella patted her hand. 'Don't let it prey on your mind, child. It'll only make it worse. Just remember that every one of us started out as terrified amateurs once upon a time. I bet even Pam was shaking in her baby bootees the first time she was on stage.'

Pam laughed. 'My mam said I screamed my head off and completely ruined her performance of "Ta-ra-ra Boom-de-ay" so I think you're right.'

'Are your parents happy for you to be here?' Fenella asked Molly. 'Some old folk can be terribly stuffy about the stage.'

'There's only my mam now,' Molly said. 'She didn't oppose me joining ENSA. She knows this is what I always wanted to do, and the salary means I can support my family far better than I could working in a mill. But she was a bit worried about me falling in with "theatre people", as she put it.'

'Like us, you mean,' Pam said with a laugh.

'My parents were the same,' Fenella said. 'Thought the life of an entertainer was nothing but orgies and depravity.' She toasted them with her wine. 'If only, eh, girls?'

The restaurant had become busy with evening revellers pouring in. Angelo brought the women their food and instantly bustled off to serve the new customers, to Pam's ill-disguised disappointment.

Molly looked with interest at the meals her friends had been served. Lasagne seemed to be a sort of pie, with cheese on top and mince inside between layers of what looked like thin pastry. It didn't look too frighteningly exotic, and it smelled wonderful. She made up her mind to try it the next time they visited.

'So that was why you wanted to join ENSA?' Pam asked. 'Because the wages were better than in the mills?'

'Yes.' Molly thought about Shack and shivered. 'Well, that was one reason. I always wanted to perform professionally though. I couldn't believe it when Jack said he thought I might be good enough for ENSA.'

Fenella paused with her fork halfway to her mouth. 'Jack Forrester sent you?'

'Sort of. He spotted me playing in my grandad's pub and gave me an ENSA card.'

'You're honoured then. He's not an easy man to impress. I don't dare tell you what he said about my act the first time he saw it.'

Molly wasn't sure why, but for some reason she found herself asking the question, 'Do you know him well?'

'Everyone in ENSA knows Jack,' Pam said. 'But we know him better than most. He did half a tour with us back in December, when he wasn't attached to another unit and we needed a last-minute substitute for an act who got called up. Tabby was his best girl for a while.'

'Was she?' Molly felt a pang of jealousy, and then a pang of annosance at feeling any such ridiculous thing for this man she had met for all of half an hour.

'Yes, for a month or so. I don't think it was serious, but he was with us a lot,' Pam said. 'Who is it you have to support at home?'

'My mam and sister both rely on my wages. My little sister Daphne is at a grammar school, preparing to take her certificate, so that's one drain on our finances. She needs to be under the doctor too.'

'Sorry to hear that,' Fenella said. 'Is it anything dangerous, or would you prefer not to say?'

'She's healthy now, but she had polio when she was a little girl and it left her with weakness in her legs,' Molly told them, a trace of emotion in her voice as she thought back to that terrible time when her baby sister had fallen ill. 'She needs to wear calipers and walk with crutches while she builds up her muscles.'

'Oh, the poor lamb,' Pam said softly. 'And poor Molly too, to have so much to worry about when you're only young yourself.'

Molly swallowed a mouthful of food. 'I do worry about her, but she's a tough little thing. I'm glad I can earn enough from this to get her the care she needs though.' She sighed. 'For now, at least. I wouldn't be surprised if Philip's thinking about sending me home.'

'He won't send you home,' Fenella said. 'You really weren't as bad as you think.'

'I wasn't nearly as good as any of you. You all seem so self-assured and confident. Pam's right: it's obvious I'm an amateur.'

'It's only obvious because of your nerves,' Pam said. 'Once you relax, you'll be perfect.'

Molly took a sip of her wine, appreciating the way it warmed and numbed her.

'What if I can't get them under control?' she said in a low voice. 'I always hoped I would be able to with practice, but what if it's just… part of who I am? I'd hate to go home now.'

'That won't happen,' Fenella said firmly, topping up Molly's glass. 'Stop worrying about it and drink some more wine. We promised to show you a good time tonight and so we will. You're one of us now.'

This made Molly smile. It was nice to feel accepted. Obediently, she drank a little more wine. If she were going to be sent home, she might as well enjoy everything this new life had to show her before it was snatched away again.

'Will Diana come out with us?' she asked.

'Oh Lord, I hope not,' Fenella said fervently. 'All she does is look down her nose at everything and ruin everyone's fun. I think that's the reason she comes.'

Pam shook her head. 'I don't know why you dislike her so much.'

'Of course you don't. You're her pet, aren't you? It's different when it's obvious she despises you.'

'Why is she that way?' Molly asked. 'Are her people terribly well-off or something?'

Fenella snorted. 'Which people?'

'Pardon?'

'She's acquired a few of them over the years. Five husbands and counting, I heard, and that's only the conservative estimate. One divorced, one pushing up the daisies somewhere in France and goodness knows where she stashed the other three. The most recent one was a Frenchman, so he came with the convenient addition of an exotic-sounding name she could bill herself under.'

'I don't believe half of that,' Pam said. 'She told me she'd only been married twice. The first died and the second, the French one, abandoned her for someone else. Poor Di, she's had some dreadful luck.'

'She would say that, wouldn't she?' Fenella said, relishing the opportunity for a truly sensational gossip. 'You're not going to deny what she was doing for a living before ENSA, I suppose, Pam. We all know it had nothing to do with Sadler's Wells.'

'Well, no,' Pam said, flushing slightly. 'But I don't see what's so wrong with that. Work's work, and we've all done our share of jobs we're not proud of.'

Molly couldn't follow what all this was about.

'What do you mean?' she asked.

Fenella lowered her voice and nodded to one of the theatres that could be glimpsed through the window. 'If you want to know the secret behind Diana Chastain, Molly, it's right there.'

Molly looked at the theatre: The Windmill. It was small and a little grimy, with a sign that said '*Revudeville*: continuous daily from 12.15. The only non-stop theatre in the West End!' She wasn't sure why Fenella was smirking so about it. It looked like just another small theatre to her – not much different from the one in which they'd been rehearsing earlier.

'I don't understand,' she said. 'Is that where she was working? What's wrong with that?'

Fenella shook her head. 'My darling, haven't you heard of The Windmill? Don't you know what they do?'

'The sign says they do non-stop revues.'

'Yes, well, so they do. Only they do them without any clothes on.'

Molly nearly choked on her stew. 'They do what?' she gasped.

'That's what The Windmill is.' Fenella seemed gleeful at having managed to shock her. 'A peep show for gents who like to look at ladies in the altogether – which is most of them, in my experience. It's practically a bawdy house, my pet.'

'They're *tableaux vivants*, not peep shows,' Pam told Molly. 'Really quite artistic, I'm told. The nudes who take part never move, as if they're living sculptures. It's not nearly so sensational as Fenella likes to make it sound. Lots of respectable people go to The Windmill.'

Fenella shook her head. 'Pam, my darling, your naivety is simply adorable. You're going to tell me next that you don't believe Di ever posed for French postcards, I suppose.'

'You're right, I am going to tell you that.'

'Um, what are French postcards?' Molly asked. She could guess from the way Fenella used the term with such relish that they were more than simply views of the Eiffel Tower.

'You know, photos of girls in the buff,' Fenella said in a low voice. 'I'd love to get hold of one. I'd like to see Di looking down her nose at us if I could wave a picture of her starkers in her face.'

Molly hadn't thought she was a particularly naive person, but she couldn't help feeling shocked at all this. Of course she knew that some poor women earned their daily bread selling themselves to men, but the idea that there were places like The Windmill, where otherwise respectable girls showed their bodies for money, had never occurred to her. And Diana, who looked at Molly as if she was some lower order of the species, had actually made her living in such an establishment!

Anyhow, that was one more thing she wouldn't be mentioning in the letter she was planning to write to her mother tomorrow...

'How do you know she was working there?' she asked Fenella. 'Have you been?'

'No, your good friend Mr Forrester let it slip, back when he and Tabby were keeping company. He was the one who recruited Di for ENSA.' Fenella snorted. 'I bet he's been "talent-spotting" in The Windmill a few times. Men, I mean to say.'

'Why would Diana join ENSA if she could earn more there?' Molly asked. 'She was sneering at ENSA wages at breakfast.'

Fenella shrugged. 'Perhaps she'd got to an age where she wasn't quite so willing to bare all. She's hardly an ingénue any more, is she? She must be twenty-seven if she's a day, and things don't stay pert forever. Or perhaps she just got chilly.'

'I'm sure the Revudebelles don't earn as much as all that,' Pam observed. 'A friend of mine only got three pounds a week for doing the *tableaux*.'

'It's probably just swank,' Fenella said, finishing her wine. 'Di's still trying to kid us with that Sadler's Wells fantasy of hers.'

Molly fell silent, chewing thoughtfully on her chicken. She couldn't help thinking about Diana, more beautiful than Clara Bow, naked on stage in front of all those admiring male eyes – Jack's eyes, even. And poor, insignificant Molly Clough couldn't even stomach the idea of performing without a piano to hide behind.

'You see what you've done now, Ellie,' Pam said with a smile. 'You've stunned the poor girl into silence with your nonsense. I thought we were going to show her a good time.'

'And so we are,' Fenella said, pushing away her empty plate. 'She'll be dancing on a table in no time, singing "Knees Up Mother Brown" with the best of them.'

'It's a pity we'll have Phil keeping an eye on us. I feel guilty whenever a boy tries to talk to me, even if it's only to make friends.'

'Well, perhaps we can distract him with a pretty face,' Fenella said, grinning. 'He won't care what we get up to if he's got someone of his own to play with.'

This broke through Molly's thoughts. She wouldn't have imagined serious-looking Philip to have an eye for the ladies, but that seemed to be what Fenella was suggesting. It reminded her that she had stored a question away earlier, to ask when they were alone.

'Do you two know what upset Philip at rehearsal?' she asked. 'Diana asked why he didn't sing for the troupe, and he turned away as if he didn't want to talk about it. I didn't realise he was a performer as well as the manager.'

'That's the way it tends to work in ENSA,' Pam said. 'Like Little Davy said, troupes can't afford to be carrying spare bodies. Usually, one of the performers manages things. That was the way it worked for the Follies too, until— but perhaps I shouldn't say anything.'

'Why, is it a secret?'

'Well, no,' Pam said slowly. 'But Phil doesn't like to talk about it, and none of us know quite what happened. He lost his partner, you see. He was one half of a duo called The Brooks Brothers who joined ENSA at the start of the war. They both sang and played – Phil wrote the music and Pete, his partner, wrote the lyrics. Then Pete left to join the RAF, and Phil wouldn't go on stage without him.'

'Why? He can still perform without his brother, can't he?'

'Oh, they weren't actually brothers,' Fenella said. 'It was just the name they used for the act. And like Pam said, none of us really know why he was quite so adamant he wouldn't perform after Pete went away. But he was a good manager, and he had the advantage of being able to speak fluent French, so the Follies kept him on.'

'I think a few of us secretly hope he'll change his mind, one day,' Pam said. 'He's very good.'

Fenella nodded to the remainder of Molly's wine. 'Well, drink up, girl. This good time isn't going to have itself. I know the perfect little club we can take you to.'

## Chapter 25

A short time later, Molly arrived at Fenella's 'perfect little club': a fashionable West End nightspot called Revels.

Although dark on the outside just like everywhere else, the club was filled with dazzling illumination within. There were mirrors on every wall, magnifying the light until Molly felt quite dizzy. A band played popular dance tunes while the club's patrons – nearly half of the men in a uniform of some kind – threw themselves energetically around the floor. Molly had hoped it would be the sort of place where she and her new friends could retreat to a quiet corner for more conversation, but it was far too crowded for any such thing. Fenella seemed as thrilled as Molly was disappointed to discover how busy the place was, and regarded the dancing servicemen with delight.

'Look at them all,' she whispered gleefully to Molly. 'We won't have to buy a drink all night. I'm going to dance until my feet fall off.'

Tabitha, Philip and Diana were already there. As Fenella had predicted, Diana was looking around the place with her nose in the air as if everything about it was beneath her. Molly found herself blushing, thinking of what Fenella had told her about Diana's previous job.

Her thoughts kept coming back to Jack. Molly had wondered, that night they met, whether he might have an amorous interest in her. His enthusiasm for her singing and his easy flirting had charmed her, even while she tried to maintain a distance from this posh boy whose motives might be anything but honourable. It seemed she had been right to do so, if he was someone who regularly visited peep shows. Apparently he had already toyed with Tabitha's affections as well. With all that experience of the fairer sex, it was no wonder he was an accomplished flirt.

She'd really had a lucky escape, Molly reflected. A boy like that could be nothing but trouble. Yet still she found herself wondering how serious things might have been between Jack and Tabitha, and if her path would ever again cross with his.

–

An hour after arriving at the club, Molly was leaning against a wall and fervently wishing she could go to bed. The others were too busy to notice that she was unhappy – Fenella was dancing with a young naval officer, Philip had seemingly abandoned his chaperone duties and was deep in conversation with a guardsman at the bar, Pam had discovered a fellow music-hall juvenile from days gone by and retreated into a corner with her to discuss old times, and Molly wasn't sure where Tabitha and Diana had disappeared to.

Her head was throbbing from the too-bright light, the loud music and the wine she had drunk, but she didn't want to leave by herself and have to pay for a cab. The money she'd brought from home had to last until she'd earned out the advance for Daphne's calipers, and she'd already spent more than she intended.

A small sob escaped on thinking of her sister. Suddenly, she felt very homesick. She missed the dark, friendly pubs of Bradford, where she could sit quietly in the snug with Rita, nursing a milk stout while they chatted confidentially about their innocent secrets. She missed the talks she had with Daphne at bedtime, when she would counsel her sister about all the things that troubled the minds of fifteen-year-old girls. She missed resting her head on her mother's knee at the end of a difficult day, and having Mam soothe away her worries. She liked the people she had met here and God knew she had no wish to go home just when her life finally seemed to be beginning, but she did feel the absence of her family deeply.

Daphne would be in bed now. Would she cry, missing her sister? Could she sleep? Tomorrow would have been their day to go to the pictures. Molly had promised the child fish and chips the next time she could afford it...

She was distracted from her troublesome thoughts by the approach of a young soldier, grinning in the lopsided way that suggested he'd had one beer too many.

'Give us a dance, darling,' he said. 'If you're worth it, I'll buy you a drink after.'

Molly blinked woozily at him. 'What?'

'Come on, girl, move your arse. What're you waiting for, the war to end?'

Molly made an effort to focus on him. 'I... no. I'm not dancing, thanks. I have a headache.'

'Course you're dancing. This is a nightclub, that's what it's for. Come here.' He grabbed her arm and tried to drag her to the dance floor, but Molly resisted.

'I said no.'

'Frigid, are you? I'm the man to fix that for you.'

Before Molly had time to protest, the soldier pulled her into his arms, swung her backwards so she was off balance and pressed a kiss to her lips.

Molly struggled, but she couldn't free herself. She wanted to scream. She felt like she might faint. All she could think of, helpless in the man's arms, was Shack: kissing her, holding her hard so she couldn't get away, trying to drag her to the floor...

Summoning all her strength, she pushed the soldier away.

'Get *off*!' she yelled. 'Don't touch me!'

'Bloody hell, you really are frigid,' he said, laughing at her distress. 'It was just a bit of fun, darling. I thought you girls liked that David Niven stuff, getting swept off your feet and all that.'

She was sobbing now. 'Just get away from me. Get away!'

'You heard the lady,' a man's voice said. 'Run along, sonny.'

Molly looked round to see who had spoken. His face was blurry behind her tears, but she recognised the voice.

'Jack?' she whispered.

The soldier put his hands up. 'Sorry, mate. Didn't know she had a feller. No need to make a song and dance out of it, eh? You're welcome to her for my money.'

The soldier was absorbed back into the crowd, and Molly found a handkerchief being held out to her. She took it and wiped her eyes.

'I think my line is "we must stop meeting like this",' Jack said. Molly blinked, bringing him into focus. He was in civilian clothing tonight, looking rather dapper in a single-breasted navy-blue suit. 'Are you all right, Miss Clough?'

'Yes.' She took a deep breath as she tried to calm her racing heart. 'Sorry. You must think I'm mad to get so upset over a silly thing like that.'

'Not at all. He was taking liberties. Besides, you aren't used to this wild London nightlife.'

'It wasn't that. It just reminded me...' She paused while she mastered her sobs. 'Never mind. What are you doing here?'

'Meeting a friend.' He nodded to Tabitha, who Molly could now see was sitting with Diana at a table they'd managed to bag. 'Then I saw you struggling with your soldier and thought you might appreciate some help.'

Molly felt her heart sink. If he was meeting Tabitha, did that mean things weren't really finished between them? Not that she had any right to care, but...

'I'd have been all right,' she told him, a little curtly.

He smiled. 'Yes, I imagine you would, but I needed some excuse to renew the acquaintance. Can I get you that drink now?'

'No.' She pressed a palm to her head. 'No, I don't want to drink anything else. The girls gave me wine earlier and it... didn't agree with me.'

'Which girls?'

Molly gestured vaguely to Fenella dancing with the naval officer. 'The Forces Follies girls. I'm here with them. I mean, I'm one of them.'

Molly experienced an odd combination of pride and fear as she spoke those words. She was proud to be one of the Forces Follies, yes, but she still couldn't shake the feeling that she was an impostor.

He looked at her curiously. 'You're with the Follies?'

She managed a smile. 'Didn't think I'd make it?'

'It's not that. It's… well, never mind about it now. Do you need to sit down, or can I take you outside to get some air? You're very pale.'

Molly certainly felt like she needed to free herself from the bright lights, loud music and smoky atmosphere of the club. The idea of being escorted outside by Jack felt risky, however. His presence was reassuring, but she didn't know him very well, did she? All she knew about him was that he was apparently a regular visitor to nude revues. She mustn't let her naivety put her in danger.

'Didn't you say you had a date with Tabitha?' she asked, a slightly bitter edge creeping into her tone.

'I'm here to discuss some ENSA business with her, yes. Tabby won't mind waiting though. I'd feel better knowing you were out there with someone to look after you.' He smiled. 'But I can see what's on your mind. You think I've rescued you from one wolf only to press my own disgusting attentions on you, don't you?'

Molly flushed. 'I didn't think that.'

'Well, you're right to be cautious. We're practically strangers.' He glanced at Philip talking to his guardsman friend. 'Your chaperone seems to be otherwise occupied though. If Tabby will give me a testimonial as an old-fashioned gentleman and defender of the fair sex, would that satisfy you?'

'I… suppose so.'

The music was overwhelming, the smoky air oppressive, and Molly was desperate to get outside the club, but she didn't want to disturb the other girls while they were having fun. She allowed Jack to take her elbow and manoeuvre her through the crowds to where Tabitha and Diana were.

'Oh good, you're here,' was the decidedly un-lover-like way in which Tabitha greeted him. 'I thought you'd never turn up.' She frowned when she noticed Molly swaying at his side. 'Is everything all right, Molly?'

'Your friend's had an unpleasant experience, and a little too much wine, I think,' Jack said. 'I just scared away a soldier who was trying to take advantage of the situation.'

'Oh, my dear.' Tabitha stood up and put her finger under Molly's chin to look into her face. 'Did those naughty girls give you wine when they must know you're not used to it? I'll ask the barman to call a cab for us all at once.'

'No,' Molly said quietly, every word jarring her aching brain. 'Let them enjoy themselves. I'll be all right. I need a little fresh air, that's all.'

'Nonsense. You need your bed, and it'll do the rest of us no harm to have an early night after being up with Millicent until the early hours. I can talk to Jack about what we were planning to discuss another time.' She turned to Diana. 'We might have to wait a little while for a cab though, on a Friday night. What do you think, Di?'

'At least half an hour, I should think,' Diana agreed, buffing her nails unconcernedly.

'I'll take Molly outside and look after her,' Jack said. 'But I'll need your endorsement first, Tab. I can tell from the look in her eye that she thinks I'm the worst sort of cad.'

Tabitha smiled. 'Don't worry, Molly, you'll be safe with Jack. I'll arrange the cab, round up the others and we'll meet you out front, all right?'

Molly was too tired to argue further. She nodded weakly and allowed Jack to escort her out of the club.

'Do you want to sit down?' he asked when they were outside, Molly breathing in lungfuls of fresh air. 'I'm sure I can find a bench hiding somewhere in this blackout.'

'I feel like I ought to walk a bit. It'll help to clear my head.'

'Good idea.' He offered her his arm.

Molly took it, still wary despite Tabitha's reassurances but in need of some support, and allowed him to lead her through streets lit only by the dim 'starlight' blackout lighting and a waxing sickle moon.

There was the sound of a plane overhead. Jack glanced up.

'Sounds like a Whitley,' he said. 'Wonder where they're going.'

Molly started to feel a little better, the cool air soothing her temples.

'Have you not been called up yet?' she asked him.

'ENSA managed to get a deferment for me, which makes me one of the privileged few. I sometimes wonder if I ought to feel guilty about that. I'm not much of a singer, but then this isn't much of a war, is it?'

Molly glanced dizzily around the unfamiliar streets. They were already a little way from the club.

'Where are we going?' she asked.

He shrugged. 'Nowhere particular. You wanted to walk.'

'Not too far though. The girls will wonder where I am.'

'Not yet they won't. It'll be at least half an hour until your taxi arrives.' He looked up at the crescent moon, smiling slightly. 'You know, it's a long time since I was out for a moonlight walk with a girl.'

'Are you sure? Sounds to me like you've got something of a reputation as a ladies' man.'

'Honestly. I don't even know what the proper etiquette is. Am I supposed to serenade you?'

Molly smiled despite herself.

'I am curious to hear you sing,' she said.

'Ah well, in that case, I'd better save it for a future occasion. I don't want to scare you away with my caterwauling just when I'm getting to know you.'

Molly looked up at him. She couldn't see him well in the dark but he looked very relaxed, as if he did this sort of thing all the time.

'I thought you were on tour with your unit,' she said.

'I was, but it didn't last very long. Our troupe had been reduced to a five-hander as it was. When one of the girls got engaged and our comic received his call-up papers, we had to call it a day.'

'Oh. So… you're unemployed then?'

'Only temporarily. I'm just waiting for ENSA to slot me in somewhere else, then I'll be back at work.' Jack glanced down at her. 'And you, Miss Molly Clough. How did you end up here? I'd half broken my heart over the fact that I was unlikely ever to see you again. I kept asking Dennis if a Margaret Clough had been in touch, but he always told me no.'

'That's because I auditioned under a stage name.'

'Did you? What was it?'

'I'm not telling you,' she said with a smile. 'It's been consigned to the humiliating past now. It didn't suit me a bit.'

'And now you're with the Forces Follies.'

'Yes.' She sighed. 'For the time being, at any rate. I can't help feeling I've got no right to be here. Like they'll get wise to what a phoney I am and send me back to the mill.'

'Rubbish. They're lucky to have you.'

'Do you mean that?'

'Of course. Why wouldn't I?'

Molly felt embarrassed to ask, but she had to know. She took a deep breath.

'What I mean is… that night we met. You weren't just trying to flatter me when you said my singing was good enough for ENSA, were you?'

'Why would I want to do that?'

'Because… because sometimes men do that with girls. Say things they don't mean to get pally with them.'

'Ah. I see.' Jack stopped walking to look at her. 'No, Miss Clough, I wasn't just trying to flatter you.' He smiled. 'But all the same, I wish you'd let me buy you that drink.'

Molly wasn't sure if that answered her question or just raised another. Jack's gaze had drifted away from her, however. They had strayed into a rather unsavoury part of the West End, she noticed, and stood now in a dilapidated street of abandoned slum housing, half demolished. Jack was looking at one of the remaining buildings with a thoughtful expression.

'Kemble's Rookery,' he said quietly. 'I'd have thought they'd have knocked this old place down with the rest. It's certainly not fit for habitation. Mind you, it never was.'

Molly followed his gaze to the tiny, broken-down terrace house. It was a bleak, disreputable-looking place, like something out of Dickens. Her old house in Bradford might be humble, but it was a palace compared to this.

'Do you know this place?' she asked.

'You might say so. At least, I was born in it.' He seemed to be talking half to himself. 'Funny how I managed to wander down here. I haven't thought about the Rookery in years.'

Molly stared at the house, then back at Jack. 'You were born here? In that house?'

'You sound like you don't believe me.'

'No, I… it's a surprise, that's all.'

'Why should it be?'

'Well, you sound so, um… I thought you must come from a well-to-do background with an accent like yours.'

'Never judge a book by its cover, Miss Clough. Or a man by his accent.'

Molly looked again at the horrible, cramped house. It made her flesh creep to think of a little baby being born into such a dirty, unhealthy place.

And this was where Jack had come from. The night she met him, she had wondered if he had a mansion filled with butlers to wait on him. The reality seemed to be very different. Molly wondered how he had come to be singing with ENSA, and how he had ended up with an accent so mismatched with where he had sprung from. She would have bet money on the fact he was a gentleman born and bred, yet his life had begun in even more humble circumstances than her own.

Jack Forrester seemed to delight in filling her life with mystery. He was smiling now, apparently thrilled to have produced the look of puzzlement she knew she must be wearing.

'I suppose if I ask you for your story, you'll refuse to give it to me,' she said.

'It isn't refused. Let's say it's deferred. That way, Fate will have to arrange another meeting for us.'

Molly smiled. 'Is that the way Fate works?'

'Of course. The universe hates an unanswered question.' He tucked her arm through his again. 'We ought to go back to your girlfriends. Hopefully they've managed to find a taxi I can pile you into.'

# Chapter 26

Molly thought about Jack often over the weeks that followed, as she started to get used to her new life. She had been too disoriented at the time to absorb it fully, but she pondered with growing frustration his remark that Fate would bring them together again.

Honestly, she couldn't understand the man. If he wanted to see her again, why didn't he ask to do so? She'd certainly say yes, if only to get an answer to the mystery of his birth. Yet he hadn't even attempted to find out where he could reach her.

The obvious conclusion was that he was only toying with her, and there was no serious romantic interest. She was a useful person to hone his flirting skills on, that was all – otherwise he would never let her slip out of his life so easily. Molly was irritated with Jack for using her that way, and irritated with herself for caring. But still she thought about him.

Her days were now filled with rehearsals for the revue they would be taking on tour, care for the kittens around whose little furry presence life at The Larches had come to revolve, and letters to her people at home. She spent a lot of time with Pam, Fenella and Tabitha too. They played games of gin rummy in their digs, went to Cortesi's or ventured out to see exciting new films just arrived from Hollywood: films like the much-anticipated *Gone with the Wind*, starring Molly's favourite screen heart-throb Clark Gable, which to Daphne's great envy was now playing in the cinemas of the capital.

Molly avoided Diana as much as she could, however – an easy thing to do, since Diana seemed keen to remain aloof. Molly was already struggling with doubts about her abilities as a performer.

She didn't need Diana's perpetually curled lip to remind her of her inadequacies.

Molly had finally confronted her fears and managed to perform her repertoire of songs without a piano to hide behind, with Tabitha playing her accompaniment. She hadn't fainted, but she still wasn't happy with her performance. Her arms just seemed to hang limply at her sides as she sang, and she had no idea what to do with them. She trembled visibly without the piano stool to lend support. Phil wanted to present her as a personality singer, like Gracie, but it was hard to show off any aspect of her personality other than blind terror.

She could tell that Phil and Little Davy – who, as the oldest member of the troupe, tended to be looked on as an unofficial assistant manager – were less than impressed with her. Nothing had been said about sending her home yet, but Molly was sure they must be considering it. She felt her act was getting better, but her nerves, which she had prayed would improve with practice, plagued her as much as ever.

Letters from home reassured her that things were all right there, although of course she was missed. Daphne was doing well with her new calipers, and wrote that the doctor was very pleased with her progress. She was eager to hear all that Molly could tell her about life in the capital. Daphne seemed to think her sister's residence in that glamorous fairy-tale place would be nothing but rubbing shoulders with Hollywood stars and attending champagne parties until dawn. In fact, Molly tried to avoid sampling the London nightlife too often after her first experience in a club.

While letters from Daphne and Mam satisfied her that her family were well, Molly's latest letter from Rita had been filled with worries. Rita's sweetheart Harry had finally got his call-up papers and was to report for basic training with the army in a fortnight. The prospect of going to war seemed to have triggered a romantic fit in the boy, who had begged to be allowed to make an honest woman of Rita. This had left her in a double panic: both over what answer she should give and her fears for what would happen to him now he was to join the forces.

It was this war malarkey that was making people so impulsive in matters of the heart, Molly supposed. A copy of *The Times* belonging to Diana was lying on the coffee table in the living room at The Larches, where Molly was sipping her morning tea. She picked it up and glanced at the front page, which carried a report of the latest debate in parliament over the prime minister's handling of the Norway invasion.

Molly didn't fully understand everything that was happening on the world stage. She didn't have Diana's head for politics, but she could tell that things were hotting up. Suddenly the Phoney War didn't seem nearly so phoney, with Norway and Denmark – countries that felt so much closer to home than either Poland or Czechoslovakia – now occupied. Those people who had talked confidently about an end to the war this year, perhaps even before autumn was upon them, had fallen silent now. Chamberlain's approval was at an all-time low as he struggled to regain the upper hand.

Everything felt so insecure and frightening, no one knowing what tomorrow might hold or what Hitler's next move was going to be, and always Molly's thoughts were with the one soldier in whose fate she was most invested: her brother Ted. She could well understand why Harry wanted to be sure of his girl before marching into danger, and why Rita was so afraid for him.

'Away with the fairies?'

Molly looked up from the newspaper to discover that Tabitha had come in with Diana.

'Sorry, Tabby,' she said, running a palm over her brow. 'I was just... thinking, I suppose. About the war.'

Tabitha glanced at the photograph of Neville Chamberlain on the front page as Molly put the newspaper down.

'He looks like such a frail old man, doesn't he?' she said softly. 'It must take its toll, leading a country in wartime. You have to feel sorry for him.'

'No you don't,' Diana said, with unusual vehemence. 'This is all his fault, with his appeasement nonsense. If he'd only been willing to see the writing on the wall when it came to Nazism, as Churchill and Duff Cooper could, all this could've been prevented. It was only for Chamberlain refusing to act earlier that Hitler was able to grow as strong as he has. If we'd taken action after he remilitarised the Rheinland, this war would never have happened.'

'Well, you're right, I suppose. Still, hindsight's a fine thing, Di. Chamberlain couldn't see the future.'

'He could if he'd gone to the trouble of looking for it,' Diana said darkly. 'It was all in that tedious bally book – Hitler's book, the one he wrote in prison. The man wrote down every wicked thing he believed, and exactly what he was planning to do as well. Trust me, I'm one of the few people who actually read the horrible thing. And would they take him seriously? No.' She wrinkled her nose at the photo of the prime minister. 'I haven't got a lick of pity for Chamberlain. He was responsible for this country and he failed it. He ought to have known better.'

Molly might struggle to like Diana, a feeling she was sure was mutual, yet she had a great respect for the woman's intelligence and breadth of knowledge – particularly when it came to political matters. Diana's eyes were sparkling with anger now as she scowled at the photograph of the prime minister.

'Do you think he'll last much longer?' Molly asked her.

Di shrugged. 'I doubt it. Still, nothing's ever certain in wartime. It all depends on Hitler's next move.'

'What do you think that will be?' Molly asked. 'You said the answers were in his book.'

Diana didn't reply. She only looked worried, and cast a fearful glance at the newspaper.

'All right, girls, that's enough politics,' Tabitha said firmly. 'We've got a transport coming to collect our things from Drury Lane at midday. Molly, are you packed?'

Molly rubbed her head, as if to clear it of worry about the war so she could redirect her worrying to what was directly ahead of her: their departure on tour that afternoon.

'Yes,' she said. 'I've got a case with my clothes and things, and essentials in my small bag like you told me.'

'Costume?'

'Phil was going to pick out a dress for me from ENSA stores. Are Pam and Ella ready?'

'Ella is.' Tabitha smiled. 'Pam's saying goodbye to her cats — sobbing her eyes out, the poor love. I think we might have trouble dragging her away.'

—

In the end, it was only through reminding Pam of Angelo's promise to visit the cats at least twice a week that they were able to persuade her to leave. She left a long letter for the ENSA members who would be occupying the house while they were away, telling them what each kitten was named, their favourite spots to be tickled, what they liked to listen to on the wireless and what Millicent's preferred treats were.

At nearly four weeks old, Millicent's babies had grown into mewling, precious bundles of fur, their baby-blue eyes open now as they began to play together and tottered around on legs still getting used to walking. That morning, the ginger and white kitten that Pam had named Marie — who as the runt of the litter tended to lag behind her siblings — had taken her first wobbly steps. This had made Pam sob all the more, devastated at missing the opportunity to watch them grow up. By the time the troupe returned to London in six weeks, the kittens would be independent beasts ready to go to new homes.

'I do wish we could keep one,' Pam said as they arrived at Drury Lane. 'Millicent will grieve so when they're taken away.'

'It isn't very fair to keep pets when we're on tour so much, cherie,' Di said, giving Pam a squeeze. Molly had noted a protective, sisterly quality in Diana when it came to Pam that rather surprised her. She wouldn't have believed the woman was capable of tenderness like that. Unfortunately this only extended to Pam as the baby of the troupe, not to the rest of them.

Pam sighed. 'I know. And Angelo has persuaded his father to take Marie as a mouser for the restaurant, so that's something. It means we can still see her whenever we go to Cortesi's.' She smiled softly. 'He's a terrible flirt but he's a sweet boy, and ever so kind. I promised I'd give him a tinkle whenever we're near a phone so he can tell me how my little puss-cats are getting along.'

Molly was sure Angelo would have leapt at the chance to have a reason to stay in touch while Pam was away. She had been to Cortesi's enough times now to see that he was at least as smitten with Pam as she was with him, although for a confident lad, he seemed shy of confessing it. If they weren't about to go on tour, Molly might have tried to cook up a plan with Fenella that would bring the two aching hearts together.

They found Phil, Nobby and Little Davy in the foyer of the Theatre Royal, surrounded by trunks filled with props, costumes, backcloths and various other things they needed to take with them.

'Just leave your cases with the rest, loves,' Phil said. 'There'll be an army truck along for them shortly. Meanwhile, a couple of cars will drive us to the station. Someone from ENSA will be waiting there with our orders.'

'Where are we going?' Molly asked. They hadn't been told anything about where they might be performing – whether it would be army barracks, aerodromes, garrison theatres or some other venue – or even where in the country.

'We'll find out soon enough,' Little Davy said. 'ENSA don't like civvies knowing too much about where the Army's keeping its troops, in case one of us is slipping information to Fritzy. They always keep it under their hats until the last minute. It'll all be in the orders.'

The two cars turned up shortly afterwards. ENSA drivers took them to King's Cross station, leaving behind cases and props to be driven separately.

Molly sat in the back of one car beside Fenella, with Phil on Fenella's other side. He leaned over to smile at her.

'Got something for you, Moll,' he said.

'What is it?'

'This. I kept one out when Davy and I were packing the trunks.'

He took a piece of paper from his pocket and handed it to her.

'Oh!' Molly said when she unfolded it. It was a playbill promoting their show.

ENSA PRESENTS

The Forces Follies Concert Party in a hilarious new revue

'Keep Smiling Through'

Laughs! Girls! Novelties! And even more laughs!

With

**MADAME CHASTAIN**

Ballet beauty of Sadler's Wells

**PAMELA SHERIDAN**

Of the famous Sensational Sheridans

**A MOONLIGHT SERENADE**

Songs for lovers and dreamers

**DOLORES DE DIAMOND**

Celebrated female impressionist

**'LITTLE DAVY' and his partner FENELLA**

Light comedy and amusing impersonations

And introducing a new discovery from Yorkshire

**MOLLY CLOUGH**

Personality songstress to sing along with

Molly stared at it for some time, blinking in case her name disappeared again. It might not be quite up in lights, but it was printed on a real playbill and that was almost as good.

'Can I keep this?' she asked Phil.

'Of course, I saved it for you. Thought you'd get a kick out of it.'

'Nothing like seeing your name in print for the first time, is there?' Fenella said with a smile.

'I can't wait to send it home for my mam and sister.' Molly laughed. 'Wines and spirits though. Right at the very bottom.'

'Hardly. You're "a new discovery". That cancels out being bottom of the bill.' Fenella pointed to her own billing. 'I haven't even got my full name on there, look. I just get tacked on as Davy's stooge.' She lit a cigarette. 'Doesn't bother me, long as I'm getting paid. I get more annoyed at Pammy being billed under Di despite being a million times more talented.'

Phil gave her a stern look, and Fenella rolled her eyes.

'All right, I won't start a row,' she said. 'You know I'm right though, Phil, even if you're not allowed to say it.'

Phil looked at the playbill with pride. 'It's a good line-up – best we've had yet. Four girls to get them filling the seats, or five if they don't read the small print about Dolores. I've got high hopes for this tour, ladies.'

'What's this moonlight serenade business?' Fenella asked. 'Don't tell me you're actually going to sing for us?'

Phil grimaced. 'No, it was Tabby who insisted on it. She was convinced we'd be able to find ourselves a male crooner to bring us back up to a seven-hander, so we put some suitably vague wording on the bills. Not sure what we can do except send Nobby on in his civvies to do a quick Al Bowlly number.'

'He won't like that. He says it ruins the gag if the audience sees him out of costume.'

'Well, needs must when the devil drives.'

Molly wasn't really listening. She was still gazing at her name. It was certainly something to be proud of, but the words around her name – 'new discovery', 'personality songstress' – sounded like they were about someone else. Always there was the feeling that she was an impostor. A phoney.

Nevertheless, nerves aside, she did feel she had improved since rehearsing with the troupe. She felt more confident in how she looked as well. The bruises from the looms had faded, her calloused hands were beginning to regain their softness, and thanks to Angelo's grandmother's cooking, she had started to fill out in all the places she had been accustomed to envy Rita her appealing plumpness. Her act was better too. Phil had had the inspired idea of giving her a signature song that would play into the personality she was trying to project: the old favourite 'My Girl's a Yorkshire Girl'. Molly had never performed this for an audience, but she had been warbling it for her own amuse-ment since childhood. It was also Phil who had suggested more community singing, getting the boys to join in with their favour-ites. This, he said, would help the show end on a cheerful note. He didn't say so, but Molly could tell he was trying to think of ways to help with her nerves too.

It worked to some extent. It certainly bolstered her confidence when the girls joined in during rehearsals, just as it used to do in the pub. But her big worry was – what if the troops *didn't* join in? If they had been forcefully marched to the concert by an over-zealous sergeant major and told to look like they were enjoying themselves *or else*, that would be unlikely to put them in a festive mood. And if they were actually ordered to join in… she couldn't imagine anything worse than trying to entertain a bunch of grumpy soldiers who'd been told it was either singing along to Gracie Fields numbers or three weeks' latrine duty.

It had started to dawn on Molly as well that this was important, in its small way. She hadn't thought about it much before. She had only thought that ENSA could be her doorway into the world of variety, and that the salary would enable her to take care of her family. Over the past four weeks, however, she had heard numerous stories from the other women about ENSA concerts they had played that had made her think more deeply about exactly what the organisation had been set up to do.

Tabby had played a show at a remote aerodrome in the Outer Hebrides, where the men had been so starved for entertainment that they had practically wept for joy when ENSA arrived. The revue the troupe had been doing hadn't been anything amazing, she told Molly, but they had got a standing ovation from their grateful audience all the same. The airmen had seemed so young that Tabby said she'd wanted to hug every one of them on behalf of their mothers far away. And Fenella had told of a small field hospital they had visited in France – how one young soldier, injured during a training exercise, sobbed to hear news of home and begged them to take a letter back to his sister. Fenella said that after seeing the men in the hospital, she had sworn never to complain about a cold billet or poor-quality rations on tour again.

Perhaps troops did joke about ENSA, like they joked about a lot of things, because that's what people do when they're afraid. Perhaps they cared more about a shapely figure than they did about the quality of talent on offer. But it still *meant* something to them. They were tired and frightened and far from home, many of them for the first time in their young lives, and here was something that – for just a few hours – could distract them from how that felt. Remind them of their civilian lives, and what the world had been like when it was normal.

Molly understood. She was often afraid herself in these uncertain days, and she knew what it was to be homesick and missing loved ones. She did want to do her best for the men, but the idea that they were relying on her to bring them relief from fears she could hardly imagine couldn't help but set her ever-active nerves jangling. Perhaps it was 'only ENSA', as her fellow performers would often say, but to her, entertaining the troops felt like an awesome responsibility.

## Chapter 27

When they arrived at King's Cross, Phil glanced around for their ENSA contact, who was supposed to meet them there. There was plenty of khaki, but Molly couldn't see anyone with the shoulder tabs that marked them out as belonging to the organisation.

'Probably waiting for us on the platform,' Davy suggested.

'We don't know which platform to go to,' Phil pointed out. 'Not without the orders.'

'Ticket office then. Come on.'

Davy led the way into the station, the others following.

'I really don't see why they couldn't arrange for cars to take us all the way,' Diana observed with a sniff. 'They can manage a vehicle for the equipment. Why not for us? We're supposed to be the talent.'

'ENSA aren't made of money, Di,' Tabitha said. 'Petrol isn't cheap these days, you know. Suppose we're performing in John O' Groats?'

Diana shuddered. 'Oh darling, don't. Anything but the Highlands again. I was freezing to death in that damn dress the last time. And the men always look so… hungry in those remote places. I swear I was half afraid they'd rush the stage and devour me.'

'You'll be used to that sort of thing though, won't you, Di?' Fenella said brightly. Diana shot her a look.

'I hope it's France,' Pam said. 'I wasn't with the troupe when they were posted overseas before.'

'Might it be France?' Molly asked her.

Pam shrugged. 'Who knows? If the orders say Dover, it certainly could be.'

'What happens when we get to our station at the other end?'

'There's supposed to be someone to meet us,' Pam told her. 'Either the welfare officer for wherever we're performing or a local ENSA organiser. They'll take us to where we're billeted and arrange for transport to the venue. Mind you, it isn't always as smooth as that.' She gave a dry smile. 'Communication isn't ENSA's strong point.'

'So we play one show there and then move on?'

'Two, usually, unless it's a very small barracks. Then we have to go through the whole rigmarole again for the next destination. They really don't like telling us where we're going.'

Phil was squinting through his half-moon spectacles at a dark-haired man standing under the clock, in the unadorned khaki of an ENSA uniform. 'There's our chap, I think.'

'That's right,' Tabitha said, smiling. 'And a surprise too.'

'Oh Lord,' Molly muttered.

'What?' Pam said.

'It's him. Jack Forrester.'

Pam looked more closely at the man. 'So it is. I didn't think ENSA made a habit of using him as an errand boy.' She glanced at Molly. 'Is everything all right, love?'

'Yes.' Molly felt warmth creep into her cheeks and tried to smile unconcernedly. 'Just a little overheated. If I'd known it was going to be such a warm day, I wouldn't have worn my coat.'

Jack smiled at them as they approached. Or not at *them*. At Molly. His first words were to her as well.

'See?' he said. 'Fate. Told you, didn't I?'

Tabitha shook her head. 'What on earth are you jawing about, Jack?'

'Just a little joke.' He handed Phil an envelope from his ENSA blouse. 'Here you are. Not to be opened until you're on your train.'

'Not this business again,' Davy said with a groan. 'It was bad enough last time, when they ordered us to go to Lincolnshire without telling us where in ruddy Lincolnshire.'

'We can't open the orders on our train if we don't know what train to catch,' Phil said impatiently to Jack. 'What am I supposed to do, ask the man in the ticket office for eight tickets to the back of beyond, nor'-nor'-east of the middle of nowhere?'

'Nine tickets,' Jack said.

'What do you mean, nine tickets?'

'I'm coming too. Didn't Tabby tell you?'

'I was saving you as a surprise,' Tabitha said with a smile. She turned to the others. 'Everyone, meet Mr Moonlight Serenade. Didn't I tell you I could get us a crooner before the tour? Don't worry, Phil, I already notified the billeting officer we'd have one more to squeeze in with the boys.'

Phil blinked. 'Jack's coming with us?'

'He is, and a devil of a job I had persuading him as well.'

Molly was staring at Jack, who was smirking in a way that seemed intended solely for her. Had he known he'd be joining the troupe when they had seen each other at the nightclub? He had joked about moonlight serenades too, that night…

Oh, the man was infuriating! Why could he never just say what he meant? Why did he delight in dangling mysteries before her? Molly turned so she was no longer in his line of sight, doing her best to look aloof.

He would be on tour with them though. That would mean a whole six weeks in close proximity. Molly didn't know if she was more excited or fearful about the prospect. And Tabitha would be there as well – his old flame. Or perhaps not such an old flame, if they had been secretly meeting to discuss him joining the Follies…

'So what about these orders then?' Nobby asked. 'We can't just hop on a train and hope it goes to where we need to be, can we?'

Davy looked at Jack. 'What is this cobblers about not opening them until we're on a train?' he demanded. 'We've had some absurd instructions in the past, but we've never had that before.'

Jack shrugged. 'Don't blame me, I'm only the messenger. I suppose with things starting to look hairy on the continent, they've decided to bring in extra security.'

'Well their extra security is going to make it impossible for us to do our jobs,' Phil snapped. 'I've a good mind to telephone Basil Dean now and demand to know what he's playing at.'

'To hell with Basil Dean. I say we open them,' Diana said decisively. 'Honestly, ENSA's becoming quite ridiculous. If we're fifth columnists, we're going to be just as much fifth columnists on a train as off it.'

'I suppose they think if we open them now, we might run to the nearest telephone and place a call to the Führer,' Fenella said. 'Has anyone got his number? If he can meet us at the venue, perhaps he'll do a turn impersonating Chaplin.'

Molly was sure Diana almost smiled at this, but she managed to restrain herself.

'We could get into bother if we open them before we're supposed to,' Phil said doubtfully.

'What else are we supposed to do?' Tabitha took them from him. 'Here, I'll do it. Then you can tell Basil Dean it was my fault.'

Jack took them from Tabitha. 'I'll do it. I've been too useful to ENSA for them to court-martial me.'

He tore open the envelope and took out the paper inside. Molly felt herself flinch. She was too accustomed to obeying the rules to feel comfortable with this act of rebellion. With all this talk of fifth columnists, opening their orders before they were supposed to felt tantamount to treason.

'Right,' Jack said when he'd read them through. 'It's Bognor. Army barracks on the coast. Their welfare officer's going to meet us from the train.'

Diana rolled her eyes. 'Bognor. Oh, the glamour of it.'

'Keep your voice down, for God's sake,' Phil muttered to Jack. 'We really will be for it if ENSA get wind that you've been standing in the middle of packed railway stations, shouting out troop locations to anyone who might be interested. I'll fetch the tickets.'

'I'll come with you,' Nobby said. 'Want to buy a paper before we set off.'

When they were gone, Little Davy cleared his throat import-antly, drawing himself up to his full height – all five foot one of it.

'Right then, girls,' he said. 'Army barracks. You know what that means.'

Fenella rolled her eyes. 'I imagine it means you're going to give us your usual tedious lecture about behaving like nuns for the whole time we're there.'

Davy glared at her. 'It means you're going to be in company with a lot of young lads who miss the women they left behind – whether that's mums, sisters, wives or sweethearts. Some of 'em might want you to mother them, but there's a lot more who'll want you to do something else. You know what I mean?'

'I don't,' Fenella said innocently. 'Can you explain please, Davy? With drawings, ideally?'

Diana actually did smile this time, and Molly had to stifle a snort as well.

'Just behave yourself, that's all,' Davy told her sternly. 'As ENSA girls, you're there to do more than just entertain them. In the NAAFI after, you'll be expected to chat, be friendly, cheer them up – and *that's all*. Don't lead them on, don't engage in any loose behaviour, and if anyone starts getting a bit too friendly, come and tell one of us men and we'll sort it out.'

Molly tried not to catch Jack's eye during this sermon on sexual temperance. She knew she'd blush if she did, and then he'd grin and look pleased with himself. Why did Davy have to give his lectures when Jack was here?

'And never forget that this matters to the war effort, just as much as what those girls who are nurses or WAAFs are doing,' Davy went on. 'Made a hell of a difference to me when I was a young lad in a field hospital in France, wondering if I'd ever make it home again. It felt like a bit of colour and hope to see a Pierrot troupe or Lena Ashwell concert, at a time when there was precious little colour or hope to be had. You're doing your bit, girls, and you should be proud of that.' He eyed them sternly. 'Just be sure not to do too much of it.'

'We've heard all this,' Fenella said.

'Well, not all of you have toured before,' he said, glancing at Molly. 'Just remember that you're there to give those poor boys a taste of home – a reminder of what they're fighting for. And remember that for some of 'em, it might be the last taste of home they ever get.'

'They're not on the front line yet, Davy,' Diana said. 'It's Bognor, not the Somme.'

Davy flinched at this. Fenella shot Diana a look, and went to slip her arm through his.

'All right, Davy, we won't forget,' she said, in a softer voice than before. 'I know we tease, but we do understand it's important – cheering up the boys. Thanks for reminding us.'

Phil and Nobby had returned with the tickets, and Tabitha clucked at them as she ushered everyone to the appropriate platform. Jack fell into step with Molly.

'Not brimming with tact, is she, your friend?' he said in a low voice, nodding to Diana.

'She's not my friend.' Molly looked at him. 'In fact, I'd say you know her better than I do. You've certainly seen a lot more of her.'

He looked thoughtful. 'Yes, I suppose I have. You're quite new still, aren't you? Strange how it feels like you belong here.'

If he was embarrassed about the way he had discovered Diana, he didn't show it. Well, Molly wasn't going to drop any more hints for him.

'So, are you reformed of your immoral ways after that little talk?' he asked, smiling.

Molly ignored this question.

'You knew, didn't you?' she said. 'That night in the club. You knew you'd be joining us and never said a word.'

'I didn't know then that I was going to join. That's why I was meeting Tabitha. I thought it might be jolly to let her try to talk me into it.'

'Well, you knew you might do, at least.'

'Actually, I'd pretty much made up my mind not to. I had an offer from another troupe with a couple of well-known names in their ranks that could have got me into some big venues.'

'So what changed your mind?'

He shot her a half-smile. 'You did.'

'Me?'

'I said Fate would make sure we crossed paths again, didn't I? I didn't think it was cheating to give her a little nudge, when she'd been helpful enough to bring us together twice before.' He grinned at her expression. 'Oh, don't be cross. We're colleagues now. That must make us friends too.'

Molly found herself smiling, although she was trying hard not to.

She wasn't sure how to feel about the fact that Jack would be joining their tour. On the one hand, she couldn't deny that she enjoyed his company. He was always so relaxed, in a way that rubbed off on her anxious little soul and made her feel at ease too. She liked the way he flirted with her in that entertaining, easy way, although she knew her mother wouldn't approve. Given everything she knew about the man, she probably shouldn't approve either. She simply couldn't help it.

Still, she couldn't take him seriously as someone keen for her favours. Not when he had already walked out with Tabitha, who was five times prettier and a dozen times more confident than Molly could ever hope to be, and especially not if he had really seen Diana in the altogether. Molly had fears enough for her first tour without adding worries about Jack Forrester's intentions towards her to the list. She vowed to enjoy his company sparingly, and not allow him to get her alone until she knew him better – although she was still keen to uncover the mystery of his birth.

They had arrived at their platform now. Molly noticed that Phil was watching her and Jack curiously. She wondered if he had been listening to their conversation. She couldn't remember exactly what they had said but she was sure it must have sounded like foolish nonsense, and flushed at the idea that Phil would think she had been allowing Jack to make love to her.

'Is everything all right?' she asked Phil when he didn't withdraw his gaze.

'Yes.' He glanced thoughtfully from her to Jack. 'The pair of you reminded me of something, that's all.'

## Chapter 28

ENSA's communication failures were again in evidence when the troupe reached Bognor Regis. There was no army welfare officer on the platform to escort them to wherever they were to sleep that night.

'I hope they haven't forgotten to arrange billets again,' Diana groaned.

'Forgotten our billets?' Molly said, blinking. 'Does that happen a lot?'

'More frequently than it should, certainly,' Tabitha said. 'We've had to borrow tents from the soldiers and make camp in a field before, when there wasn't a room to be found anywhere else.'

Molly felt a shiver of excitement. She had been a Girl Guide, and had loved learning how to make camp, build a fire and other outdoor skills. She was sure she could still pitch a tent. It was the 7th of May and not exactly summer weather yet, but Molly found herself half-wishing the billeting officer at ENSA had blundered so she could experience the thrill of camping.

There was a certain elation, too, that went with the smell in the air: a sharp sea breeze, tangy with salt and fish. Seagulls called raucously overhead. It reminded Molly of coach trips to Blackpool during Bradford's annual Bowling Tide week, when the mills would close and a carnival spirit would take over her home city. Perhaps their troupe might even camp on the beach, if there was no billet for them. There was nowhere like a beach for feeling free.

Molly looked at Diana, tall and regal in an elegant white fur stole she seemed determined to show off despite the warm spring day. It was hard to imagine her bedding down in a tent.

'What do we do then?' Molly asked, glancing around the station platform as it emptied. 'We can't wander the streets demanding to know where the army barracks are. Then they really will have us locked up.'

'I'll ask to use the telephone in the ticket office,' Phil said. 'I can ring HQ and ask where we're billeted, then we'll make our own way there. I only hope our props and things have arrived safely. It always makes me nervous when they travel separately.'

Phil made the call and wrote down directions to where they were staying, then they followed him out of the station. To Molly's disappointment, billets had in fact been arranged and she had to abandon her dream of a night under canvas.

She wondered if Jack would walk with her again. Girls and boys had separated into different compartments on the train, so she hadn't been near him for the journey. He wasn't given the chance to do so, however, as Pam and Fenella claimed one of her arms each. Molly smiled as she fell into step between them.

She was still homesick, but there would be another sort of sickness if Phil did decide to send her back to Bradford. Molly had grown increasingly fond of her new friends here. They felt like a sort of sisterhood, and she would miss them enormously if her time with the troupe was cut short.

'Watch him, Moll,' Fenella murmured, nodding to Jack walking with the other men. 'He's got his eye on you.'

Molly flushed. 'Don't talk daft.'

'Why shouldn't he have? You're not entirely gruesome, you know.'

'What she means, my dear Molly, is that you're beautiful and any man with red blood in his veins knows it,' Pam said.

Fenella grinned. 'Well I didn't want her to get a big head, did I?'

'I thought you said he was walking out with Tabby,' Molly said.

'That's ancient history, my pet.' Fenella looked at Jack thoughtfully. 'I wonder if he's planning to work his way through the lot of us. I wouldn't have minded being next. Still, by all means take your turn first.'

Pam shook her head, smiling. 'Ignore her jokes. Jack isn't one of those men. Tabby said he was always the perfect gentleman with her.'

'Definitely not my type then,' Fenella said. '"Perfect gentleman" is just code for "colossal bore" in my experience.'

'So, um, how many nights will we stay here for?' Molly asked, feeling a change of subject would be very welcome.

'It depends how big of an army camp it is,' Fenella said. 'We'll do one show tonight and possibly two more tomorrow if there are a lot of men, then if there are no other venues nearby, we'll be on the move again.'

—

The girls discovered they had rather a nice billet. The Follies men had been given rooms in a guest house requisitioned by the army, but the women were staying in a private home occupied by an officer and his family, right on the seafront. All ENSA members were civilians but for billeting purposes they were given officer status, so they could make use of facilities reserved for the commissioned ranks.

Captain and Mrs Chambers' children – two little girls – were fascinated by the entertainers sharing their home, following the women around with wide-eyed wonder. It made Molly feel like quite a star. Pam, predictably, doted on human children just as much as cat ones, and entertained the girls with magic tricks and acrobatic feats until they begged her never to go away.

It was quite a small barracks they were to perform at, they were told – an infantry training camp that accommodated five hundred men. The Forces Follies had been granted the use of the large hut used for physical training, and would put on one show that evening for half the men and another tomorrow for the other half. The day after that, they would move on to their next mysterious destination.

It was around 1 p.m. when they arrived at their billet, so there was time for a walk along the pier before they began getting ready.

Spending time on the coast was a treat for Molly, even if the beach felt rather lacking in holiday atmosphere. The seaside in wartime was very different from the place it was in peace: eerily quiet, and a little bleak. There were no tourists in deckchairs now, no donkeys, no candy-floss-sellers, and coils of barbed wire ornamented every slipway. The only other people on the beach were soldiers carrying out training exercises. But it was a new town to her, a town by the sea, and Molly regarded everything with high delight.

The captain's wife, Mrs Chambers, was so grateful for the way Pam had entertained her little girls that she insisted on buying them all fish and chips instead of cooking up the uninspiring tinned rations they had brought with them. This was another big treat for Molly. By teatime, however, her old friend Mr Stage Fright had started to make his presence felt and she only felt able to pick at her food.

She had been trying to avoid thinking about it, but tonight was the night she would really, truly earn her stripes as a performer. Tonight, for the first time, she would be a professional: standing in front of two hundred and fifty men, trying her best to be a 'personality songstress'.

A million and one frightening thoughts fought for dominance. What if the men didn't join in with the songs, or worse, actually jeered? What if her panic overcame her and her jelly-like legs gave way on stage? What if she threw up? There were so many things that could go wrong.

Molly wasn't sure if it was better or worse to be performing last. On the one hand, it meant the men would have been nicely warmed up beforehand. There were comedy sketches between acts, mostly involving Davy and Fenella with one or more of the other performers, so there was plenty to get them laughing. It also meant that if Molly's spot seemed to be going badly, she could run away and let Davy end the show.

On the other hand, performing after her significantly more talented colleagues would surely emphasise her inadequacies to the watching men. It would certainly make Molly more aware of them, and consequently a hundred times more nervous.

Oh Lord, two hundred and fifty men! She had never played to an audience of more than a couple of dozen before.

Still, at least after tonight, it would be done. She would have performed her first show as a professional entertainer. What would tomorrow's Molly look like? It felt as though she would be a different person from the one she was now.

The minutes dragged like hours between arriving in Bognor and being picked up by the army truck that was to take them to the show, and yet in some ways time seemed to fly by. In no time at all the truck was pulling up outside their billet, with just an hour to go until the show.

Molly was glad, as she climbed in after Pam, that she hadn't been able to eat much of her fish and chips. That only meant more chance of them coming back up. It also meant that Fenella, who could eat for England, had had nearly a double helping. She was beaming with a well-fed, cat-like contentment as she climbed into the truck behind Molly.

Molly shot her an envious glance. Fenella was certainly never bothered by stage fright, or by anything much. It didn't seem fair.

'The boys walked over earlier to set everything up,' Tabby told them. 'We should have half an hour to prepare before the soldiers are shown in.'

Molly clung to the canvas sides of the truck as it juddered along the roads of Bognor, and then over a rough track towards the camp. She felt ill at ease in the costume Phil had found for her: a black dress with broad lace collar, paired with a pale blue sash, a string of pearls and silver high-heeled shoes that left her very wobbly on her feet. All the ENSA costumes seemed to be old-fashioned and past their best, presumably donated by theatres and concert parties from old stock, and Molly felt sure that hers didn't suit her. It seemed mismatched, with the silver shoes, sash and pearls suggesting glamour while the dress was in a matronly style that belonged to someone much older than Molly was.

There had been a fur stole too, but Molly had drawn the line at that. It would be far too hot to wear on stage, and she already tended to flush from nerves. Add the stole and she would look like an over-dressed tomato.

In the PT hut where they were to perform, they found their four men hard at work preparing the stage. This was a makeshift affair, constructed of trestles with planks laid over them. A very small piano sat to one side: a battered old thing scarred by cigarette burns, which Molly guessed was a loan from the men's NAAFI canteen. There was a microphone on a stand at the front.

Molly shuddered when she saw the benches arranged in rows. So many of them, just waiting to be filled by men…

'I hope they let their soldiers drink beer,' she whispered to Fenella. 'I'm relying on them being at least a little tiddly by the time I have to go on.'

'Relax, darling,' Fenella said, giving her hand a squeeze. 'If you can tame those pesky nerves, you'll blow them away. We'll all be there, cheering you on from the wings.' She nodded to the 'wings': two curtains of blackout material suspended from rails at each side of the makeshift stage.

'Yes.' Molly took a deep breath, trying to conquer the sick feeling in her belly. 'Ta, Ella.'

'Speaking of getting tiddly, here, have a bit of this.' Fenella produced a small bottle from her bag. 'ENSA spirit rations – rum, I think. Tabby made me custodian of it, which I must say was mighty trusting of her.'

Molly eyed it warily. 'I'm not sure that's going to help. It'll just give me a headache, like the wine.'

'A little tot won't hurt. It'll get your courage up.' Fenella demonstrated this by unscrewing the cap and taking a swig, then gave a genteel hiccup behind her hand. 'See? I feel braver already.'

Molly smiled and took the bottle from her. 'Well, a tiny mouthful then. It can't make me feel any worse, I suppose.' She swallowed a little and coughed, then handed it back. 'Shame ENSA don't issue us with a hogshead of the stuff so we could get the audience tight as well.'

'Share it with that lot? You must be joking. This is all for us.' Ella took another mouthful before putting the lid back on. 'I'd better make sure the rest get their share or I'll be in bother. A quick swig of something before a show is a Forces Follies tradition.' She left to offer the rest of the party a drink.

The alcohol did help a little. It produced a pleasant, fuzzy numbness that for a few moments almost made Molly feel ready to face the crowd of men. She felt sure it would have worn off by the time she was due to perform, however, and she didn't dare have more. It might make her slur, or worse, forget her words. She wasn't used to spirits like the others were.

Jack, in tails and black tie, was hanging the backdrop for Diana's number. He leaned back on his stepladder to admire his handiwork. 'And like that, this humble army hut becomes a Garden of Delights.'

'Are you coming down for a drink?' Fenella called up. 'I'd claim your share before Davy and Diana get their hands on the bottle if I were you. It never seems to last long after that.'

'You lot have mine,' Jack said, climbing down. 'I can't drink and croon. It gives me a frog in the throat.'

Molly had been too preoccupied to think about it – in fact, she was still reeling from the unexpected arrival of Jack in the tour party at all – but of course she would get to hear him sing tonight, wouldn't she? She had been curious about this ever since she had first met him.

What sort of crooner was he, she wondered? A Crosby? A Buchanan? A Bowlly? He seemed too young to summon the urbane suavity of those singers, all a good ten or even twenty years older than Jack. His charm was of a different sort – fresher and less worldly.

Phil approached and patted her on the back.

'Well, did the rum help?' he asked.

'A little, but I don't think it'll last until I'm on,' Molly said.

She turned to face him. He was smiling kindly, with perhaps a little pity for her obvious nerves mixed in, but not in a way she was offended by. Molly had come to like Phil a lot in the time she had been working with him. He had placed himself in the role of mentor, and made several excellent suggestions on both how she could improve her act and ways to conquer her nerves. If he did decide to send her home, she wouldn't hold it against him. He had tried so hard to help her.

'Phil, look,' she said. 'I just wanted to say… thanks. I mean, thanks for trying to help me get better. And I'm sorry, really.'

'What for?'

'For not *being* better. And if you did decide I wasn't good enough, then…'

Phil took her arm and led her a little way from the others.

'Moll, why do you think I spoke up for you after your audition?' he asked. 'Tabby told me you heard us. Did you think I was trying to do you a favour?'

'Well, no,' Molly said, blinking. 'I suppose I thought you were just being kind.'

'For what reason? I didn't know you from Eve's aunt, did I?'

'Because… you felt sorry for me?'

'Darling, I'm the manager of an entertainment troupe. If I'd taken on every girl I felt sorry for since the start of this war, I'd have a party the size of the British Army. I care about one thing and one thing only: making this troupe the best it can be so we can put on a good show for the boys.'

'Then why pick me? Because you didn't have any other options?'

'There are always options. I've got a skilled bunch of kids here. I'd rather put Pam or Nobby on for a second spot than fill the programme up with charity cases.' He looked earnestly into her eyes. 'You're here because I could see that under the shakes and the self-doubt was some first-rate talent struggling to get out. I still believe that. You need to conquer those nerves, that's all.'

'I'll try not to let you down,' was all Molly could think to say.

She looked at Phil curiously. He always carried the air of someone older than he was, although she supposed he was no more than twenty-seven. Partly it was in the way he dressed, rather like a professor at a university, and partly it was in his general demeanour. But his face was youthful – even good-looking in a pale sort of way – with soulful green eyes peeping from behind his spectacles.

'Phil?' Molly said as he prepared to leave her.

'Hmm?'

'Why don't you perform for us any more?'

He paused for a moment before turning back. 'Someone's been gossiping.'

'Not really. I heard Diana ask you about singing and I was curious, so I asked the other girls about it. They said you used to sing as part of a duo, but you won't go on stage now. I just wondered why.'

Phil remained silent, frowning, and Molly flushed.

'Sorry,' she said. 'It's really none of my business. It's just, you play the piano as well as anyone I've ever heard, and the girls said you've got some singing voice.'

Phil's frown lifted, and he sighed.

'Molly, have you seen a comedy picture called *Elephants Never Forget*?' he asked.

Molly blinked, wondering what this had to do with anything.

'Er, no,' she said.

'Oliver Hardy's in it. Just Hardy, no Laurel. And when you watch it, it's got lots in it that's pretty funny, but all the time you can't help thinking, "That's not right. That doesn't work." Because some double acts are just meant to be double acts, you know?'

'I suppose they are.'

'That's the way it was for me and Pete. We sang comic stuff mostly, from both sides of the Atlantic – Durante, Hope, Flanagan and Allen – and we wrote our own songs too. But after Pete went to the RAF, I found I didn't have the heart to make people laugh any more. I couldn't make them laugh on my own, and I couldn't stomach the idea of making them laugh with anyone else.' He shrugged. 'So I just… stopped.'

'I can understand that,' Molly said. 'It seems a shame though. I mean to waste all that talent just because your partner got called up.'

'He didn't get called up, he joined up of his own accord. Anyhow, it's more than that.' Phil paused. 'You remember the first time you performed without your piano, you told me you felt exposed on stage without it? Almost naked? That's how I feel if I try to perform without Pete. Like there's a part of me missing up there, and everyone in the audience must be able to see it.'

'But I did go on without the piano. It made me nervous as heck, but I did it.'

'Yes. Because even though you don't realise it yet, Molly Clough, you're a far, far braver person than I am.' He looked at the stage, set for Diana's performance with the garden backdrop and a couple of dusty cloth plants, and clapped Molly on the back. 'Break a leg tonight, kitten. Just remember we all believe in you.'

Half an hour later, the troupe waited in the wings as they listened to soldiers pour in. The men sounded rather raucous, but not belligerent or hostile as Molly had feared. She could hear them chattering excitedly while they found their seats, and there were a few wolf whistles too. A military, masculine smell of tobacco, sweat, liniment and Blanco drifted to her nostrils, accompanied by the faint whiff of beer.

'Oh God, they're drunk,' Diana said, wrinkling her nose. 'Some of these commanding officers are so lax. Why must they let them loose in the NAAFI before the show?'

'They're probably just excited,' Tabby said. 'Either way, it works well for us if they're in a good mood.'

'What are they whistling at?' Molly asked. 'There's no one on stage.'

'At the playbills we left on the benches, I suppose,' Pam said with a smile. 'You can guarantee they'll be in a jolly mood when they've been told to expect girls.'

Molly felt her stomach do a somersault, and covered her mouth in case she belched. Preoccupied with worries about the men not liking her act or refusing to join in with the songs, she had forgotten to worry about what would happen if they didn't fancy her. She glanced down at her unbecoming costume – the dowdy dress and mismatched sash – with some trepidation.

And after performing, she would have to face the men in their NAAFI, wouldn't she? Little Davy's speech at King's Cross came back to her. *Cheer them up, but don't lead them on.* Flirt but don't go too far, in other words. But what if one of the men wanted to go further, and stopped listening when she told him no? Molly knew she was no Diana Chastain, but she guessed these women-starved soldiers would be no different to other men: happy to get fresh with anything in a skirt. She thought of Shack and gave a little shudder.

A hand materialised on her shoulder, making her jump.

'Nervous?' Jack murmured.

'That's a ridiculous thing to ask, when you can see I'm practically made of jelly,' Molly muttered back. 'Do bugger off, Jack.'

He smiled. 'Ah, there's that mouthy Bradford lass I met in the pub. By all means take it out on me if it makes you feel better, Miss Clough.'

'Oh, stop with that "Miss Clough" business, it's absurd. A posh voice don't make you bloody Jack Buchanan, you know. Call me Molly like a normal person.' She turned around to glare at him. 'Why aren't you nervous? Why is it only ever me?'

He shrugged. 'Perhaps you feel like you've got more to lose.'

Phil, who had been speaking with the commanding officer, appeared amongst them.

'Right, they're ready for us,' he said. 'Break a leg, chaps. Remember, these barrack room shows are more about morale than professional polish. We're not in the West End now. Just do your best, try to establish a rapport with the men, and in the best tradition of "the show must go on", if you make any mistakes then pretend it was all part of the act. Davy, out you go and warm them up.'

'How was their CO, Phil?' Davy asked. 'Am I behaving myself tonight?'

'He's quite young, and seems jolly,' Phil told him. 'Not a stern sort, I'd say.'

'No padre with them?'

'Not tonight. I think you could get away with a little blue stuff. I'll go do the lights.'

Phil went to dip the house lights, and Davy's face took on a set, determined expression as he went out on stage.

'See?' Jack murmured to Molly. 'It isn't only you who's nervous.'

Molly blinked. 'What, Little Davy?'

'Can't you see it in his face?'

'But he's been doing this the longest of any of us, hasn't he?'

'By a long way. That's just the way it is for some people.'

Tabby held a finger to her lips when Davy, as compère, launched into a bit of patter before he introduced Diana. Molly and Jack fell silent.

Molly sensed that Jack had been trying to make her feel better when he had drawn her attention to Davy's stage fright, but if anything it made her feel worse. The idea that someone could have been doing this as long as Davy and still feel nervous before going on stage made her dread never being cured. Davy could manage his nerves – there was no trace of them now as he established an easy, joking banter with the men. Molly couldn't.

She had always assumed that with enough experience she would get used to performing, but what if that never happened? She held up a hand to watch it shake.

Her gaze drifted to Diana, standing erect at the side of the stage in her revealing sequinned gown. There was no sign of a tremble there, or a single twitch in the haughty expression to suggest anything other than complete confidence. Molly felt a flicker of envy. If only she could be that way!

What must it have been like to have stood in the wings of a theatre without a stitch on, waiting to go out so a crowd of strangers could scrutinise every lump and bump on your body? Even then Diana would have maintained her perfect poise and dignity, Molly supposed. She had been shocked when she had learned what Diana had once done for a living, but there was a large dose of awe and respect mingled in. She would love to have confidence like that.

Molly couldn't see the troops from the wings, just Davy out on stage, so it was hard to judge the size of the crowd. She could hear them though. They were making plenty of noise while Davy ran through the more risqué gags that he saved for when there was no chance of anyone telling tales on him to Basil Dean. They certainly went down well with the troops, who guffawed, clapped and cheered at each cheeky punchline. But that was nothing compared to how they cheered when Davy introduced Diana and she went out to them. Tabby followed to take her seat at the piano.

As Molly had observed earlier, the NAAFI piano was a poor one: tinny, old and more than a little out of tune. The men didn't care about that though. They whistled and cheered from the moment Diana began her dance to the end, and were so vocal in crying out for more that Diana was obliged to perform it again.

Fenella shook her head, reluctant admiration creeping into her expression. 'I have to admit, as much as I complain about her being top of the bill, they really do love her. Makes you wonder why the rest of us bother turning up, doesn't it?'

'I doubt she had any more rousing reception at Sadler's Wells,' Jack said.

Fenella smiled. 'Sadler's Wells my dainty little foot. Come on, Jack. You know full well where you found her.'

'I couldn't possibly say what you mean,' he said with an answering smile.

Molly looked at him curiously.

'Did you really—' she began, but she was silenced by a look from Little Davy as Diana's music came to an end. He beckoned to Fenella, and they went out to perform a short sketch with Diana before he introduced the next act.

The men fell quiet as Davy began introducing Pam. Molly sensed they resented this new act for driving their beloved Diana away, but Pam quickly won them over. It was hard not to fall under the spell of her energetic act, and they very much approved of the circus-style costume of corset and tights that showed off the full length of her legs. They loved the way she teased and flirted with them, and when she summoned their drill sergeant on stage to enter her disappearing cabinet, they applauded fit to bring the hut down.

'That's why Pam's second on the programme,' Fenella whispered to Molly. 'Because she's the only one of us who has any hope of following Diana.'

After another short sketch, it was Jack's turn.

'Good luck, Jack,' Molly couldn't help whispering as he passed her. His eyes widened, and he shook his head at her before going out.

'Oh, you've done it now, Molly,' Pam whispered, looking genuinely horrified.

Molly blinked. 'Me? What do you mean?'

'My darling, you must *never* wish a performer—' She bit her tongue before the words slipped out. 'You must never wish them what you just wished him. That's why we say "break a leg". You must always say the opposite of what you want to happen in the theatre, otherwise it works like a curse.'

Molly laughed. 'Oh, come on. That's just daft superstition.'

'Maybe it is, but theatre folk take that stuff pretty seriously,' Fenella said. 'Honestly, Moll, you need to watch what you say.' She cast an ominous look at Jack as he prepared to sing. 'I just hope you haven't summoned some terrible disaster on us during this tour, that's all.'

—

Curiosity overtook nerves for a brief time as Molly listened to Jack sing. He had told her he wasn't much of a singer, but she had assumed that was just modesty. She supposed he must have some talent if ENSA had managed to get him a deferment from call-up. Fenella had told her it was very hard to secure deferments for entertainers, because while Basil Dean campaigned tirelessly for service with ENSA to be recognised as a reserved occupation, the powers-that-be worried about it becoming a funkhole for shirkers looking to dodge military service. That was why so few ENSA performers were young men.

Jack wasn't bad – at least, his singing was perfectly tuneful, and he had a pleasant, smooth baritone – yet Molly couldn't help feeling that the sort of songs he was performing didn't really suit him. They were all romantic, with Jack doing his best to imitate Bing Crosby as he gave them 'Pennies from Heaven', 'The Moon Got in My Eyes' and other soft, slow numbers. As Molly had observed before, though, Jack wasn't really that type. He was good-looking, yes, but in a way that exuded boyish charm more than old-fashioned matinee idol. He would be better suited to something a little livelier, she felt, with a touch of humour.

It brought back something Jack had said the night they met – that she ought to stop trying to emulate Gracie Fields and show off a little more of her own personality. She wondered why he didn't take his own advice.

The men clapped heartily when Jack had finished. Molly suspected this was less a mark of appreciation than it was hopeful anticipation that there would soon be another girl for them to look at.

Jack spotted her watching him as he returned to the wings and smiled.

'I can guess what you're thinking,' he said.

'Can you?'

'You're thinking I'm no Bingo. Aren't you?'

Molly flushed, well aware that that was exactly what she had been thinking.

'Not exactly,' she said. 'I just couldn't help remembering how you once told me I should stop trying to be Gracie Fields and be more myself.'

'Ah. "Physician, heal thyself", eh?' He shrugged. 'I told you I wasn't much of a singer. The best I can do is try to sound like someone who is.'

'But you're a great singer. I mean you would be, if you picked songs that were a better fit for you. Why don't you?'

'Because ENSA wanted a Crosby-style crooner under forty and I was one of the only men not in the forces who fit the bill,' Jack told her. 'It's good to have a male crooner in the outfit for gigs with a mixed audience, but it doesn't matter what I do when it comes to an all-male group like this. They want girls and they want to laugh. They don't want some bloke pulling faces while he sings "Somebody Loves Me". I'm here to fill up the programme, that's all.'

Molly noticed that Phil was once again watching the two of them with a curious expression. She wondered what it meant.

–

After Nobby, Davy and Fenella took the stage. This was followed by Fenella's impressions spot, which went down well with the men. They seemed a very appreciative audience, eager to be pleased.

Far from making Molly less nervous, this only made her feel more keenly what a dreadful thing it would be to let them down when she was the last act on the programme. Fenella was asking the men to shout out names for her to impersonate now, which meant Molly would be on very soon.

Except… now her stage debut was mere minutes away, she wasn't sure she could go through with it. Her heart raced, her breathing was ragged, almost a pant, and her legs felt so wobbly she could hardly support herself. Everything felt too bright, even in the dimness of the wings, and her head throbbed painfully. If there had been any way out other than through the crowd of soldiers, she wasn't sure she could have stopped herself from bolting.

'Molly, are you all right?' Pam whispered, noticing her blanched face and how badly she was trembling.

Molly pressed a hand to her brow. 'No, I don't think I am. I… I feel a little faint.'

'Oh, sweetheart. Here, sit on the floor, before you fall down.'

'It'll make my costume dusty,' Molly murmured vaguely.

'Not as dusty as if you keel over.' Pam raised her voice. 'Here, everyone, clear some space so Molly can sit.'

Molly didn't resist as Pam helped her to sit on the grubby hut floor.

'What's the matter?' Jack asked.

'Molly feels faint,' Pam told him.

'Does she need some water? I can ask the corporal on the door to fetch a glass.'

'That might help. Thanks.'

Jack disappeared to get the water and Phil knelt by Molly. 'What's up, kitten? Are you sick?'

Everything around Molly seemed to be spinning, and she held on tightly to Pam's hand. 'I… no. At least, I don't think so. It's just my stupid nerves.'

'Can you go on?'

'I don't know.' She clutched his arm. 'Phil, can I… can I play?'

'What?'

'Please, you have to let me play my own accompaniment. I don't think I can stand there in front of them all. Not without fainting. If I've got the piano, I might be able to get through it.'

'But it's a NAAFI piano,' Phil told her. 'You can hear how out of tune it is. Tabby's used to getting the best out of instruments like that. You aren't.'

'It's the only way I can do this. Please, Phil. I want to do my spot.'

Fenella appeared from the stage, her eyes widening when she saw Molly. 'What on earth is the matter? Can't she go on?'

'She says she can if she can have the piano,' Phil told her.

'Then for God's sake, let her do that. Davy's out there now preparing to introduce her.'

Phil beckoned to Tabby at the piano, and she slipped quietly into the wings.

'What is it, Phil?'

'Molly's doing her own accompaniment.' He nodded to Molly on the floor. 'She says she can't go on otherwise.'

Tabby looked down at her with concern. 'Well if she's sick, she certainly shouldn't go on. Send Jack and Nobby out to lead them in a sing-song.'

For the first time, Molly understood how her sister must feel to have people constantly talking about her as if she wasn't there.

'I want to go on,' she murmured. 'I... I don't want to let you down. I'll be all right, if I can only sit.'

'You'd better be all right quickly,' Fenella said, nodding to the stage. 'That applause is for you.'

Jack reappeared with the water, but there was no time to drink it. Besides, it might go down the wrong way and make her choke. Molly allowed Phil to help her to her feet. She swayed for a moment, then stumbled out on her wobbly silver shoes.

'Gentlemen and... gentlemen, the Forces Follies' very own Yorkshire songstress, Miss Molly Clough,' Little Davy said, gesturing to her. Molly managed a very shaky curtsey, and immediately sought the comfort of the piano stool. Davy looked surprised, but he adjusted quickly. He carried the microphone to her, lowered the stand so it was level with her mouth and went off.

Molly stared in horror at the men, who watched her expectantly with eager eyes.

Oh Lord, there were so many! All of them packed shoulder to shoulder, some on benches, some cross-legged on the floor, waiting to be entertained. By her.

This was the point where she was supposed to engage in some teasing banter before launching into her new signature song, 'My Girl's a Yorkshire Girl'. But her voice was trembling too much to speak directly to the soldiers and she didn't know the music for the new song, only the words. Instead, she started playing what had been the opening song for the act she had done in her grandad's pub: 'Sally, Pride of Our Alley'.

Her voice quavered as she sang. She prayed that the men would take the hint and join in. It wouldn't calm her nerves, which were utterly out of her control, but it would at least cover her shaking voice. But they didn't join in. They only looked puzzled at the abruptness with which she had started singing.

Obviously there had been some words whispered in the wings, because Little Davy emerged again.

'Come on then, lads, let's hear you,' he called jovially. 'You can't tell me you don't know this one. Is this a knees-up or isn't it?'

To Molly's relief, the men gradually began to join in, and soon the hut was ringing with their voices. They were even louder on the second song, 'Kiss Me Goodnight, Sergeant Major', but still Molly struggled. Phil was right: the piano was hellish to play, and her shaking was getting worse and worse. She could barely hit the right notes, she was trembling so badly. What with that and her quavering voice, it must sound awful.

She was supposed to do five songs and then an encore, but she knew she had no hope of getting through so many. Instead, she played one more – 'Beer Barrel Polka' – then stood abruptly, gave another stiff curtsey, and bolted into the wings.

This produced murmurs of disappointment among the men, who had started to enjoy the sing-song, and Davy looked bewildered at her sudden disappearance. However, he led them in a round of applause before going on to close the show.

In the wings, Molly slumped to the floor. Jack handed her the water he had brought, and she sipped it gratefully.

'Sorry,' she whispered to the others. 'I let you all down, didn't I?'

Phil patted her shoulder. 'You did your best. And you went on, even though we could see it nearly killed you to do it. That's what it's all about – the show must go on, as I said earlier. Well done, Molly.'

But despite the words of comfort, Molly could hear the disappointment in his voice.

# Chapter 30

After the show, the hut started to clear as the troops made their way to the NAAFI canteen to discuss the merits or otherwise of what they'd seen.

'We should join them,' Phil said. 'Is everyone ready?'

'Just… leave me a moment,' Molly murmured, still sitting on the floor.

'They'll expect to see us all. It looks standoffish if we don't show our faces.'

'I'll come over when I'm back to my usual self. I'm sure I can find my way.'

'We're hardly going to leave you on your own in a camp full of soldiers,' Fenella said firmly. 'Pam and I will stay with you until you're ready.'

'No, you two go,' Jack said. 'It's you girls the men want to talk to. I imagine they've forgotten I was even on the bill. I'll stay with Molly until she feels better.'

Pam hesitated. 'Is that all right with you, Molly?'

Molly gave a slight nod.

'Right, come on then,' Davy said. 'I'm gasping for a pint.'

The others disappeared, leaving Molly alone with Jack.

'You need anything?' he asked.

Molly didn't speak. She just stared fixedly for a moment, then burst into tears.

Jack sighed and slumped down next to her, putting an arm around her shoulders.

'Go on, let it out,' he said gently. 'I don't suppose it'll make a jot of difference if I tell you it really wasn't all that bad.'

Through swimming eyes, Molly stared at him in disbelief.

'Not that… bad?' she said between sobs. 'I dried up. I ruined… ruined the whole show.'

'You're really becoming one of us if you've got the vanity to think the whole show hinged solely on your performance,' he said with a smile. 'What you actually did was go on after several well-received acts, lead them in a bit of community singing and come off. I'm not going to insult your intelligence by telling you it was your best work, but it was far from the disaster you probably think.'

'It was a disaster… for me,' Molly sobbed. 'I'll be sent home. And… and even if Phil doesn't send me, I'll have to go. I can't do that again. It was awful.'

'It wasn't that awful.'

'I mean it felt awful. For me.'

'Yes, I suppose it must have.' He shuffled to look into her face. 'Why do you want to do this, Molly?'

'Because… because it's what I always wanted to do.'

'That's not a reason, it's a length of time.'

'All right, then I suppose… it's the only thing I was ever any good at – not that you'd have thought I had anything approaching talent tonight, but it got me praise as a bairn. It was the only thing that could offer a way out.'

'A way out of what?'

'Of the mills. Of a life with nowt in it except toil and hopelessness. There aren't many ways out for lasses like me except to try for a good marriage, but if you've got a talent…' She wiped her eyes with the handkerchief he handed her and met his eyes. 'I suppose that's hard for you to understand.'

'Is it?' He smiled, a little sadly. 'You sound like my ma.'

'How do you mean?'

'I really shouldn't tell you. Once I do, I'll be all out of mysteries to keep you interested with. But since you're upset…' He was silent for a moment, staring at his knees. 'I was a dead-end kid too, you know. My old man was a labourer, like all the men of the family, and the women did what work they could get. They worked damn hard, the Flaherty men, and they almost always died young.'

'Flaherty?'

'That's right. Irish descent, like most folk where I came from. I changed it to Forrester when I went on the stage.'

Molly blinked at him.

'Surprised?' he said with a smile.

'Very. So how did you, um...'

'Escape?' Jack smiled grimly. 'When my dad died at twenty-eight, my ma said she'd be blowed if she'd see her only child with no better future. So she set out to make a gentleman of me, Philip Pirrip-style.'

Molly thought of the slum house he had shown her, and wondered how a poor widow could ever hope for such a thing for her child. It had been a huge struggle for her family just to send Daphne to the local grammar school.

'She sent you to a boarding school?' she asked.

'No, she'd no money for anything like that. When I say she set out to make a gentleman of me, she was more concerned about me having the appearance of breeding than the education to go with it. In her mind, a gentleman was someone in a smart suit who knew how to talk. So she spent what little money we had on elocution lessons and nice clothes – second-hand, but in good enough nick that they got me looking the part.' He laughed. 'It earned me some beatings, I can tell you. You soon learn to fight when your mother sends you out to play somewhere like Kemble's Rookery dressed up like ruddy Little Lord Fauntleroy. But Ma was determined to make me look like something better than I was, and I couldn't bear to hurt her. She had the idea that if I looked the part of a gentleman, that was no different from being one.'

'She thought it would help you to a better job?' Molly asked, gazing at him wonderingly. If she had been invited to guess the story of Jack's life that first night in the pub, she would never in a hundred years have guessed this.

'She wanted me to make a career on the stage, where everyone would be able to see what a fine gent she'd made of me,' Jack said with another bleak laugh. 'Like you said, for people like us it was one of the few ways out. The only other avenue for me was the army – the same way it was marriage for you, I suppose. Ma was always dead set against that.'

His mother had certainly done a good job, Molly thought as she looked at him. There was nothing about Jack to indicate he was anything other than a gentleman. It wasn't only in the way he spoke or dressed but in his bearing; his manners; the way he carried himself with such easy, careless grace. When she had first met him, Molly had felt that the obvious difference in their class would be an insuperable barrier to any romantic entanglement, although she had worried that Jack might well have other things on his mind. Yet here he was, telling her that his origins were even more humble than her own.

'I imagine your mother's very proud of you,' she said.

Jack bowed his head. 'I hope she would have been.'

'She's…'

'It killed her, in the end. She sacrificed so much for me, living practically in squalor, that it…' Jack trailed off in a sigh. 'I wanted to do so much more, Molly. To earn enough to give her a better life. Perhaps if I'd worked harder when I was a kid… but I never really wanted to be on stage.' He let out a dreary laugh. 'And that's the real irony, because now I'm stuck with it, aren't I? Lord knows I've got no remarkable talent, but I couldn't let the old lady down now.' He closed his eyes, and his voice sank to a whisper. 'She was the best woman I've ever known, and she gave up her life to get me this chance. The least I can do for her sake is keep at it.'

Molly wasn't sure what to say to that. Jack's face twitched, struggling with emotions that seemed to dwarf her own distress. Her heart went out to him when she thought of his need to provide for his mother, and his guilt that he had been unable to do so. She knew what that felt like well enough.

She took his hand and pressed it gently.

'Your mother sounds like an impressive woman,' she said softly.

'She was. Tough as old boots and tender as velvet. Not a day goes by that I don't miss her.' Jack summoned a smile. 'So we're not very different, you see. We're both here because it was our only way out, doing our best to make it despite our natural disadvantages.'

'You don't get stage fright the way I do though,' Molly said, shivering at the memory of her earlier attack. 'I don't know if I can conquer it, Jack.'

'You're not going to give up after one show, are you?'

'I doubt I'll have a choice. Phil and Davy are probably having a conversation about what to do with me right this minute.'

'Then fight it.' He looked earnestly into her face. 'Fight it, Molly. I'll take your side, and so will the girls – well, three of them. Phil Brooks is a fair man, and he likes you. He'll give you a second chance.'

'I can't help feeling it'll make no difference. That the way I was tonight is a part of me that can't be changed.'

'That's defeatist talk, that is. Practically a hanging offence in wartime.'

'It's not defeatism, it's the plain truth,' Molly said dismally. 'I've heard enough stories to know that not all audiences are as friendly as the one we had tonight. If I couldn't manage the stage fright in front of them, how will I cope when we've got a group who've made up their mind not to like us?'

'So you'll go home and what – go back to the mills? You don't feel like that's a huge wasted opportunity?' Jack demanded, sounding impatient with her. 'I know you've got a good voice. If you give up now so you can spend your life twiddling bobbins in your clogs and shawl, I'll… I'll never speak to you again. And then what will you do?'

That made Molly smile, but it didn't quite have the power to cheer her up.

'You really mean it, don't you?' she said. 'I thought you might have been trying to pick me up when you said you liked my singing that night in the pub.'

'Maybe I was, but that doesn't mean I wasn't serious,' Jack said with an answering smile. 'That's why I encouraged you to apply to ENSA. I'm sure the others have told you by now that when it comes to talent, I'm not an easy man to impress.'

'They have.'

'Well then, you're not really going to go home just like that, are you? I didn't give up, and you've got a damn sight more talent than I have. Do it for your family if not for me.'

Molly grimaced at the thought of going back to Bradford with all her fine dreams in tatters, and before she'd even earned back the advance on her salary. And what then? Beg Mr Taylor for her job back, and submit to the horrifying attentions of Shack just so she could bring in enough to support her mam and sister? How could she return to that old life now, after everything she'd experienced with the Forces Follies?

'I don't want to,' she whispered. 'I just don't know what the future can be for me here, after what happened tonight. I'm sorry, Jack.'

Once her tears had dried, Jack persuaded Molly to join the others in the NAAFI. She hoped her red eyes and dowdy costume – she had removed the sash and pearls, so she was left in the matronly black dress – would mean she wouldn't be too much of a target for amorous servicemen. With a beauty like Diana nearby and the attractive faces and figures of the other women to tempt them, no soldier was likely to notice skinny little Molly Clough.

When she and Jack arrived, however, they found that there was no sign of Diana, or of Pam either. Fenella and Tabby were sitting at a table, laughing as they chatted with a group of soldiers, while Phil was deep in conversation with Little Davy near a battered wireless set that stood in one corner.

Molly wondered if the two men were talking about her. She tried to read what they were saying from the movement of their lips, the way she had learned to do at the mill, but they were muttering and she could only pick up the odd word. Chamberlain, Norway… the usual war talk, it seemed.

She had never been in a NAAFI canteen before. It was housed in one of the many Nissen huts that formed the barracks, but it felt more like a pub than a canteen. The place was thick with the smoke of dozens of cigarettes and pipes, and the smell of beer and over-brewed tea hung in the air. There was a long counter staffed by NAAFI girls, who sold the men beer and cigarettes or served the ever-popular 'char and a wad' to those just off duty – buns and cups of hot tea, poured from a large urn.

'Um, what do we do?' Molly murmured to Jack, glancing nervously at the gangs of soldiers. Despite her frumpy dress and male companion, a few of them had turned to examine her with interest. They really must be starved of female company.

'Just smile for them,' Jack whispered back. 'We'll join your girlfriends, then you don't have to say much if you're not in the mood for chat.' He grinned. 'Not that you could get a word in if you were, with Fenella one of the party.'

'You'll stay with me though?'

'If you want me to.'

Jack wasn't able to join her, however, as he had no sooner escorted Molly to the table where Tabby and Fenella were chatting than he was beckoned over by Phil and Little Davy. He shrugged apologetically before going to them, and after a moment's hesitation, Molly pulled up a chair between Fenella and one of the soldiers.

There were about six men seated at their two tables. All were privates and all were flushed with beer, merriment and the smugness that went with having three women in their party while their comrades had none. Fenella was chatting ten to the dozen, absolutely in her element. Tabby smiled politely and answered questions when they were put to her, but it was Fenella who really held court.

'Ah, here's our Molly,' Fenella said as her friend sat down. 'I'm glad you weren't here earlier, Moll, or no doubt you'd have been swept away with the other beautiful people.'

Molly blinked. 'Beautiful people?'

'Di and Pam,' Tabby said with a smile. 'They were invited to the officers' mess to hobnob with the top brass. Phil sent Nobby with them to make sure everything stays respectable.'

'Rough luck for them,' one of the soldiers observed. 'Who wants to be with a bunch of stuffed-shirt officers when you could be here with us salt-of-the-earth Tommies having real fun, eh?'

'Oh, we got the best part of the deal all right,' Fenella said cheerfully, raising her beer bottle to him. 'I've never met an officer who wasn't a bore and a half. I'd rather have privates any day.'

There were nods of approval for the insult to the officer class and then a guffaw when they belatedly registered the deliberate innuendo. Fenella grinned as if well pleased with herself. Tabitha rolled her eyes.

The soldier beside Molly had been sitting quietly while his friends joked, and he turned shyly to her. He looked younger than the rest. In fact, he was almost a boy – no older than nineteen, she was sure.

'Sorry,' he said, with the nasal twang of a Liverpool accent. 'I hope you aren't offended by this lot and their mucky sense of humour. We're not used to there being ladies present when we're letting off steam in the NAAFI.'

Molly smiled. The young soldier wasn't much like her brother, but the fact they were a similar age made her think of Ted. Was he in his NAAFI now, she wondered, hiding behind jokes to mask his fears about what the next day might bring?

'I'm not offended,' she said. 'It's good to hear you all laughing.' She put out a hand to him. 'Molly Clough.'

'Alfie Fox.' The boy looked at her hand for a moment, as if unsure whether he was supposed to shake it or kiss it, before settling on the former. 'Um, do you want a beer?'

'No, thank you.' Molly felt that while alcohol might help her to relax a little, she would prefer to stay alert.

'That was a good show tonight,' the lad observed, taking a pull on his own beer. 'I've never been at an ENSA concert before. Only been here a month. Everyone says they're a load of tosh, but I haven't laughed so much in ages.'

'It's kind of you to say so.'

'Pretty girls too,' Alfie observed. 'Shame the officers nicked the other two. I'd have liked to meet the one with the nice legs who did all the magic tricks. You were the lady who sang "Roll Out the Barrel", weren't you?'

Molly flushed. She had been hoping none of the men would mention her awful performance earlier.

'Um, yes,' she said. 'Sorry.'

'What for?'

'For the way I sang. I hope it didn't spoil your evening, Alfie.' Molly glanced at the others and lowered her voice. 'Tonight was my first performance for a service audience. I don't think I've been more nervous in my life. I'm sure you could tell.'

'Not at all,' the boy said, and he sounded genuine enough. 'I wish you'd done a few more though. I was enjoying it.' His face took on a dreamy expression. 'Reminded me of Christmas, back home in Liverpool.'

'What, my singing did?'

'Yes, and my mam at the piano. She'd always lead us in a singsong on Christmas night – all our favourites. She's got ten of us, so it's quite a party when we're all home. For a moment, I was back there with the old girl.' He heaved a wistful sigh. 'Wonderful lady, my mam.'

'You must miss her,' Molly said softly.

Alfie glanced at his comrades. When he saw that they were too busy being entertained by Fenella to listen in on his conversation, he nodded slightly, flushing.

'I don't mind saying that to you, what with you being a girl, but it's not the sort of thing you want to admit in front of your mates,' he said in a low voice.

'No. I'm sure they feel the same about their own mothers though.'

'Not that I'm a nancy or anything, tied to my mam's apron strings. It just sort of brings it home, when you realise there's a chance you might not see her again.' Alfie cast a sober glance at the wireless. Several men had gathered around it, including Phil, Jack and Davy, and were listening intently to a news bulletin. 'Says on the news we've pulled out around Trondheim. Can't be many of our lot left in Norway now. Guess that means we're giving up on the poor buggers, don't it? Leaving them to the Jerries. Some think Hitler'll try for France next.'

'Do you think that'll happen?'

'Who knows? It's what people say, that's all. Just like it happened in the last war.' He shivered. 'And if they do… my God, those poor bleeders with the BEF. That could've been us lot. Maybe it will be still.'

Molly looked at the boy's youthful face, still bearing the pimples of adolescence even though the British Army had decided he was man enough to fight, and thought again of her brother. People said the Maginot Line was impregnable, but if the Germans managed to get through to where the British and French troops were waiting... it didn't bear thinking about.

It was some time later when an army truck arrived to drive them back to their digs – all except Diana, Pam and Nobby, who were still drinking with the officers, and Tabitha, who had been sent by Phil to join them so she could make sure the other women got home safely. They would be driven back at whatever hour of the early morning the officers could bear to part with them. Props and backdrops had been left on the stage, ready for the second show tomorrow. After that the troupe would be moving on to a destination as yet unknown, to perform before another group of strangers.

The NAAFI portion of the evening hadn't been nearly as frightening as Molly had worried it would be. She knew she was supposed to mingle but she had left that to the others, instead sticking closely to Alfie, the young soldier she had befriended. It was clear he had no romantic intentions concerning her, but he had seemed grateful for a sympathetic female ear – someone he could confide his fears to without being judged a 'fairy' or 'nancy' as he might be by his male peers.

It was foolish, Molly thought, how hard it was for men to be open with one another about what they were afraid of. Surely it was natural that Alfie Fox, more a boy than a man and only one month into his military career, would be afraid for the future when he heard the worrying reports coming through on the wireless. It was natural that he missed his mam. Molly had been very happy to fill the role of a big sister as he poured out his youthful fears and talked fondly to her of his mother and siblings, hoping that somewhere in France, some kind woman might be doing the same for her own brother.

There were a couple of metal crates in the back of the truck that was to drive them home. The men naturally offered these to Molly and Fenella as seating while they stood for the journey. Molly was exhausted from her evening and sank on to them gratefully. Fenella, who had had a little too much to drink, dropped her head to Molly's shoulder and was soon snoring there contentedly.

Molly would quite happily have joined her friend in dreamland. If she had drunk beer that evening then perhaps she, too, could have ignored the bumping of the truck enough to fall asleep. She couldn't, however, and settled for leaning back and closing her eyes.

She couldn't wait to get into bed. Then tomorrow… she was dreading tomorrow. That was when her future would catch up with her, and she would know whether the next step on her journey would take her forwards with ENSA or backwards to the life she had known before. But all she could think about tonight was sleep: lots of it, and as soon as possible.

After a while of sitting with her eyes closed, Molly gradually became aware of the murmured conversation of the men.

'Don't like this Norway business, do you?' Jack was saying.

'It's all up for old Nev now, I suppose,' Phil observed. 'Right bloody mess he's made of it. Do you think they'll try for France next?'

'Only a matter of time, I reckon,' Little Davy said.

There was silence as words unspoken hovered in the air: that if France fell, it was inevitable Hitler would set his sights on Britain next.

'We'll beat them though,' Jack said. 'The RAF and the BEF boys will see them off.' But Jack's voice sounded more eager to believe this than convinced it was true.

'Those poor lads,' Phil said with feeling. 'You look at that bunch of kids we played for tonight, more like a Wolf Cub outing than trained soldiers, and try not to think about the Germans making mincemeat out of them. Try to make them laugh, and try not to think about why they need to laugh so damn badly.'

'You're not wrong,' Davy agreed glumly. 'Not much we can do about it though, is there?'

'Hmm,' Jack said, a grimness in his tone.

The conversation stopped for a minute and the air filled with the scent of tobacco, from which Molly concluded that they had paused to light cigarettes.

'What are we going to do about the Clough girl?' Davy said in a low voice. 'It ain't no good bringing Tabby in on this – not now. She's got too bleeding fond of her. It's up to us blokes.'

Molly tensed on hearing her name, but she tried not to make a movement. The men clearly thought that she, like Fenella, was fast asleep. She wanted to hear what they were going to say, so that if she was to be sent home tomorrow she could try to prepare herself.

'I know, not a good night for her,' Phil conceded. 'Poor kid. She did well in the NAAFI though, with that young private she adopted. I thought we might have to take him with us, the way she was looking at him in that motherly fashion. Reminded me of Pam and her cats.'

There was a rumble of laughter.

'I'm not saying I don't like the girl,' Davy said. 'She's improved a lot since we took her on, in looks and performance. But if she can't get on top of those nerves, she'll never make it. Believe me, this is something I know about.'

'She's got good stuff in her, I've seen it.' Jack was speaking now. 'Give her another chance. It was only her first show.'

Molly heard a sigh that sounded like Phil.

'I mean, you're both right,' he said. 'I feel like she's got something – or she could have, if we could only coax it out of her.'

'That's what I thought,' Jack said.

'But she needs to conquer her nerves. That was a serious attack of stage fright. I was amazed she even managed to crawl on stage, let alone get three songs out.'

'Surely that alone entitles her to another chance,' Jack observed. 'She really pushed herself, because she couldn't bear to let us down. It took guts to go on in that state.'

'I know it did,' Phil said. 'But at the same time, my priority has to be the Follies. We've got a reputation for putting on quality revues that's unusual for ENSA. As the manager, it's my job to see nothing puts that at risk.'

'Phil's right,' Davy said. 'She'll have to go, boys. We haven't got the luxury of letting her use concerts as rehearsal time. Maybe if she gets a bit more experience, builds her confidence, she can apply for another audition. ENSA's not a charity for every amateur who dreams of being on the stage though, is it?'

'You'd really send her home after just one show?' Jack sighed. 'Poor Molly. She'll be devastated.'

'I didn't say that,' Phil said. 'We can't have a repeat of tonight, but I did have one idea.'

At that moment, Fenella snorted and abruptly opened her eyes.

'Who's smoking?' she mumbled. 'Give me one, will you, darlings? I'm gagging.'

Phil lit a cigarette for her and the conversation ended, leaving Molly to wonder what Phil's idea might be, and whether they were going to send her home after tonight's disaster or not.

# Chapter 32

Molly awoke early the next morning, after very little sleep. As soon as she woke she started worrying about what would happen to her, and then there was no chance of any further visit to the land of nod. She didn't get up, but lay in the darkness listening to Fenella's throaty breathing beside her.

Images flashed through her mind. The men in the audience, so young, so eager, their eyes seeming to beg for relief from the fears that dominated their lives. Her old life at the mill. Shack's hands on her bottom and his acrid breath on her neck. That awful day he had tried to force himself on her, which so often haunted her nightmares. Daphne, and the new calipers that Molly hadn't even earned enough to pay for in her short-lived show business career. Her heart thumped wildly in response to the stream of pictures, almost as if she were again in the wings, waiting to go on stage.

Molly didn't know what Phil's idea could be. He hadn't sounded like he was planning to send her home immediately in spite of Little Davy's urging, but nor had he sounded entirely convinced by Jack's arguments on her behalf. She supposed the most likely thing was that he'd offer her one last chance, at the concert they were to play tonight. If that went as badly as yesterday's, the troupe would go off to their next engagement while Molly took the train back to Bradford. By tomorrow night she might be back at home, where she would be forced to announce herself a failure to her family after they had invested such high hopes in her.

She was awake when she heard Diana, Pam and Tabby roll in from their night in the officers' mess, at about three in the morning. Mrs Chambers was indulgent to the frivolities of young people and hadn't set a curfew. The giggles and loud whispers as the women tried unsuccessfully to creep quietly upstairs suggested a good time had been had by all.

Molly wondered what happened in an officers' mess. Clearly an invitation to this hallowed place was a privilege reserved only for the most beautiful and talented. No doubt Diana had never even seen the inside of a NAAFI, or been courted by anyone of a lower rank than lieutenant.

At about eight o'clock, Molly could smell bacon being cooked and felt it was safe to dress and descend. She found Pam already at the breakfast table, with the Captain and Mrs Chambers' youngest daughter, Sadie, perched on her lap in her nightgown. Pam looked tired, but far brighter than Molly suspected she would have done if she had been cavorting with officers into the wee small hours.

'Tell me again about the lion,' Sadie was begging Pam when Molly entered.

'Please,' her mother said in a warning voice from the cooker.

'Please,' Sadie chanted dutifully.

Mrs Chambers nodded a good morning to Molly. 'Do sit down, Miss Clough, and I'll bring you some breakfast.'

'Thank you,' Molly said, sitting beside Pam.

'Good morning.' Pam frowned. 'Are you feeling all right, Molly?'

'Why do you ask?'

'You look pale.'

'I'm OK. Just tired.'

'Please, please tell about the lion,' Sadie demanded again, tugging at Pam's sleeve.

Pam smiled fondly at the child. 'Well, all right then. One more time.'

She launched again into a tale she had told the children twice already: of when she had been a girl not much older than them, performing in her parents' act during a stint with a travelling circus. She had made a friend of a lion cub during that tour – Rajah – and the children couldn't get enough of his exploits. It seemed that Pam's love of cats had started with a rather larger pet than little Millicent.

'Oh, he was ever so clever,' Pam told the child. 'His trainer had taught him to sit up and beg, just like a dog, and play dead and all sorts of wonderful things. I tried to teach him tricks too, but he was always a naughty boy for me and just wanted to play. We used to have such a lot of fun together. I begged my parents to adopt him when we finished working for the circus, but of course they couldn't.' She laughed. 'I thought they were being so cruel when they said no. Couldn't you imagine it though: a nine-year-old girl walking a fully grown lion on a lead down the streets of Burnley? I must've believed he'd stay cub-sized forever, daft little madam that I was.'

'Gosh!' Sadie said, round-eyed.

Pam smiled sadly. 'I cried and cried when I had to say goodbye to Rajah. I think that in his little lion way, he cried for me too. He was such a sweet boy.'

'Weren't you terribly afraid he'd gobble you up?' Sadie asked wonderingly.

'Do you know, it never even occurred to me. I don't think my lovely boy would have hurt a soul. He sometimes played at biting me in our games, but he only mimed it.' She sighed. 'I often wonder where he is now. He must be getting to be an old man in lion years, but I would love to see my darling puss one more time. I feel sure he'd remember me.'

Mrs Chambers shook her head, smiling, as she served Pam a plate of bacon and eggs. 'You'll be giving her ideas, Miss Sheridan. Sadie, if you write to Father Christmas asking for a pet lion then I'm afraid I shall have to intercept the letter. Now run along and let these young ladies have their breakfast in peace. Go get ready for school.'

'Yes, Mum.'

Reluctantly, Sadie climbed off Pam's knee and left the room.

The Home Service was playing on the wireless. A news report had started, and Molly cast it a nervous glance. She'd started to dread hearing them. Every day seemed to bring bad news.

Today was no different, it seemed – at least, it was a bad news day for Chamberlain, who had only barely survived a no-confidence vote in the Commons over his handling of the Norway situation.

'Di says Nev won't last the week,' Pam said quietly to Molly. 'Frightening times, aren't they?'

'Yes,' Molly murmured. 'They really are.'

The news report ended, and Pam summoned a smile. 'Ella's still asleep, I suppose.'

'Snoring away,' Molly said, smiling too. 'What about Tabby and Diana?'

'Di's still sleeping off the champagne cocktails. Tabby got up an hour ago and went for a walk by the sea to clear her head. She's always an early riser.'

'Did you have a nice evening?'

Pam flushed. 'Yes, sorry about abandoning you. It's embarrassing when we get invited to the mess but of course we can't very well say no. Diana nearly always gets an invitation, which is natural when she's the star. I suppose when I get asked, it's because one of the officers remembers when "The Sensational Sheridans" was still a name that could open doors. I'd far rather stay in the NAAFI though.'

'I wasn't trying to make you feel guilty,' Molly reassured her. 'I was genuinely interested. I'd love to know what goes on in an officers' mess.'

'Exactly the same as goes on in the NAAFI, but with more expensive booze,' Pam said, laughing. 'Well, my love, what shall we do today? Our time's our own until the concert. A little sea breeze ought to blow away the cobwebs, don't you think?'

Mrs Chambers came back over with some breakfast for Molly. She thanked her hostess before tucking in, glad to have an excuse not to answer Pam's question right away.

Molly still had no idea what today was going to hold. The whisper of conscience told her the honourable thing would be to go to Phil, resign from the troupe and go home. After last night, she was convinced she had been under some mad delusion when she'd believed she had it in her to become a professional entertainer. Phil had been kind to her, and she owed it to him to leave the troupe without placing him in the difficult position of deciding whether to sack her. But every time Molly thought of returning home, defeated after only a single performance, her brain recoiled.

She might not have any choice, of course. Phil might be on his way at this very moment, armed with bad news. It hadn't sounded like his plan was to dismiss her right away though. If he was planning to offer her a second chance, ought she to take it? She was sure that if she tried to perform again tonight, exactly the same thing would occur.

Molly jumped at the sound of a telephone. Captain Chambers naturally had a phone installed in his home, so he could be contacted by the barracks when they needed him. Pam started at the sound as well.

'I wonder who that can be at this time,' Mrs Chambers said. 'It can't be for Jim. He was driven early to headquarters. Excuse me, ladies.' She left the kitchen to answer it.

Pam looked a little flustered, and gave an embarrassed laugh as she attempted to compose herself.

'Sorry,' she said. 'I thought it might be Angelo. I wired him yesterday with the number, in case he was able to telephone with news of Millicent and the babies. But I doubt he'd ring quite so early.'

Pam was right: it wasn't Angelo. When Mrs Chambers returned, it was with a message for Molly.

'From a Mr Brooks,' she said, reading the name from a notepad.

'That's our manager,' Molly told her, exchanging a worried look with Pam. 'Did he, um… did he say he needed to see us?'

'Just Miss Clough, he said. He wants you to meet him on the seafront as soon as you've breakfasted, by the pier.'

Molly's breakfast was over as soon as she received Phil's message, since that instantly killed whatever was left of her appetite. She passed the remainder of her food to Fenella, who had joined them ravenous as usual, and wandered upstairs to wrap her hair in a scarf before she went down to the windy seafront.

This was it, she supposed. She was to be let go. Phil was a sensitive enough man not to want to humiliate her in front of the others, so he had summoned her to the lonely sands to sack her in private. She was glad her friends wouldn't be there to see her cry.

Molly gazed at her suitcase. Should she pack now, and say goodbye to the friends she had made? It all seemed so sudden. So... final.

In the end, she decided not to. It felt too much like tempting fate, and if Phil wasn't intending to let her go, she would look ruddy daft turning up with a bulging suitcase and tears streaking her face. So Molly only put on her coat, squared her shoulders and set out alone for the pier.

She found Phil waiting for her. He was leaning against one of the pier supports, smoking a pipe as he watched the seagulls hopping in the shallows. Molly was surprised to see he wasn't alone, however. There was another man beside him: too tall to be Little Davy and not broad enough to be Nobby. She realised on drawing closer that it was Jack.

What was he doing here? Phil was the troupe's manager, although he seemed happy to be counselled by Davy and Tabitha when it came to making decisions. Jack had only just joined them though. Molly failed to see why he should be present while Phil sacked her, and she had no idea why he was smiling the way he was. He had sounded like he was on her side last night in the truck. Why should he look so jolly now, in stark contrast with Phil's earnest expression?

Phil straightened up when she reached them, taking out his pipe.

'Molly. Thanks for coming.'

Molly didn't trust herself to speak. He sounded so serious, she was sure it was going to be bad news. She only nodded.

'Look… this is difficult,' he said after a moment. 'I didn't want to do it in front of the others. And really, I don't want you to be offended. I did believe your act had potential, but after last night… well, you must see that we have to do something.'

Molly bowed her head. 'I understand.'

Even now, Jack was smiling. What was *wrong* with the man? Had he begged to come just to witness her humiliation? If so, she had been sorely mistaken about him. All that stuff he had told her, about his mother and their poverty… had any of that been real, if he was mocking her at this of all moments?

'I asked Jack along as this concerns him too,' Phil said, reading her expression. 'I'm sorry, Molly, but I'm not letting you go on tonight.'

Right. No second chance. How that concerned Jack she had no idea, but right now Molly was too busy struggling with tears to worry about that. She took out a handkerchief to wipe her eyes, hoping Phil would blame the stinging wind.

'All right,' she said quietly. 'Do you mind if I say goodbye to the girls before I go? I ought to be allowed that.'

Phil frowned. 'Before you go where?'

'Well, home.' She blinked at him. 'You are sending me home?'

For the first time, Phil smiled. 'I'm not sending you home – not yet, at any rate. And if my plan works like I think it will, hopefully not ever.'

Jack's smile had widened into a broad, beaming grin now. Molly glared at him. Taunting her with mysteries seemed to be the man's favourite hobby, and now he was relishing having something new to dangle.

'Do you know about this?' she demanded.

'Phil told me at breakfast,' Jack said. 'I'm not going on tonight either. Davy's going to do a couple of Marriott Edgar monologues to fill up the programme.'

'*You're* not going on?' Molly shook her head. 'I don't under-stand.'

Phil came to put an arm around her shoulders. 'You asked me yesterday why I didn't perform any more. Remember?'

'Yes, I… I remember.'

'And I said that some double acts were just meant to be double acts.' He nodded to Jack. 'Well, the two of you are exactly what I meant. I've been thinking about it ever since I first saw you together.'

Molly, still none the wiser, only stared at him helplessly.

'You're good together is what I mean,' Phil said. 'There's something about the way you are with each other that reminds me of me and Pete – as if you understand one another intuitively, which is what makes a strong double act. Jack's a good singer but he knows his Bing Crosby routine doesn't suit him, and your attempts to be Gracie Fields are turning you into a bag of nerves. This could be the answer to both of those problems.'

Jack nodded. 'I took a little convincing that changing the programme one day into the tour was a good idea, but Phil soon talked me round.'

'Haven't I got an act and a dozen original songs dying to find a new home?' Phil said. 'If you ask me, Forrester and Clough could be just the home they need.'

Molly wondered if she had woken up this morning at all, or if this was all a dream. It sounded like madness.

And yet… could it work? A new act, her and Jack?

'But we haven't rehearsed it,' she said dazedly. 'I don't know any of the songs you and your partner used to do, Phil.'

'We'll start you off with some hits from the wireless, and I'll give you examples of the patter we used,' Phil said breezily, as if doing a whole new act on a few hours of rehearsal time was the simplest thing in the world. 'It's more about the personalities than the music anyhow.'

'What would we sing?'

'I'm thinking Ethel Merman, Jimmy Durante, Fred and Ginger – you know the sort of thing. Funny duets but romantic too. A few of those then into the community singing, and we can gradually introduce some original pieces once you're comfortable. You can sit out the next couple of shows while you rehearse, then if I think you've got something, we'll try it out wherever we play on Friday. All right?'

'I'm game if the lady is,' Jack said, catching Molly's eye. 'What do you say, Molly?'

Molly wasn't sure what she said. Whatever decision she thought Phil might have made after her nervous attack last night, this one she couldn't have guessed in a million years.

Performing an act she'd never done in her life before in just two days' time was about as terrifying a prospect as she could imagine. On the other hand, the idea of having someone on stage with her was a reassuring one. And after all, could her act with Jack really go any worse than the solo one she had attempted the night before? It was a second chance, but it was something different. It would mean she was spared the ignominy of returning home after a single failed performance.

'It's only a twenty-minute spot,' Phil said, seeing her hesitation. 'A couple of duets – no more than three, with a little patter between – then you move on to the community singing. You don't need anything new for that. The three you did last night were ideal, Molly.'

'That doesn't sound too daunting,' Jack agreed. 'I haven't rehearsed the community songs but I know them well enough to lead the boys.'

'What do you think?' Phil asked Molly.

Still Molly hesitated.

'Can I have a new costume?' she said at last.

'If it helps you feel more confident. You can pick a dress from the box.'

'Well… all right, we'll give it a try. But Phil, if we go on stage on Friday and I dry up again, you have to let me resign, all right? It's kind of you to have done so much to help me but there comes a point when we'll both have to face the fact that it isn't working.'

'Molly, I promise if it comes to it, I'll put you on a train to Bradford myself,' Phil said with a smile. 'But I'm convinced this has got a really good chance, if you're willing to give it everything. Are you?'

Molly smiled too, echoing Jack's words a moment earlier. 'I'm game if the gentleman is.'

'Good girl.' Phil clapped her heartily on the back. 'Well then, what are you waiting for? The pair of you have got rehearsing to do.'

There was no time that day for Molly to explore the seaside delights of Bognor, as the other members of the Forces Follies were able to do. She was immediately ensconced with Jack in a weatherbeaten Scout hut Phil had secured them the use of, as they attempted to develop the new musical double act of Forrester and Clough.

Phil made a few phone calls and managed to arrange for a gramophone and records of three duets he believed would work for them to be delivered that same day, as well as writing out the lyrics – these weren't numbers he had performed with his old partner, being for a man and a woman, but Phil seemed to have a brain full of songs. Molly had assumed he would then coach them on how he wanted the act performed, but he didn't. He just guided them to the Scout hut, showed them how to set the gramophone going and left them to it.

'It has to feel natural,' were his last words before he abandoned them. 'It's not a lick of good my telling the pair of you what to do. Pretending to be me and Pete is going to come across just as wrong as it did when you were pretending to be Crosby and Fields. You have to make the material work for you.'

Which Molly thought was all very well, if she had even the slightest idea where to start. She picked up one of the songs Phil had written out, a Cole Porter number called 'It's De-Lovely', and looked dazedly over the lyrics.

'Do you know this?' she asked Jack.

He came to glance over her shoulder. 'I've heard Frances Day sing it on the wireless but I've never performed it.'

'It says in Phil's notes that it was originally a duet. It's from a stage musical, *Red Hot and Blue*. Bob Hope and Ethel Merman.'

'Wonderful, so I can go from failing to be Crosby to failing to be Hope,' Jack said. 'Maybe next week, I can try my hand at being Dorothy Lamour.'

Molly laughed. 'Nobby would never let you get away with it.'

'I think we just have to trust that Phil knows what he's talking about and give it a try.' Jack slid out the accompanying record. 'Let's listen to it first before we try singing it.' He put it on the gramophone, gave the handle a few cranks and set the needle in place.

Molly listened closely to the song, which was the well-known version performed solo by the popular American singer Frances Day. It was catchy, certainly. The lyrics were romantic but humorous and she could see how it would work for a pair, with the couple alternately crooning to and teasing each other. She found herself unconsciously singing along as it played.

'Will we dance as well?' she asked Jack when it had finished.

'I suppose we'll need to do more than just stand there, won't we?'

'I never know what to do with my arms,' she admitted. 'What do you do on stage?'

'Mostly I pretend the microphone's Betty Grable and snuggle up to it a bit.'

'Well you're jolly well not pretending I'm Betty Grable.'

'I don't think I could ever pretend you were anyone but you,' he said with a smile. 'Let's try singing it first, shall we? Maybe the dancing will come to us as we go.'

'Diana Chastain style?'

'Ah, now there's an idea.'

Jack started swaying from side to side, trailing an imaginary scarf over his head in such a good impression of Diana's sensual dance that Molly couldn't help but laugh.

'I take back everything I said about you not making a good Dorothy Lamour,' she said.

'I don't know why I didn't think of it sooner. It's a shame I won't fit into Nobby's costumes, otherwise you might find him tied to a lamp post while I'm on stage dripping sequins.'

Molly narrowed one eye. 'Did you really discover Diana where the girls said you discovered her?'

'At The Windmill?' he said absently, his gaze flickering over the lyrics once more. 'She won't thank me for telling you but it's hardly a secret. Yes, that's where I found her.'

'What were you doing there?'

'I was lost,' Jack said, exuding a highly unconvincing innocence. 'I thought it was the Sadler's Wells Theatre.'

'That's two miles away.'

'I was really very lost.'

Molly raised an eyebrow, and Jack smiled.

'It was work, all right?' he said. 'I know everyone thinks it's nothing but bottoms and breasts at The Windmill but they put on some decent variety turns between the girls. I've found a lot of good acts for ENSA there.'

'It sounds like you've found a few other things there as well. Diana, for one.'

'Diana wanted a job and I was in a position to find her one. Strictly business.'

'You're sure that's all it was?'

Jack shrugged. 'I can't deny it was an attractive view, but it's a strange sort of fun, looking at people you don't know in the buff. Makes me feel rather awkward, if you really want to know. Obviously I'm too British to enjoy that sort of thing.'

'Hmm.'

'Honestly.' He raised an eyebrow. 'Why so interested, Miss Clough?'

She turned away. 'I'm not. Just curious.'

'You know, I might almost think you were jealous.'

Molly ignored him. She went to the gramophone to set the 'De-Lovely' record going again.

This time they attempted to sing along, but soon collapsed in fits of laughter as they stumbled over the lyrics. A second attempt was more successful, however. Molly felt the teasing vocals were a far better fit for Jack's voice and personality than the straight romantic numbers he had been doing before. It reminded her of the way he flirted with her. It was hard to judge how well it suited her own singing voice, but she did feel she was able to put her own stamp on it in a way she struggled to do with the Gracie Fields numbers. It was difficult, when she had spent so much time listening to Gracie, to do anything other than an impersonation of her idol. This felt fresher, like something that could mould itself around her rather than the other way round.

Molly could feel herself blushing at the romantic lyrics though, and at the way Jack would insist on looking into her eyes while he sang them. She wasn't sure if she could cope with him looking that way at her in front of an audience. Before, she had worried about the possibility of fainting on stage. Now, she was more worried she might start giggling.

As soon as they had finished singing, she averted her eyes.

'That was better, wasn't it?' she said.

'It was, but we definitely need more practice,' Jack said. 'Plenty of time though. We only need a couple of fresh numbers by Friday. What do you think to taking a break and investigating that little pub around the corner?'

'Are you joking? We've only done it twice.'

'Exactly. A good time to discuss how we can improve over a drink.'

Molly shook her head. 'Are you always like this?'

'Like what?'

'So laid-back about it all. Being on stage, I mean. I could never be that way.'

He shrugged. 'That's my secret to dealing with nerves – enjoy yourself and don't take it too seriously. You ought to take a leaf out of my book. After all, it's only ENSA.'

'Honestly, I'm so sick of you people saying that,' Molly said, scowling. 'It might be only ENSA to you, but it matters a heck of a lot to those poor sods who might be about to march into hell for our sakes. The organisation pays us a bloody good salary to give it our all and you treat it as an excuse to loaf around in pubs.'

Jack blinked, taken aback by her outburst. 'All right. I didn't mean anything by it.'

Molly pressed her palms into her eyes. 'Ugh. Sorry, I don't know why I snapped at you. I'm just worried, that's all – I mean about the war. Every time I put the wireless on, there's more awful news.'

Jack met her eye. 'Someone you care about out there?' he asked softly.

'My brother,' she whispered. 'My little brother, Ted. Only nineteen. He's with the BEF out in France.'

'I'm sorry. If I'd known, I wouldn't have been so offhand about it.' He smiled. 'You know, it's funny how little I know about you. I feel like I've told you half my life story, but all I know about Molly Clough is that she can belt out a tune, her grandad runs a scary sort of pub, and she can't swear without wrinkling her nose.'

Molly smiled back. 'That is a scurrilous lie.'

'I'm afraid not. I noticed it the first time I met you.'

'Yes, well, I went to a very strict Sunday School. Now are we rehearsing or not?'

'If you agree to make a deal with me.'

'What deal?'

'That if, after another hour and a half of practice, we've managed to make this "De-Lovely" number something we won't be ashamed to show Phil tomorrow, you'll let me take you for a walk on the beach before I escort you home.'

Molly narrowed one eye. 'A walk on the beach? What for?'

'For rehearsal purposes, naturally,' he said innocently. 'I can't sing romantic duets with a girl without seeing her in the proper setting. There's going to be at least a sliver of moonlight tonight.'

He was smiling in the usual easy way, but there was a serious-ness underpinning it. Molly found it hard to understand why Jack seemed interested in her, but she was more and more convinced that it wasn't just meaningless flirting. He actually seemed to mean it.

'You used to do that sort of thing with Tabitha, I suppose,' she said, trying to sound careless.

He grinned. 'Aha!'

'Aha what?'

'Aha and you're jealous. That's the second time you've interrogated me about women in the last half an hour.' He came over to give her waist a squeeze. 'Well, it's nice to know you care.'

'Get off.' She nudged him away, but she was smiling.

'All right, for your edification, here's the full story of my love life insofar as it involves any of our mutual acquaintances,' he said. 'I have seen Diana Chastain naked, as have a significant portion of London theatregoers, but I promise it was strictly business. As to Tabby, despite what her girlfriends have no doubt told you, we were never more than good friends. I looked after her on tour when she was nervous about being abroad for the first time, so people naturally assumed we were walking out together. But if you ask Tabby, she'll tell you the truth of it.'

'Oh.'

'So, are you going to stop being jealous?'

'I'm not jealous,' Molly lied. 'I just like to know what sort of man I'm agreeing to go on moonlit walks with.'

'So you are agreeing?'

'Well… all right,' she said. 'But the deal is two hours of solid practice. Not a second less.'

'Done.'

They spent some time rehearsing 'De-Lovely', and managed to improvise a dance copied from an act Jack had once worked with. Molly doubted the variety act's dance had included quite so much of the romantic clinching that Jack assured her was necessary to give a convincing performance. Still, she went along with it, trying not to shiver when he took her in his arms. She was soon surprised to find that she was enjoying herself.

The only feeling she had ever associated with performing was anxiety. Yes, there was satisfaction in having given a good performance, but that came afterwards, not during. Even rehearsing with no audience present, there was a large dose of panic involved. Molly felt such pressure to get it right, just like Gracie would – to be perfect.

It was different with Jack. As she had noted, he was a very laid-back performer, relishing the rehearsal process as he might a leisurely cigarette, and it wasn't long before a little of his attitude started to rub off.

It was one of the few times Molly felt she had actually performed well, without needing anyone to tell her so. Of course it would be a different experience in front of an audience, but she was trying not to think about that. Worrying about audiences and their hundreds of eyes would only make her nervous.

The one thing that marred the otherwise enjoyable experience of rehearsing with Jack was how Molly felt when he took her in his arms as part of their dance. At first, the feel of his breath on her neck, his heartbeat against her back and the sensation of a pair of strong arms around her made Molly shiver with an excitement that she did her best to conceal from her dance partner. But the longer Jack held her in place, the more she started to feel panicked. Trapped.

It reminded her too strongly of that day in the mill with Shack – how he had held her, wrestled with her, and she had felt powerless to get away from him. She found herself holding her breath and counting in her head while she waited for Jack to release her, and exhaling with relief when he spun her away from him again. It was only a tiny part of their dance – no more than five seconds – but it felt a lot longer.

Molly didn't know how much time had passed when Jack eventually looked at this watch. With the blackouts down, it might be any time of day.

'We must have been having fun,' he said. 'We've been rehearsing for two and a half hours, and I only promised you two. It's after six.'

'I bet that's the hardest you've ever worked, isn't it?' Molly said with a dry smile.

'I know, I'm exhausted. It's a man's life with ENSA.' He picked up her overcoat. 'But not too exhausted to claim my reward. You owe me a walk in the moonlight.'

Molly let him help her into her coat.

'What about the gramophone?' she asked, nodding to it. She had wound it so many times that afternoon that she had an ache in her shoulder from turning the handle.

'Well, we can't carry it,' Jack said. 'Phil will arrange for it to be picked up when we leave tomorrow, I suppose, before a lot of snotty-nosed Scouts turn up and start tying clove hitches to it.'

'It feels strange to be leaving Bognor,' Molly said dreamily as she followed him out and he locked the hut. 'Time passes differently in ENSA, doesn't it?'

'When you're on tour, certainly.'

'We shouldn't linger long. The girls might worry if I'm late back.'

'The girls will be swigging cocktails with swathes of second lieutenants for at least four hours yet. They'll be at the barracks performing now, or did you forget?'

'Oh.' Molly rubbed her head. 'You're right, I did.'

'Come on.' Jack escorted her down some steps to the shingle-covered beach.

He held a dimmed blackout torch to light their way and there was a crescent moon as he had promised, reflected enticingly on the soft-shushing waves. However, even with the combined efforts of torch and moon, there wasn't much light. Molly clung to Jack's arm as she picked her way down the steps, careful not to fall against the barbed wire coiled around the railings.

It was funny, but apart from the horrible, panic-inducing memories of Shack when she had been in Jack's arms, Molly never felt unsafe when she was alone with him. She wondered why she had that instinct to trust him, and why it felt as though they had known one another so much longer than they had.

They wandered along the silver beach, breathing the night air in comfortable silence as shingle crunched underfoot. When they were close to the pier, Jack stopped to look at the reflection of the moon on the sea.

'It looks so peaceful, doesn't it?' he said quietly.

'Is it France on the other side?' Molly asked. 'I never could get along in geography.'

'Yes, France. We'll be about level with Dieppe, if you were to swim in a straight line right across the Channel.' He glanced at her. 'Do you know where your brother is?'

'Somewhere near Lille, we think. Not far from the Belgian border.'

'He's young to be out there. When was he called up?'

'He joined up, right at the start. First lad on our street,' Molly said, with some pride.

'Brave kid.' Jack was silent for a moment, looking out to sea. 'You're right, I ought to take what we do more seriously. You get into the habit of being flippant, but that doesn't mean I think it doesn't matter.'

'And I ought to take it a little less seriously, perhaps,' Molly said with a smile.

'Like you did today, and performed all the better for it.' He smiled back at her. 'We had fun, didn't we?'

'Yes,' Molly said simply. There didn't seem any point in being coy. That was how she felt, so why not say it? Jack had slipped an arm around her shoulders, and she didn't draw away.

'Who else do you have at home, Molly Clough?' he asked softly. 'If the answer's a strapping husband and twelve little Cloughs, you'd better tell me now.'

Molly smiled. 'Just my mam and sister, Daphne.'

'They miss you, I suppose.'

'They must do. Poor Mam, she's never had us away from home before. Now I'm travelling the country with what she ominously calls "the theatre folk", Ted's overseas with the Army, and our Daph gets more grown up every day.'

'What age is she?'

'Fifteen, and her head bursting with thoughts of romance and adventure. She's only got two ambitions in life: to marry Errol Flynn and become Yorkshire's first woman Spitfire pilot.' Molly smiled fondly. 'I wouldn't be surprised if she did it as well. Once she sets her mind on something, there's nothing much can stop her.'

'She sounds like another girl I know. Would Daphne approve of me courting her sister, do you think?'

Molly felt her cheeks heat. It was the first time anything had been said about courting, for all Jack's seeming interest. His arm tightened around her, drawing her close to his side.

'She'll just be surprised you aren't more like Clark Gable,' Molly said, with an awkward laugh.

'Am I a terrible disappointment then? I could grow a moustache if it'll help.'

He had the same teasing tone as always, but his voice had become soft. He moved to take her fully in his arms, and looked down into her eyes. His own held a floating silver crescent in each dark iris.

'No,' Molly whispered. 'No, I don't think you're a disappointment at all.'

He gently stroked her cheek.

'What do you think then, Molly?' he murmured. 'Forrester and Clough, on stage and off? Could we make it?'

'I… Jack, I…'

'That's all right. You don't need to give me an answer now. When you're ready, I'll be there.'

'Why?' Molly found herself asking.

'Why will I be there?'

'Yes. No.' She felt her cheeks growing hot in spite of the sea breeze, flustered by the closeness of his face to hers. 'What I mean is, why me? You must meet so many pretty girls scouting for ENSA.'

'I do, and sometimes they've got no clothes on as well, as you took pains to remind me earlier,' Jack said with a smile. His hand was still on her cheek, his thumb stroking her gently. 'And yet...'

'And yet?'

'And yet somehow... it has to be you.'

Molly's eyes closed as his lips met hers.

For a moment, she was lost in the kiss: soft at first, then steadily more passionate. Jack's arms tightened around her, pulling her close.

Then came the familiar panic – the same panic she had experienced when they had been rehearsing, and that night in the club when the drunk soldier had surprised her with a kiss. But above all, it was the panic that went with that terrible night in Shack's office, when she had last been held by strong arms that wouldn't let her go – arms that weren't tender and affectionate, but had wanted to hurt her.

'Mmm... no!' She pushed Jack away and took several stumbling steps back. 'Get off me. Get off!'

Jack blinked. 'Molly? What's wrong?'

'You mustn't.' She choked on something that was half gasp, half sob, struggling to take in enough air to fill her lungs. 'Jack, you... you mustn't.'

He looked thoroughly bewildered by the sudden change in her attitude. 'I'm sorry. I didn't think I was taking a liberty. If I was, I apologise, but I thought... well, I thought it was what you wanted.'

'No.' Molly was too choked to speak easily. 'No, I don't... don't want it. Just... leave me alone, please.'

She turned from him, blinded by tears, and fled in the direction of her billet.

'Molly!' Jack called after her. 'It isn't safe in the blackout. Let me walk you home.'

Molly paid no attention. She just ran and ran, as fast as she had run away from Shack that day at the mill, until she had put as much distance between herself and Jack as she could.

# Chapter 34

The next day, the women of the Forces Follies rose early and prepared to move on. As before, they were to travel by train while props and cases went ahead by truck. Fenella was chattering to Molly about the events of the night before while they packed, but Molly was only half listening.

'Oh Lord, the officers here are a lark and a half, I'm telling you,' she said happily as she stuffed her clothes into her case. Fenella didn't believe in wasting precious minutes on mundanities like folding. 'I take back everything I said about anyone over the rank of sergeant being a bore.'

It seemed that the show had gone down even better the previous night than it had the first time they had performed for the Bognor recruits – probably because she hadn't been on, Molly thought wryly. Afterwards, the whole troupe had been invited to the officers' mess to attend a drinks party in their honour.

'I suppose it must be knowing they might have to face death at any moment that gives soldiers such passion for life,' Fenella mused, shoving a handful of French knickers into her case. 'That's why I stay in ENSA. I've never met a group of men that suited me better than servicemen, no matter how humble their rank. Mind you, it's nice to mix with the officer class occasionally, if only for some good alcohol. Oh darling, I wish you could have been with us! It isn't fair of Phil to make you rehearse from morning until night.'

For perhaps the first time since she'd woken up, Fenella paused to let her friend speak. She frowned when Molly didn't say anything, but continued quietly packing her own case.

'You are all right, aren't you?' she asked.

'Yes,' Molly murmured. 'Tired from rehearsing. I'm sure I'd have been no fun at a cocktail party.'

'Nonsense. All the officers would have stopped drinking champagne from Diana's slippers immediately and fallen madly in love with you.' Fenella examined her more closely. 'Hmm. But you don't look as well as you should. You ought to sleep on the train, so you can be ready to make conquests wherever we end up tonight. Except I forgot, you're not on until tomorrow, are you? Well, that should give you plenty of time to rest. I hope the next lot of officers are as good as the ones from last night.' She hugged herself. 'Oh, I do love being on tour!'

Molly couldn't muster the energy to reply. The scene with Jack the previous evening had sapped her. She wasn't sure if she would be able to sleep on the train but she would certainly pretend to, if only so no one would make conversation with her.

And when they got to the next destination, Phil would expect her to put in another full afternoon of rehearsal with Jack, ready for their first time on stage together tomorrow. She didn't know how she was going to face him after what had happened, or how she would cope being alone with him.

Molly knew she owed Jack an apology, but where did one even begin apologising for something like that? The fact was, she *had* wanted him to kiss her. When he had talked about her being his girl, it had sent a thrilling shiver down her spine. The absurd way she had reacted hadn't really been about him at all. It had been about Shack, and the memories of how he had touched her.

Oh, how she hated and despised that man! How could he be ruining her life still, here, when she was so far away from him?

Would she never get to experience the excitement of kissing a lover now, or being held by someone who cared about her? The panic she suffered when she was trapped by a pair of arms felt like her stage fright – something she might never be able to break free of.

'Are you sure you're all right?' Fenella frowned. 'Jack didn't try anything on when the two of you were on your own, did he? It's plain he fancies you. We've all been talking about it.'

If Molly wasn't feeling so rotten, she might rather sharply ask if her friends could stop gossiping about her love life behind her back. She didn't even have the energy for that, however.

'We thought Phil must be crackers, letting Jack have you all to himself without even asking what his intentions were,' Fenella went on. She perched on the end of their bed, eager for fresh gossip. 'Well, what did he do? Tell me absolutely everything.'

'Nothing,' Molly mumbled.

'Are you sure? Tabby says he's one of the well-behaved ones, but I'm not sure I believe in well-behaved men myself. At least, if there is such a thing then I've never met one. It's how they lull you into a false sense of security before pouncing, that's all.'

'He didn't try anything,' Molly said, in the same listless tone. 'He was… the perfect gentleman.'

—

Molly didn't see Jack until she and the other women arrived at the railway station. As before, an army truck had collected their cases so they had only themselves to bring.

She could feel herself blushing as soon as she noted Jack's figure, standing among the other Forces Follies men on the platform. Even from a distance, it was easy to pick out their people: Phil slight and a little hunched, as if trying to make himself less conspicuous; Little Davy short and stocky, with a sizeable belly; Nobby broad-shouldered and towering, and Jack, tall and erect with unconscious confidence in his bearing, like the gentleman his mother had so longed for him to be.

Molly wondered how he would greet her. If he was angry at the way she had run away from him, or puzzled, or guilty. If he now thought she was the sort of woman to deliberately lead men on, seeming to invite his kiss one minute only to scream at him the next. She was sure he must think she was quite mad, whatever else he thought.

Jack summoned a rather forced smile when the women approached, but he didn't catch Molly's eye. He looked tired, she noticed, as she imagined she must herself. When he spoke, it was to address them as a group.

'We've headed ENSA off at the pass this time,' he told them. 'None of this messing about with sealed orders. I rang them up this morning and demanded they tell us our next few destinations or the lot of us would go on strike.'

'That didn't work, did it?' Tabby asked.

'You wouldn't have thought so, would you? But the girl on the phone handed over details of our next four destinations like a lamb. I feel very pleased with myself.'

'Well, cherie, where are we going?' Diana asked.

Phil shot Jack a warning look before he started blurting out troop locations for any passing Nazi sympathiser.

'They seem to be sending us on a bit of a coastal tour,' Phil said in a low voice. 'Three nights in Ramsgate, the best part of a week in Whitstable, a one-night stand in Deal and on to Dover at the end of the month.'

'Where are we playing tonight?' Fenella asked.

'An aerodrome somewhere near Ramsgate.'

'Oh goody.' She beamed at Molly. 'Airmen are my favourite. They always look so handsome in their uniforms.'

'Just behave yourself, that's all,' Davy told her sternly.

'Don't I always?' she said, radiating innocence.

Jack patted his breast pocket. 'I've got the tickets. There's a train in half an hour.'

Molly wondered if Jack would speak to her, but he didn't. In fact, by the time they were boarding their train, she was convinced he was ignoring her. They managed to find a compartment all together for the trip to Ramsgate, but he didn't so much as glance in her direction throughout the journey. He just read his newspaper, frowning. Whether his frown was for the news or for her, Molly didn't know.

Honestly, she could have cried. Until she had made such a colossal mess of everything, yesterday had been one of the best days of her life. For the first time she had really found joy in performing, even if it had only been a rehearsal. And it had been the day Jack had finally and unambiguously declared that he wanted her to be his girl — something she hadn't realised how much she wanted until she heard the words. Now their blooming romance had been broken off in the bud, because of her stupid, absurd panic. Molly didn't know whether to blame herself or Shack, but if there had been no one to see her, she would have sobbed and sobbed.

# Chapter 35

Molly spent the journey to Ramsgate pretending to be asleep. That felt easier than having to witness Jack's indifference. The pair of them were collared by Phil as soon as they alighted, however.

'All right, you two,' he said. 'No time for you to relax with the others, I'm afraid. Half an hour to settle into your digs, then it's rehearse, rehearse, rehearse. There's an ARP hut on the promenade that you can use until the warden comes on duty – I cleared it with them. Gramophone's already there. I'll be coming down later to see what you've got, and if I think the act's ready, you'll be on stage with us tomorrow night.'

'I'm happy to settle into digs later,' Jack said. 'I'd prefer to get straight to rehearsing if you're coming to see the act today.' Even now, he didn't look at Molly.

'That all right by you?' Phil asked her. Not trusting herself to hold back a sob, she only nodded miserably.

Jack was perfectly entitled to be angry. He had been very clear in his intentions towards her. He'd behaved nothing but honourably. She had encouraged him; invited his kiss. Molly could only imagine how it looked from his point of view: to be with a willing partner one moment and see her running away from him the next.

She wanted to apologise, to explain, but she didn't know where to begin. The thought of what Shack had tried to do to her filled her with shame and disgust, so that she felt she could hardly speak the words aloud if she tried.

Phil escorted them to the ARP shelter. This was an even more humble rehearsal venue than the Scout hut in Bognor. It was little more than a piece of bent corrugated steel: like an unsubmerged Anderson shelter, only larger.

There was no opportunity to talk about what had happened until Phil had left them alone in the draughty tin hut. Molly wondered whether to bring it up, or whether Jack would, or if he might try to act as though nothing had happened. She half hoped it would be the latter, yet she knew they ought to have it out. They were a double act now, weren't they? That involved a certain closeness, whether the two halves were romantically involved or not.

There was an awkward silence.

'Well, shall we get on with it?' Jack said at last, still avoiding her eye.

The way he spoke gave Molly a pang. There was none of the usual teasing in his tone, but he didn't sound angry either. He sounded hurt, which was worse.

She longed to release the tears she was holding back, to sob out the awful story of what had happened to her and beg his forgiveness. But all that came out of her was a shaky 'all right'.

He nodded and went to wind the gramophone.

'Jack, wait,' Molly managed, before he could set the record playing.

He paused. 'What?'

'Look, I…' She closed her eyes. 'Last night.'

He was bent over the gramophone, not looking at her, but the back of his neck pinkened.

'I think the less said about last night the better, don't you?' he said. 'I've still got plenty of humiliation left over so don't think you need to heap on any more.'

Molly shook her head. 'You don't understand. It wasn't what you think. I mean, I don't know what you think except that you must believe I'm some sort of crazed lunatic, but…'

Finally he turned to look at her, and she winced at the pain in his eyes.

'What I think,' he said quietly, 'is that I made the biggest mistake of my life. I don't know how I made it. I thought I could tell when a girl was keen on me. I certainly thought I knew when she wanted me to kiss her and when she didn't. Clearly I ran away with a very wrong idea, and God knows I'll be more cautious the next time the moon gets in my eyes.' He turned away again. 'Let's just forget about it and rehearse this bloody act.'

'I never meant to hurt you,' Molly whispered. 'Will you let me explain? Please?'

'What is there to explain? I made a mistake. I won't make it again.'

'You didn't make a mistake.' Molly swallowed, trying to stave off the nausea that rose whenever she was forced to think about Shack. 'When I ran away, I… that wasn't about you, Jack.'

He frowned. 'Not about me?'

Molly felt her cheeks growing hot, but she was determined to explain and apologise, whether he forgave her or not.

'I did want you to,' she said, rather desperately. 'Hold me, I mean. And when you talked about courting, it was what I wanted too. I wasn't trying to lead you on or anything like that. When you kissed me, it was… nice.' She swallowed, flustered. 'Not that I've got many kisses to compare it to, but I'm sure if I did it would be in the top five easily. Maybe even top three. So… I'm sorry, is what I'm trying to say. I really am so, so sorry.'

Jack stared at her for a moment. Then his lips quirked, amused by the strange nature of her apology. Molly almost laughed with relief to see him smile again.

'Only the top five?' he said. 'I don't know whether to be flattered or offended.'

'Possibly both,' Molly said with a damp laugh. 'Sorry. That came out all wrong. What I was trying to say is that I never meant to run away. It was an accident.'

His lips quirked again. 'So… you accidentally ran away?'

'Yes. I couldn't help it, I mean.'

'Why?' His tone softened. 'Did I do something wrong?'

'Not a thing. You were perfect.' She swallowed again, trying to banish the lump that had risen in her throat. 'It's… hard for me to talk about.'

'You don't have to tell me if it's going to upset you.'

'I want to though.' Molly closed her eyes. 'There was… a man. Someone from my past. He's the reason I ran away, not you.'

'A man?' Jack's brow knit into a scowl. 'A man who did something to you? Did he hurt you?'

'He tried to. Not only me either. A lot of girls.'

'Who was he?'

'The overlooker at the mill where I worked. Shack, we called him.' She shivered. 'Even saying his name makes me feel sick.'

'I hope he got his comeuppance.'

'He got a kick in the you-know-wheres, but he deserved a lot worse than that.' Molly met his eyes. 'I'm sorry, Jack. The last thing I want to think about when I'm with you is him. I don't ever want to think about him again. But when I feel trapped like that… it's like the soldier in the club. It makes me panic in a way I can't control. I can't help thinking of that night, and *him* trying to pull me to the ground so he could…' She broke off, trembling.

'Oh God. Poor Molly.' Jack looked as though he wanted to take her in his arms, but he restrained himself. Instead, he took her hands and pressed them gently. 'I'm sorry. It never occurred to me that might be the reason. I thought I'd got completely the wrong idea, and it hurt me when I believed you'd been toying with how I felt about you.'

'It must have seemed cruel,' Molly whispered. 'I ought to have told you about Shack before. I didn't know I'd react that way to being kissed until it happened.'

'Is that why you tremble when I hold you in the dance?'

'Yes,' Molly said, bowing her head. 'It's not that I don't trust you, Jack. It's more like… a memory that's trapped in me, and being held like that brings it to the surface.'

'Well, we can change the dance.' He looked into her eyes. 'What about the other thing?'

'What other thing?'

'The thing where I'd very much like to hold and kiss you, and prove to you that I ought definitely to be at the top of your top three, but I'd quite like to do it in a way that doesn't end with you running away screaming.'

'I want that more than anything,' she whispered. 'But I'm not sure that's something I can have, now. I'm so afraid it's like the stage fright. That it's just… part of me.'

'I don't believe either of those things are part of you. Not forever.' He stroked her cheek with one finger, just as he had on the seafront the night before. 'But I can wait,' he murmured. 'We'll go as slowly as you like. No kisses, no cuddles – just spending time together and seeing how we like one another. How does that sound?'

'But what if I can't ever…'

He planted a soft kiss on her lips – so gentle, dropping her hands so her movement was completely free. Then he drew back.

'There,' he whispered. 'That wasn't so bad, was it?'

She smiled. 'No. I liked that.'

'Well, then let's start with that. No more than you feel comfortable with, all right?'

'You'd really wait for me?'

'Strange, isn't it?' Jack said, almost dreamily. 'How long is it since we met – six weeks? Yet something tells me that out of all the girls I've known, you're going to be the one who's worth the waiting for.'

–

Molly felt that when she looked back on her life, she would always remember that day as one of the happiest she had spent. Once the air had been cleared and mutual understanding restored, everything slotted into its proper place again. With no pressure to be closer to Jack than she was comfortable with and the joy of rehearsing an act she was coming to love being part of, Molly was able to enjoy herself again. Jack held her loosely during their dance, so she never felt trapped. At lunchtime, she allowed him to take her into the town and buy them fish and chips, which they shared with the seagulls on the promenade.

'Look at that one,' she said to Jack, nodding to a particularly pushy specimen who looked as though he would make off with their chips if they dared turn their backs. 'Does he not remind you of Fenella?'

Jack laughed. 'Oh, *that's* who it is. I knew I'd seen that evil grin somewhere before.'

'I realised it the moment I saw him with one of my pilfered chips poking out of his beak.'

Jack smiled, and leaned over to plant a soft kiss on her cheek. Molly flushed happily.

'We'd better eat up and get back to work,' he said. 'Don't forget Phil's coming to see us soon. And he'll be judging us by Brooks Brothers standards, so we need to be good.'

'Did you ever see him and his partner perform?'

'A few times. They were well-matched. It's a shame the war had to come and break up the act. Mind you, lucky for us that it did, eh?'

Molly didn't speak. She only nibbled thoughtfully on a chip.

'Sorry,' Jack said in a softer voice. 'I oughtn't to joke about the war when I know you've got a brother in the fight. Performers must sound a cynical bunch, but it's mostly bravado, I promise. All I meant was that I'm glad what's happening out in the world gave us a reason to meet.'

'I know.' Molly roused herself. 'I wasn't offended. I was just wondering… what next, I suppose. For the war.'

'That's what the whole country's wondering at the moment.' He offered her his arm. 'Come on, let's go back.'

—

Later that afternoon, the brand-new double act of Forrester and Clough prepared to perform before an audience for the first time – well, before an audience of Phil, at any rate. Jack went to wind up the gramophone while Phil sat on the warden's stool, pencil in hand, watching them with an inscrutable expression over the top of his half-moon glasses.

They had worked on two song-and-dance numbers – more song than dance, but with enough movement to give them something to do. The first was 'It's De-Lovely', the Cole Porter number first performed by Bob Hope and Ethel Merman, and the second was a new song called 'Friendship', another Porter composition. The third song in their repertoire was going to be 'A Fine Romance', as sung by Fred Astaire and Ginger Rogers, but they hadn't had time to rehearse that one yet.

They had worked on some patter and jokes too, but they hadn't written those down. It sounded more natural if they just let it flow, Jack felt. This rather worried Molly, who couldn't help thinking about what would happen if she dried up on stage with no memorised script to fall back on, but she followed Jack's advice. To finish, they were going to lead the men in three of the most popular numbers from Molly's old act.

'Just focus on me,' Jack whispered to Molly as he put his hands on her waist for the start of the number. 'Don't think about an audience. Pretend you're telling me off as usual – only keep it clean this time. No naughty words.'

Molly laughed. 'You do seem to bring them out in me.'

'I have that effect on a lot of women, funnily enough. And one, two, three…'

Molly tried to do as Jack had told her and focus only on him while they performed. She was a little stiff at first, but she quickly found herself relaxing. Jack's easy grin and warmth almost seemed to cancel out the existence of an audience.

When they had finished, Phil remained silent. He looked down at the notes he had made, frowning.

'What?' Jack asked anxiously. 'Didn't you like it?'

'Hm.' Phil glanced up at last. 'You put that together in two days?'

'Um, yes,' Molly said. 'That was all we had.'

'Where did you get the dance routines?'

'We pinched them off another act, in the finest tradition of ENSA,' Jack said. 'So… you did like it? You're not smiling.'

Phil's frown finally lifted.

'Sorry,' he said. 'Professional jealousy, that's all. I'm just wondering why it took the pair of you two days to do what it took me and Pete weeks of rehearsal to achieve.'

Molly allowed herself to breathe.

'You really thought it was OK?' she said.

'I'd say it's what the two of you were made for,' Phil replied. 'I knew my instinct was right about teaming you up.'

'Will you put us on tomorrow then?' Jack asked.

'Tomorrow?' Phil stood up. 'No, I'm putting you on tonight.'

Molly looked at Jack, blinking.

'Don't you want us to learn the third song?' she asked.

'You've got nearly enough there to fill twenty minutes, and Tabby knows the music. I'd rather have something fresh than risk giving Davy a sore throat reciting "The Lion and Albert" again.' He came forward to clap them both on the back. 'Besides, you're ready, I can tell. Molly, we'll find a costume for you now.'

*Chapter 36*

The boys and girls of the Forces Follies were sharing a billet in Ramsgate: a large seafront guest house, closed for the duration so they had the place to themselves. The women had rooms on the second floor while the men occupied the third, and there was a lounge area on the ground floor with a radio, a gramophone and a few other home comforts. It was here that Molly, Jack and Phil found the other women, lounging in plush armchairs while they listened to dance music on the wireless and shared a plate of sandwiches.

Molly shook her head. 'Phil, why have we been rehearsing in a tin hut when there's this big warm room we could have used?'

'I didn't know that till we got here, did I?'

'I'm not rehearsing with this lot watching,' Jack said, nodding to the girls.

'Go away, Jack,' Fenella said lazily. 'This is girls' territory. We need it to ourselves so we can talk about you.'

'You've banished Nobby and Little Davy to their bedrooms, have you?'

'No, they went out to look for a pub,' Tabby said. 'You boys ought to join them.'

Phil shook his head. 'No time for that. We have to leave in an hour and a half. You ought to finish your sandwiches and get ready. You too, Jack.'

'Is he going on with us tonight then?' Diana asked.

'Yes, him and Molly both. You'll be in for a surprise when you see what they've cooked up.'

Diana looked unconvinced, but she didn't say anything.

290

'Right, all boys out,' Fenella said, in a voice that brooked no opposition. 'If Molly's going on tonight, she needs a pep talk from her sisters of the stage. Go on, you two, sod off.'

'If I'm being banished then the least you can do is let me have a couple of sandwiches,' Jack said, helping himself to some.

He stopped to squeeze Molly's arm before following Phil out. 'I'll see you later, all right?' he said in a low voice. 'Try not to worry, darling. It's going to be a smash, I can feel it. And for God's sake, no using the L-U-C-K word before we go on.'

Molly smiled. 'Don't worry. I'll confine myself to wishing broken limbs on you, like a good little theatre person.'

'That's my girl.'

For a moment Jack looked as if he might kiss her cheek, but he stopped when he noticed Fenella grinning at him. He only squeezed her arm again, then left the room.

'Well someone's a dark horse,' Fenella said when he'd gone, fixing her grin on Molly.

She flushed. 'I don't know what you mean.'

'Come on, we've got eyes. You and Jack Forrester, with your blushing and squeezing and "darling"-ing. You haven't been rehearsing at all, have you? You've been naughtily enjoying yourselves on ENSA's time.'

'We have been rehearsing, I promise.'

'Are you two walking out then, Moll?' Pam asked, smiling warmly. 'I love it when there's a sweet little tour romance.'

Molly wasn't sure how to answer that. She didn't know whether what she and Jack were doing constituted walking out together or not, when the sort of kisses she would associate with courting had to be off the menu. She only knew that spending time with Jack made her happy, and she very much wanted it to continue.

Tabitha noted her pink cheeks and came to her rescue.

'Pam, Ella, stop teasing the poor girl,' she said. 'It's none of our business. And Molly, sit down and have a sandwich. What's that over your arm?'

'Oh.' Molly held up the rather shabby baby-blue ballgown she had picked from the box in the back of the truck parked outside. 'It's my new costume. I thought this would pair well with Jack's tails. It isn't in the best condition, but it's better than that awful dowdy dress I had before. I can still wear the pearls and shoes.'

Pam beamed. 'Sweetheart, you're going to be a beauty. It's just your colour too. I am glad you're going on with us.'

Diana gave a superior sniff. 'What's the new act like? It must be rather rough around the edges with only two days to work it up.'

'You'll find out tonight,' Molly said coolly. She was in no mood for judgemental sneers, and she didn't see why she had to justify herself to Diana Chastain. Phil had liked the act and that was what mattered.

'I just don't want it to be an embarrassment to the troupe, that's all,' Diana said.

Fenella snorted. 'That's rich, from the woman who waves a scarf about and calls it dancing.'

Diana ignored her.

'Just try not to keel over this time, cherie,' she said to Molly, with false sweetness.

Molly glared at her. 'I didn't keel over.'

'Really? That's not how I remember it.'

'What is this we're listening to?' Tabitha asked, jumping in before a bigger row could develop. The music on the wireless had stopped, and a man with a heavy German accent was speaking.

Pam gave it a listless glance. 'The Bremen station. Ellie put it on.'

Tabitha shook her head. 'We don't want to be listening to that propaganda rubbish. Put the Forces Programme on.'

'Just a minute,' Fenella said. 'I want to listen to Lord Haw-Haw. He's repeated at half past five.'

'What on earth for?'

'I need to, don't I? Helps me get my impression right. Besides, he's a scream.'

'Three months ago, perhaps,' Diana muttered. 'Funny how he doesn't seem quite so hilarious these days.'

Molly couldn't argue with that. She rarely listened to the propaganda broadcasts from Germany now, although early in the war, she and Rita had tuned in nightly to the traitor they called Lord Haw-Haw to laugh at him along with everyone else. He had been a figure of fun then, with his clipped upper-class accent boasting of imagined and exaggerated German military successes. It had been a huge joke to the people of Britain: the idea that this absurd figure believed he had the power to sap their morale or cow them into surrender. Now, with the Phoney War seemingly at an end, his broadcasts had become far more sinister.

Molly shivered as the programme opened with the man's signature greeting – 'Germany calling, Germany calling' – delivered in his snide nasal voice. She wished Fenella would do as Tabby said and tune it back to the BBC. It didn't feel right, listening to German propaganda with Ted in danger across the Channel.

Then again, her friend was an impressionist and Lord Haw-Haw one of her most requested impersonations, so of course Fenella had good reason to listen. Molly nibbled an egg sandwich and tried to ignore whatever nonsense might be coming out of the man's mouth.

'Oh!' Fenella said when she caught the word *ENSA*. 'Listen, girls. He's talking about us.' She turned up the volume so they could all hear.

Tabitha laughed as Haw-Haw proceeded to tell them how ENSA shows were now so notoriously terrible, the British armed forces were having to pay their men to attend. 'The cheeky sod!'

Fenella looked thrilled. 'Oh, that's priceless, that is. That's going straight in my act. I'll ask the airmen how much it's costing the taxpayer for them to be our audience tonight. It ought to bring the house down.'

Haw-Haw had moved on from ENSA now. He was talking about the combined might of the Wehrmacht, and the Luftwaffe's supposed superiority over the RAF. He taunted them gleefully with the feebleness of the British Expeditionary Force, soon to come face to face with their better trained and better equipped German counterparts. Molly's eye twitched to hear him, thinking as always of her brother, and Diana looked uncomfortable too.

'Turn it off, Fenella, for God's sake,' she said. 'You've got what you need for your act. I can't stand to hear any more of him.'

'Yes, do, Ellie, please,' Pam said. 'Let's put on a gramophone record or something.'

'Don't you think he's funny?' Fenella asked. 'He has me in stitches.'

Pam shook her head. 'Not any more. Not now. Please.'

Reluctantly, Fenella turned off the wireless. Pam went to put a record on.

'He's a nasty piece of work, isn't he?' Tabby said. 'It's awful to think one of our own would turn against his people that way. Honestly, I think I almost hate him more than Hitler. I hope there's something unpleasant in store for him at the end of all this.'

'I know what you mean,' Molly said. 'My mam won't have the Bremen station on at home. It gives my little sister nightmares when Haw-Haw starts talking about what's going to happen to the troops in France.'

Fenella reached for her hand. 'Sorry, Moll. If I'd known he was going to start talking about the BEF, I wouldn't have put him on.'

'He's right about some things though, isn't he?' Diana said.

'Rubbish,' Tabitha told her shortly. 'He says what Goebbels tells him to say. If he gets anything right, it's by coincidence rather than design.'

'Well, he's right about ENSA. I mean, not about paying the audiences, but there are some dreadful acts working for them.' Diana shrugged. 'Not that I'm complaining. It just means we don't have to work so hard to impress the men.'

Molly glared at her.

All right, so it was true that she hadn't exactly joined ENSA out of patriotic duty. She had wanted to perform professionally, and she had wanted to earn the sort of wage that would allow her to look after her family. Still, it was starting to annoy her, the way the others ran the organisation down. Every day there was some comment about the quality of performance not really mattering because it was 'only ENSA', or smug boasts about the Forces Follies' superiority to every other ENSA concert party. It made it feel as though the work they were doing, entertaining the troops, hardly mattered at all.

'I don't believe that for a moment,' Molly said stoutly. 'I'm sure there are plenty of good acts with ENSA, and even those that aren't so good are probably giving it the best they can. We all should be, for the men's sake. Why should we talk down the organisation that pays our wages when there are plenty of bad eggs like Haw-Haw to do it for us?'

'No need to get so worked up about it, cherie,' Diana said. 'After all, it's only—'

'Only ENSA, I know,' Molly snapped. 'Well perhaps it can't compare to Sadler's Wells or The Windmill or wherever it was you were really working before, but I for one am proud to be a member. So should we all be. We're making men smile who've got precious little to smile about. We're bringing them some relief from the war, even if it's only for a few hours. Isn't that something to be proud of?'

Tabby and Pam nodded, and Fenella gave her a small round of applause. 'Hear, hear.'

'She's right, girls,' Tabby said. 'There are enough gags about ENSA going around without us joining in.'

Diana was glaring at Molly, however.

'Who mentioned The Windmill to you?' she demanded.

'We all did, Di,' Fenella said. 'I don't know why you keep up this Sadler's Wells baloney. Everyone knows where you came from, and if you weren't such a stuck-up prig then no one would give a damn about you taking your clothes off for a living. But it's hard to take superior sneers from someone who used to get paid by the nipple.'

Molly almost laughed, but she didn't. Diana certainly wasn't taking it as a joke. She had coloured, and looked rather hurt.

'You've been talking about me behind my back?' she said quietly. She looked at Tabby, then at Pam. 'You two as well?'

Pam rested a hand on her arm. 'Not in a mean way. I promise, Di.'

Diana didn't say anything. She just stared at the carpet for a moment, then stood up and left the room.

Tabitha shook her head at Fenella. 'Now you've done it.'

'What?' Fenella said, looking a combination of ashamed and defiant. 'She's not exactly the tact queen, is she? What about that comment she made to Davy about the Somme, when she knows what he went through there? What about what she said to Molly ten minutes ago about her act not being good enough?'

'Still, you didn't need to hurt her feelings to get your own back,' Pam said.

Fenella sighed. 'All right, fine. I'll apologise before we go to the aerodrome. Not that she didn't have it coming.'

'See that you do. I can't stand going to a gig with bad blood in the group.' Tabitha turned to Molly with a smile. 'That was quite a lecture you gave her.'

'Should I apologise too?' Molly asked. 'I didn't mean to upset her, as much as she makes me cross.'

'No, I don't think so. That lecture she deserved – we all did. I was impressed, that's all.'

'I just get annoyed when people act like ENSA's nothing. I was so proud of myself for getting in.'

Fenella smiled at Pam. 'I'd say our rookie's finally ready, wouldn't you, Pammy?'

Pam nodded. 'I think she is.'

'What am I ready for?' Molly asked.

'We got something for you,' Tabitha said. 'A sort of good luck gift. We all chipped in – even Di. We were going to give it to you after your first performance with Jack, but Ella's right. You ought to have it now.'

'You got me something? You didn't need to do that.'

'We knew you'd struggle to afford it, with your poorly sister to support, but it felt symbolic for you to have one.' Tabitha smiled. 'You know how superstitious we theatre folk are.'

'Um, thank you,' Molly said, puzzled as to what this could mean.

'Pam, can you fetch it?'

'Of course.'

Pam disappeared, returning shortly after with a large box wrapped in brown paper and string. She presented it to Molly, beaming.

'Well, darling, open it,' Fenella said. 'It's your size, don't worry. I snuffled around in your things on the sly to make sure.'

Molly began untying the string, wondering if there might be a new costume inside.

'Oh!' she said when she opened it. She picked up the cap that sat on top of the neatly folded serge, and gazed wonderingly at the insignia. *E-N-S-A*. Just like the badge she had first seen on Jack's cap in the pub...

'You see? Now you're really one of us,' Fenella said gleefully.

'Try it on then,' Pam said. 'We've been dying to see how you look in it. Go into the dining room next door and we'll guard the door from any men.'

'Yes.' Molly felt rather dazed as she stood up. 'Yes. Thank you.'

She went into the adjoining room to slip into the new uniform. There was no mirror, but she picked up a spoon from one of the tables to look at her reflection. The cap was quite becoming, and Molly smiled when she saw the ENSA insignia reflected back at her.

It wasn't only that the uniform made her look like one of them. It was that the other women *felt* she was one of them, and wanted to show her so.

'Well?' Fenella's voice called from next door. 'Let's see you, Molly.'

Molly went back in, beaming from ear to ear.

'Thank you all so much,' she said. 'It was such a kind thing to do, and I know it must have been expensive. Honestly though, I shouldn't accept it. If our act goes badly tonight, I could be on a train home tomorrow.'

'But that's exactly why we wanted you to have it,' Fenella said. 'Your act can't go badly now. The gods of the theatre won't allow it, when they can see your destiny's with us.'

Pam nodded. 'If anyone can wear the uniform with pride it's you, Molly. It suits you perfectly.'

Tabitha came to rest her hands on Molly's shoulders, smiling. 'I knew you were meant to be one of us. I could tell the day I met you at your audition.'

'Thank you,' Molly whispered. 'I'll try to be worthy of it.'

'I know you will. And I know that one day soon, Molly, ENSA is going to be just as proud of you as you are of it.'

Molly was reluctant to remove the ENSA uniform and put on the baby-blue ballgown she had picked from the costume box, but it was soon time to do so. There wasn't long until they had to leave for the RAF station.

The ballgown had certainly seen better days: much darned, frayed at the hem and with discoloured patches where the dye was beginning to fade. The style was timeless though, and it fit her well. Molly felt almost vain as she examined herself in the mirror. For the first time, she seemed to have actual curves: partly as a result of the gown's flattering cut and partly due to her improved diet since joining ENSA.

Fenella came into the room they were sharing, smiling when she saw Molly admiring herself.

'Pam was right, that is your colour,' she said. 'You're a true beauty, Molly.'

Molly flushed. 'Don't be daft.'

'You are and I'm willing to put money on it.' Fenella held out her hand. 'You can owe me a shilling for every wolf whistle you get off the men tonight. If you don't get any, I'll pay you ten bob. What do you say?'

Molly smiled. 'No thanks. My father taught me never to make bets with anyone who has a glint in their eye.'

'I can't argue with the wisdom of that,' Fenella said, laughing. 'Here, sit down and let me do your hair. We haven't got long.'

The concert was to be held in one of the hangars at a nearby aerodrome. It was a big house tonight, Phil told them in the truck on the way. The hangar was large enough to hold six hundred and fifty men.

'Oh bugger,' Molly whispered under her breath. 'Bugger bugger bugger.'

'Are you whispering naughty words to yourself?' Jack murmured beside her. 'I saw your nose wrinkle then.'

'I'm sure you're making that up.'

'Honestly. I'll hire a camera one of these days and follow you around until I've proved it.' He gave her hand a brief squeeze. 'What's up? Stage fright bothering you?'

'Well it is now. Six hundred and fifty men, Jack!'

'Don't think about them. Don't even look at them if you don't want to. Keep looking at me.'

'Like that night at the pub,' Molly said with a smile.

He raised a questioning eyebrow.

'That was why I gave a better performance than usual,' she said. 'I ignored the rest of them and pretended I was singing just for you. I was still nervous, but it wasn't nearly as bad.'

Jack smiled. 'That performance was just for me, was it?'

'I suppose it was,' Molly said, smiling awkwardly back.

'Well, you can do the exact same thing tonight. And I'll enjoy it all the more for knowing it's mine.'

'I'll try. Thanks, Jack.'

—

When they reached the drome, they were escorted to their hangar by a couple of airmen wearing RAF service police insignia. Molly stared as the troupe were confronted by a huge, dark green aeroplane parked to one side of the seating.

'Is that a Wellington?' Jack asked in a hushed voice.

'Yes, don't mind her,' one of the policemen told him cheerfully. 'No space for her in the other hangars, but she's easy to please and almost never heckles. You won't even know she's there.' He nodded to them. 'Corporal Evans and I will be on the door, so let us know if you need anything. Break a leg tonight, chaps.'

Jack nudged Molly. 'See? He knows.'

'All right, all right,' she said, laughing. 'I'm never going to live that down, am I?'

Pam blinked at the intimidating mass of the Wellington bomber. 'You know, I've worked with lions, tigers, camels and even an elephant, but this is the first time I've ever performed for a plane.'

'Never mind that,' Phil said in a businesslike manner, clapping his hands. 'All hands on deck. We've got forty-five minutes to set up the stage, so hop to it, boys.'

Jack pressed Molly's elbow before joining the other men.

'I just wanted to say for the record that you look beautiful tonight,' he whispered. 'Don't worry about anything. We'll be a smash, I know it.'

'But what if—'

'No "what if". Just keep telling yourself: we're going to be a smash.'

Molly did tell herself. She repeated it under her breath while she and the girls put playbills on the seats – hastily altered by Phil with gummed paper to cover Jack and Molly's previous billings and instead announce: *Forrester and Clough: comic songs and community singing*. She whispered it in the wings as the airmen started to file in, and while Little Davy was on stage warming them up before he introduced Diana.

She wasn't sure it helped much, but occasionally Jack or one of the girls would press her hand and flash her a warm smile, which was comforting even if it didn't quiet her nerves.

The nerves did feel different today though. For once Molly's heart wasn't beating half out of her chest, and she didn't have the wobbly feeling that her knees might give way. She was trembling, although not so violently as to incapacitate her, but what she mostly felt was numb. Numb wasn't the same as calm, but it was a darn sight better than the violent panic she'd experienced last time.

Diana was by the stage, waiting to be introduced. She looked proud and unflappable as always, but her eyes were a little pink, as if she might have been crying. Molly flushed when she thought about how she had snapped at the woman earlier, especially remembering what Tabitha had said about Diana, too, contributing towards the gift of her new uniform.

She could hear Little Davy introducing 'that celebrated ballerina, Madame Chastain'. Something made Molly reach out and press Diana's elbow.

'Di,' she whispered. 'Break a leg, all right?'

Diana looked surprised, but she summoned a smile.

'You too, cherie,' she whispered back, before going out to perform her dance.

Molly could sense this crowd wasn't quite as friendly to them as the army boys in Bognor. The airmen were a quiet bunch compared to the soldiers, despite there being three times as many of them. Perhaps they had been ordered to attend by their CO, and resented being here. It didn't help that there was an RAF chaplain in the crowd, which meant Davy was forced to be on his best behaviour. He sounded as though he was having the devil of a job warming them up without any of his blue material, but they soon thawed when Diana started performing.

Fenella shook her head. 'Honestly, I wish I knew how she does it. All she does is sway, and they react like she's Pavlova performing the ruddy Dying Swan.'

'She's got sex appeal. Animal magnetism,' Pam murmured, her eyes fixed reverently on Diana. 'It's a kind of magic, really.'

Afterwards, the men seemed to warm up nicely. Pam's circus act brought the house down, as always, and then the airmen seemed receptive to whatever entertainment was offered. Molly supposed that two attractive women was enough to make them feel they'd had their money's worth – not that it was costing them anything to be here, of course – so they were happy to tolerate whatever came after.

The biggest laugh of the night belonged to Fenella. She had been right when she'd observed that a joke in character as Lord Haw-Haw, referencing his recent ENSA comments, would bring the house down. The men loved it when, in Haw-Haw's clipped nasal voice, she demanded to know how much they had been paid to attend the concert, heckling her good-naturedly with different amounts.

'Oh, wonderful,' Molly said to Jack as the men applauded. 'Now we have to follow that.'

'And we can. Here, hold my hand.'

Molly flushed, glancing at her fellow performers. Holding hands felt like an intimate thing to do in front of others, so early in their… well, in whatever this was. Still, it might help to have something to cling to if her legs went wobbly.

Fenella came off, and Davy went out to introduce Forrester and Clough.

'Remember, smile,' Jack whispered, ventriloquist-style, as he led Molly to the stage. 'If you can't do anything else, just smile.'

Molly still felt that strange numbness, as if something in her was frozen, but she didn't feel as if she might faint or throw up. The warmth of Jack's hand around hers was reassuring. She tried to focus on that instead of the hundreds of eyes fixed on her, and smiled until her face ached. Cheers – and a number of wolf whistles – greeted their arrival, which gave Jack a perfect opening for some patter.

'Thanks, gents, but I'm afraid my striptease days are over,' he said, in response to the whistles. He started loosening his bow tie. 'Well, since you're all so keen…'

Molly felt some of the tension leave her body. Something about having Jack at her side made it feel sort of… real. As if it didn't need to be a performance at all. They were just two friends, joking and teasing, and the audience were their friends too. The men were laughing now, with shouts of 'Noooo!' as Jack pretended to begin a strip.

'I think the whistles were for me, Jack,' Molly said, nudging him.

He shrugged. 'All right, you take your clothes off then.'

There were whoops and cheers for this suggestion.

'I'm not getting paid enough,' Molly said. 'Tell you what, how about we do the song instead?'

'OK, but I think you're making a mistake.' He turned to Tabitha. 'Our music, please, Miss Daley.'

Tabby obligingly struck up the can-can, and Molly shook her head. 'Not that music, our other music.'

Everything seemed to click into place after that. Molly's nerves were still present, but for once it felt as though they were just enough to give an edge to her performance rather than prevent her from performing at all. The fact the men liked her made Molly want to please them, and the fact she wanted to please them made them like her. She had never considered before how much a variety performance ought to be a communal thing. The audience didn't just want to watch you; they wanted to feel part of it.

She and Jack performed their two songs, with patter and jokes in between. Naturally, their act was far from perfect after only two days of rehearsal. Molly tripped in at least two places, unused to dancing in a full-length ballgown. Jack forgot some of the words in the second song, forcing Molly to pick up his half of the duet for a couple of lines, and she knew she was off-key on one or two of the high notes. None of that mattered though. The men laughed and clapped through it all, and when she and Jack led them for the community singing, Molly could feel the corrugated roof of the hangar vibrating. The applause when they took their bow was stupendous, and they were compelled to go back for not one but two encores. After that, much to the audience's disappointment, Davy came out to close the show.

Jack was still gripping Molly's hand when he led her into the wings after the second encore.

'See?' he said, his eyes sparkling with exhilaration and triumph. 'Didn't I say we'd be a smash? Didn't I?'

Molly laughed breathlessly. 'They really loved us, didn't they?'

He grabbed her shoulders and kissed her heartily on the lips, then immediately let her go again.

'Sorry,' he said. 'I didn't mean to do that. Got… carried away.'

Molly glanced around at her fellow performers, all politely trying to look elsewhere – apart from Fenella, naturally, who was smirking at them.

'Um, that's all right.' To be honest, despite the fact they were surrounded by people, she couldn't help feeling a flicker of disappointment that he had let her go so quickly.

'I wish you'd made that bet with me, Moll,' Fenella said. 'I counted at least twenty wolf whistles. That would've been a pound you owed me.' She came over to give her friend a hug. 'Well done, darling. I knew you could get over those nerves, if you only had the right conditions.'

'Thank you,' Molly whispered, hugging her back.

The others came over to congratulate them, and Molly beamed as she basked in their praise.

Diana approached her last of all.

'Congratulations, Molly,' she said quietly. 'I said earlier that an act you'd been rehearsing for only two days couldn't be any good. I was wrong. Perhaps I was wrong about some other things too.'

'Thank you.'

It had sounded like an apology. Molly wasn't accustomed to seeing Diana Chastain look humble, yet she did so now. Molly would have taken the conversation further, but Phil appeared at that moment bearing a piece of paper.

'Note from their CO,' he announced. 'Diana, they want you in their mess again.'

Diana, who was used to such privileged treatment, only shrugged.

Phil turned to Jack and Molly. 'You two are among the chosen as well. I'm instructed to tell Forrester and Clough to accompany Miss Chastain to the officers' mess. The rest of us will put in some time with the rank-and-file.'

Molly blinked. 'Us?'

'That's what it says.' Phil smiled. 'Quite the stars of the show, eh? The Wingco says he'll send for a car whenever you're ready to leave.'

Molly floated to the officers' mess in a daze, hanging on to Jack's arm. A young flight lieutenant had been sent to escort them, and he looked almost as dazed as Molly to have a beauty like Diana on his arm a little ahead of them.

'What are you feeling?' Jack asked in a low voice.

'I'm… not sure.' Molly blinked a few times, just to make sure she was awake. 'Jack, did we just go on stage?'

He smiled. 'We did, in front of six hundred and fifty airmen and one Wellington bomber. Something to tell your sister when you write home, eh?'

'I only hope the censor won't scratch it out. Daph adores planes.'

'So now I'm going to have to compete with a roomful of handsome officers for your favours, am I?'

'They were whistling at me,' she said, still in a state of disbelief.

'You sound surprised.'

'I don't get whistled at much.'

'Then I'll be sure to whistle at you whenever I see you from now on.' He hesitated, looking a little awkward. 'Sorry about before. Kissing you in front of everyone. As I said, I got carried away.'

Molly flushed. 'I didn't mind.'

'They'll all know now, I suppose. About us. Sorry.'

'According to Fenella, they did already. I don't think you can keep secrets in an ENSA troupe.'

Molly remembered how she had felt when Jack kissed her in the wings, briefly but passionately, while they were both buzzing with the exhilaration of a triumphant performance. What would have happened if they had been alone, she wondered, and there had been no reason for him to stop? Would she have panicked as before, and felt the urge to run?

Everything seemed different now. She had worried that her panic at being held, like her stage fright, was something that would always be part of her. But tonight she had managed her stage fright, even if she hadn't been free of it. All it had taken was a different way of looking at things. And if she could conquer *that* panic... might she one day be free of the other?

In the mess, they were greeted warmly by the squadron's commanding officer: Wing Commander Heatherly. He shook Jack's hand, and pressed Molly's fingers to his lips.

'I can't tell you how much I enjoyed your performance, Mr Forrester,' he said. 'And your good lady wife, of course. Not laughed so much in years.'

Molly flushed. 'Oh, I'm not... um, we aren't married.'

The officer blinked. 'Aren't you? I rather assumed... but nothing good ever comes of assuming.' He smiled at his men, several of whom had already crowded around Diana. 'Although you might like to keep that quiet around here. Show these chappies a beautiful woman and they're like greyhounds out of the traps. Gentlemen all, of course – nothing but youthful high spirits. Now, allow me to bring you each a glass of champagne.'

Molly felt her cheeks turn an even deeper shade of pink. Being called a beautiful woman and plied with champagne by high-ranking RAF officers wasn't something that happened to her even in her dreams. She felt as though she had stepped into Daphne's perfect fantasy, and vowed to memorise every detail for her sister.

Wing Commander Heatherly returned a moment later with a flute of something golden and bubbly for each of them.

'Do mingle and enjoy yourselves,' he said courteously. 'I must pay my respects to the other young lady. Such a talent. Sadler's Wells must have been devastated by the loss.' He left them to speak with Diana.

'Funny how no one seems to notice she barely dances at all,' Jack said in Molly's ear. 'She just runs about and sways.'

'Pam's right. Her talent is in being magnetic,' Molly said absently, watching Diana in her element, being courted by well-bred young men. 'It casts a sort of spell, so people are convinced they've seen something more impressive than they have – like sleight of hand.'

Jack glanced around the smoky room. 'We ought to mingle with the officers. We are here to represent the troupe, and there isn't enough of Diana to go around no matter how much the men might wish it.'

Molly looked warily at her champagne. 'I don't have to drink this, do I?'

'Why, what's wrong with it?' He took a sip from his glass. 'Tastes like good stuff to me.'

'I'm worried it'll go to my head. Wine never seems to do me much good.'

'One glass won't harm you. It'll help you to relax.' He smiled. 'Don't worry, Mrs Forrester, I'll look after you. I can't have a wife of mine getting tipsy in officers' messes without a chaperone.'

She laughed. 'Crikey, that was embarrassing.'

'Do you think so? I rather enjoyed my brief stint as a married man.' He offered his arm. 'Shall we go make some friends?'

'I suppose so.' Molly cast a nervous glance at the men in their smart blue-grey uniforms, chatting in impeccable upper-class English while they smoked and sipped champagne. 'I wish we could've gone to the NAAFI with the others,' she whispered. 'It's not very me, all this.'

'How do you mean?'

'Well. Molly from the mill. I've never been so aware of my accent.'

'A posh accent doesn't change the person inside, believe me. You're perfect just as you are.' He nodded to her still untouched glass. 'Have a drink and you'll soon feel like a queen.'

Molly took a sip. It was rather pleasant, and didn't make her cough like the red wine she had drunk in Cortesi's. She was sure the bubbles floated straight up to her head though.

'How long do we need to stay?' she asked Jack.

'An hour at least, just to be polite. After that we can claim you've got a headache and ask for a car home.'

—

However, several hours later, they were still there. At first, Molly hadn't liked to drag Diana away from the party – when they left, it would have to be all three together. Then she found she was starting to enjoy herself.

The officers were very gentlemanly, and their conversation courteous and stimulating. They danced elegantly, kissed Molly's hand and plied her with delicious, exotic canapés – devilled quails' eggs, pâté wrapped in pastry, smoked salmon with cream – things that seemed to belong to another world than the one she had come from. They pressed champagne on her too, though Molly did her best to drink slowly. While Jack was right that it helped her relax, she could feel her head beginning to throb as the evil bubbles did their work.

As she had said to Jack, the officers' mess really wasn't her – not Molly from the mill. But tonight she wasn't her, was she? Tonight she was a star of ENSA: applauded, feted, beautiful. Tonight she was someone who ate caviar and sipped French champagne. Molly didn't even mind when Jack left her to go mingle, surrounded as she was by so many other admirers.

'Thank you,' she said, as one of the young officers offered her a devilled egg. She smiled as another topped up her glass. 'You're very kind, all of you.'

'You're smiling, Miss Clough,' the young man who had been particularly attentive to her, Flying Officer Devon, observed. 'Are we amusing you? I do hope so.'

'I was only thinking how much I'm like Scarlett O'Hara tonight,' Molly said dreamily. 'At the Twelve Oaks barbecue in her daring dress, surrounded by admirers. It'll give my little sister the laugh of her life when I tell her.'

'You do have a look of a fair-haired Vivien Leigh,' another man observed, perhaps hoping to oust Devon from the position of favourite with a little flattery. 'You might almost be sisters.'

Molly laughed. 'It would take a lot more champagne than I've had tonight to persuade me that was true, but thank you for the compliment.'

'Do allow me to get you another drink, Miss Clough.'

'No, please.' Molly covered her glass to prevent anyone trying to pour more into it. 'I mustn't drink any more. I've got the beginning of a terrible headache. In fact, I need to go out and get some air, as much as it pains me to leave you all.'

'I'll escort you,' Devon said, jumping in before any of the other men had a chance.

'Thank you, no. I'd rather be alone for a moment.'

Devon looked disappointed. 'Well, do hurry back, Miss Clough. I haven't heard half as much as I'd like to about you, and it's half past two already.'

Molly rose, a little unsteadily, and made her way to the door.

She passed Diana on the way, who was speaking crossly to one of her own admirers. He seemed to have made the mistake of bringing up politics.

'Oh, Halifax,' she was saying in a disgusted tone. 'Where's Lord Halifax going to get us? He's just another Chamberlain, ready to stab the rest of Europe in the back to buy Britain a shameful peace. We need someone who'll stand up to Hitler, not bloody well get into bed with him.'

So Diana was enjoying herself, at any rate.

Outside the mess, Molly leaned against the cool wall and breathed deeply. It felt good to be in the crisp night air, carrying a faint aroma of hawthorn blossom.

Was it really half past two in the morning, as Devon had said? She didn't think she had ever stayed up so late before – or the old Molly hadn't. But this Molly did that sort of thing, didn't she? Tonight she was Scarlett O'Hara, and there was nothing she didn't dare do.

It was dark, of course – blackout dark, so you could barely see your hand in front of your face – but Molly could smell smoke, and see the red glow of a cigarette. She wasn't alone, then.

'Is someone here?' she whispered, a little uncertainly.

'Someone is. I wondered how long it would take you to notice him.'

She smiled. 'Jack.'

'What made you tear yourself away from your admirers then, Miss Clough?'

'I wanted some air.' She raised an eyebrow. 'You're not jealous, are you?'

'As Othello. But I'm glad you're having fun, all the same.'

'I'd like to say that making you jealous by flirting with hordes of handsome officers was my plan all along, but I'd be fibbing,' she said. 'It was seduction by canapé. They kept giving me these delicious salmon things.'

'They are rather good, aren't they?'

She fumbled in the darkness until she found his hand. 'I'm glad I found you though. It's exhausting being Scarlett O'Hara. After a few hours of it, I feel like I'm quite ready to be Molly from the mill again.'

'It's late,' Jack said with a sigh. 'I ought to do my duty as chaperone and carry you girls home. Phil gave me strict instructions not to let you stay past three.' He stamped out his cigarette. 'I only hope I don't have to fight off half the Royal Air Force to reclaim you both.'

'You might have a job tearing Diana away. She's lecturing some unfortunate young officer about who the next prime minister ought to be.'

He laughed. 'Of course she is. Are you ready to say goodbye then?'

'Yes.' She tugged his hand to stop him going back indoors. 'In a minute.'

'What is it, Molly?'

'Jack, will you…' She took a deep breath. 'Earlier, in the wings… what I'm trying to say is, um… would you like to kiss me?'

'Well, yes,' he said, sounding taken aback. 'I mean, I'd like to. But…'

'I won't run away, I promise. At least, I'll try my best not to.'

There was a pause as Jack seemed to consider this.

'You've had champagne,' he said after a while.

'I know. But not too much.'

'Are you sure you want me to?'

'I'm sure,' Molly whispered.

She still had a hold of his hand. In the darkness, she pulled him towards her and sought his lips, the champagne making her bold.

Jack seemed surprised at first, but Molly wrapped her arms around him, and the kiss soon burned through any principles that had been holding him back. He enfolded her in an embrace and pressed her close.

He remained controlled though, despite his passion. His arms were firm around her, but not tight, so she didn't experience the panic that went with being trapped. Her heart was pounding, but through excitement this time rather than fear. If she could just stop her brain letting that foul memory take hold…

Jack's embrace grew tighter as the kiss deepened, and Molly felt herself stiffen involuntarily. He broke away at once.

'Sorry,' he whispered. 'Here.' He loosened his arms, so she could once again move freely. 'Is that better?'

'Yes.' She exhaled with relief as panic fled again. 'Yes. I'm sorry.'

'Don't say sorry. We'll keep doing things your way until you feel comfortable, all right?'

She smiled. 'You know, I think you would make the top three.'

'Only the top three? Who's number one?'

'Oh, definitely Rhett Butler. You know, in my dreams.'

'I have to say, I was rather hoping for the number one position myself.'

She patted his cheek. 'Well, keep trying and I'm sure you'll get there.'

A young aircraftman rushed past them, so eager to get into the mess that he never noticed the two lovers embracing in the darkness. They ignored him.

Jack claimed Molly's lips again. He didn't hold her this time, but instead caressed her cheek and the back of her neck as he kissed her. His fingertips on her skin made her shiver.

They didn't have long to enjoy one another, however. A tumult seemed to be occurring within the mess, and somewhere overhead, a siren began blaring. Within moments, men had started pouring out, pulling on jackets and caps.

Jack frowned. 'What on earth can be going on?'

Wing Commander Heatherly spotted them as he was about to hurry past.

'Oh. Miss Clough. Mr Forrester,' he said rather breathlessly. 'I'm dreadfully sorry about this. I'm afraid we've all been scrambled. Emergency, you know. I'll order a car to take you and Miss Chastain back to your billet. Thanks awfully for joining us.'

After a hasty handshake for Jack and a hand-kiss for Molly – bound by a code of chivalry that couldn't be relaxed even for a military emergency – the Wingco hurried away.

Molly blinked at Jack. 'That was very sudden. I wonder what the emergency can be?'

Diana pushed impatiently past the scrambling officers to join them.

'Do you really not know?' she asked.

'Not know what? What is there for us to know?'

'What do you think? There's only one reason they'd scramble every officer on the drome at this time in the morning. Only one thing it could be.' She lowered her voice. 'It's the Jerries,' she whispered. 'They've marched into bloody Belgium, haven't they?'

No one spoke in the car. No one knew what to say. All Molly could think about was her brother, right on the Belgian border, waiting for the Germans – perhaps with them already advancing, when he had never been in a battle in his young life before. Diana and Jack sat grim and silent too.

'You're sure it's that?' Molly asked Diana in a whisper when the RAF Motor Transport driver had left them at their front door.

'I'm sorry, Molly. It's been clear to anyone who follows the news that it was only a matter of time until Hitler made his move. I'm certain that's all it could be.'

Molly swallowed a sob. She felt faint suddenly, the shock and the champagne combining to make her legs buckle, and she stumbled as she followed Diana to the door. Jack darted forward to put an arm round her, but he didn't look at her. He only stared grimly ahead.

'I'll help Molly to her room,' he said to Diana. 'Do you need a hand, Di?'

Diana was as pale as alabaster, but she stood erect.

'I don't need any help,' she said, in a voice that sounded strangely far away. 'Just take care of Molly. Goodnight.'

She brushed past them like a ghost and ascended the stairs to the second floor.

Molly was still dizzy, and she leaned against the Jack's arm. He didn't speak – not until they reached the door of the room she was sharing with Fenella.

'I ought to have been there,' he said in a distant, hollow voice.

'Where?' Molly asked.

'There. With them. The BEF.' Suddenly he slammed his palm hard against the wall. 'ENSA. What the hell right have I got to be hiding in ENSA when there are men out there preparing to die? I convinced myself it was important. That it mattered as much as the fight. That this wasn't a proper war anyhow, so it didn't matter what I did. That I owed it to my mother's memory. I convinced myself of all that, because I wanted to believe I wasn't a coward.' He swallowed hard. 'But I am, Molly. I must be, or I'd be there now instead of letting boys barely out of the cradle die in my place.'

'But it *is* important,' Molly murmured, still holding on to his arm for support.

'I ought to have known where my duty lay. I chose to ignore it, and now...' He turned a solicitous look towards her, as if remembering himself. 'But look, you ought to go to bed. You're almost falling down. Do you need me to help you?'

'No, I... I think I can get to bed all right.'

'Right.' His voice was flat. 'Goodnight then.'

He didn't kiss her goodnight. Molly watched him go, his shoulders slumping. She couldn't imagine how it must feel to be Jack in that moment. Too many of her thoughts were with Ted to have any to spare for him.

Molly went into her room and threw herself down on her single bed, still in the ballgown she had worn to perform in. It already felt like a lifetime ago.

'Is everything all right, Moll?' Fenella mumbled. 'I heard a bang.'

'Yes,' Molly whispered. 'Sorry for waking you. We... we had a little too much champagne, that's all.'

'And I can't wait to hear absolutely all about it, darling,' Fenella said, her voice slurred with sleep. 'But before that, I simply must get another six hours. Nighty night.'

Molly removed her shoes, but she had no energy to undress further. She just lay in the darkness, choking on noiseless sobs.

All she could think about was Ted. Her naughty little brother, who had got into scrape after scrape in their schooldays. Ted, who even as a boy could always charm his sister's older girlfriends. And now he was there with hundreds of other young lads who must have sisters, mothers, sweethearts fearing for them, waiting for the German tanks while Luftwaffe planes strafed overhead.

What would happen to him? What would happen to everyone she loved, if France were to fall and the Germans launched an invasion of this very country? Was this the end of the world Molly knew?

After an hour of lying in the dark, she gave up on trying to sleep. She pulled a dressing gown on over her foolish ballgown and crept quietly to the lounge where the wireless was. There would be nothing on the airwaves at this time of night, but she couldn't just do nothing. Perhaps there would be an emergency broadcast, or something that would give her a clue as to the fate of her brother.

When Molly reached the lounge, she found it already occupied. Diana was sitting beside the wireless in the dim light of a lamp, twiddling the tuning knob, although the set emitted nothing but an empty hum.

She flashed Molly a shaky smile. 'I keep hoping I'll find something on one of the other stations, even if it's only Haw-Haw mocking us. But it's dead all the way round.'

Molly took a seat beside her. 'Couldn't sleep either?'

'Not a wink.' Diana left off turning the knob and took a small flask from the pocket of her dressing gown. She took a swig before offering it to Molly. 'Here, have a nip of this. It'll help warm you up.'

That probably wasn't a good idea, mixing spirits with the champagne she had drunk earlier, but nothing much seemed to matter now. Molly welcomed anything that would numb her. Everything felt unreal and distorted, as if she was looking at the world in a fractured fairground mirror.

'Thanks,' she said when she had swallowed a mouthful of whatever was in the flask – brandy, she thought.

'I suppose you're thinking of your brother.'

'Yes.'

'What age is he?'

'Nineteen,' Molly said in a hollow voice. She swallowed a sob. 'Just… nineteen.'

Diana took her hand and pressed it a little awkwardly. 'I'm sorry.'

Molly turned to look at her. 'Have you got someone out there too?'

'Yes,' Diana said quietly. 'Yes, there's someone.'

'A sweetheart?'

Diana didn't answer. She just took another swig from her flask. The two of them sat in silence, listening to the crackling hum of the empty airwaves.

It was a strange thing. They were still holding hands, as though it hadn't occurred to them to relinquish the warmth of each other's fingers. Of all the women she had met in ENSA, Diana Chastain was the one Molly had found it hardest to like. She wouldn't have called them friends by any stretch of the imagination. But there was something about this night that left them needing one another.

For a long time they just sat, hand in hand, listening to the wireless crackle.

'Women don't like me,' Diana said quietly after some time had passed.

Molly started. She had been half in a daze, lulled by that strange hypnotic sound.

'What?' she said.

'Women don't like me. Men like me. I suppose that's why women don't.' She laughed bleakly, and took another swig from her flask. 'When you're young you think it's wonderful, to be envied by other girls for your beauty. To be courted and admired wherever you go. Until eventually you realise that the men who court you don't have any interest in the person underneath, and soon come to resent you for daring to have a brain under your pretty face. And then what do you have? No friends of your own sex, and a lot of male flatterers who won't even glance at you once your looks have started to go. It's all so empty. So very empty.' She held out the flask. 'Have another drink.'

Molly did so, with a wondering look at the woman who had given it to her. She wasn't sure Diana had ever spoken so many words to her in one go before.

'I wasn't kind to you,' Diana said when Molly handed the flask back, still in the same quiet, even tone, with just the hint of a tremble. 'I'm sorry for that. It becomes a sort of shield, you know? Push them away before they can push you. If someone's bound not to like you, decide you don't like them first. That way you can persuade yourself you don't care.'

Molly was quiet as she thought about this strange confession.

'I didn't like you,' she said at last. 'But I admired you. I respected everything you seemed to know. I'd have liked to be friends, if you hadn't seemed so cold.'

Diana laughed grimly. 'Even after you found out what I used to do?'

'I didn't care about that,' Molly said, flushing a little, because that wasn't strictly true. 'Or at any rate, I don't care about that now. I was rather green when I first came, I suppose. I had no idea there were places like The Windmill.'

Again, Diana fell into a blank silence.

'It's my daughter,' she said after a time.

'I'm sorry?'

'My daughter. That's who I have in France. Or rather my stepdaughter – if she was mine to keep, I'd never have left her behind.' She swallowed a sob. 'Her father doesn't want me to see her. My second husband, Alain Chastain. He says she'll grow up better with no mother at all than with a drunken tart like me. Someone told him how I was earning my keep in London after we separated – no thanks to him, since he was the one who left me without a penny.'

'Oh, love.' Molly gave the now trembling hand in hers a squeeze. 'I am sorry. How long is it since you saw her?'

'Two years,' Diana murmured. 'She was eight when I saw her last. She's ten now. Alain allows us to write, but he won't let me visit her.' She choked on a sob. 'Georgette writes such fond letters from Paris. Keeps a little place in her heart for the mama she once had, like the sweet, good child she is. I don't suppose you'd peg me for the maternal type, Molly, but I loved that little girl – more than life I loved her. Her real mother died when she was a baby, so she only ever had me. Until Alain took her away from me.' She gave a bleak laugh. 'That's why I insist on Sadler's Wells being added to our playbills – for her sake, not mine. I send her every one, so she can be happy believing her *maman* is something better than what she is.'

'Isn't there anything you can do? You are her mother, even if she's not your flesh and blood.'

'She's Alain's child,' Diana whispered brokenly. 'In blood and in law, she belongs to him. If he wants to keep us apart, there isn't a thing I can do about it.' A tear slipped down her cheek. 'And now the blasted blighted Germans are coming, and God knows what will happen to my darling girl.'

'They'll never get as far as Paris,' Molly said, with as much firmness as she could muster. 'The Low Countries aren't going to just lie down and surrender, and you said yourself the Maginot Line was impregnable. Our boys will soon see the Jerries off if they're foolish enough to try to get their tanks through the Ardennes.'

'I said it because it was what I needed to believe. Suddenly that feels a lot harder to do.'

Diana's tone had been steady all through her confession – it had felt like a confession, as if Molly were a priest with the power to grant her absolution – but she broke down now. Molly put her arms around her and tried to comfort her, even while her own tears flowed.

'It'll be all right,' she whispered. 'If there's a God, it has to be.'

'And what if there isn't?'

But Molly wasn't a priest, and she didn't have any answer to that question.

They held on to each other all through those long hours, until grey dawn started to seep through the edges of the blackout curtains. They cried when they needed to cry and drank when they needed to drink and waited, waited, waited for any news to come over the crackling airwaves. Occasionally Diana would twiddle the tuning knob, trying the German, Belgian, Dutch and French stations, but there was nothing. Until eventually, at 7 a.m., the radio came to life with the morning news bulletin.

*Here is the news and this is Alvar Lidell reading it…*

For a moment – just a moment – Molly felt a glimmer of hope.

Perhaps it had been a mistake. There were other emergencies that could have scrambled the men of Bomber Command. Perhaps the Germans hadn't moved after all, and maintained their position on their own side of the Belgian border.

Her hopes were shattered, however, as the announcer delivered the news she and Diana had been dreading. The German forces had sent bombers and paratroopers into the Low Countries early that morning, and an attempted invasion of France now seemed inevitable.

# Chapter 40

The news that the Phoney War had finally become something very real indeed soon spread to the other members of the Forces Follies.

No one seemed to know quite what to do. It felt as significant as the news back in September that the country was at war.

Fenella remained sanguine, talking breezily about how she, for one, was glad things had come to a head so they could crush Jerry once and for all. Little Davy grew pale and quiet, retreating to his room to drink alone. Pam, too, shut herself in her room and sobbed into her pillow, her tender heart breaking for every boy about to enter the fight. Diana refused to leave the wireless. Tabitha took refuge in knitting, furiously clicking her needles making comforts for the troops as if that could somehow make things right. Nobby went out in search of a pub, Phil spent much of the day in the phone box at the end of the road talking to various people from ENSA, and no one knew where Jack had got to. He had gone out for a walk some hours earlier and was yet to return.

Molly, seeking salve for the helplessness she was feeling, walked to the post office to send a telegram to her mother with instructions to telephone the nearby box at four o'clock if she could spare money for the call. After that she wrote to her sister, endeavouring to pour into the letter everything she thought might bring Daphne comfort. She spoke lightly of the developments in the war. Instead she gave a detailed description of her performance at the RAF station, the Wellington bomber she had seen, and how she had felt like Scarlett O'Hara as the handsome air officers had flirted with her – all of which she knew would be meat and drink to Daph's romantic, adventure-hungry imagination.

More news came in throughout the day. The government was in crisis. In the early evening, the Follies folk learned that the prime minister had resigned after the Labour party had refused to enter into a coalition under him. The newspapers that Nobby brought with him when he staggered back from the pub speculated about whether Chamberlain would be succeeded by the First Lord of the Admiralty, Mr Churchill, or Lord Halifax, the foreign secretary. The press kept an upbeat tone, reporting valiant fighting in Belgium and Holland and expressing revitalised hope for this fresh phase of the war under a new premier, but to Molly it felt like the bottom had dropped out of the world as she knew it.

Nobody mentioned the second concert they were due to play at the aerodrome that evening. It seemed clear that it couldn't go ahead, when every RAF station, army barracks and naval base in the country must be on high alert.

At seven o'clock, Phil summoned everyone to the lounge.

Jack had returned from wherever he had spent the day, Molly noticed. It was the first time she had seen him since the previous evening. He looked as hollow-eyed as she knew she did herself. Sleep, it seemed, had been elusive for more than just her and Di. He didn't speak, but he claimed a seat by her and instantly took her hand, pressing it between both of his. She managed a weak smile for him.

Tabitha and Pam, who were sharing cooking duties, came in with two plates of sandwiches and some cold meats.

'Sorry there's nothing warm,' Pam said quietly. 'We didn't have any heart for cooking.'

Nobody seemed to care much. A few people took a sandwich and nibbled at it listlessly.

Fenella shook her head. 'Honestly, what is wrong with everyone? You act like this is the end of the world. We all knew the Phoney War had to become real one day, didn't we? And now it has, so much the better. It only means we can end it sooner.'

'You make it sound so simple, child,' Davy said quietly.

'Well we're obviously going to win, aren't we? This is just the beginning of the end.'

'And what if we don't win, Fenella?' Diana demanded. 'Even if we do, people are going to die – a lot of people, perhaps.'

'Yes, I know, and it's sad, of course, but that's what happens in wars.' Fenella looked helplessly around the sombre group. 'I mean, it does have to happen, doesn't it, so we can beat the baddies? That's how wars work.'

No one responded. There was just a collective sigh, as of resignation. Davy patted Fenella on the shoulder.

'If you were older, you might understand,' he said, his voice slurred. 'But… you'll see. You'll all see.'

'What did you want to talk to us about, Phil?' Tabitha asked.

Phil took the hint and stood up to address them.

'Well, chaps, it'll come as no surprise that our concert tonight has been cancelled,' he told them. He glanced at Nobby, whose eyes were half closed, and at Little Davy slumped like an under-stuffed toy in his chair. Both men had spent much of the day drowning their sorrows in spirits. 'Which, given the circumstances, is probably for the best. Likewise, the garrison theatre we were booked at for a week and all the Whitstable dates have been scratched. I've spoken with ENSA and it's the same story all over. They're pausing domestic operations and granting all but a few parties a leave of absence – two weeks, starting today. We'll be moving on to Dover as planned on the 27th, however, to fulfil our obligations there.'

'What do we do in the meantime?' Pam asked.

Phil shrugged. 'Enjoy the sea air, work on your acts, take a little rest. Go home to see your families if you like, as long as you're back for the Dover dates. Try to keep your chins up, and hope it'll all be settled by the time we go back to work.'

Davy snorted. 'While the Belgians are being bombed to hell on their side of the Channel, and us likely to be next?'

'It might not come to that,' Phil said evenly. 'Let's not act as though the worst has happened already.'

'It's just hard, feeling so helpless,' Pam whispered. 'And it's awful not knowing what's really happening over there. We know the wireless and the papers will only tell us what we need to hear. It might be far worse than they're letting on.'

'You're right, it is hard feeling helpless,' Phil said quietly. 'But that doesn't grant us the right to give up. We all joke about ENSA, but rest assured, we've never been more needed than we are now. Take your two weeks' leave and use it to pull yourselves together. Then screw on those grins, stick out those chins and prepare to be the absolute best you can be for the boys. A lot of poor bastards are about to find out what a real war looks like, and it's up to us to try to make them smile in spite of it.'

–

Molly did pay a short visit home to give what comfort she could to her mother and sister, who were both in agonies about Ted. Rita, too, was grateful to see her friend and confide in her about her recent engagement and fears for Harry.

Molly was glad to see her loved ones, to be able to share their griefs and fears, but she nevertheless felt anxious about being away from her troupe. Phil's talk had struck a chord with her, and she felt her duty now was to continue working on her act so it would be as polished as possible when ENSA put them back to work. So after three days at home, she said her goodbyes to her family, returned to her billet in Ramsgate and got straight back to rehearsing with Jack.

There was a certain comfort, too, in being by the coast. It made her feel closer to her brother to know she was just across the Channel from him – barely thirty miles over the water. Molly almost felt as though she could swim to Ted if she had to. She was sure that on one sunny day she could see the French coastline, although Jack laughed and told her it was just a cloud.

Molly didn't mind him laughing at her. It seemed to have become a rare thing, Jack's laughter. He and Molly spent a lot of time together after her return to Ramsgate – rehearsing, going to the pictures, walking along the seafront – but he was often sombre. He was as fond of her as ever, yet he rarely teased as before.

Molly supposed they had all become rather sombre now the tide of the war had turned, even Fenella, who had finally begun to understand what real war meant. With Jack it felt different, though. He seemed so far away, his thoughts perpetually somewhere else. He spent a lot of time wandering the seafront alone, always with the same thoughtful expression.

Molly was the only one to take any home leave. None of the others left Ramsgate. For some reason, the troupe felt the need to cling together in this time of crisis. They were like a family in their way, Molly supposed – mismatched, but bound together in spite of that.

Every day brought fresh news of the situation on the continent, and fresh fears. In less than a week Holland had been forced to surrender, and there was talk of German tanks making breakthroughs into France at Sedan, outflanking the supposedly impenetrable Maginot Line. The newspapers and the new prime minister, Churchill, continued bullishly optimistic, boasting of advances made into Belgium by the BEF, but the propaganda broadcasts from Germany told a different story. They spoke of Churchill's folly in sending his men into Belgium, of mass retreats and refugee chaos. They warned that France was about to fall, and that when it did, Britain would certainly be next. It was hard to know who was telling the bigger lies to the British people: the Germans, or their own government.

The other Follies members wouldn't listen to the propaganda broadcasts, feeling it was unpatriotic at a time like this, but each evening Diana and Molly met in the lounge of the Ramsgate billet to tune in, hand in hand just as they had been on the first night they had waited for news. As the only two with loved ones where the fighting was, they were desperate for anything that might give a clue to their fate – even bad news. Molly listened eagerly when the German broadcasts read out messages from prisoners of war to their families, but there had been no Private Edward Clough among them.

She and Diana were listening together on the night of the 26th, the evening before the troupe was due to move on to Dover, as the traitor Lord Haw-Haw crowed over failed Allied counter-attacks at Arras and predicted the annihilation of the BEF. A million Allied troops, he said, had been forced out of Belgium and back towards the French coast, where they were now trapped in a pocket – sitting ducks for the German Stukas.

'Is your brother with them?' Diana asked quietly.

'I don't know,' Molly whispered. 'I don't know where he is. I don't even know if he's alive.' She drew the back of her hand across her eyes. 'Have you heard anything about your little girl?'

'Nothing,' she said hoarsely. 'Nothing at all.'

# Chapter 41

The next day, they packed their truck and left it in Nobby's care while they caught the train to Dover. Molly sat beside Jack on the journey. As usual he held tightly on to her hand, and as usual he seemed a million miles away as he gazed out of the window.

'Penny for them,' she said quietly.

'There's something happening, Moll,' he murmured. 'Don't you feel it?'

'Of course. We all do.'

'I don't mean in the world. I mean here, right where we are.' He nodded to a boatyard they were passing, bustling with activity. 'Haven't you noticed them?'

'What?'

'Boats. Big ones, small ones, medium-sized ones. Pleasure cruisers, steamships, fishing vessels. We've been in Ramsgate for over a fortnight and I've never seen so many boats on the waves as I did last night. There were even more ready for launch when I went out this morning. I can't work it out.'

'Isn't that normal in seaside places?' Molly asked. 'Perhaps it's the start of fishing season. I mean, if fish have seasons.'

He turned to look at her, worry in his eyes.

'And what about the pleasure cruisers?' he said. 'I saw a whole fleet ready to sail. Who's in them? There aren't any tourists in wartime.'

'No, I suppose there aren't,' Molly said, glancing curiously out of the window. 'Could it be to do with France?'

'I don't know. But it seems very strange.'

There was bad news as soon as they alighted in Dover. Phil found a telegram waiting at the ticket office, letting him know that the two shows they were due to play that day had once again been cancelled in the wake of the national emergency.

'Oh, I wish they'd give us something to *do*,' Fenella groaned. 'I'm going mad waiting around. I want to do something to help.'

Diana had gone to buy a paper as soon as she left the train. She looked serious as she skimmed the latest developments.

'What is it, Di?' Molly asked.

Diana hesitated, as if she didn't want to share what she had just read. That was when Molly knew it must be bad. Jack put an arm around her waist.

'You'd better tell us,' he said quietly to Diana.

'The Navy are evacuating troops from Channel ports under heavy air attack,' Diana said in a low voice. 'The papers are trying to dress it up but it's clearly a major withdrawal, not just small-scale evacuations. This is the end, I think.' She rested a hand on Molly's arm. 'I'm sorry.'

Molly felt the world begin to spin. She sagged against Jack.

'It'll be all right,' Fenella said, rather desperately. 'The Navy will bring them all home. And then... then the RAF can finish the job, can't they? Hitler can't be allowed to win.' Her voice choked with a sob. 'He just can't.'

'Come on,' Phil said. 'There's a couple of cars waiting. Let's get to our billets, then we can talk things over.'

There was little talk that day, however.

Boys and girls were in separate digs again, private homes that had been evacuated, but Molly begged Jack not to leave her. They sat with Diana in the cramped living room of the girls' billet, listening to the Home Service until the last news bulletin ended shortly after midnight.

Even the BBC couldn't pretend the Allies were in control now, as men were herded like cattle into a small pocket at Dunkirk. The German propagandists crowed that all the troops in the Dunkirk cauldron would be slaughtered within days. Diana quickly retuned the set at this, seeing how Molly blanched.

'Do you want to go to bed?' Jack asked Molly quietly, a little while after the National Anthem had marked the end of the day's broadcasting and Diana had retreated to her room.

'I don't think I could sleep.'

'No, nor me. Let's go for a walk.'

'Yes. All right.'

She put on her coat and they ventured out into the night. The sky was cloudy, covering the waning gibbous moon, and only the dim light of Jack's blackout torch showed the way.

They wandered to the chalky clifftops and looked out to sea. There was nothing much to be seen in the black ocean, except for a faint red-orange glow on the horizon.

'St Elmo's Fire,' Jack whispered, wrapping Molly in his arms – gently, so as not to cause her panic. 'That's a good omen, the sailors say.'

'Is that really what it is?'

'No. It's them, I suppose. The troops. They're probably setting fire to fuel depots before they disembark, making sure Jerry can't get his hands on them.'

Molly gazed at the faint orange light. If she narrowed her eyes, she could see silhouettes that might be Navy ships. Gunfire and the distant sound of explosions drifted across the water: whether from bombs or the flaming fuel depots, she didn't know.

'Oh, please bring him home,' she whispered fervently, trying to will her words to the captains out there in the dark. 'Please, please bring him home. Bring them all safely home.'

'There was a whole fleet of fishing boats crammed into the harbour when we came,' Jack said. 'Now they're gone. Every one.'

'Where have they gone?'

'I don't know. We'll find it all out soon, I suppose.'

There was silence. Molly watched the orange glow and prayed as hard as she ever had in her life. Jack just held her.

'Would you like to get married?' he said after a while.

Molly blinked. 'What?'

He turned her to face him. 'I mean it. If you'll have me.'

Despite everything, Molly laughed.

'Don't talk daft,' she said. 'We've only been walking out a few week.'

He stroked her hair away from her cheek.

'I'll have to go soon,' he said quietly. 'You know that, don't you?'

'Go? Go where?'

'Where I ought to be right now – to do my duty with whichever service will take me. I telephoned in a request for a medical the day after the Ramsgate concert. I've been summoned to a recruitment centre in London in a few days' time.' He smiled wanly. 'I'm sorry to break up the act just when we've got it nearly perfect.'

Molly stared at him in the faint light of the moon, shining through the clouds. It was a surprise, yet… it wasn't. She felt as though she had known Jack was going to tell her he would be leaving for the war some day soon.

'Are you disappointed in me?' Jack asked.

'Not disappointed. Proud.' She rested her head against his chest. 'But I wish you didn't have to go,' she whispered.

'And yet you know I have to, don't you?'

'I suppose I do.' She swallowed a sob. 'Oh God, I'm going to miss you. I'll worry about you every minute. The world's such a terrifying place.'

'Hey.' He tilted her chin up to press a kiss to her lips. 'It isn't forever.'

'It feels like it might be.'

'It won't. We're Forrester and Clough, aren't we? It's like Phil said: some double acts are just meant to be double acts.'

Molly laughed damply, her tears soaking into his overcoat. 'Daft bugger.'

'I could feel your nose wrinkling then.'

'That is such a huge fib.'

He stroked her cheek. 'So, will you marry me then? I'm going to war. That ought to entitle me to certain privileges.'

Molly smiled. 'No. But… ask me again sometime.'

It took Molly a long time to fall asleep that night. When she did, it was fitful, her dreams haunted by visions of soldiers – sometimes they seemed to be Ted, sometimes Jack – trapped on a flaming beach, encircled and under fire as German planes rained bombs and machine-gun bullets down on them.

It felt as though she had hardly slept before someone was shaking her awake. It was Fenella, dressed in a siren suit with her hair pushed untidily into a headscarf. She looked equal parts frightened and excited.

'Molly, you have to come,' she said, still shaking her even though Molly was now awake. 'Throw on whatever's quickest and come.'

'What?' Molly was alert at once. 'Ella, what's happened?'

'Tabby went for a walk this morning and she came back with such news. Soldiers, Moll – hundreds of them! Maybe even thousands. There are ships full of them arriving, and boats of all sizes. The men are all over town, wandering around in a daze. Tab says they look dead on their feet, and so many hurt.'

'Oh my God!'

'She says you can't move around the railway stations, there are so many trying to get on trains,' Fenella went on. 'There are ambulances zooming about, and nurses doing triage on the piers, and WVS ladies handing out tea and sandwiches. We're going down to the Admiralty Pier now to see if we can help.'

Molly jumped out of bed at once. She pulled on the simplest outfit her wardrobe could furnish to be ready as quickly as possible.

The other women were all up and dressed when Fenella and Molly hurried downstairs.

'How many did you see, Tabby?' Molly asked breathlessly, not entirely trusting Fenella's estimate of thousands knowing her friend's tendency to exaggerate. Tabitha was in her ENSA uniform, as if she felt it appropriate to look as military as possible.

'Five big destroyers with hundreds on board, waiting to disembark,' Tabby said, excitement banishing her usual unflappable calm. 'And small boats too. Fishing boats and things. There are men everywhere you look.'

'All from Dunkirk?'

'I suppose they must be,' Pam said. 'There was nothing about it on the morning news so I guess they don't want the public to know too much. Oh, and Belgium's surrendered, and they say the Germans have crossed the Lys.'

'Poor France,' Fenella whispered. 'All those poor people.'

Molly exchanged a look with Diana, whose eyes were red, and pressed her hand.

'Well, ladies, are we going to do something or not?' Pam demanded. 'I might not be much of a nurse, but I can butter a sandwich as well as the next girl.'

'Yes, let's go,' Tabby said. 'I hope they let us help. I couldn't bear to sit here doing nothing.'

There was hubbub on the streets of Dover as the women made their way into town. Just as Fenella and Tabby had said, the place seemed to be filled with servicemen, particularly around the railway stations and public buildings like the town hall, which had been designated as processing centres.

Oh, and these men were a shocking sight! Some were sleeping in what must have been the first place they could lie down, on benches and on the pavement, oblivious to tramping feet around them. Some drifted along like ghosts, muttering to themselves, as if they didn't know where they were. Others sat and sobbed like lost children, hugging their knees pitifully and calling for their mothers.

All were dirty and many wore only the ragged remains of their uniforms, barefoot, their boots lost somewhere on the journey. One bootless man, his feet bloody and torn and with a makeshift sling on one arm, smiled vaguely at the women and lifted what remained of his cap.

'The poor loves,' Pam whispered, her eyes filling with tears. 'Why are they being allowed to wander the streets in such a shocking condition?'

'Because there aren't people enough to take care of them,' Molly murmured.

Her gaze fixed on a Navy destroyer now in the harbour. Hundreds more men were disembarking, or preparing to do so: men on stretchers, walking wounded, and only a few lucky enough to be merely tired rather than hurt. Nurses triaged them and volunteers pressed sustenance on them, but Molly could see there weren't nearly enough volunteers to cope with the influx.

'So many,' Diana murmured. 'I can't believe we were able to get so many out.' She looked to the horizon, which was filled with ships as far as the eye could see. 'How did we do it? It feels impossible.'

But all Molly could think was that it was a retreat – a retreat on an epic scale. These tired, wounded soldiers had been fortunate enough to make it home, but France was now left to the Germans. And as Haw-Haw said, if France fell – and that must surely be inevitable, now – Britain would be the next target.

Molly looked at every man she passed, hoping to see her brother's face, though she knew it was a foolish hope when there must be hundreds of men filling the streets. But oh, she prayed Ted was somewhere among the rescued! How many of the hundreds of thousands of men who comprised the British Expeditionary Force had made it home, and how many lay bleeding and dying on the sands of Dunkirk? Had half been lost? More than half? Nearly all?

The five women weren't quite sure what to do when they reached the pier. There was a cordon of naval personnel to prevent anyone getting too close, regarding nosy civilians with suspicion.

As usual, Tabitha took charge. She tapped one of the naval officers on the shoulder.

'Excuse me,' she said briskly. 'My friends and I want to help.'

He regarded her warily, taking in the uniform. 'ATS, are you?'

'No, ENSA.'

He snorted. 'Good God. Don't you think the poor sods have suffered enough?'

Tabitha glared at him. 'Look, we want to volunteer, all right? There must be something useful we can do.'

'Like what, juggle for 'em?'

'We thought we could make sandwiches and things,' Diana said. 'Or roll bandages. Anything that needs doing.'

The man sighed. 'Hang on. Let me get the old girl in charge of the teas.'

He returned shortly with a no nonsense member of the Women's Voluntary Services, who beckoned them through the cordon. Within moments, she had dispatched Fenella and Tabitha to fill buckets with drinking water to brew more tea, while Diana, Pam and Molly were put to work handing out drinks, sandwiches, cigarettes and blankets to the men coming off the packed ships.

Molly didn't think she would ever forget that day – the things she saw. Men who fell asleep standing up with a half-chewed sandwich still in their mouths, they were so exhausted. Men who had walked for days without sleep. Men whose feet were torn to shreds from too-small boots they had taken off dead comrades after losing their own trying to swim to a boat. Men in shock, unable to speak a word, staring with terrified eyes. French troops too, forced to abandon their country and continue the fight in exile, murmuring words of gratitude in broken English. Every one of them made her want to cry for pity, but she didn't. Instead, she remembered Jack's words, the night they had performed at the aerodrome.

*Remember: smile. If you can't do anything else, just smile.*

So she smiled, and gave them tea and what comfort she could, and listened when they told her about the loved ones waiting for them at home. After weeks of hell they beamed on Molly as on a guardian angel, though all she had to offer them was a smile and a cup of lukewarm tea.

She must have seen hundreds of men that day, and she said a prayer of thanks for every one whose life had been spared. But they weren't Ted. Not a man she saw that day was Ted.

## Chapter 42

All ENSA concerts had been cancelled for the foreseeable future as the country dealt with the returning men. Molly and her friends spent the next day again at the pier, and the day after that and the one after that. May became June, and still, every day, the ships came. The stream of returning soldiers showed no sign of slowing down. Thousands were pouring into Dover, with trains arriving every twenty minutes to move them on.

Of course, everyone in the country now knew that the men had been forced to retreat from Dunkirk. A defeat like that ought to have been a crushing blow to public morale, and yet somehow… it wasn't.

The boats that Jack had noticed sailing from Ramsgate and Dover had been part of a civilian flotilla – the 'Little Ships', as the press dubbed them: pleasure cruisers, fishing boats, private yachts, all heading out to bring back what men they could. Between them and the Royal Navy, they had managed to return with more than three-quarters of the troops who Lord Haw-Haw had confidently told them just days earlier would be mercilessly slaughtered. It ought to have been cursed as a defeat. Instead, it was hailed as a deliverance.

'It's a little like us, isn't it?' Diana said dreamily during one of her and Molly's now nightly wireless-side vigils, after they had listened to the news. Molly felt as though she never wanted to hear another announcer's voice, and yet as long as Ted was unaccounted for, she had to be there for each bulletin.

'What's like us?' she asked.

'The "Little Ships" thing. What I mean is, people need hope. They need stories like that to bring them hope, in just the same way as they need us. It makes people feel better about being people.'

Molly smiled. 'You weren't always so patriotic about ENSA.'

'Wasn't I?' Diana said, smiling back. 'You should know by now not to believe everything I pretend to think, cherie.'

'I do. And I'm very glad I found it out.'

'Had your mother heard anything of Ted when you spoke with her tonight?'

Molly sighed. 'No. But perhaps… perhaps tomorrow.'

She hadn't neglected to locate the nearest phone box to their billet when she was spared from her volunteering duties. She had wired her mam and told her she would wait in the box every day at 6 p.m., in case there was any news, but so far there hadn't been a word about Ted. They didn't know if he had been rescued, if he was still making his way home by boat, or if, God forbid, he was… But Molly couldn't bear to think of that. Not until she had to.

–

The next evening, Molly was about to leave the phone box and return to her billet. It was 6.15 p.m., and growing chilly. If her mam hadn't rung by now, it usually meant she didn't want to waste their precious shillings on a trunk call when she had no news to give. But something persuaded Molly to wait a few more minutes, just in case.

She was thinking about Jack when the phone rang. He had gone for his medical and been passed A1, as she had known he would. It might be any day that he would be summoned to basic training. Molly knew that joining up was the right thing to do, and she was proud of him for it. But still, even though she knew it was an unfair and selfish thing to want, she wished he didn't have to go. She wished he could stay safe in ENSA, with her, and they could continue to be Forrester and Clough. With a brother and now a sweetheart out in the fight, she didn't know how she would ever sleep again.

*If she still had a brother in the fight*, a treacherous voice whispered. Molly tried to ignore it, tried not to think of those bodies on the beach in France, as she picked up the phone to speak to her mother.

'Heyup, Mam,' she said wearily. 'Oh Lord, I've seen some things today. Is our Daph with you? I don't want to talk about anything gruesome if she can hear.'

'Whisht, our Molly. Whisht while I catch my breath.' Her mam sounded excited, and she was panting heavily.

Molly frowned. 'What's up? Is there news?'

It was a moment before her mother could answer her.

'The phone near the house was out of order,' she said. 'I had to run to the next one and hope you'd still be waiting. It's come, love.'

'Oh my God! A telegram? Not…'

'Nay, not one of those. He's all right. Well, not all right, but he's alive.' She laughed tearfully. 'He's alive, Molly. He's in a hospital but he's alive.'

Molly laughed too, although her laughter was half sob. 'Oh, thank God. Thank God! Where is he? How badly hurt is he? Have you spoken to him?'

'Not yet. I only got his telegram an hour ago. He says he had one of the nurses send it for him but it don't say what his injuries are. It's a field hospital they've got him in, I don't know if you can phone it up.'

'Where?'

'Folkestone, our Teddy says. An old war sanatorium on The Leas.'

'Folkestone! But that's near where I am.'

'Aye, he'll have come in at one of the ports, won't he?' Mam said. 'Can you go to him? I'll feel better knowing you've seen him, and I'll come down as soon as I can find someone to look after Daph.' She choked on a sob. 'He'll… he'll want his mam.'

Molly thought of all the young men she'd seen over the past week. For so many of them, the first thing they'd told her was how much they were longing to see their mothers.

'Yes he will,' she said, shedding a quiet tear. 'But for now, he'll have to make do with his sister. I'll go to him tomorrow, on the first train I can get on.'

—

'Do you want one of us to come?' Fenella said the next day as Molly said goodbye to her friends. 'I should think you could use some support.'

'No, stay here and help the men. They're going to need the four of you more than I am.'

'Evacuations are slowing now,' Tabitha observed. 'We're not needed as much as we were. You ought to have someone with you, Molly, in case… well, in case there's anything to upset you.'

'I will have someone. Jack's coming with me. I called on him last night.'

'Why the uniform?' Pam asked.

'I thought it might help get me to Ted,' Molly said, brushing down the stiff serge of her ENSA jacket. 'The military seem to narrow their eyes at any civilian who looks like they're snooping around. A little khaki can't do me any harm, can it?'

'I do hope your brother's all right.' Diana came to kiss Molly on both cheeks. 'Hurry back and tell us the news, cherie. Whatever it is, good or bad, we'll be here for you.'

Molly pressed her hand. 'Thank you. All of you.'

—

Jack met Molly on the platform at the Marine Station. Even now, though evacuations had started to slow, the place was packed with men. Jack, dressed in his ENSA uniform as Molly had requested, was just one more khaki-clad figure among the crowd. For some reason, seeing him in uniform brought a tear to Molly's eye.

'Are you all right?' he asked when she had pushed through the crowd to join him.

'Yes.' She dashed the tear away. 'Seeing you in your uniform made me think how soon you'll have to swap it for the real thing, that's all.'

'Well, ENSA's loss will be some unfortunate regimental concert party's gain, I suppose.' He slipped an arm around her. 'Although it won't feel right performing without my partner.'

'I wish we could do our act one last time,' Molly said dreamily. 'It doesn't seem fair we only got to perform it for an audience once.'

'It feels foolish to have been on tour nearly a month and only managed two shows. I wish ENSA would put us back to work so I could earn my keep for the few weeks I'm likely to remain in their employment.'

'I don't know how I'll be able to go on stage without you,' Molly said with a sigh.

'You'll be all right, now you've worked out how to tame those pesky nerves. Just pretend I'm there and sing your little heart out to me.'

'I wonder when they'll give us a show to do.'

'Not until things have settled down, I suppose.' Jack looked around at the throng of men. 'I hope we can get on a train.'

'We'll stay here until we do,' Molly said firmly. 'I'm going to see my brother today, no matter what. If I have to walk to Folkestone, I will.'

'How are you feeling?'

'Relieved, I suppose. All those days of worry about whether he was dead or captured, and he's safe, thank God. But...' She closed her eyes, thinking of the men she had encountered over the last week. 'Jack, I'm so afraid of what I might find when I see him.'

—

It was a considerable time before Molly and Jack were able to get a place on one of the packed trains out of Dover. They had to stand all the way, pressed in on all sides by weary, smelly, grim-faced soldiers heading for dispersal camps.

As they travelled, Molly saw for the first time just how the Dunkirk miracle had touched ordinary people. At every station there were civilians lining the platforms, cheering, waving flags, pushing packets of sandwiches and flasks of tea through the windows for the men on board. The soldiers themselves looked more dazed than pleased by these welcome committees, although they seized gratefully on the tea and sandwiches.

'They're treating us like heroes,' she heard one man murmur wonderingly to his mate. 'Don't they know we lost?'

—

'Do you know where the field hospital is?' Jack asked when he and Molly alighted from the train in Folkestone.

'Ted's telegram said it's a sanatorium from the last war, some-where on the cliffs called The Leas. I suppose we just wander around until we find it.'

They didn't have to look too hard, however. A crowd of walking wounded marked the spot, with triage stations set up all around the building. As in Dover, men slept where they had fallen. Weary-looking nurses tended to broken bones and bleeding wounds while exhaustion did the work of an anaesthetic.

'Oh my God,' Jack muttered. He had been away in London for much of the past week, and hadn't seen the men coming from the boats at close range as Molly had. 'Look at the state of them. Poor, poor devils.'

But Molly had only one thought, and that was to find her brother.

She accosted the first officer she saw, in the uniform of the Royal Army Medical Corps. 'Excuse me, Doctor,' she said. 'I'm looking for a patient here: Private Edward Clough. He was brought in yesterday.'

The man looked irritated at being interrupted in his work, but he answered civilly.

'I'm sorry, Miss, but God knows who we've got in there,' he said. 'It's all we can do to get the men treated, the rate they're coming in at. There's been no time to process them.'

'Well, may my friend and I go inside and search for him?'

The doctor glanced at the ENSA insignia on their caps. 'Here to put on a concert, are you? They could use some cheering up, I can tell you that.'

'No, I'm just looking for my brother. He telegrammed to say he was here.'

'Hm. We really can't have civilian visitors filling up the place. We've barely enough room for the men.'

'I won't stay long.' She met the doctor's eyes. 'Please. I just want to see him. I… need to know he's all right.'

The doctor sighed. 'All right, go on. I hope you've a strong stomach though, Miss. There's a lot in there who aren't a pretty sight.'

'Thank you.'

Jack gripped Molly's hand tightly as they made their way into the hospital.

'I'm here,' he whispered. 'I won't leave you until it's done.'

The first thing that struck Molly was the smell: men who hadn't washed for days, damp khaki and leather, sweat and urine and blood. The rows of beds seemed unending, with army doctors and nurses bustling around them.

Some of the men only had broken limbs. Others had wounds from bombs or machine-gun fire. A few looked like they were barely clinging to life. Molly saw a nurse pull a sheet over one man who hadn't made it, and prayed it wasn't her brother.

None of the medical staff paid her or Jack any attention. They were too busy for that, hurrying from man to man, freeing up beds where they could and filling them with new men.

'Ted?' Molly called. 'Ted Clough? Is there a Ted Clough here?'

There was no answer.

She hurried along the aisles of beds, repeating the call with her heart in her mouth. Finally, a faint 'Moll?' echoed back to her.

She laughed. 'Oh my God, Teddy! Teddy! Where are you, love?'

A hand waved from one of the beds, and Molly rushed over.

And… there he was. Her little brother: pale, weary and with a blood-soaked dressing on one shoulder, but he was Ted and he was alive and he was here, safe on British shores.

'Moll.' He laughed faintly. 'It's not really you, is it?'

'It's me. How hurt are you?'

'Bloody Messerschmitt got me in the shoulder and another in the leg. I'll live.'

Molly embraced him, gently so as not to hurt his shoulder. Softly he sang a few lines of 'Molly Malone', as he used to do to tease her when they were children. She guessed from his pupils that he had been given morphine.

'Where's Mam?' was the first thing he asked when she released him.

'On her way.'

'Good. Good.' For the first time, he seemed to notice her uniform and Jack hovering behind her. 'What are you got up like that for? You're not in the ATS, are you? And who's this bloke?'

'The uniform's for ENSA,' she said, turning so he could see a shoulder tab. 'Didn't you get my last letter?'

'Not had a letter in ages.' He laughed. 'Seriously, you in ENSA? What did you do to deserve that then, our Molly?'

She smiled. 'Don't you start.'

He looked up at Jack. 'You ENSA too, mate?'

'For now.' Jack leaned over to shake his hand. 'Jack Forrester. Glad you made it, son. It would've broken your sister's heart if you hadn't.'

Ted narrowed one eye. 'Take a lively interest in my sister's heart, do you, Jack Forrester?'

'Oh, don't start getting protective,' Molly said with a smile. She turned to Jack. 'Sorry, love, but do you mind leaving us alone?'

'Of course. I'll wait for you outside.' Jack kissed her cheek, then nodded to Ted before disappearing. 'Good to meet you, Ted.'

'I don't like him,' Ted said as soon as Jack had gone.

Molly smiled. 'Why not?'

'Because I'm your brother and it's my job.'

'Well I like him so you'd better get used to having him around.' She took in his pale face and blue-ringed eyes, the dirty, matted clumps of straw-blond hair, and the expression in his eyes that seemed to carry more than his nineteen years. 'You look like hell, kid.'

He slumped back against his pillows, wincing at the pain in his shoulder. 'I feel like hell.'

'Mam'll swoon when she sees how mucky you are. You look like you used to when you came back from Saturday football.'

'Our Daph's going to kill me too. I lost her perfume swimming out to a boat.' He closed his eyes. 'It's been like a nightmare, Moll,' he whispered. 'Like a living nightmare.'

She took his hand. 'I know, love.'

'You don't know. The stuff we saw...' He shuddered. 'Refugees, thousands of them. French and Belgian, trying to get away while we retreated and left the poor buggers to their fate.' His voice shook with emotion. 'Kids, Moll – women and kids. And then days trapped in that hellish bloody pocket in a crush. The bodies on the beach... pals. Lads I...' He broke off, a sob stopping his words.

'It's over now. You're safe.'

Ted couldn't speak for a moment.

'It's not over,' he said hoarsely. 'They'll be coming for us. It's our turn next.'

'We won't give up. We'll keep fighting.'

'We? What we? There's men here say they won't go back, even if they're shot for it. That they've seen enough of hell for one life.' Ted winced as he shifted his weight. 'It's all so bloody bleak,' he whispered. 'Like the end of the world. Like the end of joy.'

Molly didn't know what to say to that. There was nothing she could say to make it better. She just held her brother's hand, and wished their mother was here.

She stayed with Ted for as long as she was allowed, but eventually a nurse came to shoo her out.

'Mam ought to arrive in the next few days,' Molly told her brother as she prepared to leave. 'And I'll come again. Perhaps they'll let us take you home soon. Daph'll be desperate to see you.'

'Aye.' Ted's eyes were closed, as if the conversation had drained him. 'Aye, I'd like to remember what home looks like. I could half fancy I'd dreamt the place.'

Molly glanced at the men in the beds on her way out. Many were in shock. Some had lost limbs. Others were delirious, or groaning in pain. Some slept, some read newspapers, some played cards, some muttered to themselves or stared blankly. But what struck her most was the hollow, hopeless despair in every pair of eyes. These were men who had seen horrors, and they felt so keenly the heavy burden of their defeat. Ted's words echoed in her brain. *It's like the end of the world. The end of joy…*

Outside, Molly saw the army doctor she had spoken to before.

'Oh. Hello,' he said when he spotted her. 'Did you find your brother?'

'Yes,' Molly said quietly.

'One of the lucky ones?'

'Are there any lucky ones?'

'I suppose not.'

The doctor made to go, but Molly put a hand on his arm. An idea had seized her.

'Doctor?'

'Yes?'

'Did you mean it, what you said before? I mean about cheering up the men.'

'They could do with something to put a smile on their faces, certainly,' he said. 'Anything that might take their mind off what they've seen and make the world feel normal again. I've put in a request for a mobile picture unit from ENSA, but then so has every hospital on the east coast, I should imagine.'

'I might be able to help. Let me see what I can do.'

'Anything you could arrange would certainly be appreciated.' He nodded to her and went back to his work.

Jack had approached, and Molly turned to him with kindling eyes.

'I recognise that look,' he said. 'You're cooking up a plan, aren't you? And I think I can guess what it is.'

'Well, what sense is there in ENSA lying fallow when there are all these men desperate to smile again?' Molly said. 'It's ridiculous that we've been stood down, now of all times.'

'You want to get us back to work?'

'You're absolutely right I do. You remember what Phil said, the day we heard about Belgium? He said that the Follies were going to be needed now more than ever. And if we can't go to barracks or aerodromes, we can bloody well go to hospitals. That's where we're really needed.'

'ENSA's stopped operations though.'

'Sod ENSA. What are they going to do, court-martial us for doing our jobs? That army doctor made it sound like we'd be welcomed with open arms if we offered our services.' She beamed at him. 'We're going back to Dover to get everyone together, then we're going to put on the best damn show of our lives.'

# Chapter 43

Just as Molly had hoped, the troupe seized on her idea with enthusiasm. It felt like a balm to the helplessness they had been feeling, knowing there was something they could do for the returning troops.

'It could get us into trouble with ENSA, when they've told us to wait for orders,' Phil observed, when all nine members of the Forces Follies had squeezed into the living room of the girls' billet for a meeting.

'And is that going to stop us?' Molly asked, raising an eyebrow.

'Not a bit,' he answered promptly. 'I'll wire whoever's in command at your brother's hospital right away and offer our services.'

'Oh, I think it's a wonderful idea,' Pam said, coming over to give Molly a squeeze. 'Well done for thinking of it, Molly.'

'It's a good idea, but how will we do it?' Diana asked. 'The hospitals must be crammed. There won't be any space to set up a stage, and I don't know how we'd squeeze in a piano. Or where we'd get a piano from, for that matter.'

'That is true,' Molly conceded. 'Ted's hospital was packed to the rafters.'

'If a bunch of fishing boats can get those lads across the Channel with the Germans doing everything in their power to stop them then us lot can put on a show, no matter how limited our resources,' Davy said firmly. 'Tabby can hum the ruddy accompaniment if she has to.'

'Leave everything to me,' Phil said. 'After this, none of you will be able to say I'm not worth my weight in posh fags as your manager.'

Phil was as good as his word. He sent a wire to the medical officer in command at Ted's hospital that afternoon, asking for permission to put on a show. This, of course, was readily granted. He then spent a good hour in the telephone box, arranging everything they were going to need.

Two days later, Molly found herself once more alighting from a crowded train on to the platform at Folkestone – this time accompanied by all eight other members of the Forces Follies, in their costumes ready to perform. They had got some funny looks on the train full of soldiers, Nobby in particular, but no one was in a mood to care about that.

'We're changing the programme order,' Phil said as they walked to the hospital. 'Molly and Jack, I'm putting you on first. Just your duets, then you can come on again at the end to lead them in the community singing. While I'm sure these lads will be as keen on a pretty girl as any young soldier, they need to laugh more than anything else. See if you can get them warmed up, then we'll bring Di on to give them a thrill.'

Molly nodded vaguely, but she wasn't thinking about the programme order. She was thinking about the men she had seen in the hospital, and the empty, hopeless look on their shattered faces. So many faces, but only one expression between them.

Would she and Jack be able to get a smile from them? They had looked so weighed down by despair, as if they might never laugh again...

They found a large lorry parked outside the hospital, a platform extending from the back to create a little stage. A battered miniature piano had been placed beside it. There were no wings, no backdrops, no props – Pam's unicycle, lasso and the pieces of her disappearing cabinet were all they had brought with them, strapped to Nobby's back – but they had everything they needed to put on a show.

In front of the lorry-stage were the men, or all those fit to be moved, sitting in rows of chairs – some sixty or so. The door to the hospital had been propped open so that those who were bed-bound could at least hear the show, even if they couldn't see it.

The army doctor Molly had first spoken to, who seemed to be in command, came over to shake their hands.

'I can't thank you enough for doing this,' he said. 'These men are in sore need of anything that might make them feel like human beings again. Do you have everything you need?'

'I think so.' Phil nodded to the piano. 'What do you think, Tab, can you play it?'

'I can play anything,' Tabby said, her face painted with determ-ination. There seemed to be a shared consciousness that this wasn't just any old ENSA show. The stakes felt so much higher than at any concert they had played before.

Molly noticed several of her colleagues flinch when they saw the men, many of whom looked rather gruesome. In some cases, there were bound stumps where arms and legs had been. Little Davy didn't hesitate for a moment, however. He instantly started mingling among them, shaking hands and cracking jokes.

Molly had wondered what was in the large bag Davy had slung over his shoulder. It turned out this was filled with packets of cigarettes and bottles of beer – Lord knew where he had got them, unless he had robbed an off-licence – which he started handing out to the troops.

The other members of the Follies exchanged looks.

'Well, what are we all waiting for?' Jack said. 'Come on.'

And over they went to join Davy in greeting the men.

There was a hopeful look in the eyes of the soldiers, Molly noticed as she drew closer – or perhaps not hopeful but eager, as if desperate for something that might make a little sense of the world again.

She was scanning the crowd for her brother when she felt a tap on her shoulder. She turned, and squealed when she saw who was there.

'Mam!'

'Hello, love.'

Molly threw herself at her mother, feeling like she had never been so glad to see someone in her life.

'Oh, thank God you're here,' she whispered. 'You don't know how much I've wanted you, these past few weeks. When did you come?'

'Yesterday. I'd have sent a wire, but Teddy said you were coming today anyhow so I might as well save myself a tanner.' She held Molly back to look at her. 'You look fair blooming, our Molly. Tired, mind, but I don't wonder at that. I doubt there's a soul in the country who's been sleeping well lately.'

'Is Daph all right?'

'Aye, Rita's gone to stay with her. The child made me promise I wouldn't go home unless I could bring your brother back too.'

'Where is Ted?'

'Here, I'll take you to him.'

She guided Molly to her brother. He was having one hand shaken by Davy, and rather dazedly looking at a bottle of brown ale that had been pressed into the other.

'Ta very much,' he said to Davy. 'Here, you're going to get a right earful off our matron.'

'If she wants to argue you lads don't deserve a drink after what you've been through, she can have an earful from me right back.' Davy pressed Ted's uninjured shoulder before moving on. 'Thanks for all you've done, son.'

Ted looked up at his mother and sister. 'Look. I got beer.'

'Then you'd better drink it quickly, before someone tries to take it off you again,' Molly said with a smile.

'It will feel strange to see you on stage, our Molly,' Mam said. 'Not that I'm supposed to be here, but they've given over trying to shoo me away. I told them I'm not leaving until I can take my boy home.'

She rested a hand on Ted's good shoulder, and he gave it a squeeze.

'Stubborn old lady,' he said with a smile.

'I don't mind the stubborn but less of the old, my lad.' She regarded him fondly. 'It's good to have thee safe again, love.'

'I'd better go talk to some of the other men,' Molly said, watching her fellow performers mingling with the patients.

'Hang on.' Ted pointed to Jack. 'Mam, that's him.'

Mam raised an eyebrow. 'Is it indeed?'

Molly shook her head at her brother. 'Have you been telling tales on me?'

'Just looking out for the womenfolk, now I'm restored to my place as the man of the family.'

'Well, Molly, call him over,' Mam said. 'Let's meet this young man you've been courting with while saying never a word to your mother.'

Sighing, Molly beckoned to Jack.

'For some reason, this lady wants to meet you,' she said when he joined them. 'My mother, Sarah Clough. Mam, this is Jack Forrester. He's my, er...'

'Her double act partner,' Jack said, shaking hands with her mother. He glanced at Molly. 'And her young man, I hope, unless she's had enough of me.'

'Er, yes,' Molly said, flushing. 'I mean yes to him being my young man, not that I've had enough of him.'

Mam didn't say anything. She just looked Jack up and down, eyes narrowed.

'Well, you seem a tidy, gentlemanly sort for someone in the theatre,' she said at last. 'I could be prepared to give you the benefit of the doubt.'

He smiled. 'If it makes you feel any better, Mrs Clough, I won't be in the theatre much longer. I'm going off to the Army soon.'

'I'm glad to hear you'll be doing your duty.'

Jack turned to Molly. 'We'd better get ready, Moll. Davy's about to open the show. Break a leg, eh?'

-

Molly felt some return of her nerves as she and Jack waited by the truck for Davy to introduce them. She had never felt under more pressure to put on a good show. The nerves she was experiencing now only spurred her on, however. Every beat of her heart reminded her that never had light entertainment mattered so much.

They climbed on to the lorry-stage by means of a ramp, and Jack opened with a little cross-talk.

'Ahhh,' he said, sniffing the air. 'Can you smell that, Molly?'

'I can smell beer, if that's what you mean.'

'That's not beer, it's apple juice.' He winked at the nurse in charge. 'Honest to God, matron.'

Molly was almost knocked backwards by the gale of laughter that came from the men: far louder than the joke warranted. She had worried she and Jack would struggle to get a laugh from people who had seemed so sunk in despair, but it was just the opposite. These men were desperate to laugh. They needed it, as their medical officer had observed, just to feel human again.

'That wasn't what I was talking about anyhow,' Jack said when the laughter had died down. 'I meant the smell of my favourite sort of ENSA audience.'

'What sort is that?' Molly asked. None of this was scripted — they were making it up as they went along.

'A captive one, of course.'

Again, that loud, almost desperate laughter — but there were sobs mixed in with it. Not crying with laughter, but crying *and* laughter: grief, relief, joy and despair, mingling together in the sort of confused cocktail that could only belong to these men, here, at this time. Molly had no need to fix her focus on Jack to calm her nerves. Today, her performance was for every man there.

Jack nodded to Tabitha. 'Maestro, music please.'

She launched into 'It's De-Lovely' and they began their duet. It was rather more polished than the last time they had performed it for an audience, although the dance proved difficult in the smaller space. Molly felt herself wobble at the edge of the platform as they finished the number, and Jack gripped her tightly around the waist so she wouldn't topple off.

'Sorry,' he whispered, releasing her immediately she was steady again. 'Didn't mean to frighten you.'

'It's all right.' She glanced up at him. 'I think… it might be all right.'

The show was a roaring success – literally roaring, with the men showing their appreciation as vocally as they could. The community singing must have been audible in France.

Afterwards the medical officer in charge shook each performer warmly by the hand, visibly moved.

'Thank you,' he said. 'That was exactly what they needed. To see cheerful, pretty young faces, and to laugh like the boys they are instead of men old before their time. It was wonderful. Just… just wonderful.'

He left to oversee the removal of his men back to their beds, and the members of the Forces Follies sat with legs dangling on the edge of their strange little stage. For a while there was silence, which was eventually broken by Fenella.

'Well, if you ever again hear me say "it's only ENSA", I grant whichever of you is closest the right to give me a slap,' she announced.

Tabitha nodded. 'The same for all of us, I should think.'

Suddenly, Pam burst into tears.

'Oh Lord, I'm sorry.' She took the handkerchief Diana handed her, laughing. 'I must be half silly. It's just… their faces. The way they cried.'

Everyone nodded. They all knew what she meant.

'Don't get too comfortable, you lot,' Phil said. 'We need to get back to our digs and pack. We're moving on today.'

Nobby frowned. 'Have ENSA sent us some orders then?'

'I'm not sitting around picking my nose while I wait for that bunch to buck up and get organised. I contacted another six coastal hospitals yesterday offering our services and it was a yes from all of them. I've arranged billets for us in Margate next. There are a lot more men who need us, chaps.'

Jack was sitting beside Molly. He gave her hand a press.

'Let's leave this lot to pack up while you and I go for a walk,' he whispered. 'I want you to myself.'

Molly nodded. It was what she had been thinking too. No one seemed surprised when they detached themselves from the group and wandered off, although Fenella would insist on smirking at them.

They didn't speak for a while when they were alone. They just stood at the top of the cliffs looking out to sea, holding one another and listening to the whisper of the tide.

'I used to love the seaside,' Molly said after a little time had passed. 'After the last week, I don't think I'll ever be able to enjoy it in the same way again.'

'I know what you mean.'

'How long until I lose you?'

'Not long, I suppose. I hope I'll have time to finish Phil's hospital tour before they summon me to basic though.'

Molly breathed a soft sigh, her eyes fixed on the horizon.

Over the waves was France, with the Germans making advances every day. It could be only a matter of time until Britain's neighbour across the ocean was forced to surrender. And… what then? A battle to defend this very island from the same fate. From Nazi subjugation, and the swastika flying over Bradford Town Hall. It had given Molly comfort to feel, as she waited for news of her brother, that Ted was practically only a swim away. But now she imagined the Germans just twenty miles across the Channel, poised to attack…

She shivered when she thought of the man she loved joining the fight too. But she knew it was right that he did so.

'I'll miss you,' she said quietly.

'I'll miss you too.' Jack caressed her hair as she watched the movement of the waves. 'Would it make any difference to your decision about marriage if I told you I loved you?'

'No. But tell me all the same.'

He smiled, and turned her to face him. 'If you aren't going to have me, I think the least you could do to soothe my wounded pride is to take your turn first.'

She smiled too. 'All right, I love you then. Happy?'

'Heh.'

'What?'

'Nothing. Only, you wrinkle your nose when you say that too.'

Molly rested her hand on his cheek. 'Kiss me again, Jack,' she whispered.

'You won't run away this time?'

'I feel quietly confident.'

Jack pressed his lips to hers, his arms tightening around her, but there was no panic today. No horrible memories of Shack, or a desire to flee. All Molly felt as Jack kissed her was safe – safe in arms that loved her, and grateful to have his body against hers for this brief, untouchable moment of love and contentment before the war came to separate them.

'Top three?' Jack whispered when he broke away.

Molly smiled, and stroked his cheek with her thumb. 'Number one.'

'Still Forrester and Clough?'

'Always.'

# *A letter from Betty*

Hello, and thank you for choosing to read *The Variety Girls*. This is the first in a new series following the exploits of an ENSA concert party, tasked with entertaining the troops and keeping up morale during World War II.

In this story, Bradford girl Molly Clough sees an opportunity to escape the hard life of a weaver in a woollen mill by using her talent as a singer to get a place in an ENSA troupe. What with homesickness, stage fright and the jokes about ENSA's 'Every Night Something Awful' reputation, however, she soon questions whether the world of entertainment is everything she had hoped it would be. It's only when she and her new friends get caught up in the events surrounding the Dunkirk evacuation that she comes to realise, in spite of the jokes about ENSA, that keeping up morale in wartime is a huge and important responsibility.

I do hope readers will fall in love with Molly, Fenella, Pam, Tabby and Diana just as I have, and join me for the further adventures of the Forces Follies concert party as the so-called Phoney War becomes something very real indeed.

I'd absolutely love to hear your thoughts on this book in a review. These are invaluable not only for letting authors know how their story affected you, but also for helping other readers to choose their next read and discover new writers. Just a few words can make a big difference.

If you would like to find out more about me and my books you can do so via my website or social media pages:

Facebook: /BettyFirthAuthor

Instagram and Threads: @BettyFirthAuthor

BlueSky: @maryjaynebaker.bsky.social

Web: www.bettyfirthauthor.co.uk

Please do stay tuned for announcements about further books in the 'Sweethearts of the Forces' series. Thank you again for choosing *The Variety Girls*.

Best wishes,

Betty

## *Acknowledgements*

As always, I'd like to thank my amazing editor at Hera, Keshini Naidoo, and my agent Louise Buckley at Hannah Sheppard Literary Agency, as well as the rest of the team at Hera and Canelo for all their help in making the book what it is.